LUCY FERRISS

is

"A MASTERFUL STORYTELLER."
—#1 *New York Times* bestselling author WALLY LAMB

and

A SISTER TO HONOR

is

"An urgent and ultimately political work of literary fiction that is also a brilliantly paced page-turner."
—AMITAVA KUMAR, author of *A Foreigner Carrying in the Crook of His Arm a Tiny Bomb*

"A bold and engaging novel, one you'll find impossible to put down."
—A. MANETTE ANSAY, author of *Vinegar Hill* and *Good Things I Wish You*

"A wrenching story...told with compassion and insight."
—JENNY WHITE, author of *The Sultan's Seal*

"A powerful exploration of faith, family, and the deep cultural divides that threaten to destroy these in our modern world. Ferriss has written a remarkable novel that strikes the perfect balance between the global and the personal."
—IVY POCHODA, author of *Visitation Street*

"[A] brave novel...about love in its many forms—romantic, maternal, filial."
—LISA ZEIDNER, author of *Layover* and *Love Bomb*

ACCLAIM FOR

The Lost Daughter

"An unflinching study of parenthood . . . Convincing, Franzen-style realism . . . A powerful domestic novel." —*Kirkus Reviews*

"*The Lost Daughter* delivers the goods: flawed but sympathetic characters and a plot that will keep readers turning the pages voraciously. From its harrowing prologue to its final sentences, I was emotionally engaged with this fine novel. Ferriss is a masterful storyteller." —#1 *New York Times* bestselling author Wally Lamb

"[A] complex, engaging novel about guilt, secrecy, and the mysteries of family. Lucy Ferriss is a courageous and thought-provoking writer." —*New York Times* bestselling author Tom Perrotta

"This achingly beautiful novel about marriage and love, pulsing with complex life, is the work of a master American realist, up there with Richard Yates or anyone else. With spellbinding attentiveness and intimacy it explores what a husband and wife can be sure they know about each other but also, in prose wearing night-vision glasses, the inaccessible places where the hidden past lies threateningly coiled, and which love must also find a way to reach."
—Francisco Goldman, author of *Say Her Name*

"In the same way that Judi Dench won an Oscar in 1999 for eight minutes of screen time in *Shakespeare in Love*, Ms. Ferriss's prologue is a doozy at a mere eleven pages . . . [Ferriss] has a real knack for creating dramatic tension." —*The New York Times*

"An emotionally riveting story . . . Ferriss moves the plot along at a fast clip, deftly weaving together recollections of the past and, as the disturbing truth of Brooke's secret slowly emerges, the present. All the while, Ferriss infuses the story with a heady dose of realism . . . *The Lost Daughter* manages to be a romantic family novel with a palpable atmosphere of impending calamity." —*Booklist*

"A compelling story." —*St. Louis Post-Dispatch*

MORE PRAISE FOR THE NOVELS OF LUCY FERRISS

"Tough, grave, and sweet . . . a book that will stay with me for a long time." —Lee Smith

"Ferriss's strength as an author is her uncanny ability to layer so many emotions in her fiction." —*St. Paul Pioneer Press*

"Beautiful . . . sympathetic, well-defined characters." —*The Advocate*

"Sad and soaring and sexy . . . lyrical, honest prose."
—Susan Straight, author of *Between Heaven and Here*

"Bittersweet but often laugh-out-loud funny." —*Foreword Reviews*

"Sharp humor and dazzling writing . . . one of the best books of the year, period." —*St. Louis Riverfront Times*

"Thought-provoking and disturbing . . . subtle and original."
—*Contra Costa Times*

"If in this novel Ferriss makes you think, she will also make you feel."

—*Publishers Weekly* (starred review)

"A gripping coming-of-age story . . . dense and richly evocative."

—*The Washington Times*

"A complex, satisfying work."

—*Ms.*

"A beautiful novel about family and love, from one of the best writers around."

—Oscar Hijuelos, author of *The Mambo Kings Play Songs of Love*

"Tight, cleanly structured, and polished . . . The author's voice is intelligent and her analysis shrewd . . . Interiors—the parts that matter—are brilliantly drawn, and the prose itself is often superb."

—*St. Louis Post-Dispatch*

ALSO BY LUCY FERRISS

THE LOST DAUGHTER

A SISTER TO HONOR

A NOVEL

Lucy Ferriss

Berkley Books, New York

THE BERKLEY PUBLISHING GROUP
Published by the Penguin Group
Penguin Group (USA) LLC
375 Hudson Street, New York, New York 10014

USA • Canada • UK • Ireland • Australia • New Zealand • India • South Africa • China

penguin.com

A Penguin Random House Company

This book is an original publication of The Berkley Publishing Group.

Library of Congress Cataloging-in-Publication Data

A sister to honor / Lucy Ferriss.—Berkley trade paperback edition.
p. cm.
ISBN 978-0-425-27640-2 (softcover)
1. Brothers and sisters—Fiction. 2. Muslim women—United States—Social life and customs—Fiction. I. Title.
PS3556.E754S56 2015
813'.54—dc23
2014029571

PUBLISHING HISTORY
Berkley trade paperback edition / January 2015

PRINTED IN THE UNITED STATES OF AMERICA

10 9 8 7 6 5 4 3 2 1

Cover design by Lesley Worrell.
Cover photo by Vanessa Skotnitsky / Imagebrief.com.
Interior text design by Kristin del Rosario.

For the women of Khyber Pakhtunkhwa

Woman is the lamp of the family.

—PASHTUN PROVERB

ACKNOWLEDGMENTS

I am deeply grateful to the entire Kakakhel family, but especially Shazia Sadaf, without whose hospitality, generosity, and wealth of sympathy this book could not have been written. Others in Pakistan were equally gracious and helpful in breathing life into both characters and story: Yawar Mumtaz and his family, the Ashfaq Chaudhry family, Aslam Khan, Tahir Malik, Zoia Tariq, Hina Jilani, Mohibullah Khan, and the faculty and students of the University of Peshawar all devoted time, energy, and insight to welcoming a stranger to their home and helping her understand its customs and challenges. I am grateful to Trinity College for a sabbatical and research funds that allowed me to travel to Pakistan. Paul Assaiante provided valuable expertise in competitive squash. For reading countless drafts and never giving up on me, I have the honor of thanking three irreplaceable editors: Jackie Cantor, Al Zuckerman, and Ann Patty. Amy Schneider's sharp eye brought the manuscript into focus, and the art department at Berkley rose beautifully to the occasion. Thanks to Eric Goodman for reading an early draft, and to Don Moon, as always, for his unflagging patience, honesty, and encouragement at every step along the winding path.

For background on Pashtun culture, the history of honor violence, and the changing roles of women in Islam and in Pakistan, I consulted perhaps three dozen volumes. Especially helpful were

Sadaf Ahmad's *Pakistani Women*, Jan Goodwin's *Price of Honor*, Benedicte Grima's *Secrets from the Field*, Amir Jafri's *Honour Killing*, and Kathleen Jamie's *Among Muslims*. Among a plethora of fine novels by Pakistani authors, Jamil Ahmad's *The Wandering Falcon*, Nadeem Aslam's *Maps for Lost Lovers*, and Uzma Aslam Khan's *Trespassing* were particularly evocative. Those interested in ongoing advocacy for women in Pakistan may wish to consult AURAT, http://www.af.org.pk/index.php; or Women Living Under Muslim Laws, http://www.wluml.org/node/5408.

Book One

CHAPTER ONE

In the valley below Farishta's house, the mulberry trees clung fast to their leaves. When the sun rose over the eastern hills they looked plated in gold; but as the wind lifted the dry leaves, they whispered like yellow-haired girls sharing secrets. Seated in a circle in the warm sun, the village women pulled stripped branches from the stacks piled up during the monsoon pruning. From these they made baskets they would use in the spring, when the trees had returned to flower and to fruit and the dead leaves had scattered in the tall grass.

Farishta was looking out from the *hujra*, the main room of the house. Her stepson Khalid lay sleeping on a charpoy, his injured arm dangling. His breath seemed to catch in his adenoids with a sound that gave her a prick of irritation, at which she felt ashamed. Soon her girls would be home from school; her husband, Tofan, would take time from overseeing the harvest to fetch them and check quickly on Khalid, and then he would be off again. At that point Khalid might wake. He would take from her a lunch of chicken wings and rice. He would ask where his father was.

Slowly she turned from the window, knelt by the charpoy, and touched her palm to his forehead. It had gone clammy; the fever had broken. Tonight, perhaps, he would haul himself from the bed and make his way into the village, to the Internet café, where he drank tea and shouted at whatever political news he could find on the flat screens they lined up along the wall. Farishta didn't like to admit how much easier she breathed when he was out of the house.

She stood, adjusting her dupatta. She was a compact woman, of middling height, but her firstborn son, Shahid, stood head and shoulders above her, and she was now eye to eye with her thirteen-year-old, Sobia. Even Afia, once the smallest and frailest of her children, could throw an arm around Farishta's shoulders. She smiled, thinking of Afia. Though Shahid still lit her heart brightest, Afia gave her the warmest hope. They were both half a world away, but not forever. In two months, there would be a wedding for Maryam, one of Tofan's cousins, and the women would all ask about Farishta's absent children. Afia, they would assure Farishta, would one day make a brilliant marriage—to a doctor in Islamabad, or a rising star in the army—and be one of the new women of Pakistan, bringing medical care to other wives and mothers while being one herself. If any female could manage such a thing with honor, it was Afia. As to Shahid . . . Farishta's eyes burned. He might not, she admitted to herself when she had moments alone, come back. In his letters, she could read the truth: He was becoming part of the West, comfortable among its gleaming towers and atomized citizens. Her husband, Tofan, still spoke of Shahid's returning with his business skills to help Khalid take over the farm. But that was a fantasy. Khalid would have the farm to himself, and he would fill it with his jihadi friends, and Farishta's old age, her daughters gone, would be spent among sneering men not of her blood.

She tried not to feel this way. She had been trying, now, for almost twenty years.

In the kitchen the cook, Tayyab, was rattling pots. She went in to him. In the corner, her mother-in-law sat embroidering a shawl. Two years ago, the old woman had suffered a loss that had robbed her of speech, but her sight still seemed keen enough. Once, her needlework had been among the finest in the village. "Asalaam aleikum, Moray," Farishta said, and touched her on the shoulder. The older woman looked up quickly, her eyes watchful as a bird's. "As soon as Sobia gets home," Farishta said to the unspoken demand. "I will speak with her."

Beneath his white beard, Tayyab harbored a knowing grin. How did servants come to know so much? He was hacking a chicken, the dull crunch of small bones beneath the cleaver. Tayyab's age was a mystery. He looked as old now as he had the day Farishta was brought to the Satar compound here in Nasirabad, almost two decades ago. Since then he had had five more children and lost the two daughters he had managed to marry off. Diabetes was affecting his eyes. But his face was as lean, lined, and sober as ever below his white cap. One of his remaining daughters, in the corner, was grinding cardamom, and the sweet tang filled the air.

Farishta took a wooden spoon and tasted the spicy sauce. Her eyes watered. "Good," she said. "Khalid likes it spicy."

She lifted a piece of warm bread from the rounds stacked by the stove and stepped out onto the veranda. The mulberry trees seemed to float on the million wings of their gold leaves. The breeze this time of year was luscious, free of the monsoon but not yet locked into the stony chill of winter. Far off, Tofan's cotton fields stood brown and stubbled, the harvest just finishing. She could hear the hum of the threshing machines. Every day for months now, her husband had risen before dawn and returned home only to fetch and deliver the girls. When Khalid, Shahid, and Afia had been young, she had done that duty herself; but things had changed. Her husband spoke of getting a driver for Sobia and little Muska. But today he would bring them home, and Farishta would draw Sobia into her bedroom alone and bring out the pair of bloodstained panties she had found stuffed under Sobia's mattress. The girl had become a woman. Patiently Farishta would explain to her—as she had explained to Afia seven years ago, as her own mother had explained to her when this awful-seeming thing suddenly happened—that a new and wonderful burden was laid upon her. From now on, Sobia would need to learn how to keep her chest covered with her dupatta. She would fast this year during Ramadan. She would no longer play in her old rough ways with her cousin Azlan. She would walk with a new, firm carriage, protecting the treasure of her womanhood.

Tayyab eased open the door from the kitchen. "Tea, memsahib?"

She smiled as he set down the tray—teapot, cup and saucer, biscuit, sugar bowl. Tayyab was fond of the niceties. He followed Farishta's gaze down the valley, to where the family's Suzuki van would be making its way from the school. "Only the little one left, now," he said.

"Muska, yes. She'll be my last." By which Farishta meant, and Tayyab understood, that she was done having babies. After three daughters, she was not confident of bringing forth another son. But Tofan had Khalid, and even though Shahid had been his brother's child, he treated him like a full son. Farishta had tried to do the same with Khalid, but her efforts had hurled themselves, always, against the mortar of his jealousy. Three years ago, when he'd gone to the mountains to join a new madrassa there, she had sighed with relief. But each time he came home, his beard was longer, his skin darker from the sun, his eyes more shifting and suspicious.

"You will be rich in grandchildren, memsahib," said Tayyab. Farishta watched as he bowed, backed away, and returned to the kitchen. When she turned back to the valley, she saw the Suzuki chuffing up the hill.

Muska dashed out from the backseat, waving the drawings she had done at school. Farishta kissed her and sent her back to take a snack from Tayyab and to feed the goat kid she had been nursing. Sobia exited the car more slowly and walked as if she held a coin between her knees. Her downcast eyes looked bruised. Inwardly Farishta smiled. She remembered the time she had felt this way, unaccountably filthy and out of sorts, wads of tissue paper between her legs, hoping no one would detect that she was slowly bleeding to death. "Come talk to me, Soby," Farishta said, holding out her hand.

"Something's wrong with her," Tofan said. A big man, he had stepped out of the car and stood quaffing a Pepsi. He scarcely paused when he dropped the girls off, especially during harvest. "She has been sullen all the way home, and when I asked—" He stopped when he looked up and caught Farishta's glance. "Ah," he said. Whether he understood what was happening with Sobia, what Farishta needed to do, was impossible to say. But he ducked his head back into the car, waved once, and drove off.

Farishta pulled the sack of sanitary napkins she had been saving from the bottom of the bathroom cupboard and went into the girls' room. Sobia was curled up on the bed, crying quietly. Farishta sat down and put a gentle hand on her daughter's hip. "Do you want to tell me?" she asked.

Sobia sniffled. Then she said, "I wish Afia was here."

"Because you could talk to her." The girl nodded. "About what you are experiencing." Another nod. "Well, I miss her, too. But I will speak to you as I spoke to her, when she was just your age." She reached over and tipped up her daughter's chin. The girl's eyes glowed with tears. Farishta felt a surge of pride. "You are bleeding," she said.

"Yes."

"But you are not ill. There is nothing wrong with you."

"But, Moray, it is awful, it comes—"

"You are bleeding because you are a woman now. It is a sadness and a happiness too. At Ramadan, this year, you will join the fast. Now I will show you how to use these," she said, pulling out the pads, "and how to begin thinking of yourself. Because you will never be the same again."

That evening, as she changed Khalid's dressing, her husband slit open the mail. "A fortunate day," Tofan exclaimed. Farishta felt Khalid's arm stiffen beneath her fingers. The *hujra* was spacious, filled with the warm light of the setting sun. Along the east face, they had shut the doors that turned the space, in summer, to an open-air living room. At the far end her husband's two living brothers were watching the news—another drone attack in the mountains, a gang murder in Sindh. When Farishta first came to Nasirabad, she had done the menu planning with her sister-in-law Mahzala, who was kind and protected her from Tofan's mother. Then Mahzala had died. That brother, Roshan, had never remarried; the other, Saqib, had never married at all. And with the change of customs, Farishta shared her meals more and more with her mother-in-law and her children, so that her husband and his brothers seemed to drift away even as they lounged on charpoys in the very next room.

"A fortunate day," Tofan repeated, "when we have letters from both our wayfarers."

Behind the door to the kitchen, Sobia had turned on the smaller television and was laughing at whatever comedy was being broadcast from Lahore. Despite their talk of womanliness this afternoon, despite her walking around the house as if she held a pot on her head, she sounded still like a little girl, giggling at sight gags. She was not a scholar, like Afia, who used to bend over her books by candlelight when there were rolling blackouts. Muska, at ten, was more studious than Sobia, but she was very shy. Only Afia had challenged her teachers. When Farishta had explained to Afia about menstruation, she had asked one question after another about female biology, until Farishta found herself stumped for answers.

She dampened a washcloth in the bowl she'd brought over and bathed Khalid's lacerated arm. "Indeed a fortunate day," Khalid was saying to his father, "when Allah sees our house pure and upright."

"And why shouldn't he?" Tofan said, opening the first letter. Farishta recognized the handwriting, Shahid's. She wanted to read it herself, to savor each word. But she kept washing the arm. "Here is your brother," her husband went on, his eyes scanning the page, "with A's on two of his midterm exams, and he has won the individual prelims, in Boston. He says there is a coach there, at Harvard. Might help him get into the business school." Tofan snorted. Folding up the letter, he flexed his eyebrows toward his older son. "You'll be needing someone who can keep a close eye on the accounting," he said, "when the time comes for the farm—"

"Baba, please." Khalid held up a pale hand. "Don't start on me about the farm. I know my responsibilities. There are things more important right now. There is a war, coming our way—"

"There is no war!" Tofan slapped the stack of letters onto the floor.

"Husband," Farishta said under her breath.

Tofan took a deep breath. His mustache rose and fell as he tightened his upper lip. In the corner, the TV gabbled. "You want to be a soldier, join the military. That's a respectable career. Shahid is a great athlete now, but he also has a head for business. No law says the blood son must take over. If you're not up to the task—"

"Shahid will do it better," Khalid said. Farishta finished the bandage just as he swung his legs over the edge of the charpoy and sat up, facing away from her. "Shahid does everything better except respect our ways."

"And what slander," said Tofan, "are you hinting at?"

Farishta sent him a warning glance: *Calm yourself. This is your son whom you love.* She felt a quiver of pleasure, knowing her husband cared for Shahid, but she wanted no quarrel between him and his firstborn. Khalid would only blame her.

"No need to hint," said Khalid. "Not when he takes our sister to Amreeka to show her off, with no concern for the consequences."

Farishta flushed with irritation. So typical of Khalid, to claim Afia as his sister and denigrate Shahid as if he were an interloper. But as if to prevent her from speaking out of turn, a bell tinkled from the kitchen. "That's Tayyab," she said, rising. "Shall I bring dinner out, or will you eat with us?"

"The men will eat alone," said Khalid.

"We will eat where I say we will eat," snapped his father. Bending to retrieve the mail, he slit open another envelope. Farishta hovered. "Afia writes," he said, replacing his reading glasses on his nose, "that she is taking four science classes this fall, and she studies so hard her head hurts. What she wouldn't give right now, she writes, for a good tikka dinner and her own bed. This does not sound like a girl who is being shown off."

Khalid grunted. "That's because you have not seen the photograph."

"What photograph?"

"On a certain website. You would find it interesting, Baba."

"Is it"—Farishta heard the hesitation in her husband's voice—"objectionable?"

"Judge for yourself. Come with me to Ali Bhai's."

Farishta could not constrain herself. "Afia is a modest girl," she said. "Shahid sees to her safety."

"I'm sure he does." This was Saqib, leaving the television to scoop some nuts out of the bowl. "Only they are gone so long, it is easy to be fearful. Why not bring them home, Tofan? For Maryam's wedding."

Tofan frowned. "Bring them home? But the expense—"

"Nonsense. The price of your cotton soared this fall."

"Yes, Baba," Khalid put in. "Why not celebrate? I would love to see my brilliant stepbrother."

Farishta caught the note of sarcasm. At the same time she thought of Sobia, wanting her sister home to whisper with her about blooming into a young woman. "I don't know," she said hesitantly, "if they can spare the time from their studies."

Thoughtfully Tofan folded his reading glasses and tucked Afia's letter into his breast pocket. "They may have a break," he said as if to himself, "in December."

"You bring her home," Khalid said, rising, "and I'll ask her about that photo."

Roshan had disengaged from the television and come to pour himself a glass of water from the pitcher by the door. "You bring your daughter home," he echoed in his sonorous voice, "mothers of many sons in Nasirabad will think you are prepared to entertain proposals."

"Hardly prepared," said Farishta quickly. "She has three more years of school."

"Nothing wrong with proposals," said her husband. "Khalid, where are you going?"

"I told you. To Ali Bhai's, the Internet café. I'll be back for dinner."

"Mind you are. This is not a hotel."

"And shall I serve out here?" Farishta asked again as her stepson shut the door to the *hujra* behind him. "Or will you join—"

Tofan gazed after his firstborn. He sighed and pulled at his mustache. Then he turned back to her. "Bring the food out here," he said, his voice suddenly wistful. "Tell my daughters I will come see them when they have finished their homework. How is Sobia . . . how is she feeling?"

"She will be fasting at Ramadan."

"Ah." He cast a look at the door to the kitchen, as if his daughter had left through it and would not return.

"And will Shahid and Afia—"

Tofan's eyebrows still drew together. "We should embrace our children while we can," he said. "And show the doubters how wrong they are."

CHAPTER TWO

At the start of every season, Lissy Hayes gave both her varsity squash teams the honor talk. It was corny as hell, made worse by how much she believed it. But she couldn't stop. Even though she was athletic director, wrapped in the power of her office, she never gave lectures other than this one. Bringing the women and men together in the big conference room next to her office, she used the whiteboard just like a professor.

"Honor," she began, "is one of the oldest concepts we have. It comes before love. It comes before victory. It comes from the same Latin-French root as honesty, and honesty is one of its chief components." She wrote *honesty* on the whiteboard. "In our sport, that means you don't call a let when you couldn't make it to the ball. You call yourself on obstruction when you obstruct. When you're judging, you call the fouls on your teammate the same as on his opponent. And no, it doesn't matter what the other guy is doing. Dishonesty needs its tubes tied. It shouldn't breed.

"What else makes for honor?" she went on. Tall, her blond hair spiky, formidable in sea-blue Enright University warm-ups, she paced the conference room. Enright's athletes were the Rockwells, from Norman Rockwell, who made his name in the Berkshires; their logo was a jutting promontory of rock from the hill overlooking the campus. "Does winning make for honor?" The new recruits started to shake their heads. They knew they weren't supposed to admit how much they wanted to win. "Well, sure," Lissy surprised them by saying. "If you win by playing your best game, you demonstrate your respect for your opponent, who wants nothing less—nothing less—than your best." *Respect*, she wrote on the board. "Pandering to an opponent, throwing him or her a few points, that's dishonorable. Giving up on a squash match when you're down two games and nine points, that's dishonorable. The point of a competitive game is to compete, and to compete with everything you've got is to act with honor, and don't let anyone tell you different.

"Then there's courage," she said, adding it to the list. "Now, this ain't war. You're not getting shot at. But you are trying a back-wall boast when you're down ten-three, or you're pounding the rail until you grab your moment. You're not playing wild, but you're not playing safe. You're playing with heart, which is the only honorable way to do anything in this life."

To her left sat Shahid Satar, her first starter on the men's team. Squash was the only sport Lissy coached, though she could have taken on tennis, soccer, field hockey in a pinch. Everyone in athletics called her Coach Hayes, which was more than fine by her. She knew all the players on both men's and women's squads—knew them intimately, their loves and hates, their daily habits, their family backgrounds, what foods they refused and what jealousies they harbored, what drew forth their greatest effort. In the three years since he came from a remote town in Pakistan to this small town in the Berkshires, Shahid had done more than his best for Enright. He had given Lissy back her sense of magic. With Shahid, she'd come to feel, any given moment held the possibility of perfection, of the opening to a new world. She hadn't felt this way since she tore her Achilles in the midst of a streak at the Cleveland Classic, twelve years ago, and walked away from the lights of her own squash career. So she glanced at Shahid as she continued, and in return received his slow, enigmatic smile.

"Integrity"—she added the word to the board—"refers to wholeness. If you compromise one part of your life to serve another, you have no integrity, and you are playing without honor. This means the athlete who cheats on her exams is a dishonorable athlete, even if nothing about the exams shows up on the squash court. It means the athlete who stays up all night with a friend at the hospital has to weigh the cost of coming onto the court. Got to be honest—remember that part, about honesty?—about his ability to do his best. Bowing out may be the most honorable thing. On the other hand, staying up all night with a friend who's drinking herself into a stupor because her boyfriend broke up with her? Then calling at noon to say you're not a hundred percent for the match? That's a lack of integrity. So to play with honor you have to know yourself, every bit. You've got to keep that self whole.

"And the team." She was tiring now, her voice going husky, keeping the speech rolling because it all had to be said, though voicing this many words at once seemed to knock the stuffing out of her. Writing *Loyalty* on the board, she went on. "Keeping the team whole. Loyalty and honor, you know, they're like fraternal twins. They don't share quite the same DNA. The player who showboats, the player who sneers at his teammate who just muffed the match, the player who entertains her sorority sisters with tales out of her squash squad—she is disloyal. She's a blight on the team. How do we treat her? With honor. We do everything we can to get the glue working again, and if we have to let her go we do so with a lot of pain. The opposite is the player who does something magical and invisible for one of his teammates, who gets no credit for it but does it out of pure loyalty, and we all feel his honor, it's like a warm breeze."

She squared her shoulders. She glanced at Shahid, and at Margot, the lead on the women's squad, a chunky fighter from Minnesota. These were her kids. "Loyalty can be dangerous, too. Confirming a let when there was no let, because your teammate needs it so bad? Dishonorable. Informing the coach that your teammate plagiarized, or hawked cocaine, or left the scene of an accident? Honorable. Yeah, I know," she said, when Yanik and Gus, her up-and-coming starters, shook their heads. "There's a code. You deal with your friends first, sure. Do everything to get them to come forward. Only if they don't, then you're being loyal to something that's rotten, and it'll rot your loyalty too. If you feel different about this," she said, targeting one after the other with her eyes, "you should find a different squad."

"But you're the A.D.," a first-year put in, feeling the speech wind down.

"Find another college then," she said. "There are plenty of sports teams that don't bother with honor. But this is Enright, and we do."

Occasionally an athlete dropped off the squad after the honor speech. Two years ago, she lost her top male recruit, a tall Argentinean who went out for soccer and told those players that the A.D. was a Class A bitch. Six months later, brought up on sexual assault charges after a frat party, he was suspended. So the speech did serve to weed out some bad apples, but it also put a shine on the good ones. Without it, getting them to cohere—a band of brothers, a circle of sisters—felt like herding cats.

The first team match of the season, an exhibition against Dartmouth, fell a week after Halloween. Standing in the middle of Court Four, Lissy and the Dartmouth coach, Brad, a sharp-faced pro with a dense tire at his waist and a chip on his shoulder, introduced their teams. The players shook the hands of each player on the opposition and of the coaches, then launched routines of high-fiving, chest-punching, and back-slapping before they broke into paired matches.

"What've you got this season, two Americans?" Brad asked as the guys started warming up.

"Four, counting Tom. He sprained his ankle skateboarding." Lissy nodded toward a player on the bleachers, among the couple dozen spectators who'd come out. If her kids did well over the season, the numbers would grow.

"You're joking." Brad moved his finger down the list of Lissy's players on his clipboard.

"Yanik's from Virginia," Lissy said without looking. "Gus Schneider is from right here in Devon, Jamil Brown's from Queens."

"He's Jamaican!"

"His parents are. It's called the melting pot, Brad."

"Well, yours make a spicy stew."

"They're student athletes. Like yours."

Brad was assistant A.D. at Dartmouth, which had a much higher profile than Enright. But if Lissy's teams beat a couple of Ivies, she'd be serious competition for the Brads of the world. She beamed at him and went to watch Court One.

Shahid looked fluid. Two weeks ago he'd placed first in the

prelims, setting the individual rankings for the season and bolstering his confidence. Andros, the guy he was playing, was a thick-necked South African; Brad recruited abroad, like Lissy, but among the Anglo and Aryan sort. Two years ago, Andros had called Lissy's Kurdish player, Afran, a raghead. Afran had almost lost his cool, but Shahid had stepped in, made a joke of it. He helped the others keep a lid on epithets. They got plenty, both from opposing players and from the crowd. Worse, when they first started at Enright, they got it from each other. Since forming her team, Lissy had learned more hate terms than she knew existed. Desi, banana, camel jockey, chi-chi, cholo, kaffir, paki, malaun, slopehead—they'd razzed each other on and off the court until Lissy decided to begin the year with a shouting match: Every offensive name they could think of got tossed out, never to be heard again. When she witnessed Shahid, the paki, go hoarse with cheering for Chander, the malaun, she punched one hand into the palm of the other, flush with success.

"We don't just preach diversity," went her standard line to the donors she was sent to woo. "We play it." In the endless, *endless* meetings about the capital campaign, the *d*-word, *diversity*, always brought a marked stiffening from Don Shears, Enright's president. But since she had taken over as A.D., Enright's athletic gifting had almost doubled. Maybe the alums weren't such bigoted blockheads as the administration imagined.

"Keep it flowing," she shouted to Shahid. She never looked at him without a certain softening, almost like a bruise, in her heart. It wasn't simply the assurance with which he played, or his bird-like qualities, the way he flew diagonally over the court to retrieve a drop shot or how his brows became a hawk's brow as he stretched for the volley. It was mostly the look of wonder he wore as the ball arced high in a cross-court lob coming down to the back wall, coming to him. As if physics itself astonished and seduced him.

She watched him finish the point with a nick that died off the right wall, then turned to the others. Afran, at number two, was down 0–4 to a big lug of a kid recruited from Andover. The other courts were trading points. She moved into the bleachers to shake hands with a few stalwarts from the faculty. On the fourth bleacher she spotted Shahid's sister, Afia, a shy girl who had come to the States last year to attend Smith. She was wearing a loose purple tunic over a black turtleneck, with loose black pants and flats. The only parts of her exposed were her face and hands. No wonder, Lissy thought, she couldn't recruit women from countries like Pakistan. "Hey there," Lissy said, making her way over. Afia was flanked by a redheaded girl sporting a Dartmouth sweatshirt. "Early in the season, for fans."

"I am helping Shahid to study tonight," said Afia.

"Attagirl. He could use some focus. What's your excuse?" she said to the redheaded girl.

"This is my friend Taylor," said Afia.

"Got a guy out there, Taylor?"

The redheaded girl grinned. "He's up against Afran."

"Well, it's just the start."

She turned back to Afia. Behind her reserve, Lissy had always detected a vibrancy, almost an exultation at the challenge of academics. Such a great thing Shahid had done, giving his sister this chance.

"Your family must be proud of you," she said now. "And Shahid." She perched briefly; she needed to get back to the courts.

"Oh, they are proud of Shahid," the girl said. Her voice cracked a little.

"Come on, Chase!" Taylor jumped up and clapped. Lissy glanced at the scores. Shahid had taken his first game and was on a ninety-second break. But Afran was in trouble. By the time she'd excused herself and made her way back down, the first of his games was over: 11–7, Dartmouth.

Stumbling off the court, Afran collapsed on the bench. Shahid was already crouched by his side. "So," Lissy said. "What's going on?"

"Just don't have it today, Coach."

Normally she knew how to do this, to let a player talk his way through defeatism to the other side. "Let's hear it," she said.

"He's crowding me, you know? So I try cross-courts to get him off the T, but he volleys, and then I'm just hitting straight again, playing defense."

"So what are you going to do about it?"

"C'mon, Coach. Don't make me go through this."

She sighed. This was her third season with Afran. He could be his own worst enemy. "You want me to tell you?"

"I can't do anything right today, okay?"

Shahid leaned in. "You can nick the ball," he said. "You're rad at that. If he's geared up to cover a drive, he is not ready to dash up and cover the nick."

Afran lifted his face from the towel. His eyes were bloodshot. "I guess I could try that."

"What else?"

"Or I could show the kill and then just flick the ball to the back."

"Now you're talking." Shahid tapped his racquet against Afran's. "And what about the T?"

"Dominate it," Afran said. "But, dude, he obstructs me."

"So ask for a let."

"Yeah, and let him call me Muhammad."

"You think that lughead's not calling me Muhammad?"

"Fifteen seconds," said Yanik. He had the job of referee for Afran's match. It was one of squash's great features, Lissy thought, the way it called on players to shift from competing to judging.

Shahid stood up. "Whose game you playing?" he said to Afran. "His or yours?"

As Shahid turned away, Lissy touched his arm. "Thanks," she said.

"He'll be okay," said Shahid. He glanced over at the score on Chander's match, which had drawn even. "Go Rockwells!" he shouted. Then he replaced his goggles and stepped back into the glass cage.

Losing, Lissy knew, was never an option for Shahid Satar. When the coach at the Pakistan Squash Federation first called her, Shahid had played professionally for a year. You'd have thought he'd spent a year at hard labor, the coach said, so crushed was his spirit. Not that he had done badly. He had risen up the way boys did in countries with Olympic-sized aspirations: not through his family's wealth or connections, but through the national sports system. Everything he had, all the medals and rankings, he had earned. There were simply better players on the international scene. When Lissy first spoke with Shahid on the phone, he had apologized for his failures, sure he was wasting her time, so many had believed in him but there he'd gone, again and again, losing in the third round, the fourth round. He'd been forty-eighth in the world in juniors, Lissy had pointed out. A long silence had ensued, in which she realized he was transforming her praise into pity. Finally he said, as though lying prostrate, that he would do his very best for her. He would fight for every point. And yes, yes, he would study. He wanted to learn things. Things besides squash.

His grades from Edwardes College in Peshawar had been good enough to get him an academic scholarship at Enright; the rest, Lissy understood, was being paid by a childless uncle in Peshawar. Already in this, Shahid's senior year, doors had started to open for him in the States—a chance to coach at Harvard, internships in the corporate world that knew of squash through the elite clubs in New York. He impressed people.

A half hour later, his match was over in three games. As the others went into a fourth, the three-sided block of bleachers looking over the U-shaped set of courts filled with spectators. The players glanced back at the growing crowd and played more fiercely.

Amazing, Lissy always thought, the power of a cheering crowd. Her brothers and their friends, ruffians cheering by the swanky squash courts at the Missouri Athletic Club, called themselves Lissy's Love Boat. Inspired by them, she used to hit rail after rail in the community center after school let out. To build her speed, she strapped weights onto her ankles. To train her reflexes, she sometimes hit blindfolded, trying to guess from the sound where the ball would bounce.

She resembled Shahid, she thought now as she joined him to watch Afran play his fourth game, more than she did his sister. Like Shahid, she hated to lose; she accepted no excuses from her weaker self. And like Shahid, she was more fragile than anyone knew.

Down 7–9, Afran hit a trickle boast, a tricky shot that came off the side wall and ricocheted low on the front, stretching his opponent into the front corner. Chase caught the effect of it too late and missed before he sprawled on the floor. "That's my boy," said Shahid, pumping his fist.

Lissy took her place on the bottom bleacher. If Afran lost this game, he'd be tied at two games all. Chase, she noted, had dropped twenty pounds and put on muscle since last year. He darted around the court more nimbly than Afran.

"I think he's going down," she said to Shahid.

"No way, Coach," Shahid said. "Watch him now."

Sure enough, Afran took the score to 9–9, then 10–9 with a looping lob that Chase wanted to call out and shanked instead. Though Chase nicked a ball for 10 all, Afran served an ace, and followed it on the next point with a series of rails until he pulled the ball off the wall and slammed a volley—a move that Lissy would have called pure Shahid. "You've been coaching him," she said.

Shahid grinned. "A few tips," he said. Then, as Afran shook Chase's hand and the spectators began to gather their things, he glanced up to the bleachers and frowned. "You seen my sister, Coach?"

Lissy twisted to look up at the top bleacher. Afia was gone; not a hijab to be seen. "Her friend's there," she said. Taylor didn't look happy at her boyfriend's loss. "She's probably in the ladies' room."

"Hey, man," said Afran as he came off court. "Did it make a difference?"

"Three-two so far, thanks to you," said Lissy.

"Thanks to him, you mean," Afran said, fist-jabbing Shahid. "This is your year, man. We're taking it all the way."

"Inshallah," said Shahid.

With a portion of the crowd drifting off, Lissy looked around for her second tier. She had four more matches to coach, and then the women. In the corner by the snack machine, Yanik was stretching his hamstrings. "You seen Gus?" she asked him.

Yanik jerked his head in the direction of the unlit hallway toward the lockers. Sure enough, there stood Gus Schneider, in his uniform, his unruly hair tied back, squash bag at his side. But he wasn't stretching. He was embracing a girl. For good luck, Lissy thought. She took two steps, then stopped. She recognized the girl. Her head bent back to receive Gus's kiss, her head scarf had fallen away from her dark hair. Shahid's sister, Afia.

Lissy smiled. *How sweet*, she thought. Discreetly, she turned away. She counted to ten. When she turned back, Gus was coming toward her briskly with his bag. And the girl was gone.

CHAPTER THREE

Gingerly Afia stepped out of the restroom. She looked both ways before she scurried back to the bleachers. Gus was on the far right court now, three other Enright players on the nearer courts. Shahid's woman coach prowled back and forth like a blond lioness watching her cubs. Afia perched on one of the top bleachers, out of Gus's sight, to wait for her brother. She tried to look into the middle distance, as if she were thinking about her biology class, or Maryam's wedding, or anything other than the salty taste of Gus's mouth on hers five minutes before.

It wasn't the first time he'd kissed her. That had been last week, the night he had taken her out for her first hamburger, to Local Burger in Northampton, where he said they got the beef from nearby farms so it was probably close to halal anyway. She'd had a chocolate milkshake with the sandwich. She hadn't thought much of the meat—she liked her mother's kofta better—but the shake was creamy, delicious. When he'd pulled the car over to the curb to drop her off, Gus had put his hand gently on her jaw and turned her to him. Pulling away, she had felt a stirring deep inside, like the froth on the milkshake.

But that had been in Gus's car, in the dark. This kiss had come suddenly as she'd been heading toward the restroom, in the hallway where anyone could be passing by. Suddenly Gus had been in front of her, his squash bag slung over his shoulder, and before she could speak he had cinched her waist with his free hand. *Wish me luck*, he had said, and his lips were on hers, his tongue flicking quickly in and out of her startled mouth. His fingers had feathered against her hips before he kept going. Anyone could have seen them, anyone.

But no one had. No one, she reminded herself as she practiced her absentminded gazing. Just like the first time the plane lifted away from the tarmac in Peshawar and she was sure it was going to fall, it was turning, it was falling, and then it didn't fall but rose safe into the blue sky, a free-floating panic grabbed at her breath and pumped through her veins long after the danger was past. And she thought—as she'd thought then—*never again*, while at the same time the rush of pleasure slipped back and she realized terror wasn't the only feeling in her veins. And this time, as she pushed herself back onto the bleacher, to look as though she had been there a long while, she felt also the damp warmth and tingle between her legs that Gus's kiss had ignited. In the restroom she had soaked a paper towel and held it cold to her face, then a dry towel; she had wiped her glasses and fixed her scarf. All she had to do now was appear mildly distracted.

"Hey, Shahid, man," she heard. She turned to see her brother's friend Afran rounding the corner from the locker rooms. "Your sister's right where you left her!"

She smiled modestly at Afran. Behind him, Shahid bounded out. "You go invisible, or what?" he asked in Pashto.

"That's my power," she said. And as she lifted her book bag to follow him out, she knew it would be all right. He hadn't noticed a thing. Though he talked to the coach before they left, she didn't even stop in front of Gus's court. She had become expert at dividing her life into compartments, the way fetal cells differentiated until one group could function only as a heart, another only as bone marrow. When Shahid had told her about Maryam's wedding and the tickets Baba was sending, she had felt only a surge of excitement and homesickness—not the homesickness she'd felt last year, when Massachusetts food made her ill and the winter cold threatened to kill her, but a longing to be back in Nasirabad, with its smells of spice and animal dung, with her sisters' silly games and the clack of knitting needles from her grandmother, her *anâ*. By contrast, when Gus rang on the dorm phone—he knew not to ring her mobile—she felt only her heart rising in her chest, as if his call meant their future was unfurling before them as unblemished as a fresh carpet. Now and then she reminded herself that the heart and the bone marrow have to work together, or a person will not survive. But normally she put off for another day the question of reconciling her two separate lives. Only now did she have the memory of that sudden encounter, his hand on her waist, his lips. Like a jewel that glows in the dark.

When they'd picked up a pair of halal burritos and settled into Shahid's dorm room, he put on the DVD of *Othello* he'd checked out of the library. Outside was windy, with fat gray clouds scudding across the sky, the last yellow leaves of fall dancing across Shahid's window. Already the hours they had spent together last spring, with her hauling him through Principles of Physics, were a distant memory. He wasn't taking any more sciences, just this lit course and then business and economics. Shahid was a better writer than she, Afia kept telling him; Shakespeare should be easier for him. But he had trouble grasping these plays.

When the video was over, all he could talk about were the scenes that weren't in the version he'd read for class.

"And they show a lot of sex, you know," he said in Pashto, not looking at Afia. "Because it's for the Americans, they need that."

"They show it between married people," she said quickly. "They wouldn't show it on the stage."

She had read the play, for his sake. If he could nail this class, he'd bring his GPA above 3.5, which was what the fellow at Harvard said he needed for that job, next year. She had her own paper to write, for Microbio, but she could do that tonight, with lots of tea. She marked a few places in Act Three. "You see how it's morning when Cassio asks Desdemona for a favor? Emilia's with her. She's never alone with Cassio. But by that night, Othello's sure his wife has been unfaithful and he strangles her."

Shahid shook his head. "I'm lost already," he said. "And it's all in this old English—"

"But remember in the movie. There's just the one night that Othello spends with his wife."

"Yeah, when she marries him against her father's wishes. I thought I could write about how it's fated not to work because she's so headstrong. And in the movie, what they do—"

"Shahid, it's an American movie. We see that stuff all the time."

"We don't write about it."

"Ignore the sex. If you look at the time frame—"

"Still, he's a Moor. She's Italian. Maybe it's kismet, you know, that they die."

"Where would you find the evidence, Shahid lala?"

He stood and stretched. His dorm room was smaller and more cluttered than hers. He'd drawn a single this year. "You don't need evidence," he said, looking down on the leaf-strewn quad. "This isn't science."

"I took a class in poetry last spring. You needed evidence even for that." Carefully she pointed out to him that Shakespeare's play let only twelve daylight hours elapse between the time Othello first becomes jealous and the moment he kills Desdemona. "And see here," she said, pointing to where she had highlighted lines in yellow, "how he says she's committed the act of shame with Cassio a thousand times. But she hasn't had the chance to do it once!"

In the end, Shahid couldn't stop talking about Desdemona's planting the seed of suspicion by the way she dishonored her family. That was, Afia thought later, the way Baba would see it, and Khalid too—especially Khalid. So she helped Shahid write his paper about Desdemona's disobedience and kismet. Even if the evidence wasn't strong, she thought it would get him the B he needed.

Just as they were finishing, three of the squash guys came by to persuade Shahid out for a hamburger. Afia adjusted her hijab and averted her eyes. She knew all Shahid's teammates. But Gus was among the three, and she didn't trust herself. "I have to take my sister back to school," Shahid said to them.

"Both of you come out with us," said Yanik. "You're not keeping halal anymore, Shahid. Don't give us that bullshit."

"My sister is," said Shahid.

"Valerie's hostessing tonight," Yanik said. "C'mon, dude."

"I have to get back," Afia said. It hurt not to lift her eyes to Gus. He was the only secret she kept from her brother—well, he and her job. Three afternoons a week, she bagged groceries at the Price Chopper in Northampton. The scholarship she had from Smith covered tuition and housing, but she had told her family it covered everything, just like Shahid's scholarship and his allowance from Uncle Omar. The older women at the Price Chopper knew about Gus and didn't mind when he came by. She called them all "Aunty," the way she would have at home. At the end of the day, they usually gave her a bag of dinged cans and boxes they'd found, and she sorted through for what was halal. It lifted her spirits, to tie on her apron and spend the dark evenings in a bright place where she felt cared for.

But she could not tell Shahid about the shameful job she held, bagging other people's food and mopping up their messes; and she could not let him see how well she knew Gus. She put the Gus-feeling away, like moving a wayward cell with a tweezers back to the organ it was meant to serve. As they stepped out of the brick dormitory onto the parking lot, she saw the clouds that had been threatening all day had opened, and rain was coming down. She slipped off her flats and waited barefoot on the cold sidewalk for Shahid to bring his Honda around.

"What, no Wellingtons?" he said when she slid in.

"I bought some last year. They leaked."

"Where'd you buy them?"

"I think it's called Payless?"

He chuckled. "Silly sister. Those are cheap, you can't expect them to last." He glanced at the clock on the dash. "We'll swing by the outlets," he said. "Get you something for rain and snow too. What'd you wear last winter for the snow?"

Afia shrugged. She didn't want to tell him she had ruined her sturdiest leather shoes, the only ones that could keep her warm enough. She couldn't expect a brother to notice such things. That he thought she could buy anything at all was odd, since he didn't know about the grocery job—but even with her own money, she was a burden. Shahid had had to ensure she was safely transported and cared for on weekends and school breaks. He had to answer to Moray and Baba for any tarnish on the gleam of her promise in America.

"They have good boots here," said Shahid, pulling up in front of Clarks. "Britisher boots, rains all the time there."

Afia hung back while he pulled one model after another off the shelves and examined them critically. Her eye was drawn to a pretty pair with a buckle on the side and a stacked heel, but she let Shahid ask the saleswoman questions about waterproofing and warmth. "Here," he said in English when the woman had fetched her size, "try these."

He handed her a pair of strangely elegant workmen's boots. They laced up from a padded toe but ended in a flap of shearling. When she stood up in them her feet felt hugged. "These are the kind Patty wears in winter," she said in Pashto.

"That's the idea. They'll keep you dry and warm too."

She glanced at the tag dangling off the shelf. "But Shahid," she said, "these are more than a hundred dollars. You can't spend this on boots!"

He snorted. "You don't know what Uncle Omar sends me for allowance, do you?"

"But that money's supposed to be for you—"

"Do you like them? Do they fit?"

Her eyes strayed to the pretty pair. But they were even more and would not keep the rain off. Her toes began to feel the way they felt when she wiggled them in front of a fire. "They're perfect," she said.

The rest of the way to Northampton—her boots on in the car, her feet a pair of little ovens—they talked about Maryam's wedding, the tickets Shahid would buy with Baba's credit card, the dates they would each be finished with exams. Afia was excited to fly home in the middle of the year. She had told the other girls in her suite about Maryam's wedding. She had even told her favorite professor, Sue Glasgow, about it. It would be fabulous, Professor Glasgow said, for her to see her family. She didn't ask, the way the girls did, how long Maryam had known her fiancé; she didn't ask if

Afia liked this young man. Professor Glasgow taught biology, but she understood a lot more about the way families could be organized than the members of Al-Iman, which Afia had been invited to join when she arrived at Smith last year. The Al-Iman girls were mostly Jordanians, and they wore the hijab in the Turkish style, not at all like Pakistanis. The famous Muslim feminists they talked about were from the Middle East, and they all seemed wealthy, with winter vacations on the Black Sea or in Cancun. She didn't have any more in common with these students, she complained to Shahid, than with the women in the South Asian club, who were all Indians and Sri Lankans.

"It's the same for me," Shahid said. "The only one who even starts to understand is Afran, and he's from Turkey. That's practically Europe."

"So strange they are bringing us home now," Afia said. "Our cousin Geeta was married when we were on spring break, but they didn't even talk about flying us back. It's so expensive."

Shahid's mouth twisted. "Baba probably wants to talk to me about the farm."

"He's not ready to turn over the farm!"

"No. And when he is, it should go to Khalid. He's Baba's true son."

"Baba doesn't think that way. He's never made a distinction."

Shahid shrugged. "Khalid's the oldest. And I have no interest in the farm."

"So why—"

"Baba will dangle something. To persuade me to return, not now but sometime, maybe with a Harvard degree."

Afia's stomach hollowed out. "And you won't?"

"There's nothing for me there. I love home, Afia. Just as much as you. But I can't be a doctor, tending to poor women in the tribal areas. I'm not going to be an engineer. And I don't see myself at the Peshawar Sports Academy." They were turning up Afia's narrow street. Shahid's wipers squeaked across the windshield; his headlights shone on a carpet of wet leaves. "Inshallah, Baba could find you a husband who's emigrating to America," he said. "Another doctor, or something."

"What, so I'll stay in America and keep you company? It never works that way, Shahid. When does Moray see Uncle Omar?"

"She sees him."

"Well." He'd pulled over in front of her dorm. She gathered up her cloth bag of books and her old shoes, and hoisted her pocketbook over her shoulder. "I have almost three years still to go," she said. "Let's not talk about being separated yet."

Impulsively, she leaned over and planted a kiss on her brother's cheek. He turned to her, his eyes wide with shock. "What's got into you?"

"Thank you," she said, "for my boots."

"Thank you for my essay."

She made her way up the puddled walk and through the old-fashioned foyer of the dorm, so much cozier than Shahid's. Gus had not reentered her thoughts—not since she had glimpsed him in Shahid's room, and not yet, not until the tie to Shahid loosened and this strange life of her own slipped in. She climbed the curving stairs to the third floor, where her room was open. On the floor sat Patty and Taylor, eating pizza. "Hey, girlfriend," Patty called out. "I hear your bro did good."

"He did. About Chase, I am sorry he loses, Taylor."

"'S'okay," Taylor said, not taking her eyes from her laptop screen. "Chase is a punk."

"They had a fight," Patty explained.

"Oh! I am sorry."

"But look here," Patty went on. "You're a total celeb, my hijabi roomie."

Afia sat on her bed and pulled off her boots. They were not beautiful boots, but she would treasure them. Already, on the thin carpet, her feet began to cool. That Chase and Taylor would fight seemed a tragedy, but no one in the room was acting that way. "What is a celeb?" she asked.

"A famous person! Look here."

They made room for Afia by the coffee table. At Patty's nod, she lifted a slice of the pizza. Then she peered at the screen Taylor tilted toward her. "This is Smith College," she said.

"Look closer. Look at the faces. It's like a slide show."

Chewing, she watched while a photo of a girl in a graduation cap gave way to one of a girl hitting a hockey ball, which faded to a pair of girls with a professor—she recognized Sue Glasgow—staring at a test tube. That image, too, rolled away, and there was a crowd of excited young women, holding aloft pieces of cardboard with slogans: *We are Smith! Diversity = Strength!* There, at the right edge, stood Afia herself, her right hand in a high five with a girl from Somalia and her left holding a hand—oh, Allah be merciful, a man's hand—that connected to a figure who had been cut from the frame. She remembered the event, in late September. She remembered Gus's hand.

"Roll it back," she said, the pizza slice poised in the air, halfway to her mouth. Though what she wanted to say was, *Take it back, erase it.*

"Just wait," Patty said. "It'll come around again. Cool, huh?"

As the photos rotated through, a knot of fear gathered under Afia's rib cage. The rally appeared again. "Cool," she managed to say.

CHAPTER FOUR

Waiting outside Coach Hayes's office the first week of December, Shahid drummed his foot on the tight carpet. He had thc itinerary in his back pocket. The past three Januaries, he had played the Tournament of Champions in New York, with Coach Hayes at his side, the week before spring classes began. It was a so-called amateur tourney, but the best in the world came to America for it, and he had the chance to see guys he'd played in the juniors, now struggling like him to figure out their next path to glory. This year, as luck had it, Afia could not leave Smith before December 22. Baba would not hear of a visit shorter than two weeks, and the championships were four days after New Year's.

He loved squash. It was difficult to say why, to put the feeling into words. Only to say that if he couldn't play squash, he wasn't sure how he could live. He would miss this tournament, not that he had any chance of winning, but just for that pulse of life beating within its glass cages.

He hadn't felt this way at first. It had been Uncle Omar's idea, one weekend when he'd come to Nasirabad. Squash, Omar had said to Baba. That's the sport for Shahid. We have a great training center, right in Peshawar. Makes champions. Were not the two greatest squash players of all time Pashtun?

That first week at Omar's home had been an experiment, a strange bed and a new routine, lessons with Coach Khan every morning at the Peshawar Sports Academy. But when he returned home to Nasirabad, Shahid hadn't been able to sleep at night, for missing the din of the city. Cars had honked and people shouted inside his ears, their strange accents like distant music. The town of his birth had seemed arid and lifeless. Then he had taken the new squash racquet Omar had given him and shanked the hard rubber ball around the high-walled courtyard by the grammar school. He lost himself in the movement of the ball, the way it came off all the walls, the angles and spins. It was like getting to know a person—if you sent him that way, he bounced up, over, and low on the back wall; if you sent him this way, he hit the corner and shot back to your forehand. The ball answered you back. It surprised you. It caught you from behind, unawares. When Omar's BMW pulled into Nasirabad a month later, Shahid's bag had already been packed. His mother's eyes shone with tears. His father hosted the neighborhood for tikka. To the world championships, they toasted. To the Olympics one day!

Finally the door to Coach Hayes's office opened. Margot, number one on the women's squad, was heading out. Coach patted her back, murmuring something. "Hey, Shahid," Margot said. "How was your Thanksgiving?"

He rose. "I got caught up on work. Coach fed us turkey."

"I hear that's quite a feast," Margot said to Coach Hayes. "Can I count as an international student next year?"

"You and everyone else from New York," Coach said.

Shahid exchanged grins with Margot as they passed. He would

have liked to have her at Coach's Thanksgiving because she would have made Afia feel less alone. The other guys—Afran, Chander, Carlos—were all from countries where people knew how to keep a respectful distance, which was good. Still, Afia had spent most of her time in the kitchen helping Coach's husband or on the floor playing with Coach's three-year-old daughter, Chloe. She said she enjoyed it, but Shahid thought she would rather have been with her Smith friends.

That had been a stroke of genius, he admitted to himself with a nice dollop of pride, finding Smith College for her. After she took her O levels in Nasirabad, her teachers had recommended the university in Peshawar. But she could never have stayed with Uncle Omar, who had no wife. In America, Shahid had declared, he could keep a close eye on her. She could get her medical degree at a women's university and come home to attend to the women in Nasirabad who needed doctors, women who could not be seen by men. Baba had doubted there were such places in America. But Shahid was persuasive, and Afia's eyes shone. She had sent in the application for a scholarship, and the letter had come back by express, an acceptance. Their mother had clapped her hands even as she wept.

There were men on her campus, he knew. But the place was designed for women, sensitive to women. Afia would have been horrified by what went on at Enright during the weekends. She would have felt tainted—no: She would have *been* tainted. As it was, she had returned home last summer the same innocent she had been when she went away. Moray and Baba had been pleased beyond measure. They'd told Khalid so when he came down from the mountains and tried to persuade them to keep Afia home before *Amreeka* stained her *namus*, her purity. This fall, when school had started up again, Shahid had felt easier in his heart, able to let his sister live her college life without checking up on her every other day.

"I hear you got a B-plus on that Shakespeare paper," Coach was saying as she led the way into her office. "Good job."

He smiled sheepishly. "Thanks to my sister."

"Afia?" Coach's blond eyebrows went up. "Thought she was all about science."

"She's better at everything that is not a matter of hand-eye coordination."

"Don't put yourself down, Shahid. When you apply for that Harvard job, you'll be giving them a GPA that speaks for itself."

"Does Coach Bradley really think I am qualified?"

"I know he wants you. It's a question of the business school. You don't want to be a squash coach all your life."

"I could be an A.D. Like you."

She ignored this. She knew him too well—better, in some ways, than either of his parents. She knew he couldn't care, as she did, about twenty or thirty young people at once. He cared deeply about a few. And he was too proud to be a great coach. When he listened to Coach's honor talk every year, the parts that stuck with him were loyalty and courage because they echoed *pashtunwali*, the code of the Pashtuns, of his tribe, which he would never shake off, Harvard or no Harvard.

"So," Coach was saying, glancing over his itinerary. "You miss the Tournament of Champions. Well, they'll survive." Her mouth, though, was tight.

"I'm sorry, Coach, but my parents—"

"Don't worry about it. Let's look at the schedule for when you're back."

She turned to the wide screen on her desk. It was open to the website for Smith College. "Why are you looking at my sister's school?" Shahid asked, surprised.

"Oh, that's Margot. She's lesbian, you know. And Enright's

such a straight place. She's thinking of transferring, so we were looking it over together."

"Margot is—" he started to say, shocked at the word *lesbian*, which he'd heard before but never about an actual girl he knew. But then his eye followed the photos that drifted across the screen below the Smith College logo. "Wait, Coach," he said, as her hand went to her mouse.

"Shahid, it's not what you think, they're not all gay. I wouldn't have suggested you send Afia there if—"

"Wait." He put his hand on her wrist. "Look," he said.

He pointed to the screen. A photo bloomed into being: a rally of some kind, and his sister, his *sister*, her mouth open, shouting something, and her hand holding another hand, definitely, yes, he sat clutching Coach's wrist while the photos looped through and he could see it again, a big hand attached to a muscular arm. A man's hand.

He slapped at the screen with the back of his hand. "What the hell is this?" he shouted. He stood up. His head felt full and tight. "What is she doing?" He looked at Coach, who had a strange, pale look.

"Shahid, calm down," she said. "That's Afia, right? You're upset because—"

"Turn it off! Turn the bloody thing off!"

She peered once more at the image as it loomed up, then closed down her browser. She stood to face him. "She's at a rally," she said. "There's nothing wrong. You've had your picture on the Enright site. She's not being inflammatory or anything. If you want me to talk to her . . ."

"It's not what she's *doing*, Coach. It's what she is *holding*."

She frowned. She looked confused. Three years now, she'd been his coach. So long he'd almost forgotten how horrified he'd been when he first laid eyes on her. When he wrote home about life at Enright, he never mentioned having a female coach, much less a female A.D. They would have thought him disrespected, or thought squash was not just unpopular in the States but reviled. Even Uncle Omar, who had spoken with Coach Hayes on the phone, thought she was an underling, and Shahid had never set him straight.

But whenever Coach fixed him with her knowing eyes, Shahid couldn't imagine an authority greater than hers. She never barked, like other coaches; she didn't need to. She went to the heart of the matter, whether it was the joint you'd smoked the night before or your showing off for the girl in the third row. Even when you were at your worst, she would know at least one thing you were doing right. She never dissed your opponent. *You've got his attention*, she'd sometimes say. *Now earn his respect.* The year before Shahid came, Enright had landed Jean-Louis Nèves, a top recruit from Belgium. When Nèves got caught DUI, she suspended him without a blink; when three others threatened to quit, she opened the door to usher them out. They came back the next day, Nèves the next year. He told Shahid that Coach had kept him in therapy every week; he'd hated the bitch, he said, and yet he owed her his life.

Now, though, she was recoiling. "Shahid," she said, "*you* had a girlfriend, last year."

"This is nothing to do with that. Did you not *see?*" He waved at the blank computer screen as if the picture were still on it, his sister's hand in that paw.

"Shahid, you and Afia are in the States now. If she wants to have a boyfriend—"

"Does she? Does she have one?" He was shouting at her now, at his coach. Coach Khan had caned boys who shouted back.

But only a flicker of something—disapproval? doubt?—disturbed her gaze. Then she said, "I don't know, Shahid. It's none of my business. I'm not sure it's yours."

"It is. I have to go, Coach."

"Stay. Talk to me."

But he couldn't. He let his itinerary float from Coach Hayes's desk to the floor, exited, and hurried through the reception room. His breath whistled through clenched teeth. Outside, in the bright December air, he pulled out his phone and fired off a text to Afia. *WTF is up with that website pic?* He couldn't think what else to write. A dull panic slowed his steps as he started across the quad to his history class. Afia was the flower in his heart. He might be the son who would find a place in the world of Western commerce, whose name might be in the newspapers. But she was the daughter who would bring good to the world. When they helped each other, Afia spent hours reading his assignments and helping him shape his words; he bought her boots with Uncle Omar's money. Who was this guy creeping his fingers around her small hand? He'd kill this guy. Whoever infected Afia, infected him. And now here came a high voice, behind him on the frozen quad, calling his name. "Shahid! Shahid, you dope! Wait up!"

He turned. No, no, this he did not need. "Hi, Valerie," he said. Just speaking her name made his penis move, in his jeans.

Her books under her arms, dressed in a V-neck cashmere sweater and an open down jacket, she caught up to him. She was breathing heavily; her breasts bobbed over the books. "Haven't seen you all semester," she said. She tipped her head at him, her green eyes glinting in the bright cold sun.

"Yeah, well." He'd practiced for this encounter for months. He was going to say, *You know why that is*, and she would confess her weakness, her fickleness, and then how she had realized she needed him, at which point he would say he had no time for untrustworthy women and would leave her on her knees, begging. Now, that speech dissolved into sawdust. “Been busy,” he said. “I’m late for class.”

“We’re having a party next weekend. You know, like pre-finals. Afran’s coming. I thought maybe you—”

“Maybe I what? Maybe you’re between boyfriends and Shahid’ll do for a quick one?” This came out harsh and ugly. He wanted to snatch the words back, but they hung like frost in the air.

“Shahid, come on. We can be friends, can’t we? It’s not like we were going steady, it’s not like we made some commitment—”

“Friends,” he snorted. He shook his head, to clear it. Who was this girl? Were they all like this? Was his sister like this? That hand, the way she held that man’s hand, at her own volition. “I’ll catch you later, Val,” he managed to say, and he stumbled into the econ building.

CHAPTER FIVE

Gus's converted garage reminded Afia of the quarters occupied by Tayyab, the cook, back in Nasirabad. It was tucked the same way, behind a hedge at the end of a driveway, with a tiny, nailed-up porch and a side door. Only Tayyab had a whole family in his quarters—separated by curtains for various privacies—while Gus's was one big room with a portable radiator cranking electric heat.

"They are like swimming jewels," she said of the fish in the big tank set up at the far end of the garage. She had never known a person to keep tropical fish before. The snake and lizard—their cages by the adjacent wall, complete with heat lamps—reminded her of what anyone might see in the hotter area of her province, down by Peshawar. And the two cats reminded her of her village, where cats roamed free. Only these bright swimmers, some of them translucent, their eyes unblinking, mesmerized her.

"They have different behaviors," Gus said, standing close behind her, his hand on her shoulder. "See how the betta come up to gulp air? And this little suckermouth hides—see her behind the castle?"

"You always say 'her.' "

"Yeah, they all seem like girls to me. I don't know why."

In a week, she would leave for Nasirabad. Gus kept saying it was not a big deal. That he would miss her for the three weeks, sure, but he would be busy with vet school applications and his own family in Pittsfield, and he would write her every day. She didn't know about getting e-mail in her village, she'd reminded him. There was Ali Bhai's, the Internet café, but otherwise not much of a signal. "Anyway," she'd said, "I cannot be writing while I am home. It is"—she wanted to say *dangerous*, but then he would ask how it could be dangerous, which was not possible to explain here—"it is weird," she said.

He'd seized on this information about an Internet signal to calm her down. Not only, he'd pointed out, had the PR people at Smith cut him out of that picture, but there was also no way for anyone in her village to kick up a fuss about a web page they couldn't access. Oh, he made her brave, Gus did. He offered to talk to Shahid for her, which was not possible—*Do you hear me?* she insisted to him. *Not possible*—but with Gus in her heart, she felt able to make light of Shahid's acting like Baba, talking about her *namus* and the family's *ghairat* when it was just a photo, after all, and she was doing nothing wrong in it. *I don't even remember the guy*, she'd lied in her last text to Shahid. *Everyone was holding hands.*

She turned away from the fish tank to Gus's little stove—two burners below a microwave—where she was making him a special tikka, the first time she had cooked for him. She didn't like the yoghurt she'd found for the marinade—they were too thick, the yoghurts in America, and they lacked the tang you needed for a good lassi. But she'd managed to find a heavy iron skillet at the Salvation Army, and they'd opened the high windows behind the stove to let the smoke escape.

She knew from American TV how cooking was part of courtship in America. The men and women advanced their intimacy to where they were playing house, making the roles that would become tedious into moments of romance—candles; a tiny white apron untied to reveal a clingy top; the masculine uncorking of wine. She and Shahid sometimes watched these shows broadcast from Peshawar, and Baba would come in and laugh at the man who thought his life would forever be this way: his perfumed lady staring longingly at him over roast chicken. *It is an illness they suffer from,* he would say, *and when they recover they find themselves married.*

She was ill, she supposed. Odd feelings came over her at unexpected moments. Sometimes, it seemed her skin was not strong enough to contain the energy of her body. Other times her breath would not come right, and then it was as if she didn't even need to breathe, as if her feelings for Gus drew oxygen from the air and charged her blood.

He'd put on a song track they both liked, Rufus Wainwright, and fed the cats, and now he came to stand behind her. "Smells nice," he said, nuzzling her ear.

"The tikka, or my hair?" she asked. Because she no longer covered, now, when she was alone with him, and her thick hair curled down her shoulders. He didn't answer but wrapped his arms around her waist, and he moved with her as she chopped the onions and tasted the sauce. "Don't want to hold you and feel so helpless," he sang along with the song. "Don't want to smell you and lose my senses."

The girls Afia lived with at Smith fell in and out of love with boys and with each other every day. They talked about birth control the way they talked about food—natural versus organic, controlling what they put in their bodies. When they could have been unlocking the secrets of proteins, they were weeping in the shower or giggling on the phone. It was as Baba had said, a disease. But for her first nine months in America, Afia had been immune. Even when she went to watch Shahid play, even when he introduced her to the guys on his team, she paid no attention to any of them, certainly not to the freckly redhead at the bottom of the lineup.

Then in September she'd gone to the med school fair at the state university with Taylor, who sometimes talked, idly, of becoming a pediatrician. Forty-five American med schools were there with their pamphlets and computer videos set up on plastic-covered folding tables, and five veterinary schools in a corner by the auditorium stage. When Taylor spotted Gus by himself at the table for Tufts, she gave a little squeal. "He's that cutie from your brother's team," she'd said. "Poor lonely boy. Come on."

He reminded her, that day, of the village boys, the way they could prattle about goats or the weather but fell back to mumbling if asked about their sisters or their homes. Gus said he didn't have any sisters or brothers. He grimaced when Taylor called him a jock. You can play squash by yourself, he said; that's how he'd started, when he was a puny kid and didn't get picked for any high school teams. "You're not puny now," Taylor had said, and Afia had felt herself blushing, because her eyes had fallen on his shoulders, the way they pulled at his T-shirt. He was interested in endangered species, he'd said. He thought he might be a vet at a zoo, or go somewhere exotic like Africa. Only it was hard to get into vet school. Maybe he shouldn't play so much squash, Afia had suggested. He should be studying. That was not, he'd said, the advice her brother gave him when they roomed together. "When was that?" she'd asked, surprised, and he'd said that was all Shahid talked about, that first year—getting his brilliant sister over here for school. "He missed you bad," he said, and Afia felt her face grow warm.

It had been Taylor's idea to haul him out for pizza. When Taylor got bored with his short answers about the Greek scene at Enright or Dartmouth's chances against them in the March tournament, Afia managed to lift her voice and ask him what exotic species interested him most. "Reptiles," he said. He went on to describe what had been happening to habitats in the Amazon and sub-Saharan Africa. He told her about Pearl, his corn snake, and Voltaire, the iguana. He described the fish he'd acquired, saying that before medicine began obsessing him, he'd thought of becoming a marine biologist. Eventually, the pizza cold and her beer finished, Taylor told Afia she was going to roll, off to meet Chase at an Amherst party. Gus offered to give Afia a lift home.

No, she'd said when he'd asked if he could see her again. She did not date, she said. He promised not to touch her, he understood things were different for her. He liked her, that was all. He liked talking to her. What time was it, by then? Three A.M., they remembered later. They had spent most of it in his car, their breath steaming the windows, the air still warm back then, late summer crickets singing. She had told him things she'd never told anyone, not even Moray. About her rebellious friend, Lema, back in Pakistan, and how worried she was for her. About Khalid, how he frightened her. About her fears of the drone strikes in the mountains and what would happen to Sobia and Muska; would Baba ever let the family leave or did honor mean staying on your land even when the soldiers came? The Americans, the Taliban?

They could talk again, she said. Which they did three nights later, under a full moon by the river. The next week on a hike in Huntington. At Local Burger, the first night he'd brushed his lips to hers. On Columbus Day they'd gone apple-picking with Afia's roommates, who kept calling them a cute couple. Afterward they'd come back to this garage, where he'd introduced her to his pets. By Halloween she'd let Pearl wrap around her arm. The next week she had bumped into Gus in the squash center hallway, and there in that public place he had planted his lips on her own. Late that night, after Shahid had dropped her back at Smith, Gus had rung on the dorm phone. *I have feelings for you, I can't help it, I do,* he'd said, and she'd said without thinking, *I do too, for you I mean.*

Now, cooking in the garage, she shooed him away and flamed the tikka. The cats—Facebook and Ebay, he'd named them—meowed and rubbed at her legs even as smoke billowed up and drifted out the high windows. On her instructions, he ran the blender to make a version of lassi that wasn't the same as home but would have to do. They sat at his rickety folding table and ate. On the iPod, Rufus Wainwright crooned. *Every kind of love, or at least my kind of love, must be an imaginary love to start with.*

"Your mom taught you how to do all this, I bet," he said after he'd pronounced the food delicious and proved it by digging in. She was proud of her rice, fluffy and perfumed with clove and cardamom.

"Some from her, yes. Mostly Tayyab. Our cook. Don't look so!" she said when he rolled his eyes. "It is not like here. Servants . . . people have servants. Not just rich people. Normal people."

"I know, M'Afia. I'm just giving you a hard time." He called her that, *M'Afia*, which he said was short for *my Afia*. "What would be normal," he said, "is sharing this great meal with your brother. I bet he misses this food."

"Don't," she warned him. She held up her fork and pointed it at him.

"I'm just saying. He's my friend, too."

"He is my brother. I know him best."

He nodded. She saw his eyes go to her white knuckles, clenching her fork. "I'd like you to meet my family, anyhow," he said. "Even if I can't meet yours."

She wrinkled her brow. "You have family?"

"Sure. My mom. Sometimes my dad, I mean, they don't live together, but still."

"But—" That a mother did not make a family was not something she could tell Gus; it would hurt his feelings if he understood how many voices filled the compound in Nasirabad. "But she will not like me," she said instead. "She will think . . ." She set down the fork, drank her lassi. She was glad Gus didn't drink beer. In so many ways, he surprised her. Always wanted to know what she thought about things. When she explained about the wedding, he saw nothing wrong in Maryam's being plighted to a man she had not met. He cried at sad movies. But still: his mother. "She will think I am a bad girl."

"She'll be crazy about you."

"No, she—" She couldn't finish. A tear welled in one eye. She tucked a finger under her glasses to wipe it away. A mother would want to inspect a girl first, for her son—this, she knew, was universal, no matter what they showed on American TV. A mother would want to see how modest the girl was, how graceful. She would want to know something of the family. Such was a mother's absolute right. "I am not ready," she managed to say.

"M'Afia. I've upset you. Come here. Come on. I'm sorry."

It was infecting her, this illness, and all she could do was open her arms wide and invite it in.

He pushed his chair back and beckoned to her. When they were alone and close like this, she almost felt at home with Gus, but in a new sense of home, home as a place where their own rules made them safe. Three weeks ago, in November, they had touched for the first time beneath their clothes. The next week, again.

Each time, he had asked permission. Would she like this? Was this all right? When he touched her, it was with both wonder and inquiry. She had seen him probing his animals, just gently enough so they did not flinch away but with enough authority to detect a bowel obstruction or a tumor. One night, studying in her dorm room, he'd swung her around in her desk chair and gently, so gently, pulled off her glasses, so the world and his face lost their outlines. *Your eyes*, he'd said, *are the most amazing eyes in the universe. So blue. It's like you went to Saturn or somewhere and came back with those eyes.* Just as gently he slid the arms of her glasses back over her ears, and his face had snapped into focus, and his lips had moved to hers.

Now she sat on his lap, and he kissed her. He stroked the mole on her cheekbone with his index finger. He took off her glasses and set them on the table. "You are a blur now," she said.

"We're all blurs," he said, and kissed her again. His voice was husky. His lips pressed on hers like little warm, moist pillows. The strange feeling started up inside her. She leaned into him and felt the hard muscles of his chest against her breasts. His mouth urged hers open. Then there was his tongue, his wet and lively tongue swimming between her teeth, and her own tongue moved and was tasting his, salty and spicy with the tikka. "Is this all right?" he asked when they pulled apart for a moment, and she meant to answer but it came out as a little groan of assent. Then their lips were together again and his hand, oh his hand, under her sweater and cupping her breast as it had needed to be cupped. Since when had it needed? She didn't know, only his fingers were warm and gentle, exploring the warm skin above and below her bra, and it was safe, they were home. "Let's lie down," he said.

"All right," she said, a little frightened but not as frightened as she knew she should be, and she couldn't pretend with him. He lifted her up, rising from the chair with her in his arms. It was only two steps over to the bed, where one of the cats hissed and sprang off as he set Afia down and lay beside her.

"You tell me, okay?" he whispered when they had kissed like that some more and his hands had found the clasp of her bra and freed it. "You tell me to stop and we'll stop." A minute later he said, "It's so good, Afia," and she felt it too, how good it was, this gradual opening to each other. She wasn't just being touched now, she was touching, the curly red hair of his chest under his T-shirt and his nipples like seeds. His jeans were stiff and hard in the middle where they pressed against hers, and she held him like that, his hips wedged into her thighs. When his lips made their way down her neck to her breasts, she heard him in her mind saying, *It's so good, it's good*, because there could not be a bad thing about this loving, it wasn't possible.

She heard the slide and thump of his jeans as he pulled them off and dropped them to the floor. She raised herself onto an elbow. There was the curve of his freckled hip, the scoop of pelvic bone. So vulnerable. Softly she said, "Let me see it."

"What?"

She nodded toward his nest of hair. "Let me look at it," she said.

He lay back. She felt him trusting her. Brushing her hair back from her face, she shifted so the lamplight fell between his legs. The hair coiled there was russet, like the hair on his head. A little fat on the thighs. His penis was shorter than she had imagined, but thick, pink, curving just a little up toward his belly, the circumcised top like a smooth cap. She leaned close. He smelled like the mud floors of the village during monsoon, the sweet stink of the clay. She breathed him in. She touched her finger to the thick blue vein that ran up the inverted back of it, and Gus groaned. "M'Afia," he said. "You don't know what that does to me. I want you so much."

"You have done this," she said a little dreamily, "with other girls. Have you not?"

"One other girl. I told you about her. Ashley, in high school. Oh, Afia, please." He took her hand and wrapped it around his penis. She felt the pulse of his blood under the thin membrane. "Let go now," he said after a few seconds. "I don't want to come, not like this."

"Come," she said. "That's the bad thing. Isn't it?"

"No, Afia, no. Not a bad thing. Not when we love each other. Here." He moved her hand away from his penis. Gently he pushed her back onto the mattress. "I love you, Afia," he said. They said that in the movies. But this wasn't the movies, this was Gus. "Let me," he said.

He moved down her body. He slid her jeans off, her underpants. He studied her belly, her mound of Venus—the hair there was too dark, too thick, she never looked at it herself, but he studied the terrain with a look of wonder in his eyes. Then he dipped his head and pressed her thighs back firmly, as if opening a pair of heavy curtains, and he put his mouth there. *There.* She felt it on her in the dirty place, and his tongue that he played in her own mouth, it played down there, finding her, pulling her out. *There.* "Please," she said, and she wanted to say that her legs mustn't be apart, this was why women back home rode motorcycles sidesaddle, so nothing would get between them, nothing *there*. But he muttered something, she couldn't hear, he came up for breath and then his mouth was back, deeper in the place. *There. There.* Rising, she felt herself rising. To meet him. "Please," she said again. "Please. Please. Gus. Oh, please." And her hand went to his head, his soft curls, holding him to her. *There*, and she felt herself turn inside out. She heard herself shout. Then she was weeping, she couldn't say why, and he was on her, the whole length of him, and his hips moving, his penis like a hot iron bar rubbing against her wet patch of hair. "Don't hurt me," she managed to say.

"I won't. I won't hurt you. I'd never hurt you. Oh, Afia," he said. Something sticky spilled onto her belly, but she was past caring. He stopped moving. He wrapped his arms around her. He buried his face in her neck.

Some time passed. She didn't know—seconds, minutes, an hour? From above, the cold December air slipped through the open windows and lapped them. "Afia, M'Afia," Gus finally said, and he gave a low chuckle.

That snapped her back. She pulled her arm out from underneath his back—it had gone to sleep a little, pinpricks below the elbow—and sat up. She felt the drying mess of his ejaculate in her pubic hair. His come. She recalled what she had done, unfolding to him like that, opening her shame, delighting in it. *Shahid*, she suddenly thought. *Shahid lala*. At the thought of her brother, of her brother's knowing what she had just done, her body contracted. She curled up like a bean sprout. Her arms wrapped her shins; her head tucked into her chest. Blindly she reached for the blanket and pulled it over her body and head. She tried not to breathe. The air hurt. It kept her shame alive.

Weakly she heard Gus talking. She felt his hand pulling at the blanket. "Honey?" he was saying. "You okay? C'mon out of there, M'Afia. Knock, knock. Come on, don't get weird on me. Honey?"

"I must go," she said into the blanket. She didn't know if he could hear her. She didn't move. "I must go." The blanket was becoming damp with her breath. Her damn breath. Oh, to disappear.

"Here. Here, look. I'm sorry, I thought you wanted to."

Unmoving, she nodded. *I did want to.*

"Here, let's make it better. Cover yourself with this. It'll be okay. I didn't come inside you, right? So it's not like we did anything, really. Here."

He managed to pull down the blanket so her head was out. She sneaked a look upward. He was still naked, blotchy pink, his hair disheveled the way it got when he'd played a squash match. He was holding out his bathrobe; she'd seen it hanging on a peg by the tiny bathroom built out from the far corner of the garage. It was terry cloth, navy and red plaid, frayed at the cuffs. Sitting on the edge of the bed, he managed to lift her torso as if she were an ill child. He maneuvered her arms into the sleeves. Her hair fell into her face, but she didn't brush it back—she wished it would fall heavier, become a wall between her and the world.

"Stand back," she finally managed to say. He stepped away from the bed and she rose. But once she'd knotted the belt around her waist, she didn't know what else to do. The delicious feeling that had started when he put his mouth between her legs still crept up through the center of her body, like a heavy perfume. The intoxicating taste of shame.

"Whoa," he said as she started to sway. He got his arms around her shoulders. Gently he steered her to the bathroom. His face looked so worried. She wanted him not to worry, what had happened was not his fault, but she couldn't put the words together in English. That her legs would carry her across the industrial carpet of the floor astonished her. Blurry still, without her glasses, the fish glimmered under the light of the aquarium. Rufus Wainwright wasn't singing any more. Keeping one hand on her back, Gus reached into the rickety shower stall and turned on the spray. "You just need to wash off, Afia," he said. "Just wash me away, then you'll be okay. We love each other, okay, honey? Let me kiss you. Just once. Here."

Steam began to rise. He lifted her chin with his fingers and put his lips on hers. It was different this time, the touch like a benediction. Still she could not meet his eyes.

He untied the robe. "Go on," he said softly, slipping it from her shoulders and steering her into the stall. The water was warm and pounded her back. She stood with her hands over her breasts. Between her legs, she felt urine release. At the same time her eyes released and she began to sob. The water poured down, the tears poured. Then she felt something warm and a little rough against her shoulder blades. She turned. He was in the stall with her, Gus. Naked too, and wet, he soaped up the washcloth. He ran it over her back. Then he turned her, opened the cross of her arms so the water spilled over her front. Turned her again; knelt on the white floor of the shower. With studious care, he washed her pubic hair, her thighs. When she would not part her legs he reached around and washed between them from the back. Standing again, he lifted up first one of her arms, then the other, and soaped the delicate skin underneath, the little nests of hair that she didn't shave, and turned her again so the water would rinse off the soap. Then, quickly, he soaped and rinsed himself. When he was done, still under the steaming spray, he wrapped his arms around her, his big bearish arms. When he let her go, the water washed her again, washed away his touch. "You see?" he said, and the huskiness in his voice was gone; he sounded like a boy, a very young and hopeful boy. "It's going to be fine."

He stepped out of the shower, wrapped a towel around himself, and left her in the bathroom. After a little while, she shut off the water. The tiny room was white with steam. She groped her way out of the stall to a second clean towel that he'd left for her on the rack. She dried herself everywhere and twisted her hair up in the towel. She brushed her teeth with a finger and Gus's paste.

Before she put the robe back on she touched herself, just at the top of her pubic mound. It felt softer there, like the skin of ripe fruit. When she stepped out into the room, Gus handed her back her glasses, and she slipped them on. And it all looked as it had before. This was her home in America, this was her safe place. Shahid did not know she was here; no one knew or could know. Nothing that happened here could hurt her.

Gus was standing apart from her, by Voltaire's cage. The iguana was stretching his neck up, sniffing for food. Gus's arms hung down, the palms turned toward her, waiting. Her lips parted by themselves into a smile, the pleasure making its way all the way up now and into her face. "I'm hungry," she said.

"We've got ice cream," he said.

They sat together at the rickety table, the light outside gone now, only the yellow light from the bathroom streaming across the floor. Their knees kept knocking against each other. Afia felt famished. She couldn't stop eating.

CHAPTER SIX

Lissy managed all her job requirements superbly except the Ask. The Ask was the moment when you faced a potential donor, an alumnus or parent you'd been schmoozing for an hour or a month, and you put the question: How much would they give? She asked questions all the time: hard questions, peculiar questions, questions whose answers she didn't want to hear. But the Ask wasn't about asking. It was about favors. Big favors, money favors. The Ask was really a Beg.

The week after fall semester wrapped up, she was getting ready to leave three-year-old Chloe with a sitter and haul her patient, plucky husband down to New York to be at her side while she accomplished the Ask. The capital campaign was due to wrap up by spring. For Lissy, its outcome meant either going forward with or shutting down plans for a true fitness center at Enright. The dinner, at the Yale Club, was meant to be the final push. All the university officers were attending, plus a hand-selected group of seniors, Shahid Satar among them.

She emerged from the bathroom in the one cocktail dress she

owned, an off-red silk thing with a halter neck. "Wow," Ethan said. "You sure clean up nice."

"Speak for yourself," she said, appraising him. He looked great in a tux, she thought. More filled out, less gawky. He was a psychologist, and she sometimes imagined him in his overstuffed armchair, a jangle of legs and arms like a resting marionette, listening to people's problems.

He held her by the hips, his brown eyes behind their Buddy Holly glasses appraising her shape. She'd combed mousse into her wheat-colored hair and spiked it. "Maybe we should stay over," he said. "Brunch at the Doral."

Kissing him quickly, she turned back to the mirror and fitted the diamond earrings he'd given her last Christmas into her lobes. They had almost frightened her at first—not just because diamonds were extravagant, but because the square-cut gems, set in pale gold prongs, came from a man who knew her better than she did herself. "I told Kaitlin we'd be back by one," she said.

"So invite her to sleep over. Easier for her, and more cash."

"You've forgotten one thing," she said.

Ethan frowned, then rolled his eyes. "We're giving the star athlete a lift."

"I'm sorry, honey. But you said you didn't mind, and—"

"I don't." He stepped closer. His hands came around her midriff and cupped her breasts lightly. "But let's take a weekend sometime."

"In the city?"

"City, or up at the camp."

"I thought your sisters wanted to sell the camp."

"They do. I don't. Maybe in the spring."

"I'd love that," she said. She reached her arms back and they kissed. "When I'm out from the squash season," she said, "I'm yours."

Funny, she thought as she finished dressing, how they called Ethan's family place, in the Adirondacks, a camp. A camp, for her, had been a patch of ground in the Ozarks, not a piney cottage with vaulted ceilings and a new dishwasher.

Kaitlin, the sitter, played on the women's squash team, and Chloe loved her. "Buenos tardes!" she sang out when Kaitlin strode into the living room.

"What you got there, Peanut?" Kaitlin asked.

"Dora puzzle," Chloe said. Chloe was crazy about Dora the Explorer. She'd begged to have her hair cut like Dora's, though with Chloe's curls the Dutch-boy bob didn't bear any resemblance.

"Tacos ready to go," Lissy said, "and she needs a bath."

"Yum yum," said Chloe without looking up. "Dora *loves* tacos."

Lissy lifted her from the floor for a hug. She loved the smell of the back of her neck. "Be good to Kaitlin."

"Don't go, Mommy." Chloe was pressing Lissy's lips together to make a fish face. "I'll be *scared*."

"Is Dora scared?"

"No, not of anything."

"Just think of her then. Te amo."

"Te amo mucho, mucho!"

They drove by the university to pick up Shahid. He, too, cleaned up nicely. In a dark suit and crisp blue tie, his wavy hair combed back from his high forehead, he looked like a young symphony conductor. He had small, boyish ears, usually in need of a Q-tip. Lissy had been watchful of him since the afternoon, two weeks ago, when he had glimpsed his sister on the Smith website and dashed from her office. But his answers regarding Afia had been tersely polite. She had held off from bringing the photo up with Gus, whose hand was surely the one clutching Afia's in that image. Now she let Ethan draw Shahid out. He was good at this. When Lissy first met him, they were taking the same PATH train, she trekking from the Lower East Side to Rutgers University and he heading for the state penitentiary to talk to men convicted of violent crimes. That had been his dissertation subject, male violence and its prospects for remediation. Among other things, he knew how to charm young men. Now he was asking Shahid about his travels in the States. Had he spent much time in New York?

"Only for the squash championships, sir," Shahid said from the backseat.

"But you're trying for an MBA at Harvard—"

"Inshallah. If they admit me, sir."

"Then you might move here, one day. Wall Street and all."

"That will depend on my family."

"Who are all in Pakistan?" Ethan glanced back at Shahid through the rearview. He was working his way, Lissy could tell, to the subject that had been vexing her. "Except your sister?"

"Afia is at Smith, yes."

"That must be nice for you. To have her nearby."

Shahid's face paused midway between a smile and a grimace. "It has rewards and challenges, sir."

"You must feel very protective of her."

"She is a good girl," Shahid said quickly. Ethan glanced at Lissy. "She is very smart. Much smarter than I."

"They usually are," Ethan said. They were passing Co-op City, the lights of Manhattan before them. "But you sound worried, Shahid."

"My family has called us home. I don't know why. And . . . well, Coach knows."

Lissy turned. "I *don't* know, Shahid," she said. "Other than that you saw a picture of Afia. Are you afraid you won't come back here, after your visit?" There, she had said it, the thing she herself feared. That one day Shahid would return to Pakistan and disappear, his talent buried, her years of working with him wasted.

"I am afraid *she* may not," Shahid said.

A long pause fell. They took the Third Avenue Bridge and spilled onto the streets of Manhattan. "Because of this picture," Ethan said at last.

"Because I failed to . . . because I failed, sir. And she wishes to be a doctor. And my country needs doctors."

When they'd pulled up in front of the Yale Club, its awning stretched over the sidewalk, Ethan twisted around. "Shahid, let me ask you something. Are you upset that someone might've touched your sister? Or that it's out there where people can see it?"

"I don't see a differencc, sir."

In the overheated foyer, Lissy surrendered her coat and stamped her feet, in their stupid strappy heels. She shooed Shahid upstairs, to the Tap Room. When Ethan appeared from parking the car, she took his arm. "What difference," she asked, "did you want him to see?"

"The one between guilt and shame." He gave his coat to the attendant. "Would it be sinful for Afia to have a boyfriend, or just shameful if people knew about it?"

"Does it matter?"

"To him? It makes the difference he won't admit to."

"Well, thank you for bringing it up." Lissy wrapped her arm around his weedy waist, stiff in the tux. "You got farther with him than I have."

Upstairs, thin-haired men and frosted women were grabbing tumblers and flutes while launching into tales of Australia, Sweden, London of course, and at least one business destination in South America. Enright was a fallback college for Yale hopefuls, but somehow it still produced more than its quota of the one percent.

"You are one helluvan elegant A.D.," said Don Shears, detaching himself from a pair of trustees. Enright's president was a short man, with a shiny bald head that narrowed toward the top and arms that seemed long for his torso. He shook Ethan's hand. "Dr. Springer," he said. "Thank you for bringing your lovely wife. You're both at table two, with the jocks."

"Got it," said Lissy. Her stomach lurched. The Ask, she thought.

Don moved away toward table one, where Charles Horton, board chair for the past decade, was already seated. Beak-nosed and narrow-jawed, Horton leaned one way and the other, his shock of white hair dipping first toward an oil executive's pretty wife, then toward a leathery and squint-eyed widow. Lissy avoided him. At the last of these events, he'd introduced her as Madame Athletic Director, the Directresse of Sports, and he'd directed most of his conversation with her to her cleavage.

At table two she found her seat across from Ethan's, between a beefy donor whose name tag read *Jeff Stubnick '95* and a willowy woman, *Mona Smith-Gibbons*, who said her father had won awards in pole vaulting. Their eyes widened at the news that she was the athletic director.

"I hear you're after a fitness center," said Jeff Stubnick, when he'd gotten over the notion of a coach in a cocktail dress. "Whatever happened to the gym?"

"The weight room," said the donor next to him—square-jawed, horn-rimmed glasses, probably varsity lacrosse in his day.

"Everybody's got them now," said Mona Smith-Gibbons, who kept lifting her wineglass and looking hopefully for the server. "Our condo building, for instance. Six A.M., and you can't get a treadmill."

"All filled with women," said Jeff.

"Well, that's it, isn't it?" said the lacrosse player. "Girls like those machines. The guys—they press weights and they're done with it."

"Which isn't exactly healthy," said Ethan. "Those guys who do nothing but weights," he went on when he caught Lissy's grateful smile, "stop lifting when they hit thirty. That muscle goes straight to fat, clustered around the heart."

"Keeps my beta blockers in business," said Jeff.

"All the top colleges have fancy fitness centers," said a woman next to Ethan who had looked bored up to now. "Take it from me. I've got a senior in high school, and she didn't apply to Enright."

"And that was *why*?" asked the lacrosse player.

The woman shrugged. "They're all the same, otherwise. Good professors, swishy housing." She raised a glass, as if toasting Lissy. "It comes down to the squash team and the fitness center."

"I heard about that squash team!" said Jeff. "There's some world contenders you've got, there."

"Not a single American on it," said the lacrosse player.

Lissy beamed at him and Jeff both. You had to move carefully toward the Ask, shedding insults like water. "I'll take any good American I can find," she said lightly. "But wherever they hail from, they need a fitness center."

Soon there were glasses being tinkled, the microphone being tested. Lissy excused herself and wove between the tables. Shahid was seated toward the back, at a table of elderly donors with one other student, a pale boy with enormous glasses and a shock of red hair. "You ready, champ?" she asked.

"Tell me what to say, Coach."

"Just charm them. You know, remote village in Pakistan, lucky break in junior competition, generous scholarship from Enright, you love Enright, you love Enright."

"Tell them the truth, you mean."

"That's my man."

Her name was being announced. She stole a swig of water from Shahid's glass and approached the podium.

"What a privilege it is to share this evening with you," she began, leaning into the mike. "Not just because I admire the dedication to Enright that I see around this room, but also because of the dizzying array of accomplishment represented here. At Enright, in the Department of Athletics, we are all about accomplishment. I've brought proof of that to you this evening, in the form of a remarkable student athlete."

And then she nodded at Shahid, the string to her bow, her ace in the hole, knowing he wouldn't let her down.

CHAPTER SEVEN

Long before his father's mud-brown Suzuki crossed the river into Charsadda district, Shahid's head had started pounding. Talk, talk, talk. Ever since they left Northampton, all he and Afia had done was talk. None of it had gotten them anywhere. Stubborn, that was his sister. With his own eyes Shahid had seen that photo. *So who's the guy?* he'd asked her, shoving his laptop under her nose. Just a guy, Afia had said. A guy at a rally against bigotry, they were all holding hands, no one asked if they could take her picture, and who cared? That shrug, she'd picked it up from the American girls like a mimicking monkey.

A man's hand in hers. On the Internet. A man with reddish body hair, touching her. Did she think this was funny? She didn't put it there, she claimed. Oh, right. Didn't she know people would see this? That there would be consequences?

She didn't put it there, was all she would say. Or else: *Please, Shahid, don't be like that, it's nothing, an accident.* When he tried to ask how she'd drawn the photographer's attention, she gave him that look. That Afia look. Her head tipped to the side, her blue eyes narrowed, chin thrust forward. The look that made him feel as if he were dripping snot or drooling from the side of his mouth.

Just before they'd left baggage claim in Peshawar—both of them stretched thin as wire by the long flight, the changeover at Abu Dhabi, the crap food, the endless bottles of holy water riding by on the baggage carousel, waiting for the hajj pilgrims to pluck them off—Afia had tried to make amends. She'd touched his elbow. By then she was already in shalwar kameez, her silky dupatta looped over her hair and wound across her chest and shoulder. No one in our family, she'd insisted in her feathery voice, ever looks at the Internet. They can't get to my Facebook page. We're coming home for Maryam's wedding, that's all anyone will want to talk about.

Dotting the riverbank now were the thatched fishhouses fronted by dories unloading their morning catch. "They look like party favors," Shahid said, his hot forehead resting against the cool window.

From the front seat, his mother, Farishta, twisted around. She wore a black niqab, which she never wore when she used to come with Baba to pick him up in Peshawar. Her brown eyes loomed large in the almond-shaped space between scarf and face veil. "What looks like what?"

"The boats. You know." He turned to Afia for support. "Like those pastel cellophane things kids pull apart at American parties, and there's candy or something inside. Look at the roofs." It was true. The bright, fringed canvas tops, the sparkling streamers and little flags made the boats gay, like toys for giants' kids rather than leaky vessels for men who scraped their living from travelers who stopped, as the Satars did, to gather their lunch at roadside.

"They're always like that." Afia had shut her eyes. Her face, framed by dupatta, looked once again like the face of his little sister, smooth and sweet, that teardrop mole on one broad cheekbone.

Pulling over, Baba found a likely seller and ordered enough trout for the whole household, back home. Shahid stepped out and stretched. The brisk air felt warm compared to the bone chill of Massachusetts. Dozens of times, Baba had taken him home over this road, stopping always for fish. He waved a boy over and gave him a handful of coins. "Naan," he ordered, "and three chai."

Only since Shahid went pro had the journeys been from the airport. Before then, Baba would fetch him for weddings or funerals or Ramadan from Uncle Omar's walled compound in Peshawar. Until he went to America, Shahid had never been gone from Nasirabad for more than four months at a stretch. He tried, again, to think this homecoming was just a sign his parents had missed him and Afia, or that Baba did want to talk to him about the farm. Nothing more.

The roadside boy brought a tray. Shahid gave him another coin, opened the rusted doors of the Suzuki, and passed glasses in to his mother and sister. "I want to sleep," Afia said, her hand waving the tea away.

"You know the family won't let you, not till tonight."

Sighing, she straightened up and took the tea. It felt to him like her peace offering. Moray took hers as well, and sipped it underneath the face veil. They all broke off chunks of the naan, just baked in the ash oven under the lean-to. The elastic heart of the bread, with its tang of salt and deliciously charred edges, melted in Shahid's mouth. Bringing his tea and bread to where his father oversaw the gutting and cooking of the fish, he breathed the familiar stench of river weeds and the fishermen's kerosene fires. "These airline tickets have set you back, Baba," he said. "This wedding must be important."

His father smiled, showing the one gold tooth where he used to let Shahid see his tawny reflection. "An excuse," he said, "to see my precious children."

"Everything is all right, then? At home? The farm?"

"Oh, yes." Baba frowned. His heavy mustache had twice the gray as when Shahid first went to live with Uncle Omar. His cheeks were descending to jowls. "Your brother has come down from the mountains," he said.

"To stay?" Shahid tore the bread with his teeth and chewed it, to disguise his nerves. He had not laid eyes on Khalid in two years.

"For the wedding. But inshallah, we will talk about the farm." He laid his large hand on Shahid's forearm. "He is my first son, and of my own seed," he said. "Though, if you get that business degree . . . you could bring the place into the twenty-first century—"

It was a question Shahid used to talk about with Afia. Did you go away from your people in order to bring the world back to them? Or did you go away to shed the world you once had? Afia had always been firm: She would come back to do medicine, to help the women in the mountains. Whereas the only gift Shahid could offer his family was the stories they could tell about their famous son, out in the world. And so, bit by bit, he had let the world take hold of him. "The farm should be Khalid's, Baba," he said.

"If he will leave off jihad and take it. The village is more to his liking now than when he left."

"Still that way, then? Practicing purdah?"

"More and more." Baba stepped back from the fishmongers. He leaned toward Shahid. "I grow concerned about our *ghairat*." He jerked his head toward the car. "Your sister."

"Afia?" Shahid sipped tea to hide the catch in his breath. "I watch her, Baba."

"I know. But perhaps it would be best. . . . Ah. Thank you." A skullcapped grandfather bowed as he handed over the hot cooked fish. Near him, a pair of children drew pictures in the dirt. Behind the hut, next to a high stone wall, two fishermen laid out their prayer rugs, facing west. "We will have time to talk," Baba continued, lifting the package to smell the hot, spicy fish as they returned to the car. "You must not be burdened in your last year. American championships, yes?" He squeezed Shahid's shoulder.

Afia was dead wrong, Shahid thought as they made their way back onto the highway, gaudy autorickshaws honking around them. Internet service had been available in Nasirabad for five years. Maybe Farishta and Tofan Satar paid it no mind, but at the wedding there would be cousins from Peshawar with iPhones. Khalid used to love video games. Before he went to the mountains, he always went to the Internet café. And now Baba was talking about *ghairat*, about honor.

Shahid's father laid on the horn as they navigated the roundabout off the highway. Motorcycles crowded the lanes, women sitting sidesaddle on the back of the seat with packages or children in their laps, their husbands dodging the wildly painted buses where workers sat cross-legged on top. Back in Devon, Massachusetts, Shahid had missed this life-threatening bustle, where no one felt compelled to stay in his lane and vehicles swarmed like a school of fish. As they climbed through fields of sugarcane into Nasirabad, he felt homesickness bloom through his veins like cream in coffee. His village—the hoarse calls of its vendors, the rough bricks of its streets—suited him now. Khalid would have the farm; he understood that. But he wanted to run through the alleys the way he had as a kid, racing the other boys to the river. Baba drove the Suzuki slowly, avoiding cats and goats. With the window rolled down, he stopped every few houses to shout to whoever sat outside their mud wall—"My son, Shahid! Forty-eighth in the world in juniors, you know! Back from America, now! Going for the number one there. What a boy, hey?"

"Husband, please," Moray said quietly after glancing back at Shahid. "You're embarrassing him."

"It's all right," Shahid said. Though it wasn't really. What, after all, was forty-eighth? Not first, certainly, and not tenth, and Shahid was four years away now from having played in the juniors. That was why he had taken the scholarship to Enright, wasn't it? Because he hadn't a chance of a career as a professional. Omar had told him so, soberly and with great sympathy. Only in America, where the universities gave out money to athletes—and why? No one could say—did he have a second chance. Without such a push, he'd have resisted the call of the West. He'd have come back here after his training, learned the running of the farm, readied himself to help Khalid—or, should Khalid become a holy *maulvi* after all, to step into his stepfather's shoes.

But Baba had always needed a hint, a glint, of glory. With his squash triumphs, Shahid had brought him that. At least, so Shahid wanted to believe. And Baba looked plenty pleased as they made their way up the hill to the orchard and their own slate-roofed compound. As the sheepdogs barked their welcome, Shahid's family swarmed out from the house. Their little sisters and the servant girls enveloped Afia in a pinwheel of dupattas. Around Shahid gathered his uncles and cousins. Khalid emerged from the *hujra*. Cries of welcome and admonishment echoed. Shahid and Afia were both too thin, didn't they eat anything in America, and so pale, how deep were the snows, how long was the flight, were they hungry? His uncle Saqib's fleshy hand pressed against Shahid's bicep; he smelled the familiar mustiness of Uncle Roshan's wool coat. So many years, now, he had been coming home from somewhere—Peshawar, the squash tour, America.

Khalid jostled him as they made their way through the courtyard. The dogs pushed their wet noses against his wrists. The girls had spirited Afia away to the other side of the house, chattering like birds. "Snow," Khalid said. "They all wonder how you live in the snow. Well, I know snow, now, brother. As well as you."

Shahid set his bag down in the *hujra*. On the wall hung yellowing photos of the estate as it had once flourished, in the days before Partition, when the British had favored Shahid's great-great-grandfather and the land had stretched as far as the Swat River. The name Satar was still honored in Nasirabad, though the place was much reduced now. Only twelve families worked the land, producing cotton the likes of which could not be found this side of Peshawar.

Scratching the dogs' rough heads, Shahid looked at his stepbrother. Like him, Khalid had started a beard, but Khalid's was longer; it hung thinly from his chin like moss on an oak tree. He was an inch taller than Shahid, but lean and jumpy. He picked at his cuticles as he spoke.

Of course it should have been Khalid who went to Peshawar, to train as a cricketer for the Peshawar Panthers. Khalid had been captain of his Nasirabad team and three years older than Shahid. Only his left foot dragged a bit, hardly noticeable, from a surgery done when he was a newborn. The coach Uncle Omar had brought with him to Nasirabad frowned and said physical limitations, he was sorry.

"Couldn't Khalid come to Peshawar as well?" Shahid had asked Baba before Uncle Omar came to take him away. "He could study engineering."

"Your uncle has already been generous," Baba had replied—not mentioning that Omar was Farishta's brother, not blood-related to Khalid.

Khalid quit cricket after Shahid left for Peshawar. When Shahid came home on holidays, Khalid would take him around the town, laying wagers on his brother's ability to beat any of the boys not just at squash but at sprints, table tennis, handball. Eager not to disappoint his big brother, Shahid would steal time from squash to train at everything else in the weeks before he returned. At the thought of losing, he would break a cold sweat. But when they came home from these challenges, Khalid would berate him. Did he think he was better than everyone now, showing off like that? The next day, he would wake Shahid early, pull him from bed, tell him he had a hundred rupees on another challenge and Shahid had better not let him down.

"You live in the snow?" Shahid asked now.

Khalid jerked his chin north, toward the mountains. "Three meters thus far. We train in snow. I was grazed by shrapnel this fall." Pulling up the sleeve of his kurta, he exposed a constellation of scars, like jagged flowers, trailing down his forearm.

Shahid frowned. "Were you in hospital?"

"My comrades know how to heal such things."

"What comrades? In the madrassa?"

Khalid's lip twisted. "We are an unsettled country," he said. "Someone has to be ready."

Shahid lifted his bag onto a charpoy next to Khalid's. He did not want to know what Khalid was ready for, or how he had been wounded. Khalid and his jihadi friends had not dictated the changes that had come to Nasirabad, but the parallels were unsettling. On the walls of the elementary school hung pictures of the faculty. When Baba had been a student there, his teachers had posed with uncovered heads, the men in suits and the women in knee-length skirts and chunky heels. By the time Afia graduated, the female faculty was reduced to three, all in shalwar kameez, wrapped in dupattas, even across their noses. Shahid remembered his mother driving the car, but now she went out only with Baba and in niqab, her warm eyes like bruises framed in black cloth. The madrassa where Khalid began his studies had been built by the Saudis while Shahid was in Peshawar. So the changes were a slow tide seeping across the province. They were going back, Shahid had heard, to how things used to be, before the Britishers came and began corrupting Pashtun ways. He didn't mind. But none of it seemed worth what Khalid and his friends were willing to do, the great fight they were gearing up to wage.

"Baba says he'll be talking to you about the farm," Shahid said now.

"I respect my father," Khalid said. "But I have greater work to do. We can't all be playing games while the drones rain down."

Shahid pressed his lips together. No point in a retort. Khalid had started resenting him even before he'd been chosen for Peshawar, from the moment he came into the world. All because Shahid had a living mother. No, that wasn't all. There was Afia, too. All their growing up, they had been inseparable—picking mulberries together, raising lambs together, dreaming of America together—where Khalid had been older and alone. And then three years ago, Shahid had hatched his plan to bring Afia over to Smith College.

Had any of them stopped, Shahid wondered now, to think of Khalid, still living at home then? Had it been Shahid and Khalid in America, there might not be this awful tension, not to mention worry over a damning photo on the Smith website. But Khalid hated *Amreeka*. And Shahid had felt too frightened and guilty to reach out to his brother, to claim him.

These days his parents thought Shahid could go anywhere, do anything. But it was a relief to find himself among the men of his family. Here in the *hujra* you could relax; you could say what you thought. No blond women smirking at you or leaning forward to show the soft tops of their breasts. In the corner, the TV played last night's field hockey match, with Shahid's cousin Azlan shouting and shaking his fist at the center forward. "Two left feet! Why do they put him out there? He handles the stick like a club! Fool!" Tea was set up on the low center table, with plates of almonds and dates. Shahid's uncles pressed him to eat and asked about the journey. They lounged on their charpoys, their feet up and backs against the great bolstered pillows. This afternoon, after the Friday *jumah* prayer and a good fish lunch, they would return to work—Uncle Roshan to his dental practice, Uncle Saqib to the textile mill. For now Shahid had come home, enough reason to take the morning off.

"Your final year." His father put a brown hand on Shahid's jeans. "And a shot at that American title, hey? Will they televise it?"

Shahid smiled. "No, Baba. Squash is not such a big sport in America. But there will be a video. I can send you the link."

Baba held up a hand. "Don't talk to me about links. Links are for golf, which I do not play."

"What comes after?" asked Roshan. He was Azlan's father and the most intellectual of Shahid's relations. Even now he balanced a book in his lap, his finger holding his place. "You'll come back to Peshawar, take over that club? Or is it on to the Olympics?"

"Squash still isn't an Olympic sport, Uncle," said Shahid. "I'm trying for the MBA program at Harvard. They've asked me about an assistant coach job."

"Harvard." Tofan nodded, as if he had suspected exactly this. He turned to the others. "Do you hear the boy? The best school in America."

"A school that takes its money," said Khalid, sitting cross-legged on the rug, "from the Amreekan military. Who send their drones into our mountains."

"Harvard is not attacking us." There it was, the retort. Shahid had failed to hold it back. "America is a big place, Khalid lala," he said.

"Maybe I should visit."

"It would be my honor."

"It is good to know your enemy in their own country."

"Stop sniping at each other." Baba held up a hand, but his eyes darted only to Shahid.

"Look!" cried Azlan. "Did you see that? Offsides! Did you see it? Where is the official? He's a Sikh, isn't he? See? Look there!"

Shahid's uncle Saqib was fat and slow. The youngest, he had always been gentle with Shahid, more like a plump aunty than an uncle. He leaned in toward the TV. "Looks like a fight brewing," he said.

Khalid poured himself a cup of tea and brought a plate of raisins over to Shahid's charpoy. He leaned close. "If I visit, as you call it," he said in a low voice, "it will be to rectify the situation there."

Shahid chuckled to conceal his nerves. "What situation, Khalid lala?"

"You know." Khalid lowered his head. He had a longer face than Shahid's, fine cheekbones, ears that curled out a bit from his head, like their father's. He spoke into his beard. "Our sister," he said, "has been dishonored."

"Really." Shahid fought to keep his breathing even. "Where and by whom?"

"I've seen the photo," Khalid muttered. "Her with her paw in that monkey's paw. I've told Baba about it."

Shahid stiffened. "Did you show it to him?"

"I was waiting," Khalid said with satisfaction, "for you."

On the screen, the officials were pushing their way into the scuffle. Azlan yelled at the set. Baba and his brothers kept their eyes on the game but had started talking about the farm. "It's only an advertisement," Shahid said, "for a college."

"It is your sister holding a man. Who is this man?"

"She is not *holding* him. And I don't care." A lie: Shahid had pored over the photo, the boy's arm bare up to the elbow. "We don't notice stuff like that in the States," he said. He sounded, he thought, like a Western tool.

"They will notice it here." Khalid jerked his head toward their relatives. "And there is no *nanawate* for *tora*."

Shahid stared in both mock and real horror. No sanctuary, Khalid had said, actually said, for fornication. Those were the words of *pashtunwali*, of the Pashtun code, and they were fighting words. The same fear he had felt when he first saw the Smith homepage crept back over him. "They'll notice it," he whispered, "only if you show it to them. And shame casts a wide net."

"You need to control her."

"I do."

Deliberately Shahid rose, stretched. He always got off on the wrong foot with Khalid, especially when jet lag made him foggy. He had left New York just before midnight on Wednesday; now it was midmorning two days later, midnight for him. Tomorrow the men would go to the groom's home, over the hills in Mardan. Afia and the women would hold the *mehndi*, to henna the bride's hands. He would see little of his sister until the third wedding day. Maryam was marrying a government doctor, but a doctor nonetheless, and her family was relieved. Unlike Afia, Maryam wasn't so desirable—her skin was too dark, her hairline too low on her forehead, and her father ran a restaurant. The bride price for Afia, with her blue eyes and fair skin, and her father's newly rebuilt farm, would be much more substantial. "Baba," he said, to turn the conversation away from Khalid, "who are Maryam's new people? How are we related to them? Are they of our *khel*?"

Baba rolled his eyes. "If you stayed home instead of roaming the world with your racquet," he said in mock derision, "you would know about your own clan."

"This is your grandfather's sister's husband's family," said Roshan evenly. Keeping his eyes on the TV screen, he nodded for emphasis. "Our *khel*, yes, an honorable family."

"Maybe one of them will spot our Afia," Khalid said from his corner, "during the dancing."

"Now, now," said fat Saqib. "No men allowed at the rukhsati."

"And yet you found my mother there. Didn't you, Baba?" Khalid said.

A look of pain crossed Baba's face. Why did Khalid take every chance to do this, to bring up his mother who had been dead now for two decades? "She was a lovely girl, an innocent girl," Baba said. "She stood out."

"And the same for your stepdaughter!" Roshan said. He punched his brother lightly on the shoulder. "What is Afia now, nineteen?"

"Twenty in January," Shahid said. "But she's got two more years after this—"

"High time," said Khalid. "While she still looks—what did you say, Baba?—innocent."

Shahid felt the sting and the poison behind it. He looked at his brother sharply. But Khalid was gazing into the middle distance, out the open gate of the *hujra* into the orchard. Did Khalid care about their *ghairat*? Or did he care more about cutting Shahid down, and if Afia now provided the knife to do it, he would use her and honor be damned? *It's not been what you think over there*, he wanted to say to Khalid. *It's been hard, it's been lonely. We need each other.*

Rising to pour tea, Baba called through the door, and Tayyab emerged. Setting down a fresh tea tray, he bobbed his skullcap at Shahid.

"Asalaam aleikum, Tayyab," Shahid said.

"Wa aleikum salaam, Shahid sahib," said the old man.

"How goes it with your girls? Have they—"

His father put a hand on his arm. "Thank you, Tayyab," he said. His face a map of wrinkles, the old man bobbed again as he removed the old tray. "Died," Baba said when Shahid frowned at him.

"Childbirth, one of the two who married," Roshan added. He adjusted his glasses, a quirky grin on his face. "And the other got a kick, didn't she, Tofan?"

"In her big belly, from her father-in-law," Baba confirmed. He shook his head and sighed. "Never forget seeing Tayyab banging his head against the wall like that. Moaning about his fate."

"And his third daughter? Panra?" Shahid asked. Panra was just Afia's age; he remembered playing with her when they were children, her auburn hair the color and texture of cornsilk.

"Still in your uncle Omar's household," his father said. "They'll be lucky to marry her off, pocked like she is."

Shahid didn't want to respond to this. "He's got the one son," he said instead.

"Soft in the head," said Saqib from his charpoy.

"Worst of it is, Tayyab's going blind," said Baba. "Diabetes, your mother says. She's tried to hire him an assistant, but he scares them away. Scared we'll replace him. Meanwhile we get cumin instead of cardamom, and the rice overcooked."

"Kismet," said Saqib, and they all chuckled. Shahid felt his judgment readjusting, like a shoulder dislocated and popped back into place, the sharp, brief pain of it. This was Nasirabad, not Devon.

Baba poured tea. He was a big man, almost as tall as Shahid, and heavy in the gut these days. He smiled rarely, but when he did it was a soft curl of the lips under his mustache, as if he had waited for just that moment of happiness. His hair was thinning away from his forehead, the skin there tanned from the sun. "Your mother should take some photos of Afia," he said thoughtfully, "while she is here."

Khalid pounced. "There's that photo I told you of, Baba."

Baba's eyebrows lifted. "From America? Is it appropriate, Shahid?"

"What?" Shahid's mind had wandered. Jet lag, he thought. He was trying to remember the cook's eldest daughters. How relieved the old man had been, when they were taken up by husbands. Dead now in childbirth, and of a kick to the belly. How casual it sounded here, a strange little story about the cook. "If you're talking about showing Afia off to a suitor," he said, avoiding his brother's eyes, "I think we should take photos here. She'll show to good advantage at the wedding."

Khalid opened his mouth, then shut it. Biding his time, Shahid thought.

"Finally, a goal!" cried Azlan. A shout went up from the television. "That showed them, didn't it, Baba?"

"Just in time, too," said Saqib. "Time for *jumah* prayer."

As they rose, Shahid looked at the familiar faces of the men of his family. They thought they knew him. They had traveled to Peshawar, to Lahore and Karachi, to watch him compete. They had mounted him on their shoulders when he brought home a winning plaque. But they had never heard him say how much he feared going to America, how he would never make it professionally, how much he found himself missing Nasirabad, how hard it was for him to sit still and study, how he could never think beyond the next tournament. Since they were little, Afia had been his sole confidante. She was smarter than he, and she knew how she could contribute to the world. He had only to protect her—from the men in America, yes, but also from these men, from men who chuckled over Tayyab's dead daughters, from his family who could not comprehend what things were like, somewhere else.

Passing through the courtyard to head for the mosque, he saw Tayyab's youngest daughter scrubbing the steps. She looked up shyly at the men and went back to her work. How old was the girl now? Twelve, fourteen? How would she manage in the world without a brother to look after her?

As they piled into the Suzuki, his father plucked him back. "This American photo," he said. "It is not objectionable, is it?"

"I . . . I don't know what you mean, Baba. It's not appropriate for an engagement, but—"

"You protect her."

"I do, Baba."

"It is what makes a girl happy. To know she is safe. She is protected."

"But I worry, Baba. It's different over there. And if a rumor started—"

His father laid a heavy hand on Shahid's shoulder. "We'll get her engaged, before you go back," he said. "I have been thinking about it. I'll speak to your mother. You both need to finish your studies with a plan for the future. This is a good plan, and a good time for it. Now, we'll talk no more of women. Tell me," he said as the call to prayer rose above the village, "about this chance at Harvard."

CHAPTER EIGHT

Afia had dressed in her brightest shalwar kameez, with spring green flecking the deep turquoise silk, the bodice hand-embroidered and studded with freshwater pearls. The sleeves went only to her elbows but ended in handworked lace. She had washed her hair and doused it with the tea-scented rinse her mother always used. Brushing, she found her locks thicker, softer, brighter. She would bring a tube of this to Northampton. How far away Northampton seemed! Forty-eight hours she had been home, and already the whole world of Smith College seemed an invention.

Yesterday, at the *mehndi*, she had still set herself a little apart. Maryam was the sixth of her cousins to be married, and the others giggled and gossiped about which girl would be next. As a government doctor, the groom would receive a house once he and Maryam started a family. His father ran a sugar mill in Mardan. The groom was rumored to be short, with a receding chin, but not too old and in good health. One sticky point was that his parents had come first to the home of another cousin, Tahira, but Tahira's parents hadn't taken him seriously. Tahira was tall, fair-skinned, and blue-eyed;

over the summer she had married a cardiologist in Peshawar. So everyone knew that Maryam's parents had accepted another's leavings. But marriage was marriage; marriage was the point.

Strange, how Afia felt the pull of this gossip. Her first instinct was to make the kind of speech she imagined in the voice of her roommate, Patty, about the superficiality of fair skin or a doctor's wages, the value of the single life. But after they had gathered to watch the design spread over Maryam's tiny hands onto her plump wrists, she found herself laughing at the mother-in-law jokes, eager to hear of other visits made by other bride-seeking families to other cousins, the bright hope of a good match. They had gathered in Maryam's home, a small compound but immaculate, with a garden that would bloom brightly in the spring. All were women except for the guard at the gate, and what a relief, to be away from men! Maryam's mother and aunt had spread a feast of kebabs and fried fish on the veranda's long table. Filling her plate, Afia thought idly of the buffets at Smith, laden with vegetables and trays of meatless lasagna, with knives as well as forks, and napkins because you weren't supposed to eat with your hands or lick your fingers. But your fingers tasted good! She bit off a chunk of juicy meat and then sucked the juice from her thumb.

That was when Moray had touched her elbow and said calmly, as if she were talking of hiring a new cook, "When all this is over, my sparrow, Maryam's people will be calling on us."

Afia felt a space open in her heart. "But, Moray, we'll just have visited with them. Why—" Then she stopped, and flushed. Of course. Maryam had an older brother, another second cousin. Zarbat? Zardab? She had not seen him since she was small.

"You'll need to serve the tea," her mother went on. "We'll go shopping in a day or two, after the ceremony. Find you something in the latest fashion. See what your cousin Tahira is wearing?"

Last night, Afia had lain awake in the bed she had longed for while at Smith—the wide frame constructed from an ancient wooden chest her grandfather had brought home from the Kashmir. The chest had split apart, but the panels were solid enough for Baba to refashion into a bed, which had been Afia's as long as she could remember. All through the long flight, she had craved a good night's sleep in it. Now sleep would not come. They wanted her married, Baba and Moray. Of course she had always expected to be married off. Being educated had been part of preparing for marriage; a more successful man, Moray had declared to Baba, wanted a wife with a university degree, even a wife who could practice medicine. Afia was short and wore glasses, but behind them her eyes were blue as sea glass, and when she let her hair go, it fell thick and soft over her shoulders. Marriage was never going to be a problem for her. Only since America had it become a problem. Only since Gus.

She turned on her side and thought how neither of her parents had talked of engaging her before her studies were finished . . . until now. Would Shahid have—?

No. Not possible. There would have been howls of shame, and the shame would have covered Shahid, too. People were starting to talk, that was all; starting to ask when Afia would be coming home, what Afia's prospects were. No one knew about Gus, not even—especially not—Shahid. She could lie here and think about her beloved to her heart's content, and bring dishonor to no one.

But when she tried to dwell on Gus, the dark air seemed to swallow him. That she had lain naked next to him only a week before was now a thought too horrible to own. Even to imagine his half-shaven face, his hands with the wisps of dark hair on the backs of the knuckles—no. She couldn't. If she lingered on his touch, or his breath against her ear, her stomach would rise within her. She would vomit the strangeness of it. What she had done was risky, in and of itself. But it had happened in that other world, where honor was topsy-turvy and rules frayed at their edges. To think about it was to do something *here*, in Nasirabad, something unforgivable.

And so she stopped thinking about Gus. It happened like that, like the door of the freezer sucking closed. There was, after all, so much else to think about. Maryam's wedding, of course, and the tremendous anticipation of how Maryam would look at the close of the *rukhsati*, how her new husband would regard her, how the men of the wedding party would slip into the back of the hall to watch the girls dancing. Whether Lema would be there—Lema, her best friend from school, who had gone on to secretarial college in Peshawar and come home over the summer to be married. She had written to Lema and tried to connect with her on Facebook, but no answer. She had to think, too, about Moray and about Sobia and Muska, who were fourteen and ten now and starting to cover their little chests with their dupattas. The village was already a more conservative place for them than it had been for Afia. Yesterday Sobia had talked about three girls from her class who had quit school and were staying home, in purdah like their mothers.

She finished brushing her hair and applied a line of kohl to her eyelids before putting her glasses back on. She never wore makeup in America, but here it seemed part of getting dressed. She found her mother in the bathroom, helping Sobia drape her dupatta properly. "Don't you look all grown up," she said to her sister.

"I want to wear heels," Sobia said, eyeing herself in the mirror. She had lost her baby fat since Afia saw her last, and stood with her shoulders back, as if to show off the tiny bosom that the dupatta concealed. She'd had her period twice, she'd bragged to Afia the first moment they were alone, and Afia had hugged her and said, "Poor baby," in a way that let her know she felt not pity but pride.

"You're tall for your age already," she said. "I'd never wear them if I were tall like you."

"I'm tall too!" cried Muska, pushing her way into the bathroom. For a moment they stood together, craning their necks high like a trio of geese, while their mother stood off to the side, shaking her head.

"My silly sisters," Afia said.

Two hours later, Baba dropped Afia with her mother and sisters at the entrance to the wedding hall and drove to the lower parking lot with Khalid and Shahid. Afia had not looked at Shahid the whole drive—not because she was angry at him, she wasn't anymore, but because even a look would bring Gus into the car with them. She let out her breath as they left the men and went in their silky outfits to join the women at the *rukhsati*.

Inside the hall, the stage was festooned with fresh lilies and bloodred roses woven in with silver streamers and strings of white lights for a backdrop. On the puffy little couch at the center sat a shy, homely man in white kurta trimmed with gold embroidery, his turban-wrapped head balanced on his thin neck. He sported a wispy beard and a gentle smile for the dozen men of his family, the only men in the hall besides the DJ and the photographer, who came up to have their photographs taken with him. "He looks sweet," said Muska.

"He looks old," said Sobia, who had started trying out saucy opinions.

"He is thirty-two," Moray said. She found them a spot at a table with aunts and cousins. "You can't call that old, not when he's had to get himself established."

Moray, Afia thought, was sensitive on this subject, though she shouldn't have been. Her first husband—Afia's real Baba, whom she couldn't remember—had been young, twenty-seven to Farishta's eighteen. It was only when she married Tofan, the eldest, that she had a husband two decades older than she was. But it didn't matter, because Baba had never seemed old. He had been more playful with Afia and Shahid than either of his brothers. He would toss Afia in the air and catch her; he played cricket with Shahid and his friends. Moray knew she had been lucky, no matter the talk.

Greeting her relatives, Afia found herself scanning the room as more women entered in their silks and heels. "Moray," she said, leaning over to her mother, "do you think Lema will be here? Her brother married Maryam's sister—"

"She lives outside Charsadda now," Moray said quickly. "Long way to come."

"I came. Cousin Gulnar came." Afia nodded toward the only other female at the gathering who had traveled from North America. Gulnar had married an orthopedist and moved to his new home in Ottawa. The normally high-spirited Gulnar had been terrified of the journey, Afia remembered. Now she sat with her close relations, a baby on her lap and another in the belly, dressed in black niqab. They became more religious, it was said, the ones who were taken abroad.

"The journey's longer for some," Moray said.

The DJ put on a dancing song, a Pashtun song. Afia's cousins pulled her away from the table. In front of the stage, they danced. The spike heels felt wobbly, and Afia dropped her dupatta twice. But the music fired her blood, and she forgot about anything she'd ever done to set herself apart from the girls around her. She clapped and swayed with them, the lights spinning. Somewhere in the dark at the back of the room, a knot of boys from the other side of the wedding building had gathered to watch the girls with their shiny hair and their arms half bared. Like the others, Afia lifted her arms higher, tilted her chin so her eyes caught the light.

She couldn't help herself. They were fifteen in the circle. Virgins dancing, Afia thought. A dark question arose but she quickly scuttled it; she clapped and shouted.

Then the music slowed, and they returned to their seats, where there were trays of Mountain Dew and Pepsi, and Afia drank thirstily, wishing for plain water. Funny, how no one at Smith College drank Pepsi even though they drank beer. But the thought of Smith ushered in a thought of Gus—of his hands, his mouth, the fullness of the lower lip—and she guzzled the Pepsi and washed it away.

"Here she comes," said Sobia at last. They turned as the spotlight swung over the crowd of women. It picked out Maryam, approaching from the back of the room, on the arm of her brother.

She was, Afia thought, a work of art. A red veil edged with a broad swath of gold and green embroidery, studded with mirrors and bits of colored glass, fell from the crown of her head over her shoulders, leaving her face exposed. From the top hung a diadem of ruby and gold in the center of her forehead, echoed by the heavy necklace that lay across her collarbone, above the tight embroidered bodice of her ruby-red gown. Her face looked, not beautiful, but majestic, with the deep kohl around her eyes and several pairs of false lashes; her cheeks both whitened and rouged at the bones, her small mouth stained red, almost in the shape of a heart. Holding fast to her brother, she took a step forward. Then the lights went out.

The women groaned. "Load shedding," said Moray. "What a moment for it."

"Poor girl," said one of the aunts.

Afia sat in the dark. She had forgotten how it was always like this, the electricity going out at a moment's notice, the air dark and still and hot. She felt the anticipation in the room like that uncanny moment when the airplane leaves the tarmac, defying gravity. *This* was the journey, all the women were saying together. These heavy, glittering garments, this gold against the throat, this man waiting on a white couch. As soon as the lights came back on, they would have liftoff. What had Afia been thinking, off in that strange land, America? Had her brain gone upside down, that she should think of men and women like stray planets drawn to each other and not like stars in a constellation of family? Around her, the women buzzed. Sobia and Muska, holding hands, went scuttling in the dark between tables, headed for the trays of tiny cakes.

Zardad, that was the name. Whose parents would come to call, in a few days. She would need to look rested, healthful, humble, helpful. Zardad. She tried saying the name, silently, with her teeth and tongue. Back toward her throat, another name lingered. *Gus.*

The lights returned, along with the distant roar of a generator. In the room's center, Maryam had not moved a muscle. Now she wobbled forward on her heels, her mouth frozen in a half curl. Ahead of her, on his makeshift throne, the groom appeared pleased. He had perhaps seen a picture of her, but her real self was an improvement. She was not an ugly girl, far from it. But he did not look at her, really, nor she at him. Her brother sat Maryam on the couch, and she folded her hennaed hands in her lap, the hands they had all exclaimed over just yesterday, when the transformation of Maryam into a bride had begun.

However short her forehead, however clumsy her walk, Maryam was coming to her husband pure. Afia forced herself to study her cousin as she smiled for the cameras and nodded at the friends and relatives who approached the couch to give their blessings. Maryam's mouth, she thought, trembled a little. Her eyes, so prominent with the kohl and extra lashes, betrayed eagerness, hope, anxiety, excitement, and terror. Tonight, this girl who had not been kissed—who had not been touched—would go with her strange new husband to his parents' house, where he would undress her and make love to her, perhaps gently, perhaps roughly. The next day his family would celebrate the consummation while her own retreated home and adjusted to life without their daughter.

Afia had never dwelled on any of this before, not in such terms. Everyone knew what happened, but you didn't think about it, and she wouldn't think about it, not now. As she turned her gaze away from the new couple on the stage, she caught sight of a familiar figure, though wrapped tightly in her dupatta, her kameez shapeless as a tent. "Moray," she said, turning back to the gossiping women at her table, "there's Lema."

"Maryam's mother wants us to take a picture—"

"In a minute. I'm just going over to say hello. I'll be right back."

"Afia, I don't want—"

But she was already weaving her way across the room. Impudent, to ignore her mother. But she had been trying to reach Lema for too many months; she wasn't going to pass up this chance.

From age nine, when Lema first moved to Nasirabad with her family from the tribal areas, the two girls had been inseparable. Together with Panra, Tayyab's daughter who was two weeks older than Afia, they had climbed mulberry trees and sneaked off to swim in the river. Dark-eyed and broad-cheeked, Lema was always the boldest of them. In school, she dared other girls to sneak over to the boys' side, or to chug a bottle of bright red Rooh Afza until they choked and spewed red over their kameez. While Afia was getting high marks and dreaming of test tubes, Lema dreamed of a snug house in Hayatabad, away from the stench of chicken dung. While Afia arranged her goals like a staircase, conquering each step, Lema talked people into pulling her up the ladder. Two years ago, she had persuaded her parents to let her try a secretarial school in Lahore. *IDK how I ever lived outside the city before!* she wrote Afia. Then last summer she had suddenly returned to be married, to a small farmer in the dry valley by Charsadda. Afia had learned of it only through her mother.

"Lema," Afia said, touching her friend's sleeve.

Lema turned. There were her large, dark eyes, the high arch of her brows framed by the blue cloth over her hair and across her cheeks and nose. The eyes lit up when she recognized Afia. But across her left temple and running down into her cheek, the skin puckering by the eye, ran a deep scar, still purple with old scabbing.

"Why, look at the American, come home to Nasirabad!" Lema said. When she put her arms around Afia, the hard bulge of her belly met Afia's ribs. Afia embraced her friend, then stepped back. Carefully she lifted away the scarf. The scar ran down to Lema's chin, like the scratch of a giant's nail. She reached out a hand, but Lema flinched away.

"What did they do to you?" Afia gasped.

"I'm fine. Really." Lema wrapped her face and neck again. Nervously she glanced left and right. A heavyset woman glowered at her from a table—her mother-in-law, Afia guessed. "I'm sorry I haven't written. I've been so busy. I'm due in May," Lema said quickly, caressing her belly.

"That's . . . that's wonderful. But what did they—"

"I'm going to tell you while we admire Maryam. All right? Smile, will you? Let's turn and look at her."

Afia tried to turn toward the stage, but she stole glances at her old friend. Her joy at finding Lema had shriveled. Lema had lost weight—she could tell despite the covering, despite the pregnancy—and her hands were chapped, the nails ragged. Keeping her voice light, Lema ran through her story. She had become pregnant in Lahore. It didn't matter who the man was—it was a man, she had liked him, she had thought herself free, she had not been forced but neither had she been in love. Not that it would have mattered, because he was a Sikh. He paid for the abortion, but by then it was too late. Word had got out. When she came home last spring for Ramadan, her mother held her down while her father and brother took the knife to her face. It was a warning, they told her.

"But I don't understand," Afia managed to say. "If they wanted you married—"

"No one decent would marry me anyway. That's what they said." Lema laughed, a strange yipping sound with no humor in it. "But when I healed, it turned out they had found someone."

"And—and are you happy?"

Lema shrugged. "I live with my in-laws now," she said. "They brought me here tonight." Her eyes crinkled; she was smiling sheepishly. "I knew I'd see you," she said.

"But you didn't come across the room. I don't even know how I recognized you, all covered up. Why—"

Lema shook her head. "You looked so happy, dancing," she said. "I didn't want to spoil your evening."

"Oh, Lema." Afia reached to squeeze her friend's hand, but Lema flicked her away.

"Don't," she said.

"But can't I do something?"

"I'm fine." Lema pretended to wave at someone across the room. "He doesn't beat me. I get along with his brother's wife. Soon I'll have a child. But you." She faced Afia. With the back of her dry hand, she stroked Afia's cheek. "You're so smart," she said. "You'll fetch a fine husband. Maybe one who'll take you back to America!"

"I don't know, Lema. Things have happened." Afia's eyes filled with tears. Lema was about to turn away, back to the crowlike mother-in-law; there wasn't time to tell her the truth.

"Don't let things happen." Lema's scar deepened as she drew

her hand away. "You're not stupid, like me. You'll be taken care of. You'll be wealthy. You'll be safe."

"Aren't you safe?"

"I have to go." Lema pulled her dupatta loose. She leaned forward. She planted a kiss, moist and slightly sour, on Afia's cheek. Then she turned away, back to the women at her table, who frowned as she joined them. She did not glance back.

Afia burned for her friend. That night and the next she dreamed first of Gus and then of Lema. She woke both mornings dry-mouthed and achy.

Then, when her little sisters had left for school, she persuaded Tayyab to walk her down to Ali Bhai's Internet café, where she booted up her e-mail. And there, both mornings, was a new message from *gusschn@gmail.com*. *M'Afia*, the messages began, Gus's little cleverness. He went on about missing her, tried to tease her into sending a photo of herself, complained of the wet snow and the sudden loneliness of Devon, with only his menagerie for company. For Christmas he'd gone about ten miles away, to his mom's house in Pittsfield.

She didn't answer the e-mails. She could not write anything to Gus, not here, not in this place where even thoughts of Gus were weeds to be plucked by the root and discarded. She read the blithe sentences—*M'Afia, I know you said Internet would be spotty but what I wouldn't give to get a word from you. I worry about you. Your country is one very scary place. Not to mention how scary the thought that you'll meet some cute guy with a Kalashnikov and that'll be the end of us*—and erased the e-mail, then went to the trash and deleted it there too. When she returned home, she fished in her purse for her mobile, and for a moment she panicked. Then she found it, in the back pocket where she didn't usually stash it. She opened the photo she had of her and Gus, where she was sitting on his shoulders in the apple orchard just west of Northampton. Patty had taken that photo on Columbus Day, before Gus's lips had even come close to hers, and still the sight of it flooded her with shame. Quickly she deleted it. Then she turned off the phone and tucked it deep in her drawer, where no one could get at the photos or text messages. Seeing Lema had brought on caution; she should have felt it before. Shahid was always with the men, no chance to discover if he'd said anything about that stupid shot of her on the Smith website.

Lema had drawn a poor hand with her family, she told herself as she woke next morning—a family that came from the hills, that understood nothing of life in a city or of what Lema wanted for herself. Afia's family wasn't like that. Afia's parents had been proud to send Shahid to Peshawar. They had faced down whatever rumors arose to let Afia study in America. Yesterday, drawing extra rupees from the stash in her mending basket, Moray had taken her to the shops in Mardan and bought an outfit in the latest style, Afia's favorite, an A-line kameez with a flare from the hips, and the new ruched pants underneath. And how many times, over the years, had she heard Baba argue with Khalid? A good Pashtun, he would declare, is not a primitive Pashtun. Your Taliban with their amputations and their stonings, they are like cavemen, they know nothing of Islam.

Thus far, this visit, Khalid had been nice. When she was little he'd given her rides on his broad shoulders. But she remembered teasing him once, for the way his left foot dragged a little as he ran across the pitch in cricket. After that he'd treated her with contempt, guffawing when she first got glasses and reaching with a smirk to pull her dupatta over her chest. Since she left for America he'd ignored her. But yesterday he had asked about her studies, about whether she kept halal. He hadn't asked about the Smith website. Her family, she reminded herself, trusted her. With that thought she curled herself into a ball, as if to shield her body from its own memories. She couldn't let the wall between that distant world and this familiar one become porous; it had to stay solid, each side opaque to the other.

It was her fifth morning at home. Sounds of commotion penetrated the bedroom door. She heard her father's voice; Moray's; Khalid's, with a shrill edge. Then her mother pushed open the door, no knock.

"Afia," she said, "you've slept enough. Get dressed and help your *anâ* and me in the kitchen."

Moray was dressed in a dark kameez. Her eyes were puffy, her mouth turned down as if she held a bitter pill on her tongue.

Afia affected a yawn. "What time is it? Can we have puri breakfast?" Rich and delicious, the breakfast of fried bread and sliced fruits was one they used to share as a family, though more and more her father took most meals with her uncles while she and her sisters took stools at the kitchen counter across from her mother and Anâ.

"Too late for breakfast. Get dressed and come. None of your American jeans, either."

Afia felt slapped. She hadn't even packed her jeans. She knew better. She pulled open her closet and chose her brightest kameez, red with gold threads making little curlicue designs. Pulling her dupatta tight, she stepped from the room and down the short hallway to the kitchen.

"Anâ," she greeted her grandmother, who was knitting furiously in the corner. Not long after her husband, Afia's *niko*, had died, Anâ had stopped talking. Shock, Afia's mother called it, but Afia suspected a stroke. Anâ's eyes, though, spoke paragraphs. This was her home, and she never let her daughter-in-law forget that. All through her childhood Afia had listened to the quarrels between her mother and Anâ. Gradually she had come to understand that the bickering was not so much hostile as gregarious. Anâ and Moray, she had explained to her sister when Sobia began staring wide-eyed at the raised voices and shaken fists, were like two birds who chattered the same things over and over at each other. *My house, my house, my house*, Anâ chattered, while Moray sang back, *But I'm here, I'm here, I'm here, but I'm here.* Indeed, Moray seemed less sprightly, her voice harsher, now that she could not quarrel with Anâ but only endured her icy, darting eyes. Afia kissed her grandmother's lifted hand.

"Peel the cardamom," Moray said, setting a bag of the dusty pods in front of her. "They'll be here at two o'clock. I want the cakes to be fresh."

"Who will be here?"

Her mother frowned, as if Afia had meant to annoy her. "I told you. Maryam's people." She studied her daughter's hair. "You'll cover your head," she said, "but that new dupatta is sheer, your hair will show. You should curl the ends."

"I thought they were coming tomorrow."

Moray shrugged. "They are eager. Not a trait to discourage."

Dread hollowed Afia's stomach. She shook a bowlful of green pods from the bag and pulled a tiny knife from the set her mother kept always sharp.

"Inshallah," Moray said, shaking blanched almonds into the grinder, "they have not heard about the photo."

Afia dug the point of the knife into the first pod and twisted. Her breath stuttered. "What photo?"

"You know the one. They will say it was my fault, taking such a risk."

"I don't know what you're talking about." Afia dug her thumbnails into the crack made by the knife and pulled the husk away, spilling the black seeds. "I haven't taken any—"

"Don't lie to me, child!" Her mother slapped the bag of almonds onto the counter. The face she turned to Afia was the same color as the blanched nuts. "I have to find a husband for you, do you not realize that?" she said. Her voice rasped. In the corner behind her, Anâ's eyes blinked and glinted like the blades of a fan. "With an engagement, you have a chance. Without it, someone could do us evil. There would be no more school, no more medicine. All I have invested in you, wasted. Is that what you want?"

Afia's face burned. She tried to focus on the green pods, the seeds. She had not smelled fresh cardamom in months. "Have you seen this photo, Moray?" she said weakly.

Her mother set about grinding the nuts. She grunted with the effort. "Your brother would not show it to me."

"Shahid told you about—"

"Not Shahid."

"Oh." Afia's hand rested on the cardamom pods, their brittle skin, the secret treasure inside. Khalid, then, for all the kindness he'd shown. "Am I to be punished," she said to her mother, "for a photo you cannot see?"

"You are not being punished. You are being considered for marriage." Moray stopped. She wiped her hands on a cloth. The cook would be in soon, to clean up the mess they were making, but the important thing was that Afia and her mother prepare all the trappings for tea themselves. "People are loath to spread stories about an engaged girl," she said. "An engaged girl can finish her studies without trouble. Now if it were up to your father—"

She broke off. She shook her head. In the chair, Anâ had tangled her knitting needles; Moray stepped over and gently straightened them out. A phrase came into Afia's head. "There is no *I* in *team*."

Shahid's American coach had said that. Afia had heard her, once when she came to watch Shahid play and the coach was lecturing. Funny how it applied to Farishta. There was no *I* for her. Everything she did was for someone else, for family. Family was a team. And she bent backward, it always seemed, for Khalid, who wasn't even her own son.

Afia went after another pod, piercing the husk then tearing it apart. She swept the seeds into the mortar. From the other room came men's voices, muffled. Khalid was out there. Khalid, Afia thought, who had opposed her going to Smith because Shahid supported it. Was any of this—Maryam's family's visit, letting her mother know of the photo—really about her? Or was it all about her brothers? Was there an *I* for her? "Has Shahid said anything?" she asked.

"He claimed," Moray went on, drawing a breath, "that it was not an objectionable photo. He says he has guarded your *namus*, and we are not to worry."

Afia split open another seed. Shahid was angry with her, but in this he was on her side. "I have done nothing wrong, Moray," she said. She sank her fingers into the bowl of cardamom pods, rubbed against them as if the curved husks gave off comfort.

"You have given the appearance of wrong."

"Not over there, I haven't. It's all different, over there."

From the corner, Anâ began hawking and spitting onto the floor. Afia took a cloth and went to wipe her grandmother's chin. When the old woman lifted her eyes to Afia's face, the glassy blue bore through her. Anâ no longer recognized her grandchildren. She could barely swallow, had to be fed by hand. But she appeared to know a lie when she heard one. "Water?" Afia asked, but her grandmother pressed her lips together; her long nose flared.

Her mother set the knife aside and wiped her hands on a clean cloth. She set them on Afia's shoulders, and Afia could feel the warmth of the palms, the blunt fingers with their cropped nails. At

Smith she had heard the girls talk about Muslim women, how oppressed they were, how the Smith girls needed to help them. But Moray had never seemed oppressed. Everything in their home was her creation. A glance from her could rip a hole in a moment of false pride; an approving nod was all it took to gather hope. "All the more reason," she said, her palms firm against Afia's cherry-red kameez, "to give you an anchor here. A future you can prepare for."

"Moray, I have a future." Afia tried to wriggle from her mother's embrace. Hot tears stung her cheeks. "Only two years to go after this one, then medical school. I have not seen this photo," she added hastily, "but it must be part of a collage, or something. They like to show how diverse they are, at Smith. I'll ask the administration to remove it."

"Erasing the photo will not erase the story of the photo," Moray said, almost gently. "And that story could put a knife to our hearts, child. You wouldn't do that to us."

"Of course not."

"Then do your duty. Start cooking the sugar. Our visitors should know what a gifted baker you are. Remember when you used to make us all *chana*?"

It was only a visit, Afia told herself as she mixed the ground almonds and cardamom in with the melting sugar. A visit from a family who might find her nose too long or her tea service too clumsy and not choose her after all. Or if they did choose her, might find that Zardad—was it Zardad?—preferred a taller girl, a younger girl, a girl with more flesh on her. Or if he had no such preference, it was only an engagement. An engagement was a span of time. It was a long breath. It would not scar her face, like Lema's. And later she would be away, far away, too far for their knives to reach.

CHAPTER NINE

The long winter break tended to unravel the varsities. Even though Lissy's players came back two weeks before the rest of the students, they'd gotten enmeshed with their families or their old heartthrobs on New Year's, and all they wanted to talk about was spring break. Lissy had to work them back up to speed and into shape as teams. But this year, men's squash sprang back like a new rubber band, mostly because Shahid Satar returned from Pakistan with a spring in his step and a laserlike focus. "You must have loved seeing your family," Lissy said to him after the first practice.

"They are growing up so fast. My little sisters, I mean," he said. "And my sister Afia has been engaged."

"Engaged!" Lissy's voice betrayed her shock. "I didn't know she was . . . seeing anyone."

Shahid hoisted his squash bag from the floor. "No, no, Coach," he said, tucking his water bottle into the outside pocket. "It's all arranged. This is how we do things. Nothing will happen for some years. She is promised, that is all. To marry my second cousin. The families are very happy about it."

That night, giving Chloe her bath, Lissy tried to keep her good humor. "I'm drowning," Chloe said, flopping back into the water after Lissy washed her hair. "Save me, save me, I'm *drowning*." She paddled her hands like a pair of useless flippers.

"Aren't you Dora the Explorer?" Lissy said. "Dora can swim."

"No soy Dora. Soy Sleeping Beauty. And I am *drowwnning*."

"Okay, Sleeping Beauty. I'm coming to save you!" Lissy said in a hollow chest voice that had somehow become the voice of Beluga, the blue plastic whale, who dived into the bath from the toy basket. Chloe tipped her head up as Beluga leapt over the ripples and nudged at her underarms. "Don't drown, Sleeping Beauty!" said the whale. "I'll teach you to swim!"

As the whale entreated, Lissy lifted up Chloe's head until Chloe giggled and grabbed the whale to squeeze its spout. "Thank you, Beluga," she said. She kissed its nose. "Now," she said, "I will marry you."

"What, are you a whale now?" Lissy asked.

"No. But he rescued me."

When she'd put Chloe to bed, Lissy poured herself a V-8 and vodka and nestled in front of the fire with Ethan. She had a report due to Don Shears tomorrow, but it could wait. Outside, fat flakes of snow had begun to fall. "Our daughter wants a prince to save her," she said. "She'll grow up like your sisters, married to a Wall Street mogul."

Ethan chuckled drily. "If Chloe falls in with the wrong guy, I'll rip out his fingernails."

She sat up. "Would you really?"

"No. I'd get her into therapy and lock her in her room at night."

Lissy sighed. She returned her head to his shoulder. "They'll just marry that girl off," she said.

"What girl?"

"Shahid's sister. Afia."

"Did you ever talk to the boy?"

"Gus, you mean?" When he nodded, she sighed. "That's not an area I interfere in."

"Wise move, Coach."

"But how can she—if she doesn't even know this guy back home—can they really make something like that work?"

"You worried about the girl? Or about Shahid?"

"I don't know." She took a sip of laced V-8. "He seems so suddenly happy. But if his sister doesn't behave—"

"You might not have your star player at peak performance."

She glared at him. "I'd be a pretty selfish coach to think that way."

"Or a coach mindful of her priorities." He pulled her head to his shoulder and stroked her hair. "You're the coach," he said. "Not God."

She didn't want to be God. She just wanted a smooth season, a winning season, a dazzling future for Shahid Satar, and a new fitness center. That night she slept fitfully. Outside, the snow continued, whitening the lake. She rose before dawn and worked on the figures for her first-semester report—how many enrolled in phys ed classes at all levels, how many on the varsities, how much club-level activity was up and running. When she'd dropped Chloe at day care, she fishtailed across campus to Don Shears's office.

It was lucky for Don, Lissy often thought, that he'd been able to spend fifty-one of his fifty-six years in academe. In no other world would his natural limits have combined so successfully with his ambition. He had moved a lot, but always within College Land—like Airport Land, a sprawl of concourses with secured entrances and privileged clubs for those who'd earned their stripes. Waiting outside the president's office, Lissy wondered if she, too, was lost on the concourse. *She had potential once; now she's a bureaucrat.* No, no, no. She was breaking barriers, paving pathways. She remembered Shahid playing Afran on the court yesterday, whipping the ball back and forth. Chess at ninety miles an hour, her coach used to call it.

Don flung his door wide and waved her in. "Coffee?"

"Done that, thanks."

The office was overheated. Don was down to shirtsleeves and a crooked bow tie. Lissy felt her underarms grow damp. "I sent you this by e-mail too," she said, laying the folder on Don's desk before sitting down. "We don't have all the add/drops yet, but the numbers should be stable."

Don lifted the cover and glanced at the report, then set it aside. "Basketball team's off to a good start, I hear," he said.

"Both women and men, yes. We've been lucky with recruiting."

"And of course you've got your internationals, on the squash squad."

"Highest GPA of all the varsities," she said. "Not that we can take credit for that. Those kids come prepared."

"Which is more," Don observed, "than we can say of the football team."

Lissy felt the soft, ragged edge of misgiving scrape against her wall of assurance. Something was up. Something had happened between the elegant dinner in New York and this snowy morning in the Berkshires. "I'm not sure—" she began.

"Look, I don't want a football team any more than you do."

She frowned, tried to smooth the misgiving. "I've never said I didn't want—"

"But we get a lot of pressure. A lot of pressure, Lissy. Admissions lets these guys in, and they struggle to get up to speed—"

"And when they don't cut it, Coach Salazar throws them off the team. We're not Penn State."

"But Charlie Horton thinks we should devote more time to the big sports. Set aside the yoga studio and get regular tutoring for the kids who're struggling."

Lissy tried not to let her jaw drop. Don Shears knew his faculty would revolt if athletics got a tutoring budget and minority programs were left to flutter in the wind. Then she remembered. "Drew Horton's on the football squad."

Don adjusted the pens on his desk. "We've got to let the legacies in," he said. "And people like Horton remember a time when football took the conference title."

She wanted to rail at him. Not that she cared so passionately about yoga, or a fitness center, or any of the million-dollar touches that made a four-year college into a country club. But what she knew of Charles Horton was his direct regard of her breasts; she'd forced a smile at *Madame Director* and *La Directresse*. She didn't take well to billionaires in tuxedoes telling her how to run a sports program.

"You're telling me they want boys kept on the teams," she said, "and they want those teams to win."

"If we could make that happen, I think we'd have a better chance with the fitness center."

"Well, squash is winning." When Don started to object, she held up a hand. "Go ahead. Call it un-American. But every country club in the Northeast has a squash court. And this year we've got a chance against Harvard."

She had never made such a claim to herself, much less voiced it aloud. But when she watched Shears's shiny head lift, his chin thrust forward with interest, she knew she'd found something to work with.

"I've never had a men's squad like this before," she went on, trying to keep her voice casual. "You heard my player at the dinner."

He nodded. "South Asian kid."

"He impressed Jeff Stubnick. Jeff's pledging a hundred grand toward the fitness center."

"And you think—with this kid—you can beat Harvard." Don had edged out from around his desk. He straightened his bow tie.

"I said we had a chance."

"Charlie Horton hates Harvard." A rare smile played across Don's pallid face. "Don't know why. Maybe they turned him down when he was eighteen."

"Then he should come up from New York and cheer for us."

"Not just that." Don put a finger to his mouth and turned a circle, Sherlock Holmes without a pipe. "Do this for me," he said. "Forget football. Pull out a win against Harvard."

This wasn't the effect she'd hoped for. "Don, I can't guarantee—"

He waved a small hand. "Victory is written all over your face. I'll lay a bet with Horton. He loves a gamble. The man's in hedge funds, for Chrissake."

"What kind of bet?"

"You win against his nemesis. He forgets football for a New York minute and buys us a fitness center. I'll slap his name on it."

In the warm office Lissy felt a chill down her spine. Compete with everything you've got, she always told her teams. She met Don's bright eyes, enlarged by his glasses. "And if we lose?" she said.

"Then you and I'll have to talk again," Don said, "about football."

CHAPTER TEN

The first few nights back in the dorm, Afia couldn't sleep. Missing were the hoots of the owls, the murmur of turtle doves, and the hourly whistle of Baz, the night watchman who bicycled through Nasirabad followed by stray dogs. Slight though she was, her bed felt too narrow and sagged in the center, not like the firm harbor Baba had built from that old chest. And when she woke, what did she have? Breakfast of cold toast in a hall full of chattering girls with piercings on their bits of loose flesh and hair chopped as if they'd suffered lice.

Patty, her roommate, tried to help. "Of *course* you belong here, Afia," she said the third morning after classes had started. They were in the dining hall with Taylor. Taylor was making plans to transfer from Smith because there were too many lesbians. Afia thought maybe Patty was a lesbian, but she wasn't about to remark on it; she still didn't understand that part of things. "Don't you think we all feel out of place sometimes?" Patty went on, touching Afia's wrist. "Look at me. I'm from the deep South. I'm fat. I'm Baptist. People here think I talk as funny as you."

Afia was back in her jeans, her turtleneck, the clothes she had been so excited to wear when she first bought them. "I don't think it is the same."

"Nothing's the same, honey. That's America."

"Diversity, diversity," Taylor chimed in. "Just look at the Smith website. You're on it, Afia."

"Not anymore," said Patty.

"I told them no picture," Afia said when Taylor frowned at her.

"What, is that your religion?" Taylor said. "Like it's stealing your soul?"

"She means no pictures with boys in them," Patty explained.

Taylor laughed. "Please," Afia said to both of them. "You are my friends. This is serious. In my country, to hold a boy's hand—"

"You mean Gus's hand."

"Any hand, if he is not of my family. It could make trouble."

"Afia, I'm just messing with you." Taylor picked up her hand and kissed the knuckles. "We all love you to death."

Wrapping her head scarf tight, Afia set off across campus to her classes. Molecular Bio was her favorite. It was taught by Sue Glasgow, for one, with her print blouses and unfashionable wool pants and her standard response to questions: "Isn't it *amazing*?" It *was* amazing, Afia thought—the shiny textbooks and the small, gleaming lab, and the way Professor Glasgow helped her apply the stain to the gel after separating molecules, so she could see the proteins glow under ultraviolet light. Each day on her way to Molecular Bio, her brain growled its cravings the way her stomach growled when she hadn't eaten all day.

In that way she was excited to be back. Excited, too, to hear a lecturer from Burma on Aung San Suu Ki, and to go with Patty to a strange, slow Bergman movie about a family with a crazy daughter, the scenes full of silence and menace, and she didn't really understand the plot but afterward Patty and Taylor argued in the wee hours about the meaning of it all.

But then she went to her job at the Price Chopper. And the aunties greeted her, "Back from the dark side! Seen your fella yet?" And she felt it then, felt how she couldn't just go back to this world she had inhabited before, the world in which she was a bag girl, and she had a fella, and his name was Gus. That other world, the world of henna and *rukhsati*, of *namus* and *ghairat*, had reached its tentacles across oceans and continents.

Away from the Price Chopper and bio lab, she hung in a place in between, like between sleep and waking. In the dream that kept tugging at her feet, she had bought this life—these classes, this too-narrow bed—with a promise to marry Zardad. Zardad, who was Zardad? She must have seen him, as many as a half dozen times at one gathering or another, but she drew no memories of him. An engineer, nine years older than she. In Nasirabad, after the families had come to terms, she might have asked for a photo of him, but she did not want to think about photos. Instead she had lain awake in her big firm bed. She'd made a collage from his mother's face—she had served tea to his mother and his aunt—and what she had seen of his father's face from the crack in the door between the kitchen and the *hujra*, the day his father came to set the terms with Baba. His father's big forehead, his mother's soft chin and narrow shoulders, his father's way of thrusting his chest forward when he spoke. *We hear your daughter is ambitious.* And Baba denying it, no, no, she wants only to help people, she will be a wonderful mother, so caring.

After the tears, she had said yes. Of course she had. She saw no point protesting. It was a good match, an engineer still in his twenties and from her *khel*, and they would let her go back to Smith, to finish her degree. No promises on medical school, but a married woman could do many things before she had children. In the dream haunting her sleep now, she was anchored to the name *Zardad*. She was anchored to her *namus*, or the story of her *namus*, and must behave as if it were intact. Already a letter had come from Moray, asking all the usual questions—was the flight smooth, did she have enough warm clothing—and giving in passing a possible date for the marriage, two years from this coming May, a week after Afia would graduate from Smith.

It was when she stared at the date that she felt the pinpricks of awakening—awakening from the dream into the bags she snapped open at the Price Chopper checkout and the soft pressure of Sue Glasgow's thumb on her wrist as she directed her tweezers under the microscope. And then his voice on the phone. Not the messages, which he started leaving before she left Peshawar, his words tiny and distant, but his voice when she lifted the receiver from the ringing wall phone. "M'Afia."

She was awake. This was her dorm suite. Her Qur'an on top of the bureau. Patty's stuffed animals piled on her pink comforter. The cold sun outside the window, the bright snow like English cake frosting on the archways and roofs. Her own breath, stuttering. "Gus."

"I was about to ask Shahid if you'd stayed in Pakistan."

She sat up in her desk chair. Her skin gave off sparks. "But you didn't."

"Down, tiger. I obey orders."

She reached for the dream, tried to pull it into the world that was real again. "Gus, I am so sorry."

"Hey, you should be. I read the headlines, you know. Always violence over there. I get worried when you don't pick up."

"I am engaged."

A long silence. Then, "Don't be stupid, M'Afia. Nobody gets engaged anymore."

"I do. I am. I cannot see you, Gus."

"I'm coming up."

She looked at the Hello Kitty clock that Patty kept on the bookshelf. "In an hour I must be in lab."

"Yeah, but I'm downstairs."

The dream was shattered, now, into splinters of panic. She cleared off the desk and closed the library copy of *Jane Eyre* onto which she'd stuck Post-its for her notes. Quickly she brushed her hair before the full-length mirror on the back of the door. She had loved this mirror when she first discovered it, just as she'd loved the view from the second story. She had never lived so high above things before. She loved the desk lamps the college supplied, with their flexible necks. Only late at night, when the high-pitched laughter of drunken girls reached her through the window or the smell of pot seeped through the walls, eerily reminiscent of fish roasted with tamarind, did she feel out of place. Now she tucked her hair under a sheer dupatta that she wore back from the crown of her head. Lifting her glasses, she ran a pinkie under each eye, as if she were applying kohl. She tried to move slowly, deliberately. But her body was too full of blood, and it had to move. Sliding into her clogs she yanked the door wide. She clattered down two flights of stairs. She opened the front door just enough to pull Gus—in his yellow fleece and Icelandic cap, his short freckled nose bright with cold—into the building.

"M'Afia," he said. His hands on her cheeks were cold. "I missed you so much."

Where was her shame? In her, all around her, but lost to her senses. Gus's cold nose buried itself in her hair. Before, with him, she had forgotten shame. Everything had been reversed. Her life in America, which had proceeded with the loopy logic of a dream, became real, and Nasirabad took on the slow undertow of dream.

Even with Shahid going on about that photo, that stupid photo that the publications office had posted, the world of shame had stayed far away. Dream people couldn't hear what you said when you were awake; they couldn't see what you did.

But now she had been home, where the photo was a letter from another world, from the America that had turned, all at once, to dream, and in Nasirabad she had understood the exact terms of the life she was destined to conduct. Her task was plain—keep the rest of the dream under lock and key, accept the engagement to Zardad, marry Zardad if it came to that, and hope he never learned what she had so recklessly allowed to happen in her dream life.

Which now, again, was real. "I worried about you," Gus said, his hand cupping the back of her neck. "We heard there was a suicide bomb in Peshawar—"

"Peshawar's a hundred kilometers away from Nasirabad!"

"I know. I Googled it. I Googled every day, like you might pop up from the map and wave at me. But I know you flew in and out of Peshawar. And you weren't writing, so I thought—"

"I couldn't write."

"I know, it must be impossible to get Internet."

"No, not for that. I just . . . Gus, if I am writing you, in Nasirabad, I am a bad daughter, I am rotted like bad fruit."

"Hey, hey. It's okay. You didn't need to write me." He took her face in his hands. He kissed her mouth. Her blood sang.

"But I did not. And I cannot." With what strength she could muster she pushed away from him. "Gus, I am *engaged*."

"Yeah, you said that." He pushed unruly hair from his eyes. He was so eager, like a puppy. She envied him. All he'd needed to be set free from his shyness was to know that she loved him. No looking over his shoulder for the judgments of one world to be passed in the next. He would crow from the rooftops if he could. "Let's go upstairs, baby. Let's sit down. You look pale. What kind of mafia's putting the screws to M'Afia?"

She didn't know what he meant by *putting the screws*. Screwing was intercourse, she'd learned that much. Did he think—? Shame muffled the song in her blood. "No, no, Gus—"

"Okay. Okay, I withdraw the question. Come on. It took more than an hour to get here. It's snowing outside."

By the time they entered her room, his good cheer had drained away. Sitting next to her on the narrow bed, he rested his elbows on his knees and picked at invisible dirt under his fingernails. In the last e-mail she'd received from him in Nasirabad, he was driving to Manhattan with a couple of guys from his high school, to watch the ball drop. *If you were here*, he'd written, *we'd stay at the Ritz tonight. Pancakes in bed tomorrow. Book it for next year?* "So," he said now, flicking an invisible speck of dirt to the floor, "you've met someone. In Pakistan."

"I have not met him. Maybe, when I was small. But it is promised now."

"I don't get it." Wounded, his pale eyes turned to her. "If you haven't met some other guy, who are you engaged *to*? What's promised?"

"To marry. His name is Zardad." Slowly, sitting next to him while low light slanted through the dusty window, she explained the custom she had grown up with. The image that Khalid must have found on the website, the visit from Zardad's family. "I had to come back here," she said, "so I say yes."

"So they're forcing you," he said. He stood up, bristling. She had never seen him angry before. "That's disgusting."

"No, not forcing. This is what we expect. I expected, until . . ." She couldn't complete the sentence. She tried again. "I am the disgusting one, Gus. My family's honor—"

"No. No no no. You can't let them do this, Afia." He stood by the window, arms akimbo. "You're in America now, you can see who you want, marry who you want. I thought . . . Jesus, I thought there was somebody else. This Zardad guy—he's not a problem. He's nothing to you. You can just, I don't know, not go back there."

"No, Gus." She shook her head. What she wanted to say was like telling him the dream. But you could never explain a dream once you were awake, even though it had made perfect sense in the other world. "It is not me. It is my family. I cannot hurt them. You cannot imagine, how it would hurt them."

"Look, the photo's out there. *We* should be out there, if you ask me. But you can't call the picture back. So what do they want?"

"That I marry a good Muslim man. That is all."

"I'll be your good Muslim man, then!" He picked up the framed family photo that Afia kept on her desk. It had been taken just after Baba had rebuilt the terrace overlooking the mulberry orchard, the summer before Shahid left for the States. No one smiled the way people smiled in photos in America, but they all looked happy. Speaking as if to the picture, Gus went on, "I'll convert. Can I convert? Tell me what I have to do. Do I have to pray five times a day? I'm circumcised. Do I have to sew that bit back on? Because you tell me, baby, and I'll do it."

"We circumcise. Just like Jews."

"I'll do something else, then. Swear an oath. A blood oath."

He looked so earnest, so eager. She couldn't help herself. She laughed. "It would not work. And if it does, you would have to marry me."

"So I'll marry you." He set the photo down. "I'll convert, and I'll marry you. Only not in Pakistan. Can't let them behead me."

"And how do you know, silly boy, that we should be married?"

"I love you. We've been together four months. We're both smart, we're not crazy. If marriage is what it takes—"

"What do we know of marriage? This is something . . . our parents know of. This is why in this country you have everyone divorce. Because no one wise is choosing the partner. It is all romance, all love."

"You don't think we're wise?"

"We are young. This marriage, choosing . . ." She was the serious one, now. "It is not for us."

"Then what are we doing? Huh?" He returned to the bed and sat cross-legged. "Why are we together, if you're just going back to marry this Zarba guy you don't give a fuck about?"

"I don't know, Gus."

"I'll tell you why, then." He took her hand in his. He pressed her fingers, one by one, as if checking for sprains. "We are beginning, Afia. We are exploring. It's what people do. But you know, we can't just do it by ourselves."

"This is what we say in my country. It must be the family—"

"Or your friends. Look, Afia, I've been playing this your way. I don't breathe a word to your brother, who is my old roommate and a teammate. I don't go posting pictures on Facebook."

"It wasn't Facebook."

"But it should be. It should say, 'In a relationship with Afia Satar,' right there on my profile. And you see how you are with your friends, and how you are when your friends are away, and little by little you figure out. Whether you should get married, you know, or move on."

She shook her head. "We cannot do it that way, Gus."

"Why?"

"You know why."

"Tell me again."

"Honor"—she looked away from him, toward the family portrait on the desk—"is not just the greatest thing, for Pashtuns. It is really the only thing. And however you might think it is stupid, Gus, I am"—she bit her lip, to hold back the tears—"my family's honor. Without it, they more rather I am dead. And maybe I more rather, too."

"Well, I don't more rather. And I don't accept that you're engaged to this guy. So maybe if you don't break up with him I'll just tell Shahid—"

"No!" She grabbed his wrist. "If you tell my brother, then . . . then . . . you do not love me." She let go. She removed her glasses, which were fogging, and set them on the bedside table. She pulled her dupatta over her hair. "I am maybe to you just exotic, like your pets."

Strangely, he snorted. He leaned close. She could feel his breath on her face. He touched the mole on her cheekbone. "M'Afia," he said softly. "You are so *basic* to me."

His lips came close, very close. She could taste him, almost, the liquor of his saliva. Her lips parted. Then she tasted, instead, her own salt tears. She blinked, snatched back the glasses, pushed at his shoulder. "Go," she said.

"Afia, you can't mean this. We're here, now. All those rules, they don't exist here."

"They exist," she said, bringing a fist to her chest, over her heart, "here."

She stepped to the door and opened it. He said more things, but she had stopped speaking. Words were like hot matches on the skin of her heart. She hung her head and would not meet his eyes as he brushed past her and made his way out into the cold.

CHAPTER ELEVEN

All was settled. All settled. Shahid kept repeating this truth to himself, every time a cold lizard of anger threatened to twist inside him. He'd first felt the lizard, darting one direction then the other, when he got that call to come home to Nasirabad. Maybe only Khalid knew about that photo, he'd thought then, and maybe their father had spent all that money just to bring them back for Maryam's wedding. But that reasoning had never added up.

The marriage offer had arrived while Shahid was in Peshawar, summoned by Uncle Omar. Omar had prepared a feast of roasted chicken and curries and invited a crowd of relatives from that side of the family. Shahid saw his other *anâ*, his mother's mother, whose legs were failing her but whose mind was quick as ever and who loved hearing his stories about America. Attending dutifully to her was Tayyab's daughter, Panra, prettier and plumper than he remembered her. In the morning, Omar took him back to the Peshawar Sports Academy, where Coach Khan looked spindly, and Shahid hit a few balls and reminisced about his training days. Everything felt coated by nostalgia, even pausing at the spot by the banyan tree, just inside the gate, where a suicide bomber had broken past the guards and blown himself up, his severed head rolling down the walk toward the main office. "And I told the boys," Coach Khan said to Omar, as if he had never told this joke before, "that the fellow'd come to the wrong place. Should've dropped his head off at a football academy."

Khalid, Shahid told his uncle that evening, would not have found the quip funny. Omar listened quietly while Shahid complained about his stepbrother. In the end Shahid told his uncle of the photograph, of Khalid's veiled threat, no *nanawate* for *tora*.

"And is the photograph," Omar asked quietly, "objectionable?"

Shahid sighed. "I don't know, Uncle. It's not so easy to say, over there."

"Not so easy to control your sister, either."

"I try, Uncle."

"You should not have this problem on your mind. You have a career to focus on." Omar had lifted his glass to his lips. He drank two fingers of Scotch every night, unwitnessed by anyone except Shahid. "Let Afia be engaged," he'd said. "Married as soon as possible. You are a generous brother, Shahid, but you saddle yourself with a liability, here. I will speak with your family," he added, before Shahid could object.

On the plane returning to America, Afia had been silent, sullen. "You might thank me," he'd said at last.

"For what?"

"For the fact that you're on this flight. Khalid had a print from the website. What if I'd let him show it to Baba? What do you think would've happened to you?"

She had shrugged. "Maybe I'd be dead. Maybe that would be better."

He had felt his anger then, cold and wriggling, threatening the relief he felt at their both returning to New England, safe. "Drama queen," he had accused her, and they had not spoken for the remainder of the flight.

Well, she was getting in line. She knew what she had—a great opportunity for education, for independence. She knew what Shahid had done for her. He was pissed at Khalid, but that was nothing new—all his life he'd wanted and needed Khalid to be his mentor, his guide, and Khalid had done nothing but wish him dead. *Too bad for you, Khalid lala*, he'd thought when Zardad's offer finally came. And now, when Khalid's words came back to haunt him—no *nanawate* for *tora*—he just hit the squash ball harder and drowned them out. He focused on the GMAT, coming up in a couple of months. All was settled. All would be well.

The first Sunday in February, Coach Hayes pulled him into her office after a home match where they steamrolled St. Lawrence. She stood in the doorway for a minute, talking to two girls from the women's team, before she shut the door and sat in her swivel chair, opposite him. Her phone's red light announced messages, but she ignored it. Shahid took the stiff-backed chair. From the yellow bin she kept by the door he picked one of the old-fashioned blue hardballs she made them use, sometimes, just to keep them on their toes. From the other bin, the red one, he picked one of the soft balls and began juggling them, blue and black spinning off his hands. Coach Hayes had the largest office in the athletic building. In four years, Shahid still hadn't gotten over how weird this was. Coach took a swig from her water bottle—the woman drank like ten gallons a day—and opened a folder. "I need your honest opinion, Shahid," she said.

"Always, Coach." He kept his eyes on the balls. Blue, black, blue, black.

"What are our chances with the Ivies?"

Now here was a subject Shahid could warm to. He caught the blue ball in his right hand; the black one skittered off. "We took Brown last year," he said, "and we came close with Columbia. Princeton's out of reach—they've got those two guys from Egypt, I played them in the juniors, and now they've got one of the Khans, from Lahore. But Yale graduated three of its top contenders, so they're beatable. And Harvard . . . well, Harvard is a toss-up, Coach."

"What do we need to do?"

"To beat them?" Shahid sat back. With the relief of Afia's engagement, he had been playing well, but he hadn't really thought about team strategy. He was flattered, Coach asking him like this. Not like she wasn't sure of herself. That was one of the many things his family could never have comprehended—how well this woman seemed to know her mind, like a man. He'd Googled her athletic history. At her peak, her serve had been her signature. She struck it overhead, like a tennis serve. Her ball traveled fast enough to disorient her opponent, and she somehow recovered quickly enough from the follow-through to pick off the return. It was a high-risk strategy. "To beat them," he repeated, "we'd need to look at the bottom half of the lineup."

"That's my thinking. You, Afran, Chander, Jamil—I can't see changing anything there. Tom's out till March, probably, with that ankle."

"I've been working with Carlos." Shahid stood. He had to pace, to see how to rearrange the squad. "You've got him at seven, but he's beating Yanik. And you're alternating Gus and Johan at nine, but you know, Gus took that guy today in less than an hour. I could see putting him at eight, and trying someone new at nine."

"Gus at eight," Coach Hayes repeated. She was making notes, sipping her water.

"Yeah. His serve has got that soft little spin, you know, it's tricky. And he's got more confidence this year. You might give him a try at eight when we play Trinity, just to see." Shahid nodded at his vision. "And maybe stack the boys on the top. Switch Chander and Jamil, you're sure to get that fourth match."

"I don't approve of stacking, Shahid, you know that."

"With positions three and four, it's not really stacking." When she raised her eyebrows, he gave in. "All right, but let me work with Jamil on the side. Then we have a chance, Coach. Not a big one, but a chance."

"Well, that's your assignment. A win over Harvard." She drew a rectangle around the list she'd made in her notebook. She stood. She looked almost pleased. Then a shadow crossed her face. "How's your sister, Shahid?"

He stiffened. "She is well, Coach."

"She's . . . adjusting okay? To this idea of being engaged?"

He gave her his widest smile. "It is all settled, Coach. Everyone is very happy."

"Good." She cleared her throat. "Because—not to be selfish—we're going to need your focus, these next few weeks."

"Count on me, Coach."

If all she wanted was focus, he thought, tossing the blue ball back into the bin, he could oblige her as long as things stayed settled with Afia. Outside her office he checked his phone. No calls. He felt tender toward Afia, as he did every time the subject of her engagement surfaced. He sent her a text: *We play Trinity next Saturday. Take the bus down to Hartford? Dinner on me.*

Then he loped into a mostly empty locker room. Gus waved while he talked on his mobile. Chander was still in the shower. Afran stood by the sink blow-drying his hair. For a short, bullet-faced Kurd, Afran was touchingly vain. He bought crisp white

T-shirts by the dozen and tended his mop of soft curls like a girl. "Coach on your hide about grades?" he asked when he'd shut off the dryer. He eyed Shahid in the long mirror as Shahid stripped off his practice uniform.

"No, dude. Dreaming about Harvard."

Afran snorted. "That's like her wet dream."

"You were raging out there, man," said Gus. Shutting his phone, he clapped a hand on Shahid's shoulder. He was a bear of a guy, more like a cricket player than squash, but they didn't have cricket in America.

"Yeah, and I'm starving. You want to drive over to Bertucci's tonight?"

"Can't, man. History paper."

"Afran?"

"You just want to exercise those wheels."

Shahid shrugged. With Afran's Turkish accent, *wheels* came out like *whiles*. Yes, he wouldn't mind giving his whiles a spin. Shahid didn't have the same feeling about owning a car as the American guys did. The Civic was a pain in the ass and would always be a pain in the ass. He had it only so he could drive to Northampton and check in on Afia. "Gimme five?" he said to Afran.

He showered, the hot water sluicing through veins of fatigue. Even with everything settled, he wasn't sleeping well. In a week or two his family would expect a report—and Khalid, he felt sure, would be plinking computer keys, looking for evidence that Shahid's report was bogus and their sister was still whoring around.

"Your hair's wet, man," Afran said as they headed into the frosty night.

"Sexy new look," Shahid countered. The Civic started up fine but shifted rough, and squealed on the sharp turn to the state highway.

"You get a mechanic on this thing?" Afran asked.

"You volunteering?"

"Fuck, no. My dad runs an auto shop. Makes me sick just to slide under an axle."

"Your father fixes cars? How the hell'd you start in squash?"

"Same as you, man. The little clubs, the little competitions, the kind uncle. Not like our pig-rich American buddies."

At Bertucci's they slid into a red vinyl booth and ordered Cokes. At least Afran didn't drink, though that might have had to do more with squash than with Islam. Afran was nuts about squash. He didn't have Shahid's talent, so he worked a lot harder. He'd built up an arsenal of spins and ricocheting boasts. He subscribed to *Squash Magazine*, even though Coach would lend out her copy, and he was forever asking Shahid what he thought about Amr Shabana or the legendary Jahangir Khan, or whether the new Head racquet had a bigger sweet spot.

"When I'm number one, next year," he said after they'd chosen a hamburger pizza, "I want to start captains' practices at six. Seven's too late. Half the squad's got eight A.M. classes."

"You'll never get the Americans up," said Shahid.

"So the starters become all Pakis and Turks. What do we care?"

"When Coach's budget gets slashed, you'll care."

"She's the A.D. She's not going to slash her own squash budget!"

Shahid waved him off. Afran might be more Americanized than he was, but he didn't have a clue about politics and athletics. When Enright held another fund-raiser in New York, Afran would not be on that stage.

"Let me show you some starters I think she should recruit," Afran said. He pulled out his iPhone and began scrolling through his sites, his fingers opening and compressing like a magician's.

"I don't want to see 'em, Af," Shahid said. "I'll be gone, remember? I might be working for the competition."

"What's your sister going to do then?" Afran asked, keeping his eyes on the screen. "Schlep to Boston for matches?"

Normally Shahid would have grinned at Afran's used of *schlep*. The Turkish sponge, he'd called his friend, soaking up slang along with American customs. But at the mention of Afia he felt a tightening in his jaw. "Afia may not stay—" he began.

But Afran interrupted with "Whoa. Someone's been recruited."

"I don't care about squash right now—"

"Not for the team. To help your captivating sister."

Afran passed the iPhone over just as the waitress arrived with their pizza. Shahid watched as she exchanged winks and smiles with Afran. The guy's hair definitely did the trick. Light from the votive candle caressed Afran's dark curls and his high, flat cheekbones. Shahid turned to the phone's tiny screen. He tipped the thing into the light, then away from it. He was looking at a Facebook page. In the highlighted photo, Afia was sitting on a guy's shoulders, reaching up into an apple tree heavy with fruit. She was wearing the hijab, but her turtleneck revealed the curve of her breasts. He squinted.

"You can expand the photo," Afran said. He made the opening motion with his fingertips. Shahid tried it, then pushed the photo upward. Still all he saw was the top of the guy's head, with Afia's hand pressing down on rust-colored curls. The head looked familiar, but he couldn't say from where. In the blurry background of the photo was another apple-picking girl, tagged as "Taylor!"

"Who's the guy?"

"Ask your sister, man."

He scrolled back to Afia's face, the delight in her eyes and mouth. The lizard of anger went ice cold. Last week, the picture of Afia had disappeared from the Smith College website. But now Shahid's fingers were moving over a Facebook timeline. Above it shone a snapshot of a toothy girl, her arms around a disheveled guy in a Dartmouth sweatshirt. *Taylor Saintsbury*, the name read. *In a relationship with Chase B.* Chase—of course, the squash leftie. He tapped back to the photo. "When did this show up?"

Afran took the iPhone back and scrolled. "Last week," he said, "but the pic's from fall, you can see the leaves turning. You don't know the dude holding her up?"

"No."

Afran scrutinized the picture. "I'm surprised your sister let this go online," he said. "She's not real show-offy."

"She didn't let it go online."

Afran's eyes widened. He set down the phone and took a slice of pizza. As if he couldn't talk with his mouth empty, he bit off the point before he said, "*You* posted it, man? She might get pissed. I didn't even think you knew Taylor—"

"Of course not me!" Shahid exploded. Afran jerked back in his seat. His dark eyebrows knit together. The iPhone lay on the table. Shahid picked it up to look again at the photo. It had been taken in the fall, before the trip home. This Taylor, this stupid friend of Afia's, let someone put it on her page. He wanted to tell Afran his sister was engaged, but that would only compound the shame.

"Eat some pizza, dude," Afran was saying. "It's getting cold."

Robotically Shahid lifted a triangle and tasted the greasy beef, the stringy cheese. His first year in the States, he had tried to keep halal. It wasn't impossible—the dining hall was prepared to cook special meals—but it drew an attention that Shahid had come to resent. Slowly he gave in on one thing, then another: vanilla cake, Chinese food prepared with MSG, desserts with pig-marrow gelatin. "You get girls off social media?" he asked when he'd swallowed enough to calm himself. No reason for Afran to know what threats came out of Nasirabad. Shahid could take care of his own family troubles. "Because this Taylor looks taken."

Afran shrugged. "You can't have sex on Facebook. But they mess with my head, I'll tell you that." He looked around the restaurant, as if the waitresses in their crisp blouses and jeans were part of his problem. "I slack off in classes, you know? Coach is making me see someone. They're calling it ADD, but it's not really."

"What do you mean, see someone? Like a doctor?"

Afran looked embarrassed. "I decided to see this guy Springer. He's a sort of shrink. Smarter than the tools at the counseling center, though."

"What does he do to you?"

"He doesn't do anything. We talk. It's stupid."

Talk. Shahid didn't want to talk to anyone, not about his sister. "Springer," he said. "Isn't that—?"

"Coach's husband." Afran wrinkled his nose. "But he doesn't, like, talk to her about me. It's not allowed." Afran drained his Coke. He leaned across the table. "Look. If I could get someone to cut out whatever central lobe is all about the Prophet's commands, and what you can do and what you can't and how big a deal a girl's hymen is . . . I'd do it. Bingo. Like that." He made a movement atop his head that was similar to what he'd done with his iPhone, opening his fingers then locking them together, as if pinching off part of his brain. "Do I care about purity or marriage? No. I want to get laid."

Even knowing how Afran liked to say things like *get laid*, Shahid reddened. "But would you want someone to treat your sister the way you treat, you know . . ." He gestured at the iPhone as if it were Afran's Rolodex.

"Hey, you had a hookup last year. What was her name? Vanessa?"

"Valerie." Shahid lifted the final slice of pizza and let it flop onto his plate. "She wasn't a hookup, she was a girlfriend."

"And?"

"And then I found her in the closet at some party, making out with a lacrosse player."

"That's American women, man."

"Well, I don't understand them."

Afran signaled for a refill on the Coke. "You asked about my sister," he said when it came. "I don't have a sister, okay? But I did have a cousin. She was retarded."

"Afran—"

"No, I mean really retarded, like in something was wrong with her brain, okay? But she was this beautiful girl. And she got pregnant."

"How old?"

"Fourteen." Afran's eyes were fixed on a spot over Shahid's shoulder. "She wouldn't say who the guy was. I'm not sure she knew. But I'm telling you, man. I'd rather somebody treated her the way I treat American girls, than do what they did."

"Which was?" Shahid's mouth went dry.

"She died in a kitchen fire. The door was locked."

"That's awful, man," Shahid said. "But an accident like that—"

"It wasn't an accident. You know it. I know it. The cops knew it." He took a long swig. Then he fixed his eyes on Shahid. "So what would you rather?" he said. "A girl suffers because some guy toyed with her feelings? Or because her dad locked a door and lit a match?"

"Will that be all?" the waitress asked. Her wide-set eyes darted from one of them to the other. She was pretty in the way of local girls—a layer of baby fat on fine bones, slender nose, breasts that seemed ready to give milk. *Julie*, her name tag read.

As if he had just been bantering with his friend, Afran turned to her. "That depends," he said.

"On what?" Julie asked.

"On what you're doing after work."

Julie's blush mottled her pale skin. "I work late," she said.

"So do I," said Afran.

"Just the check," Shahid said to her.

When Julie had stepped away, Afran pulled out his wallet. "Here's my cousin," he said. He pulled out a scattering of tiny photos and pushed one across the booth. The girl was squinting into the sun. Plump cheeks made her look very young, but her mouth was a straight line, giving away nothing. Afia had never looked like this. In the photos from holiday gatherings, in the photos on the Internet, she was always beaming. But Baba had wanted a picture, last month. Had they taken one? Had they given it to Zardad's family? He remembered Afia's sorrowful eyes, looking up at him while she waited to serve the tea to Zardad's people. He found his hand shaking. He pushed the tiny square back across the table. He had been looking at a dead girl.

"Very sad," he managed to say.

"Sad, nothing," said Afran vehemently. "It is sick and a crime, and nothing I can do about it. So don't lecture me, man."

"I'm not—" Shahid started to say. But an exclamation from behind his right shoulder cut him off.

"Oh my God," the voice cried, "it's the boys!"

Shahid turned. Standing by the booth were Margot and Evie, both starters on the women's team. "Hi," he said. Margot had her arm across Evie's shoulders. *Lesbian*, he thought, and his scrotum tightened uncomfortably. Afran tucked his photos away. The girls slid into the booth, Margot on Afran's side and Evie on Shahid's. Smelling their perfume, glimpsing Evie's cleavage, Shahid felt confusion like smoke, draining his energy. After they'd chatted for ten minutes—they'd crushed St. Lawrence too, wasn't Coach Hayes the best; were the guys ready for the Trinity match—he lifted his jacket from the back of the booth. "I gotta study," he said. "I'm behind on two papers."

"C'mon, man," Afran said. "Party's just starting."

"Shahid's a scholar-athlete," said Margot. "Not like you."

"Party after the Trinity match, though," said Evie.

"Sure," said Shahid, though he couldn't even think that far.

"Your sister going to the match?" Margot asked.

"Not anymore," said Evie. She elbowed her friend.

Shahid stood and shrugged on the jacket. Everything they said was irritating. "I don't know if she is or not. She'd have to take the bus from Northampton."

"Gus'd give her a ride," said Evie, "if she'd let him." Then she flinched. Margot had kicked her. Slowly, a dread in his stomach, Shahid turned back. Resting his knuckles on the table, he leaned forward.

"Gus Schneider?" he said slowly.

"Uh, yeah." Evie glanced quickly at Margot, then back.

"Why," he went on, "would Gus give my sister a ride?"

"We gotta go," said Afran. "Sorry, ladies." He rose. He started to pull Shahid away. With one shove, Shahid put him back in his seat.

"What are you saying about my sister?" he asked Evie.

"Look, I'm sorry." Evie was averting her eyes. Her chestnut hair caught the light. "Sensitive brother," she added in an undertone. She bent her head toward Margot's. Nervously the girls giggled.

"I asked you a question," said Shahid.

The waitress came over. "Is there a problem?" she asked, directing herself to Afran.

"Thanks, Julie," said Afran. "We're fine. Come on, Shahid." He rose again.

Shahid leaned closer, on his elbows now. He stared at the girls until they met his eyes. "Gus would give my sister a ride," he said as quietly as he could manage, each word feeling to him like the lash of a whip, "from Smith."

"Look, dude, she broke up with him, okay?" Evie said. Her lips pulled back from her teeth, and her voice took on the whine he'd heard from American girls when they were on the phone with their parents. "It was like some secret romance, but he's pretty upset so he spilled. I mean, he was really good to her, and—"

"You don't have to explain, Evie," Margot said. She grasped her friend's hand and pulled her from the booth. "We just stopped by to say hi." She held up a hand, like a stop sign. "No harm, no foul, okay?" she said.

That red hair. Of course. Gus. Gus Schneider. A Jew. "A fucking Jew," Shahid muttered when the girls had tripped away, shaking their heads. "A lying, betraying, goddamn son of a whore, shit-licking, filthy—"

"It's okay, okay, we're leaving," he heard Afran say, and Shahid realized he'd started to shout, and in Pashto. The manager was striding their way. Diners stared in alarm.

"Let go of me!" he yelled when Afran had him out of the restaurant.

"Hey, I'm your friend, dude, I'm just trying—"

"Did you know this?"

"No. In Allah's eyes, man, I had no idea."

"How long? How *long*!"

"I don't know. I told you, I didn't know they were an item. Gus, you know, he's mostly into his pets. I'd seen him with your sister, but I didn't—"

"You *saw* them?"

"Not saw them as in, like, saw them. I mean, they were talking. I didn't think anything."

"I have to kill him. Do you understand that? I have to destroy the guy! He was my roommate, for fuck's sake. My sister is *engaged*."

"I didn't know that, man. I'm as shocked as you are. But listen. Just listen to me. Are you listening?"

Afran was holding both of Shahid's forearms, now. Shahid's jacket was unzipped. The cold air whistled through to his chest. His hair still felt wet, next to his scalp. Fury raged through and exhausted him. He nodded.

"Don't do anything. Not tonight. Give this a little time. They broke up already. Maybe it was never anything."

"It was something," Shahid managed to say. His tongue felt thick. "There are pictures. That one you showed me. I didn't know it was him. I didn't want to think—"

"Let me talk to him."

"No!" Shahid yanked his arms away. "Don't you tell him a goddamn thing, Afran. You hear me? I'll take care of this my own way. He doesn't need a warning."

"But those girls might—"

"Let them. But not you. *You* don't betray me." He pulled his keys from his pocket and started toward his car. Afran followed.

"Okay," Afran said. "My lips are sealed. But you don't do anything tonight. Is that a deal? We'll talk in the morning."

As Shahid turned to his friend, his eyes burned. "It's a deal," he managed to say. Then he was in his car and turning it in a wide U through the parking lot and out onto the state highway. He sped the three miles to the campus, the radio blaring ghetto rap to drown out his thoughts, before he realized that he'd left Afran standing in the parking lot. He tore back, but the lot was empty, his friend gone. He checked his mobile: nothing. For a long moment he put his head back, the radio silent, and shut his eyes. Then he shifted into first and made his way again to campus, haltingly this time, driving like an old man. *All settled.* Nothing was settled. All was chaos.

When he'd parked the car he pulled out his mobile. He punched in Afia's number. Then he stared at the tiny screen, seeing again the picture that had bloomed forth on Afran's iPhone, Gus Schneider hoisting Afia onto his shoulders in the orchard, her legs parting to grip his neck. She'd broken up with him, the girls had said, but what did that matter, when she had lied to Shahid's face, lied all fall, sneaked around like her filthy friend Lema, betrayed everything she loved for her appetite? No, he wouldn't call her. He wouldn't be lied to again.

In his dorm room his laptop awaited. The screen swirled with color, a school of fish ready for feeding. He flicked it off. He tried, and failed, to pray. He opened his mobile again. There was Schneider's number, keyed into his contacts list. But call the guy? For what? To hear him, too, saying they'd broken up, saying there was never anything, when the picture showed what he'd done? To make him confess how he'd seduced Afia, how he'd parted those legs with his stubby hands? To threaten him, the betrayer, the cocksucker, as his buttocks rose and fell over the body he was violating, the body with its cushiony breasts, its wide V of pelvic bone plunging to the dark triangle . . .

He was on the bed now, clothes stripped off in the overheated room, eyes shut, picturing it, torturing himself. The cleft between the breasts, the salty taste under the fullness. Only they weren't Afia's breasts, which he'd never seen; they were Evie's breasts, in the V-neck sweater she'd worn at Bertucci's. Then they were Valerie's breasts, Valerie from last spring, and his hand was on himself now, her pale body against the sheets, the slight fat of the belly. Girls, how they wanted it. How consequences meant nothing to them. How they touched you and drew you in, how their breasts shook when you thrust. Faster and faster his hand moved. He was almost there, almost, almost, seeing Evie's breasts, how she wanted it, when his mobile rang, but he wouldn't stop, no, he would come into those breasts, that cleft for his cock, and she wanted it, they all did, and finally he came.

He let his head drop back. His hand swiped at the mess on his belly. In a minute, when the throbbing ceased, he would get up and wash himself. The mobile had gone silent but then gave a chirp, a message for him. With his unsticky hand he reached for the thing and checked the call.

The orgasm washing over him shrank to a sour trickle, then dried up. The call came from Nasirabad, from his home. His father—who in three years had never picked up a phone to make the costly connection, who had last put his hand on Shahid's shoulder to declare how he trusted him to watch over his sister—had something important to say to his son.

CHAPTER TWELVE

The Monday after Lissy conferred with Shahid about lineups, he came to practice glowering. The next day, he was absent. He didn't return her calls. The other guys worked their games, preparing for the Trinity match, and didn't ask about their number one player. Lissy's nerves were jangling. Shahid had been on top of his game, keen for the challenge of revamping the team. It had to be something personal getting at him. It had to be his sister.

"He say anything to you?" Lissy asked Afran.

Afran shrugged evasively. "He's had papers to write."

"Don't you take Poli Sci with him?" she asked Gus, who appeared faithfully at every practice and was improving in tiny increments.

"That's right, Coach." Gus was bouncing a squash ball on his racquet, his eyes flicking up and down. She wondered. Had he seen Shahid's sister? Did he know the girl was engaged? He gave no sign, and she couldn't think of a way to ask. She'd never said anything to him about the moment she'd witnessed in the squash center. Sometimes players confided in her about their romances—certainly on the girls' team they did—but Gus kept his own counsel.

"So was he in class?" she persisted.

"I didn't notice, Coach. It's a big class."

The same with the others. They hadn't seen Shahid, or they'd caught sight of him but he was busy, going off to study. He'd been working on his car, Carlos said. But Shahid had broken a major rule: shirking practice without calling the coach or informing any of his fellow players. While the guys ran drills, Lissy brooded. They were evasive, not because they didn't like Shahid or because they were hiding stuff from her—she felt certain of that. They were confused, as she was. Shahid was their glue, their light, the wind at their backs. And they'd rather be seen as secretive than clueless about a teammate, especially one they all depended on.

Next day, again, no Shahid. Only a few days remained before the match with Trinity, the best squad in the country right then, the only one ahead of Harvard. Jamil plopped down on the bleacher beside Lissy after he'd finished a punishing series of set-ups and volleys with Chander. Even his dreadlocks sported beads of sweat. "Coach's head be in the clouds," he said.

"Sorry, Jamil. You looked good out there. Getting that wrist action."

"We going down to Trinity."

"They're the best. We'll give 'em a run."

"You playing Shahid?"

"Doubt it. He's missed practice all week."

Jamil nodded soberly. "We got to get him back for the big one, though." Looking at him—his walnut skin, aquiline nose, the dimple in his right cheek, details the likes of which she came to memorize for each player—she raised her eyebrows. "Harvard," he said.

Lissy chuckled drily. "Let's get past Trinity first."

"Without Shahid—"

"Either way."

"Man's doing a lot of sufferation, me think."

Lissy's eyes flicked to the others on court, then back to Jamil. "Are you, like, delegated to persuade me to let him play, Jamil?"

He put up his hands, the long pale fingers. "Ease up, Coach. I be on your side."

Was there another side? she wanted to ask. Instead she rose; paced the courts; harangued Chander on his footwork.

February was in full stride, with its thawings and freezings. The roads were sloppy, icy at night, a fresh coat expected to fall and then melt by the weekend. At breakfast the next morning, after cutting the crusts off Chloe's toast—spoiling her, Ethan thought, but Lissy had never liked crusts when she was a girl—Lissy said, "If Don Shears weren't breathing down my neck, I'd cut Shahid slack. But there's Trinity in two days. Harvard next week. Not even Shahid can go up against Harvard without practice."

"Have you seen his sister?"

She shook her head. "Whatever's happening with her and Gus, I'm probably best not knowing about it."

Ethan looked up from the sandwich he was fixing. He often scheduled patients during lunch hour, when they could break free from their jobs, and he ate on the fly. "You could send Shahid to counseling."

"To you? Not sure I could stay out of it. This is my number one we're talking about."

He smiled, his glasses reflecting the light. "I'm the one who keeps you out of it. But he doesn't have to see me. Send him to the counseling center. Sounds like a young man with stuff on his mind."

It was a misty morning. Outside, Chloe's latest snow creature was losing weight, its fallen scarf a wet tangle. Lissy lifted her to kiss its frozen mouth good-bye, and then they left for day care. She made it through a morning coaches' meeting with an extra cup of coffee. By noon students were slipping and sliding their way into the building for PE classes. The entrance hall carpet was soggy. Three calls to Shahid's cell, meanwhile, had gone unanswered. Putting off lunch, Lissy keyed herself into the women's faculty locker room in hope that a workout would lift her spirits. From the crisp blouse and slacks she wore to the office—male A.D.s, she'd noticed, got by in tracksuits—she changed to cycling shorts and a T-shirt in need of a wash.

The workout room wasn't a fitness center yet, but it did the trick. A half dozen stationary bikes and ellipticals, a couple of rowing machines, a full set of Life Fitness stations, a mirrored corner for free weights. One of the first things Lissy had done as A.D. was to silence the Top 40 radio station that used to blare here. Sure enough, students now came in with their iPods and earbuds, and the faculty, like Lissy, appreciated the relative silence, the sound of straps sliding over heavy metal rollers and lungs expanding. With the new fitness center they would add tiny TVs to the treadmills and bikes, but that noise, too, would pass through the earbuds.

Two of Lissy's female players, Liza and Margot, were already on the ellipticals. She waved to them. Some administrators refused to visit the run-down facility; Don Shears, she knew, had joined the local health club rather than let students see him in exercise shorts. But Lissy liked breaking through the barriers, and she didn't mind having students, especially the girls, see a middle-aged woman staying in shape. "Some guys on the team were looking for you," Liza said as she set her resistance higher.

"They'll figure out I'm here," Lissy said.

Normally she started with aerobic work, but this time she began with weights. In their heft she could feel the power of her muscles. Free weights first, to work on breathing and balance. Take her mind off the absence of Shahid, the pressure from Don to beat Harvard in eight days. Bench press, hammer grip. Tricep extension. She breathed and counted. As she turned to the leg press, she spotted Afran and

Carlos, weaving between the bikes. They'd probably tried her office first, and this was their next stop. She waved with a fifteen-pound dumbbell, then frowned when she saw the looks on their faces.

"Got a sec, Coach?" Carlos asked.

"Always," said Lissy, her standard response. Setting down the weights, she wiped her face with her towel. "You find Shahid?" she asked. "Did you talk to him?"

"It's not Shahid," said Afran.

"It's Gus," said Carlos.

"Gus?" Lissy frowned. Gus had been at practice yesterday, working hard as always. "What's wrong with Gus?"

"He's at Berkshire Med Center," said Carlos.

"Christ." She pictured a fistfight, a broken jaw. "Not one of those football guys," she began, though what she was picturing was Shahid, seeing what she'd seen that afternoon in the corridor, Shahid breaking Gus's nose.

"He had an accident," said Afran. "With his car."

With the news that no one else was involved came a hidden rush of relief. "Where? In this lousy weather? Is he hurt?"

A dumb question, she realized. Gus was in the hospital; they had just told her.

"Broke his leg, apparently, and a couple of vertebrae," said Carlos.

"Was anyone else—"

"No. On the road to Northampton. His brakes, like, gave out."

"Well, he shouldn't have been driving in this crap. Have you seen him?"

"We just came from there," said Afran. "They put him on a bunch of pain meds, he's pretty out of it."

"I imagine." Vertebrae, she thought. Could mean everything or nothing. At the least, he was out for the season. "Well, thanks, guys. I'll head over. Is Shahid there?"

"I—I left him voice mail," Afran said with a quick glance at Carlos. "I think he's on his way."

"Yeah, good." She stopped at the door. Margot and Liza had stepped off the machines and gathered around Carlos. "You boys tell the team, okay? Send out a quick e-mail. I'll announce the new lineup at practice."

"Right, Coach," said Afran.

As she scraped snow from her car, she realized. Gus must have been headed out to see Afia. How foolish, to risk country roads in this freezing slop. Did the girl know? Someone had reached Gus's teammates. They should have started with the captain, with Shahid. But it was Afran who'd come to alert her. Could it be that, after his burst of enthusiasm at the start of the term, Shahid was so wrapped up in his own life, his own future at Harvard, that he would just abdicate, hang his coach and his teammates out to dry?

"Selfish asshole," she muttered to herself. Just when you think you've got the player of your dreams, the stuff of real leadership, he falls into drugs or infatuation or self-pity, and there goes everything you've tried to teach, all the honor of the team. She wanted to hammer her fists on Shahid Satar's chest. To call him what he was: a traitor. Furiously she scraped at the windshield. When she was finished, she flung the scraper into the car. Then she leaned on the hood. She gathered her breath.

This wasn't about Shahid. She was the coach. She had a wounded athlete. Her job was to tend to him. And to pull the squad together. And to win, Shahid or no Shahid. "Got that, girl?" she said to herself. She sounded like her own coaches years ago, making herself snap out of it. She tucked herself into the dark car and headed through the snow-misted morning, toward Berkshire Medical Center.

CHAPTER THIRTEEN

Esmerelda was Afia's favorite aunty from the Price Chopper, and also the one who lived halfway between Northampton and Devon, so it was from her that Afia had begged a ride to the Berkshire Medical Center. As the car pulled to the curb under the big *Emergency* sign, Esmerelda looked out suspiciously at the figure huddled below the awning. "Don't like the looks of that one," she said.

"Oh," said Afia, keeping her voice light, "that's just my brother." And promising Esmerelda she would call if she needed a ride back to Smith, she zipped up her puffy jacket and stepped out into the cold. The sun was sinking into the horizon, leaving a sky gone cobalt in the wake of the storm. Shahid stood by the revolving door, his hands balled into the pockets of his warm-up jacket. When she tried to step around him, he blocked her way.

"Please, Shahid lala," she said in Pashto. "Don't let's argue."

"You could have told me." His voice came out tight. He must have been standing there in the cold, waiting for her—knowing she would come, she couldn't stay away—for a long while.

"Let me by," she said.

She strained for the door, and he caught hold of her wrist. "You have no idea," he said, "what's at stake here."

"What's at stake is your teammate Gus!" He frightened her, but something in his grip told her he wasn't all that sure of the ground he stood on. "Can't you bother me later?" she said, lifting her chin. "He might have died."

At that word, *died*, Shahid's grip tightened. "Afia, look," he said, keeping his voice low. "I don't want to fight. You lied to me—"

"I never lied."

"It's called a lie of omission. If you took a class in ethics you'd hear of it. You took me for a fool, and like a fool I went and pledged my life for you. Now we have a serious problem."

"My problem is I need to go through that door."

It was Taylor who'd told her about the accident—Taylor who checked Facebook the way other people checked their watches, Taylor who'd seen the post from Afran. And at once Afia had known. Gus was in the hospital because of her.

"For what?" Shahid was saying. "Think you can satisfy your lust in the hospital, Afia?" His voice cracked; he was losing control. "Is that what you need? What you—"

"It's not lust, Shahid," she interrupted. "It's called love." There, she had said the word. No hiding anymore.

"Bullshit," he said. "It's a disease you've caught."

"Thank you, Baba." With a sudden jerk, she managed to twist free of his hand. She rubbed her wrist. "Neither of you knows anything about it."

He sighed. He didn't move away from the door, but he didn't try to grab her either. He said, "I'm not just your brother. All right? I'm your friend."

"Funny way of showing it."

"Afia, listen to me. They've found another picture."

She looked up, startled. His face had softened, the forehead knit with worry. "Who found a picture?" she said. "I'm not stupid, Shahid. I wouldn't post—"

"On Taylor's Facebook? The photo you sent her, or the photo she took? I don't care where it came from—"

"None of my friends take photos of me." Afia swallowed. Could Taylor have done something so idiotic? They paid no attention, these girls.

"Well, someone did, and now it's too late. We have no choices left, okay? I'm putting you on a plane."

"A *plane*?"

"To Peshawar. I'll get Uncle Omar to pick you up. And then—"

It was too much, too much. She had broken this off, she had shoved love into a box and sealed it with tape. And now—now she would be punished? And Gus, punished? "I'm not getting on a plane," she said, lifting her glasses to swipe at her eyes. "Gus is in *hospital*."

"I don't give a shit. *I'll* be in hospital, or worse, if this keeps up."

A car door slammed behind her. A pair of worried-looking parents got out. Both she and Shahid stepped aside, to let them through the revolving doors. Then she turned her gaze back on her brother. Her glasses had fogged up; his face was blurry. "How can I go back?" she asked at last. "They will kill me."

Shahid's mouth twisted. He planted a hand on her shoulder. "Nonsense," he said.

"They will kill me," she repeated. "Look what they've already done to Gus."

"You're crazy. Who's 'they'?"

She searched her brother's face, but it betrayed nothing. Still she would press him. "Gus got his brakes checked two weeks ago."

"And there's ice on the roads. He shouldn't have been driving. If he hadn't been coming to see you—"

"I talked to him. The road was sanded. He was braking around a turn, and suddenly no brakes. They will kill me, Shahid."

His palms on her cheeks were cold. "Listen to me," he said, leaning down to her. "This story you're telling, this story about what happened to—to, you know. Your boyfriend." He pushed the word out. "This story is crazy. But if you *don't* go home? That is one scary true story, Afia. You can't keep on like this. You'll be cut off." He let go her cheeks and seized a bit of air with his right fist. "Or worse."

"I can't be responsible for what people say in Nasirabad, Shahid lala."

She tried to push past him, but he grabbed the edge of her jacket. His voice went sharp again. "You've betrayed your whole family," he said. "Baba, Moray, our cousins, our uncles, everyone. You *mark* us. And still we're being generous with you. When you go back to Nasirabad—"

He spoke truth. That was the horror of it. Her shame would spread like poison gas, rapid and uncontainable. "Go back," she repeated, "to be accidentally poisoned? Found dead in a car crash?"

"Married, Afia. That's all. Safely married."

She lifted burning eyes to him. "I turned him away, you know," she said. "I told him I was engaged. I broke his heart. And for what, Shahid? For what? So someone could go break his body, too?"

"Afia, the guy had an accident."

"Did he? Gus is a careful driver."

"Oh, you know that, do you? You've been driving places with him?"

"Not for many weeks. And I've missed him. I'll say that now, Shahid, no matter what you do to me. And if somebody hurt Gus so they could scare me away from him, they didn't know me, not on the inside."

She had hit home. She saw it. He let go of her jacket. He wanted to be on her side, she could see that, but it would do no good. There were no sides, really, only honor or death. "You should scare a little easier than you do," he whispered.

She had no more words for him, not now. Turning, she pushed through the revolving door.

That night and the next, she slept in Gus's garage. Or failed to sleep. It wasn't the sound of garbage trucks, backing up in the parking lot on the other side of the fence, that kept her awake. It wasn't the restless prowling of his cats, Ebay and Facebook. It wasn't being alone, because the animals and the sense of Gus all around her kept her from feeling alone. It was anticipation. Any moment, she felt, the door would swing open and Shahid would stand there, his dark eyes glowing, in his hand a blade to scar her face the way Lema's family had. She forced herself to get up, use Gus's moldy bathroom, pour herself a glass of water. Finally the cats settled down on either side of her, and she drifted off.

She was staying at the garage through the weekend so she could feed Gus's animals. She was missing a day of classes, but she had her books with her. It wasn't possible to go back and forth by bus; the buses stopped in Springfield, taking three hours for a forty-mile trip. And she had to be at Gus's side, at least until the doctors were sure he would be all right, he would walk and run again, he would miss nothing more than the squash season. The team would be absent two players this weekend, because Shahid was being banned from the Trinity match. Afia knew because Shahid had rang her mobile to tell her, again, that he was taking her to the airport, sending her home—and, he'd added, if it weren't for her, he'd have led his team to victory. But no, she'd messed that up, and she'd mess up his whole life if he let her stay in America.

She had to get off the phone, she told Shahid; she was at the library, studying. He didn't believe this lie, but she didn't care. If she had only a few days left in America, she would spend them with Gus. Even if his accident had been just that, an accident, she was still to blame. He had been bringing her a Valentine's present, a big box of chocolates and a slim gold bracelet that sat, now, on the crate serving as a bedside table. She hadn't broken off with him convincingly enough; he'd thought he could win her back. And now either Shahid or kismet had caused his car to go off the road. She wanted to think kismet, but Shahid's face had loomed at her at the hospital entrance: *You should scare a little easier than you do.*

This photograph Shahid scolded her about—there it was, on Taylor's Facebook timeline. Some Dartmouth guy named Kent Star had tagged Taylor, but the photo centered on Afia, perched on Gus's shoulders, last fall at the apple orchard where they'd gone, a group of them from Smith and Dartmouth. One of her happiest days, soured now. Friday night she called Taylor and ordered her to erase it. "Jeez, girl, calm down," Taylor said. "I don't even know this Kent dude, he just friended me. Must be one of Chase's crowd."

"Just take it down, Taylor. Please."

"Where are you, anyway?"

"Gus is in hospital. An auto accident."

"Ooh. Ouch. I thought you broke up with him. Can I borrow one of your scarves?"

"Take away this photo, first. Then yes, please, of course."

Saturday morning, she cleaned the lizard's cage and sprinkled flakes on the surface of the aquarium. The fish rose, nibbled delicately. The trickiest was Pearl, the snake, who was due for a mouse.

The mice lived in a tiny cage under the table. Gus bought a dozen at a time, on the same days when he bought crickets for the lizard; they lived as food-in-waiting. Quickly, blocking all thought, Afia opened the top of the mouse cage and thrust her hand in. She wasn't squeamish about death. She had dissected plenty of frogs and fetal pigs, and on the farm in Nasirabad you saw death on a regular basis. But choosing which creature's life would end in these next five minutes felt like playing God. Blindly she clutched a hairless tail, swung the gray creature over to Pearl's cage, and dropped her in. Then she went to brush her teeth. If she had been half the scientist that Gus was, she'd have stayed to watch the snake's jaws unhinge as he took the mouse whole. Instead she brushed her hair, threaded earrings into her lobes, and emerged when the snake's middle sported a telltale bulge.

When she'd fortified herself with orange juice and a stale bagel from Gus's fridge, she bundled into her down jacket and the delicious boots Shahid had bought her. She lifted her bag over her shoulders. It was a two-mile walk to the hospital, and the air outside cold enough to pinch her nose shut. Today and tomorrow she would study at Gus's side, in the hospital; tonight she would care for Gus's animals, then sleep for the last time in sheets smelling of Gus. When they discharged him from the hospital it would be to his mother's home, not the garage—but Afia would be back at Smith by then. At Smith, or in Nasirabad. What would happen with Shahid's threats to take her away she didn't know, but she couldn't stop her life while she waited to find out.

One thing she knew: She did scare easy. Nothing else bad could happen to Gus, or she would never forgive herself, whether for shaming her brother or for offending Allah or simply for tipping the scales toward bad luck. Never again would she run her fingers down the chiton-like ridge of Gus's vertebrae; never again would she taste the salt left behind by the soft press of his thumb on her lower lip. This thing that her roommates found so important—this romantic love—she could give up. What she couldn't give up was Gus's own bright future, clear as a vision in the Cup of Jamshid that Anâ used to tell stories about.

At the hospital, they brought Gus a lunch of egg salad sandwich and applesauce that his mother, Mrs. Schneider, kept urging him to eat. "Mom, please," Gus said, lifting the yolky mess with a plastic fork and letting it dribble onto the small square plate. "It smells like cat food."

"It shouldn't go to waste," said Mrs. Schneider. She tipped her head toward Afia with a what-can-you-do expression. This was Afia's second encounter with Mrs. Schneider. The first had been Thursday, the day of the accident, when she had rushed past Shahid and his threats to learn that Gus was in the casting room. She had taken a seat in the waiting room across from an ample woman with deep red hair who set aside her magazine and her reading glasses to say, "So you must be Afia." She might as well have said, *So you left the gates unlocked*, so resigned and accusatory was her low, rich voice. Afia had wanted to sink several floors down, below the hospital's basement. But once her views were known, Mrs. Schneider made no further issue of Afia's presence. She asked about her studies and what she wanted from the cafeteria. When Gus was settled in his room and visiting hours were due to end, Mrs. Schneider had said simply, "I'll leave you two lovebirds alone," and left the room, taking her judgment with her.

"You must keep up your strength, Gus," Afia said now, eager to agree with his mother.

"Really?" Gus said. "For what? For the squash match I'll be playing against Harvard?"

Afia reddened. Her eyes traveled to the floor.

"I'm sorry, M'Afia. Honey? Don't cry. I'm just pissy," Gus said.

"They keep asking me how fast I was going. Jesus. I *know* how to drive in snow. I was doing maybe forty. I wanted to get to *you*, not go ass up in some ravine—"

"Gus, I'm sorry. I'm so, so sorry that this happens."

"Just come here, okay? Here."

He held out his arms. Frightened to touch him in any setting but his garage, Afia turned to Mrs. Schneider. But Gus's mom was looking away, at a magazine in her lap. The door to the room stood ajar. Quickly Afia leaned over the lunch tray and let Gus kiss away the tears gleaming on her cheeks.

Midway through the afternoon, Mrs. Schneider left. While Gus was wheeled out for tests, Afia wrote notes from her organic chemistry textbook. She tried to puzzle out her *Introduction to Thermodynamics*, though it gave her a headache. She turned to *Jane Eyre*. Jane had been rescued by the Rivers sisters, but now they were leaving her alone with their brother. When Gus was wheeled back, she played games of hangman with him. She had never played hangman before. It was just a spelling game, she knew, but the way Gus drew *X*'s for eyes and a tongue lolling out of the mouth of the hanged stick figure gave her chills.

"You should head back," he said when he'd finished an equally bland supper—lasagne with a sweetish tomato sauce, pale salad, chalky brownie. "I'll call Afran or Carlos, they can give you a ride."

"No, no," she said. The idea of being left at the garage by one of Gus's teammates terrified her. "I like to walk."

"Afia, it's below freezing outside."

"I have my boots. I will be fine."

"Well, okay. Look, maybe my mom can pick you up tomorrow, and you can sneak Pearl in. She needs to be handled."

"I—I can handle her."

"Afia, you hate touching her."

"I fed her a mouse this morning."

"Thank you." He reached out his hand, and she took it. Still holding on, he said, "I might sleep now."

"You should do that. I will stay, a little bit."

As he drifted off, his hand slipped away, and she tucked it under the blanket. She took up *Jane Eyre*. Now and then, she looked up to watch Gus's face in sleep, its creamy skin with freckles like clusters of cinnamon.

"How's he doing?" came a familiar voice.

Quickly Afia closed the book. With a glance at Gus, she started to stand.

"Sit down, sit down." Coach Hayes, from the squash team, stepped into the room. She looked inquiringly from Afia to Gus asleep.

"He—he has been really brave," Afia said. "Just to move, it pains him." Then she remembered. "How was this match? Against Trinity?"

The coach forced a smile. "We lost. But we'd have lost anyway."

"You mean if Gus could have played."

"I mean if Shahid could have played."

"Ah." Afia concentrated on her hands. Her fingernails were chipped, the cuticles torn from absentminded picking. "Coach, that has been my fault, I—"

"Don't you say a word. Your brother's a responsible young man. He'll learn to manage sports and personal life. Now, what's happening with your guy?"

Relieved not to speak of Shahid, Afia nodded toward the charts at the foot of the bed. "The doctors do more x-rays," she said. Anatomy: this much, she could speak of. "They say T-9 and T-10 vertebrae are fractured. Also they find two cracked ribs. So they build him a brace, and they are watching the nerves also. They give him medicine, for sleep."

Coach Hayes pulled up the second chair, the one Mrs. Schneider had used. Her eyes assessed the bruise on Gus's forehead, the bandage wrapping his left elbow, the stiff length of his broken leg propped by pillows under the sheet. "How long will they keep him?"

"They say two more days."

"Have you been here all along? I haven't seen you."

That, Afia reflected, was because she stepped out whenever she knew someone from Enright was coming. She took her books to a waiting room in another wing and stayed there until the visitor had left. Gus thought this was stupid. "Mostly," she admitted now.

"Has Shahid come by?"

Back to Shahid, again. Afia clenched one hand with the other. She could not tell this woman what she feared Shahid had done. At the same time, Coach Hayes knew Shahid better than anyone else in America. She was the closest thing either of them had, within thousands of miles, to a mother. "Shahid," she confessed after a long silence, "is angry with me."

"Because of Gus?"

Afia nodded. "I am engaged now, to be married."

"So I've heard. Who is this fellow, in Pakistan? Do you love him, or—"

"Love!" As tears started into Afia's eyes, she tried to laugh them away; it came out as a kind of snigger. "Coach Hayes," she said, her words trying to reach across the wide gulf of Gus's bed, "this is not for love. This is for family. You cannot understand. Shahid says I must go home."

"But you love Gus!"

Oh, this coach. She voiced what should have remained silent, waded in where the current ran strongest. Shahid marveled at her. Afia was a little horrified. She turned her gaze away, to Gus's sleeping form, his unruly hair and injured arm, the awkward angle of the bound leg. She could not speak.

A nurse appeared in the doorway. "Five minutes," she said.

Afia sat very still, waiting for the coach to leave. But when she had gathered her things, the coach said, "Afia? Do you have a car?"

"No, Miss Hayes."

"Well, then . . . how are you getting home? Do you have somewhere to stay?"

Afia blushed. The coach might say that she loved Gus, but for her to think she was sleeping in Gus's sheets—that went too far. "I will be all right."

"No, you won't." This was emphatic. "Why don't you come home with me?"

"I . . . no, Miss Hayes, that will not be necessary."

"Ah." The coach took her seat again. Gently she said, "How about I give you a ride to Gus's place?"

"Miss Hayes, I would not want you to think—"

"Afia, please. It's a good idea. At least for the weekend. You're feeding his little zoo, right?"

Afia nodded. A hum of assent made it past her closed lips.

"Come on, then. You look like you could use some sleep."

They spoke no more of Shahid as they left the hospital. Mrs. Schneider was at the nurses' station, arguing with one of the doctors; her hefty arms gestured one way and then the other. Afia saw the nurse behind her roll her eyes. Coach stepped over to speak with them. As Afia waited in the bright light of the corridor, the nurses glided past her with their rolling carts, their clipboards. If she ever became a doctor—and how unlikely that seemed, now!—it would not be in one of these immaculate hospitals, with their precise machines, their flower paintings. Mrs. Schneider waved at her as they turned for the elevator, and she waved back, grateful to be so gently dismissed.

CHAPTER FOURTEEN

What he had done to Gus struck Shahid to the bone. But what choice had he had? The call from Baba, six nights ago, had been unequivocal: Afia had gone too far. Khalid had shown Baba the photo he'd downloaded from the old Smith homepage. Then he'd told him about the new one, of Afia on a man's shoulders, her knees splayed, pinned up for all the world to see. How had Khalid known about this other photo? Shahid had demanded, but Baba couldn't say. Khalid was claiming that the men he trained with knew of these photos. They were all over the Internet. It was only a matter of time, and not much time, before Zardad's family found them out. That would end the engagement, and with it all hope of a future for Sobia and Muska. As to what would happen to the Satars' cotton business, who could tell? Afia had to be controlled. This man—Khalid had said he was a Jew—needed to be gotten rid of.

"Your family is bleeding, my son," Baba had said. "Do you understand? You've got to staunch this."

Next day, Monday, the guys had kept looking at him. In the

dining hall, in class, at practice. Even Coach Hayes. As if they knew. Not about Gus but about Afia. What she had done to him, what he had let her do to him, degraded him worse than anything he had ever known. It was awful, Afran had agreed when they talked in the locker room. A shock. He'd thought that Facebook photo was a fluke, some random girl's boyfriend hoisting Afia. A girl like Shahid's sister, you think she's got her nose in a book all the time. And Afran had promised not to say anything to anyone, but Shahid couldn't blot out the impression that there wasn't anything to tell—because Afran had already known, everyone had known except Shahid. The way Afran acted during practice, like there wasn't any deference he had to show to Shahid anymore. They could talk all they wanted, in this country, about the tough time women had in Shahid's culture. Shame was still shame, and left him whose honor had been pulled out from under him drowning and all alone. Packing his squash bag, he'd seen a call on his mobile from Nasirabad, but he couldn't bear to answer it.

Instead he'd spotted Gus, leaving the building. Stop him with words, that was his first instinct. He'd tucked the mobile into his pocket and jogged to catch up. Gus was hitting better, he'd remarked as they walked across the cold campus. He, Shahid, had told Coach to move him up a spot in the starting lineup. Gus had thanked him, said flattering things about Shahid's game, asked how Shahid's break in Pakistan had been. It was cool, Shahid had said, my sister got engaged to this chill guy. He had watched Gus's reaction, the slight stutter in his compliment to Shahid, the disingenuous question about what year Afia was in now. They had reached Gus's garage by then, and Shahid had followed him in.

The place smelled much like the dorm room Shahid had shared with Gus that first semester: of lizards and cat litter. Shahid had wondered at first if all American students lived with animals. But

Gus had made him promise not to tell the RA about the pets, and in exchange, Gus had helped him with how to dress, how to act around American girls, how to manage the food they served on campus. Now the smell brought back to Shahid how he had told Gus about his plan to bring his sister over, how he'd shown Gus the only photo he had, then, of Afia, from her O-levels class, in the pale blue uniform with the white sash.

"You need something, man?" Gus asked.

"Yeah. A word with you."

Gus's shoulders had lifted and lowered, like he knew this was coming. He didn't look at Shahid. His mobile rang with the opening chords of "Stairway to Heaven," but he ignored it. He shooed two cats off the bed—a queen-sized futon, Shahid noted, with a quick, jagged memory of the one night he'd spent with Valerie, last spring, in her narrow dorm bed.

"Sit down," Shahid said, and like an obedient puppy, Gus dropped onto the bed. He was a midsized, broad-shouldered guy, with freckles and a short nose, not especially Jewish looking. He wore contacts and blinked a lot. Shahid pulled over Gus's desk chair and sat backward on it, facing his teammate. "I want you," he said very slowly, making sure he had the guy's attention, "to stay the fuck away from my sister."

Gus had chuckled nervously. "I got nothing special with your sister, Shahid."

"Lie one more time and I'll break your arm."

Gus had started to laugh again, but at the look on Shahid's face he went pale. "Since when do you own her?"

"When were you going to tell me? Hm? When you graduated and she moved in with you? Do you any idea what that would do to her? You fucking moron. Why do you think she wanted to keep your little—what, relationship?—a secret?"

"Because she's scared of *you*, obviously." Gus cracked open a Gatorade from the stack by the side of his bed. He offered one to Shahid, who shook his head. "You gotta let her go, man, she's a big—"

"Listen." Shahid grabbed the Gatorade from Gus's hand and tossed it across the room, where it spilled blue onto the industrial carpet. He leaned over the back of the chair. "Repeat after me," he said. "There is no God but God, and Muhammad is his last Prophet."

"What are you, insane?" Blinking, Gus rose and retrieved the half-empty bottle. Shahid rose, too; he needed to stand taller than this guy, be clear he was a threat. "Your religion," Gus said, "has nothing to do with this."

"That's how you convert to Islam. And if you convert, and you don't touch her till after the wedding, I might be able to pull a magic trick and keep us all alive."

"Yeah, well, I tried that, and guess who didn't want it? M'Afia. Afia, I mean." Gus went to the door, opened it. Shahid shut it again.

"You don't plan to marry my sister," he said. "You want to use her, like a dishrag, and throw her away when she's dirty and you're done."

"Man, it's not like—"

"Don't lie to me. I warned you."

"This isn't Pakistan, okay, Shahid? You can't go around threatening to blow yourself up in front of people because you don't like the way they dress. Or the way they touch your sister."

"It's not about me, goddammit."

"Good. We're agreed on that." Gus had opened the door again and gone onto the rickety wooden porch someone had nailed up to pretend this was a carriage house. "You don't scare me, Shahid," he'd said. "This thing with Afia is between me and her. The only one who tells me who to sleep with or not is whoever I'm sleeping with."

Sleeping with. The words had been a sock to the gut.

Two nights later, dressed in black, Shahid had slipped down Gus's driveway, taken a flashlight below the belly of his car, and drained most of his brake fluid. Not to kill the guy, only to warn him. More important, to warn Afia; to put her into a frame of mind that would make home and safety, an honorable marriage, the best and only choice. When the job was done, he'd cut across campus, tossed his tools into a dumpster, and, before he'd even showered the grime off his face and hands, gone online to buy Afia a one-way ticket to Nasirabad. He'd used his father's credit card. When it was done, when Afia was on her way safely home, he would make the call, confess the expense, tell Baba when to expect his daughter.

That night he'd slept fitfully. Before dawn he woke in panic from a dream in which he was chasing Afia down a series of corridors that echoed the layout of the airport in Doha where they transferred to Peshawar. Trembling, he'd punched in his uncle Omar's number.

"Are you not in training?" Omar had asked after Shahid had explained the photos, his father's phone call, the ticket home. "Do you not have important matches ahead?"

"Trinity this weekend, yes," he said. "Harvard next week. If we beat Harvard we have a berth in the nationals."

"And for you, personally. The individual championships."

"Yes, Uncle, yes. But that's not why I'm calling. It's Afia—"

"A troublesome girl. I counseled against letting her go, you remember. Nothing but an impediment to you."

Shahid recalled the conversation over winter break. *Let her be engaged. Married as soon as possible.* "My point, Uncle, is that I'm not sure I trust her to change planes properly, at Doha."

"And if she doesn't get on the plane to begin with? Then you miss more training? It's unacceptable. She must be got rid of without disrupting you."

"Got rid . . . Uncle, you are jumping to conclusions. I have a responsibility to my"—he started to say "sister," but reached higher—"my father. I have his instructions."

"Your stepfather is a great man," Omar pointed out, "but he has not funded your career. Have I wasted my money? My concern? My love?"

"No, Uncle, no. What I was thinking"—Shahid began to feel the hopelessness of his appeal—"was that you might forward me enough funds to go as far as Doha with her. To see her onto the plane to Peshawar. Just so everything's safe. Then I'll be able to concentrate better—"

"It's a twenty-hour flight to Doha!"

"Seventeen, actually. And there's a return flight just seven hours later. It would cost me less than two days, and the trouble's over."

"Two days! And you say you have this Trinity match—"

"This weekend, Uncle. Afia doesn't fly until Monday. I've worked it all out."

"There must be another way. I did not support ten years of training to have one wayward girl—"

"Yes, Uncle. And I am so grateful for your support. But if I am to buy this ticket, I must do it today."

"Then find another backer." He could see Omar waving his hand in the air as if batting a fly. "You are my dearest nephew. I want the best for you."

"I understand, Uncle." Shahid shut his eyes. He knew better

than to press. If he couldn't get the money from Omar, he would try borrowing from Carlos. Carlos's family had Venezuelan oil money. Or Tom; Tom came from wealth. "Don't tell my father I rang. Please. I don't want to bother him right now."

"And I don't want you distracted by some shameful mess. Is that clear?"

It was clear, Shahid assured him, though there was no way to avoid the guilt and grief. Guilt for his failure to protect Afia's *namus*; guilt for crushing her hopes of becoming a doctor; grief at this loss that felt like a death, Afia's quick blue eyes that would dull, her happy step that would slow, her wit that would sour.

That was Thursday. He slept through his classes, ignored the calls to his mobile, and shot off an e-mail to Carlos about the money. *Family emergency*, he wrote, figuring Carlos was Latino; he'd get the gist. At practice he heard the news on Gus. An awful accident, he agreed. Thank God he'll be all right in the end. The others had been to the hospital already. He'd had the flu, he'd said; he'd slept solid for two whole days.

"Well you should get to the health center," Coach had said. "And you're out of the Trinity match." She'd leveled her round eyes at him. "And I want you to get some counseling. Seriously, Shahid. You and I know it's not just your health. Go to the center tomorrow. I want proof of two sessions before we play Harvard."

It was a blow, but he could absorb it. In the locker room Carlos put Shahid's bank account number into his smartphone and promised to put through a transfer. He didn't ask what the emergency was. If Shahid didn't repay it on time, he said, he'd take it out in coaching sessions. Oh, and he'd better not fuck up the Harvard game.

It was okay, Shahid had told himself as he raced from campus to the hospital. In a month he could find the money, and everyone saw Harvard as a crapshoot.

He'd known Afia would come to the hospital. He'd known she would suspect something. That was why he'd done it, wasn't it? To scare her, just a little. To make her safe. But what he didn't know was how the brakes would haunt him. What he might have caused to happen; what, but for kismet, would have happened. That night, after facing down his sister, he dreamed himself a passenger in a car driven by his father. As they rounded a bend, snow pelting down, the brakes gave, suddenly there were no brakes, and the car swung wide, wider, right through the guardrail . . . and he woke. Sweating, his heart banging. *Inshallah*, he whispered to himself in the dark, *Inshallah he will be fine, he will forget, he will never know.*

Early Saturday, the team left for Hartford without him. Hoping against hope, he'd suited up and gotten as far as the parking lot, where Coach Hayes held the line against him in front of the whole team. Humiliated, he watched them load into the van. Back in his room, he found the number online, the office of Dr. Ethan Springer. If Afran could talk to the guy, he supposed, he could too. And the doctor was married to Coach. If he saw that Shahid was sorry about the practices, that there was nothing seriously wrong, he might persuade Coach to let him play Harvard even if he missed a couple more. By then Afia would be gone, would be on her way to marriage.

He thought he would leave a message, but to his surprise, Dr. Springer picked up. Why, he wanted to know, was Shahid calling him on a Saturday?

"My friend Afran says you are the best therapist. And the counseling center is closed today."

"So am I."

"You answered your office phone, sir."

"Only because my daughter's having a playdate down the street. I'm catching up on paperwork."

"Then perhaps Monday, sir?" Shahid calculated. He had Shakespeare first thing Monday morning; he'd have to skip.

"I'm booked solid Monday." There was a pause. Shahid imagined Dr. Springer shuffling papers, drumming his long fingers. "Oh hell. Can you be here within the hour?"

"I can do that, yes. Thank you, sir. I am grateful, sir."

But Dr. Springer was tougher than he looked with his horn-rimmed glasses and skinny arms. He wrote things down on his yellow pad in his crabbed handwriting, and Shahid couldn't tell what pieces of the puzzle he was putting together. He asked about Shahid's studies first, then about his family, about his sister. All fine, Shahid insisted. She was going back to Pakistan; everyone was happy about it. But then why had he shirked practice? Stress. One of his teammates had been injured, was in the hospital. This had been upsetting to him. "We were roommates," he volunteered. "Freshman year."

"I see." Another scrawl on the yellow pad. What was the man writing? *Looks guilty. Sounds guilty.*

Now they were one down on the team, Shahid babbled on, and the Harvard match approaching, and so the stress had affected his sleep, and his stomach; he was better now, though, and with Dr. Springer's blessing he would return and play on Friday. The doctor nodded, scribbled, asked more questions. "If you could simply speak," Shahid finally said, "with Coach Hayes—"

"Shahid, you've come to me as a therapist. Not as a personal advocate. Now, my next opening is Tuesday morning."

"You can tell her you saw me today, though."

"I can. You want that appointment?"

The man was skinny but firm. Shahid shook his head, defeated.

"I cannot come Tuesday," he said. "I've got to take my sister to the airport."

"You mean she's going back home *now*?" Dr. Springer sat forward.

"It is what our father wants."

"Is it what your sister wants?"

"I think"—Shahid looked earnestly at his watch—"we are out of time." He met the doctor's eyes. Brown like his own, behind glasses like Afia's. It came to him that Dr. Springer was a Jew. Like Gus.

They made the next appointment for Thursday morning. He would have to cut class. But by then he would have flown to Doha and back. He would throw himself on Coach Hayes's mercy for the missed practices. He would tighten his budget to repay Carlos. And with Afia safe in Nasirabad, he would be able to breathe again.

That was what Shahid was thinking as he walked away from the Victorian house where Dr. Springer had his office, down the driveway wet with melting snow. He drew in deep, welcome breaths of the moist air. He'd cleared one hurdle, two if you counted the warning he'd sent with Gus's accident. He felt bad for Afia, he felt lousy for Gus, but no one had been killed, and the outcome would be for the best. For everyone.

As he crossed the street to his car, he heard a door open. He glanced at the only other car on the street, a royal blue Hyundai at the opposite curb. The sight of the man who stepped out stunned him.

"Asalaam aleikum, Shahid."

"Khalid!"

"Someone said you had walked into town," Khalid said in Pashto. "I saw you on this street. Thought I'd wait. Give you a lift."

Khalid was in jeans and a gray sweatshirt with the Nike slogan, *Just do it*. His beard was cropped close. He looked diminished by the Western clothing, a slight fellow with a narrow face and a hairline receding prematurely. Around his neck a scarf in a tartan plaid. Smirking, he sauntered across the street. His left foot dragged a bit as it always did. Khalid, definitely Khalid. But Khalid didn't belong on this street. Or in this town. This world.

"What in Allah's name are you doing here?" Shahid asked. "When did you come? Why—"

"Let me give you a ride."

"I have a car." Shahid took a step back, as if his brother would grab him. He was fearful but also amazed. Khalid in America! Khalid almost beardless, in jeans, like a graduate student! "No one told me you were coming."

"No one knew." Khalid blew on his hands, then stuck them into his jeans pockets. The jeans were new, creases down the front. "And no one will know." He smiled briefly; raised and lowered his eyebrows. "I flew into Boston." He stamped his feet. "A cold, wet country you have here."

"It's warm for February. What are you doing here?"

"I have business in this country. And someone had to tell you."

"Oh no," Shahid said. His lips went cold. Afia self-poisoned. Afia hanging from a rope. "She didn't—"

"She did."

"No." Shahid backed against a picket fence and sank into a crouch. "No. No. No," he moaned. "I told her—if it hadn't been for—but she wouldn't—" His eyes burned. He felt Khalid leaning over him. Finally he looked up. "But you don't care, do you?" he said. "You hate her. You hate both of us."

"My feelings have nothing to do with it," Khalid said calmly. "It is the third picture she has posted online. She is not just shaming us. She is mocking us."

"Wait." Shahid pushed himself back up against the stone. "You mean Afia's not—"

"Dead? Is that what you think I came thousands of kilometers to tell you?"

Shahid shook his head. He was desperate for sleep. Of course Khalid had not come to tell him that Afia had committed suicide. Khalid must have left Nasirabad at least twenty-four hours ago, must have planned the trip even longer. And Baba, last weekend, had known nothing about what was happening with Afia; had known only of two photos. Shahid made himself back up. Pictures. Photos online. *That* was what Khalid had come to tell him. "But Baba knows about this second photo," he began.

"Third photo. And for this, brother, there is no excuse."

Shahid shook his head. "I am tired of hearing about photographs. Photographs are not witnesses."

"She is leaning over a hospital bed, in this one. There is a man in it. We see him clearly. He is a Jew. She is kissing him. He is touching her—"

"I don't want to hear it."

"Her breast. And so we know, brother, that you have lied."

"Take that back." Shahid stood up from his crouch. He stepped close. Khalid even smelled different, like cheap hotel soap and American clothes. "I don't know why you came, but you have no idea what's going on here—"

"I have a very good idea." Khalid spoke rapidly, his eyes quivering with excitement. "You pledged your life to keep your sister's virtue. Your sister who is engaged to be married. She consorts like the black whore she is with this Jew and you allow it, you encourage it. Then she flaunts her black appetite until the whole world knows."

"The whole world. Really. And this ignorant world—it thinks Jews are bad because Israel is bad because it oppressed Palestinians, which is the same as Obama sending drones—"

"Stop. We are not talking politics. Everyone in Nasirabad knows. Zardad's family knows. Farishta knows because none of the women will talk to her, no one will serve her at the market, she goes into the street fully covered and she is spat on. Her little girls know because they come home from school with their heads bloodied from the rocks that are thrown at them. Baba knows because to replant the fields they burned down he has to hire guards, guards from outside because no one in town will do the work, they are too ashamed. So you see, brother, we all have a good, an excellent idea of what is going on here. The solution? You pledged your life. Do I take it from you now that you betray your pledge? What do you think? Is this what is going on here?"

"I have not *betrayed* my *pledge*." Shahid spoke through gritted teeth. So this was what all those calls from Baba were, the calls he had ignored. The temptation to punch Khalid in the face came close to overwhelming. He jammed his fists into the pockets of his jacket. "I have an arrangement with Baba. I am sending Afia home. You have no business interfering. I could've used the money you just spent—"

"The money is nothing," said Khalid quickly, "compared to what her shame is costing us. You had better understand. If you send her home, you only force Baba to do what you are too corrupted to do."

"That's not true. We are catching the problem in time. We agreed, so long as she returns, if she remains engaged to Zardad—"

"Zardad *knows*. You think he would keep such an engagement?"

"If he knows, then who told him? Hm? You, Khalid? You, who want Afia dead no matter what? Even if it shames you, too?"

Khalid opened his mouth to speak, then thought better of it. He tucked his loosened scarf back into his sweatshirt. He rocked back on his heels. Slowly, he lifted a canvas backpack from his shoulders and reached inside. "Blood," he said, not taking his jittery eyes from Shahid's, "cleanses honor. We gave your way a chance because we loved you. I knew it was doomed, but I told Baba, I said to him, 'If you can bear the risk of letting Shahid try once more, we will all sleep easier in the end.' He said he could. And he has paid the price—a heavy, heavy price. Now it is time."

From the backpack he withdrew a white flannel bag. Shahid didn't need to ask its contents; the shape and weight were obvious. As if moving on its own, Shahid's hand reached out. The revolver slid into his backpack, its weight almost that of another textbook. He said nothing. Words seemed to form and melt in his head, leaving his tongue glued to his palate. "Where are you staying?" he said at last to Khalid. "How long are you in the States? Does Baba know you're here?"

Khalid made a fist almost playfully and tapped Shahid's forehead with his knuckle. "No need to worry your brains," he said. "I have somewhere private to stay. When our honor is restored, I can go about my business."

"What sort of business—" Shahid began.

But his stepbrother had started toward the blue car. "Sure I can't give you a lift?" he asked, sliding sunglasses over his eyes.

As Khalid started the ignition, Shahid came back to life. He reached into his pack to retrieve the gun. *This is not the way*, he would say, *and I am not the one*. But Khalid waved through the tinted window and took off down the glossy black street. Backing up against the fence, Shahid sank into the wet snow, put his arms around his knees, and rocked himself, like a mourning woman.

CHAPTER FIFTEEN

It wasn't the loss to Trinity that depressed her, Lissy explained to Ethan on Sunday morning. It was Shahid letting down the team. "Thursday he tried telling me he'd been running a fever and was all better now. I mean, really? Did he learn that from his American teammates? Next is he going to claim a grandparent's bogus death?"

All of them still sported pajamas, Ethan with the *New York Times* spread over the coffee table, Lissy and Chloe on the floor with Chloe's "Dora in the Zoo" puzzle, the pieces spilled out for the fourth time. "I'm sure the guys respected you for holding the line," Ethan said over the top of the front page.

"Fat chance. They wanted to win." She told him about finding Shahid's sister at the hospital. "I dropped her at Gus's place, I guess she's minding his pets. There's another little secret I'll have to keep from Shahid. Good Christ."

She lifted herself onto the ottoman. Chloe was finishing the puzzle now, methodically and with no hesitations.

"Good Christ what?" said Ethan. "What do you mean?"

"What's Shahid's role in this? The girl's twenty years old, not married yet, it's America." She shook her head. "Afran said," she went on, "that whatever happens next, it's not like I could have controlled any of it. That sounds like a threat, damn it."

"There!" Chloe pressed the last piece into place. Animals grinned and clapped their hands around a frolicking Dora. "I need to go potty, Mamí."

"Can you go by yourself?"

"Sí sí."

When she'd trotted out of the room Ethan came to sit in the armchair behind the ottoman. He squeezed the back of Lissy's neck. "You're tense."

"No shit, Sherlock." She bent her head, let him work his magic. "Remember," she said, "when I'm on the other side of all this—the squash season, you know, and the campaign—we said we'd get away."

"Where to?"

"The camp, maybe?"

"In Hadley?" He snorted. "I'd love that. But it needs a week of solid work. No one's been there in three years." His thumbs dug into her trapezoids. "Maybe you'll feel better," he said, "if I tell you your boy came to see me."

"Shahid?"

"He called and stopped in. I can't tell you more than that."

She twisted around. "And? What'd he say to you?"

His grin was crooked. "What is there about 'not more than that' you don't understand, Coach?"

She sighed. He was right, but still. "I just want him back. The way he was."

"For Harvard."

"For life. Look, I'm glad he came to you. He's got another appointment? Because I told him—"

"He's got another appointment. I gave him a slip for you. But Liss, honey, listen. This isn't a confidence I'm betraying. It's a central cultural fact."

He was leaning forward now, serious. "Okay," she said.

"Afia dating Gus. In the place Shahid comes from, that kind of thing doesn't happen without consequences. I've watched your boy, over three years now. He is one cool cat. Something has unhinged him. And when punishment gets meted out, in these cultures, it's often the brother doing the meting out."

"Are you implying that Shahid had something to do with Gus's car? Ethan, these guys are both on my squad. You don't get it. They are *brothers*."

"Not by blood. Anyway, I'm not talking about Gus. I'm talking about the sister. Afia."

That girl again! Lissy rued the day she'd helped Shahid get the admissions forms to Smith. "Shahid loves Afia more than anything," she said. "If he's found out about Gus I'm sure he's pissed off. But—"

"Not just pissed off. Dishonored."

"Hey, look." She slipped to her knees, across the coffee table from him. She reached out her hands and took hold of his shapely fingers. "We talk about honor all the time, on the team."

"Not this kind of honor. There are places in this world that do not tolerate a woman's baring her face to a man, much less the kind of thing that's gone on with Afia and Gus."

"You're saying because Shahid's Muslim—"

"This isn't about religion. It's about a—a sort of tribal code."

"Shahid's taking a job at Harvard next year. He eats bacon. He dates girls."

"Liss, honey, none of us really leave our roots behind. If Shahid's family's putting pressure on him, if his hand is being forced—"

"You just think that way because of the guys you've worked with. The prison guys."

"I know something about violence, yeah."

"But those are all abusive boyfriends, jealous husbands," she objected. "That's not Shahid."

"They're people who think they own someone. Crime of passion, crime of honor—people make these distinctions, Liss, but believe me, when it's someone you care about—"

Chloe was back, her pajama bottoms twisted behind her fanny. Lissy straightened them and took her onto her lap. She was getting so long, all arms and legs. "You okay, cutie?"

"I want to get dressed. Go outside."

"In a sec." She turned to Ethan. "You know what I'm going to do?" she said. "I'm going to get them together. One on one. With me to mediate. They'll come to some sort of understanding, and then we'll move on. Just to get through the season."

"Not sure that's a good idea." Ethan drained his coffee. She could feel him, wanting to tell her about his session with Shahid. But he held back.

"It's the best I've got. Can you and Chlo go somewhere this afternoon?"

"You come too, Mommy." Chloe reached her arms around Lissy's neck.

"You want to bring them here?" Ethan said. "That's nuts. You could prompt a fight as easily as a reconciliation."

"It's a neutral place. You and Chloe could go to the Discovery Zone or something. Just for like an hour."

He shook his head, but he knew how stubborn she could get. He wasn't going to argue with her. "How can you be sure you'll find these kids?"

"Oh, I will." She kissed Chloe on the forehead, then set her down and stood. "Your job may be to know how their minds tick," she said to Ethan, "but mine is to know where they are."

She got Shahid on his cell. He'd been for counseling, he said, and she said great, and could he drop by her place around four? When he hesitated, she pointed out that she had the place to herself. By afternoon, when Chloe woke from her nap, she was excited about the Discovery Zone, and Ethan had corralled another day care dad to meet them.

"Just don't get your hopes up," Ethan warned as Lissy dispensed hugs.

"That's not what we coaches say," she countered.

She headed for the Med Center. Tomorrow, she realized as she passed the town green, was Valentine's Day. Hearts and balloons had appeared out of nowhere. Devon seemed invaded by cherry reds, Pepto-Bismol pinks. She found Afia planted, as before, by Gus's bed, but this time Gus was awake.

"Hey, Coach." Gus was propped by what looked like an inclined board. His carroty hair stood out from his head in corkscrews. On the side table where his lunch might have been sat an empty plastic cage, the size and shape of a small picnic hamper. As Lissy drew close, a white rope lifted off Gus's forearm. From its tip, a tongue flicked out at her. "Meet Pearl."

"Hi, Pearl," Lissy said with forced nonchalance. Snakes made her skin crawl. "Could you put her back? Hi, Afia."

"She is not permitted," said Afia, glancing nervously at the door. With her head scarf draped across her neck, her hair fell in dark waves over her shoulders.

"And you got her past the nurses—?"

"In my girlfriend's big-ass handbag," said Gus, stretching his arm over the plastic bin until the snake slithered off and wound itself into a knot in the corner.

Afia snapped a yellow lid onto the cage and lifted it by its handle. "Gus says Pearl must be handled," she explained as she tucked it into a green leather shoulder bag that looked, as far as Lissy could tell, custom-made for transporting a snake cage. "I cannot do it. In my country, snakes are dangerous."

"Some might say they are here, too," said Lissy. "Can I borrow you for a little bit?"

"Borrow me?" Afia frowned.

"I mean, can we talk about something? I'll make you some tea. At my house."

"But why—"

"Just for a little while. Okay with you, Gus?"

Gus sighed. Lissy watched his eyes travel quickly down Afia's body. "You have to go soon anyhow," he said. "Last bus to Northampton at four."

"Hey, I'll drive her to Northampton," Lissy said, seeing an opportunity. "It's just an hour."

"I will have to take Pearl back," Afia said.

"Let me get a last peek at her, then." Gus pushed himself up the inclined bed. "And a hug from you," he added to Afia.

The girl blushed and glanced sidelong at Lissy. "I'll be by the nursing station," Lissy said. "They let you out tomorrow, right?" she added to Gus. But he was already unzipping the green leather bag, and he merely nodded.

The halls were plastered with hearts and Cupids. At the nursing station Lissy found Gus's mother, peppering the staff with questions about Gus's discharge. Ellen Schneider was a Smith alum, the daughter of a state senator, a figure of sorts in the Berkshires. But though she lived just the other side of Pittsfield, Lissy had seen her at no more than a half dozen games in three years. "You say he should get on crutches as soon as possible," Ellen was saying. "But it's winter out! What if he slips? And he can sleep downstairs in the study, but there's a step down to the bathroom. Oh hi, Coach." She pushed back her streaked hair and shook Lissy's hand briefly, her fingers small and cool. "Can you believe insurance won't cover another day here? He broke five vertebrae, for God's sake!"

"Two," countered a weary nurse. "We'll be sending a physical therapist."

Ellen pulled Lissy into the hallway, out of the nurses' earshot. "Can you do something about this?" she asked.

Raising her brows, Lissy caught a look from the nurse over at the station. It was funny, how parents believed in her power. Ellen Schneider no longer saw her as a woman, or a faculty member, or even an administrator. She was Coach, and Coach called the shots. "I don't have any jurisdiction here, I'm afraid."

Afia emerged, her scarf secured, the leather handbag tucked under her arm. "Get that thing away from me," Ellen whispered.

Afia looked frightened. "Gus says tomorrow you will start to feed her."

"I will throw food into the cage, yes. I'll fill that water bottle since it's outside. But no reptiles ride in my car or live in my home."

"That's a good reason," said Lissy, "to get Gus mobile as soon as you can. Meanwhile, Afia and I have a rendezvous."

"Rendezvous?" The girl looked wary, as if she were about to step back. Lissy took her elbow and steered her away from Ellen Schneider and the nurses.

"You'll see," she said. "It'll be okay."

A cool wind was blowing outside, harbinger of a return to

winter. As they bundled into Lissy's car, she thought she caught sight of Shahid pushing out from the revolving doors of the hospital. "Isn't that—" she started to say. But Afia was busy settling the snake cage on the car floor, and the man Lissy had mistaken for Shahid headed for a blue Hyundai and not Shahid's beat-up red Civic. As they pulled out of the lot, the Hyundai stayed behind them for a while, and in the rearview Lissy saw her error; this guy was taller than Shahid, with a cropped beard, and dark glasses despite the gray day. When he turned the other way at the top of Winter Drive, she let out her breath. Ethan's paranoia had come into her head, turning her favorite player into a stalker. She knew him better than that.

By the time they pulled into Lissy's driveway and saw Shahid's Civic, Afia's quiet good humor had diminished to an unreadable meekness. She asked quietly if she might bring the snake cage indoors so it wouldn't get cold. "So long as we don't let little Pearl out," said Lissy. She led the way inside. Her players knew she kept the Winter Drive house unlocked, and until he went home this year, Shahid had spent winter and spring breaks here. Already, as she kicked off her snow boots, she smelled the Darjeeling he liked to brew for himself.

"Coach," he said as they entered the main room. He uncoiled from the couch. He looked tired. "You said four o'clock."

"Sorry to make you wait," Lissy said. She heard Afia in the hallway, setting down the leather bag with the cage and hanging her coat; she shucked her boots before she entered the main room.

"Asalaam aleikum, Shahid lala," she said.

"Wa aleikum salaam. What's my sister doing here?" he asked Lissy.

"I picked her up from the hospital." From the fridge Lissy pulled a V-8. She considered a quick spike of vodka but resisted. "I thought you two should talk."

"We have talked," said Shahid.

"I thought we three should talk, then."

"Coach, this is my sister." Shahid went over to where Afia was lowering herself gingerly into one of the two Danish armchairs in the living room. Her scarf was neatly arranged, her sleeves tugged down to her wrists. Scattered on the floor were the pieces of another Dora puzzle. Stepping over them, Shahid circled the chair. Lissy had seen menace in him many times before, but only on the court. The girl looked straight ahead, not at her brother. Quickly Lissy moved to the other armchair. She offered Afia tea, but Afia shook her head. "This is my sister," Shahid repeated, "and with due respect, Coach, I know what is best for her. You do not."

"Shahid, sit down." Lissy kept authority in her voice. Shahid returned to the couch, sipped tea. His face was a storm. "I hear you're borrowing money from Carlos."

"Just for a couple of days. I'm expecting a wire."

"And you've been pushing Afran. To take over at number one, if you have to be gone?"

He shrugged. He did not look at her.

"It's good of you to hit with someone who *wants* the extra practice," Lissy went on, "but coaching isn't your job."

"I'm sorry, Coach." He lifted his dark eyes, bloodshot, the lids sagging. "I overstepped. But this has nothing to do with my sister and me."

"When you're preoccupied with her, it does." Lissy sipped the V-8, missed the vodka. "And she has rights, you know, Shahid. If she wants to date someone—even your roommate—"

"Miss Hayes, stop." Afia sat way forward in her chair, her palms pressed together in a plea. "My brother loves me," she said. Her voice was strained, breathy. "He is a good brother. You act as you do," she said, turning to Shahid, "because you must. I know that. And I must love Gus."

Afia stood. As she took a place on the couch next to her brother, the scarf fell away a bit, exposing her glossy hair. Shahid leaned back against a cushion and regarded her. When she took his hand he flinched, but he didn't draw it away.

"You know what Baba says," he told her softly. "It is a disease."

She smiled ruefully. "I am ill, then."

Shahid said something in Pashto, and Afia nodded. He said more, and as he pressed his case her head drooped on her neck like a flower wilting on its stem. Finally she raised her head and answered him in English. "It is not Gus you need to stop," she said. "It is me. I am not controllable, Shahid. Kill me if you must and leave me here. But I will be no good to Zardad."

"Whoa whoa whoa," said Lissy. "What do you mean, you're no good? You are good, Afia. Look, falling in love is not a crime."

"It is for us," said Afia.

"No, it is not. It is not a crime," Shahid corrected his sister. "Not when the man is approved. Not when it hurts no one. But now." He looked with soft eyes on Afia and then waved his hand uselessly, as if at a stream of gnats. "She is ruined. Her life is over. And worse besides. You know that." He continued in rapid Pashto to his sister, who began, silently, to weep. "Unless she goes back. She must agree."

"Goes back to Pakistan." Lissy was incredulous. "You mean after she graduates. Or gets her medical degree."

"I do not. I mean tomorrow night."

"What? Afia, is this what you were expecting?" She turned to the girl. But Afia's face was tucked downward, studying the weave of the sofa cushion. She turned back to Shahid. "You're going to put her on a plane," she said, "in the middle of her sophomore year, to go marry some guy she doesn't give two hoots about."

"It is our custom, Coach. It is the family—"

"Give up her whole education. Give up the love—well, we don't know if it's the love of her life, but—"

"Exactly." Shahid sat forward. He gulped his tea. "We don't know. You don't know. You give us that talk about honor, Coach. Every year I listen to it. But not once do I hear you mention the honor of a family. The honor that is a woman's duty."

"I don't agree." Afia sat erect. She let the scarf drop to her shoulders. "This duty. I do not accept it now. I am not a dirty girl. I am not a blackened woman. But you win," she said to Shahid. She finished in Pashto, talking quickly to her brother, her hands moving in the air. Then she turned back to Lissy. "I have said to him," she explained, "I do not know where this third photo, it comes from. I do not find it on Internet."

"What third photo?"

"Pictures of her," said Shahid, "with—with Gus. They are . . . objectionable."

"To my family," Afia said, "who now may . . ." She looked down at her nails, scraped at an invisible bit of dirt. "Punish me," she whispered.

"So don't go to your family!" said Lissy. "Why would you send her home?" she said to Shahid. "Is it the money? Because she could get a job here, Smith has scholarship funds—"

"It is not the money," Afia interrupted. "It is what will happen. To my sisters. To my mother. My father's business. I am angry with Shahid. But Shahid is right."

Shahid sat forward. He took both his sister's hands in his. Slowly, as if they each might break, they wrapped their arms around each other. Shahid whispered in Pashto, and Afia answered. If Lissy hadn't heard the English words they had just pronounced, she'd have thought they were comforting each other for something that was past, that was being grieved. Lissy felt flummoxed. Here she had meant to negotiate a problem, to steer Shahid to see how stupidly jealous he was acting. Now brother and sister were embracing over some insane notion of dignity that would send the girl packing. Lissy felt awful. She wished Ethan were here; she had lost her bearings. She stood, stepped into the kitchen, and tipped a healthy shot of vodka into the can of V-8. When she came back, Shahid had stood up.

"Tomorrow we go to the airport," he said.

"I must go back to Northampton first," said Afia. She looked up at him, supplicating. "To see my professors. To thank them."

"Get your stuff, then. I'll take you."

Miserable, Afia shook her head. She wiped tears from her cheeks. "I don't want you to take me, Shahid," she said. "Please."

He sighed. He held his breath. He looked at Lissy, a familiar look from all his matches: *Coach, help me out here.* She reminded herself she loved this kid. She loved his intensity, his dedication, his grace, his loyalty. But her throat squeezed closed. Finally he said to Afia, "Then you'll have to stay here in Devon," he said. "We must leave tomorrow."

"She said she would take me," said Afia, gazing at her own feet.

"She?"

"Me," said Lissy. "I said I would. And I will, Shahid. You and your sister have made your decision. That I think it's wrong isn't here or there."

"It's not your responsibility, Coach." He looked around the room, as if he had lost something. "And don't you have Chloe?"

"She's with her dad. She's fine."

"Please, Shahid lala." Afia touched her brother's chest, then moved away. "I will be ready tomorrow. Three P.M." She stepped into the hallway, pulled her coat from the rack. When she reappeared in the sitting room she had her boots on, her bag over her shoulder. "Coach Hayes?" she said stiffly.

"So you don't even want me to drive you home?" Shahid asked, a catch in his voice.

"We will fight, Shahid lala. And I honor you. I am done fighting you."

Shahid took a step toward her. She held up a hand, stopping him. He turned again to Lissy. "You are taking her straight to Northampton?" he asked. "You are sure?"

Lissy's smile, when she put her arm on Shahid's shoulder, was shaky. It was almost five. They had to stop by Gus's place, to return the snake and pick up Afia's clothes, but she didn't want to say Gus's name at that moment, when everything felt so out of kilter. Nothing about these siblings made sense. And so she lied. "Without passing go or collecting two hundred dollars," she said. "Now finish your tea, and leave the porch light on for Chloe and her dad."

Already the sky was indigo, darkening to black, no moon. Quickly, before they pulled out of the driveway, Lissy sent Ethan a text message: *GTG to Northampton. May not get back for dinner. Give Chlo extra squeeze for me.* Afia hardly spoke as they drove back up to the main road and through the town. Lissy let the silence grow. Plenty of time to talk on the road to Northampton. Plenty of time to remind the girl that she was in America, she had options. Time, too, to figure how best to get Shahid back to his old self, to the player who could stride onto the court and beat Harvard. The wind still blew, with stray flakes of wet snow slapping the windshield. The roads would be icing up.

"You sure you don't want to stay here?" Lissy asked as they pulled into the drive by Gus's garage.

"No. I would see Gus again. I cannot do that. I cannot say goodbye. To my professors, yes. My roommate. But not . . . not Gus."

Afia had freed the snake cage from the dark handbag and set it on the floor. Now she lifted it by its handle and hoisted the green bag and her own purse with her free hand. "Here, let me help," Lissy said. Leaving the engine running and the headlights on to light their way, she stepped into slush that was beginning to crisp at the edges. "I'll unlock the door. Give me the key."

"In my pocket," Afia said. Lissy dug the key out, on a keychain with a rabbit's foot, and went ahead of the girl down the soggy path. A calico cat appeared from a row of bushes and rubbed against her leg. "They are not supposed to be out," said Afia as another cat, blond and annoyed, shaking its ears against the drifting snow, trotted around the side of the garage.

"We'll get them in, then. C'mon, kitty kitty," said Lissy. She fit the key into the lock of the old door, its paint more peeled than sticking. A narrow set of windows afforded her a glimpse of Gus's den, where a blue light shone on the far side over a home aquarium. The place would reek of animals, she figured. Gus usually carried just a whiff of his hobby with him, no matter how much he sweated on the court or showered after.

She pushed the door open and flicked on an overhead light. She caught a glimpse of the room—secondhand furniture, stacks of books, throw rugs over oil stains on the concrete, a bouquet of tired flowers on the blocks-and-board coffee table, another cage in the corner, a litter box. Then her sense of smell kicked in. No, this smell wasn't right. It wasn't a smell of cats or amphibians or urine, it wasn't mold or sweat. It was a more rotten stench. Fertilizer. And something burning, something sulfuric.

She turned to Afia, whose eyes when they met hers went wide with alarm. Without explaining it even to herself, without even naming the thing she suddenly knew was there, Lissy grabbed the girl's arm. "Get out of here!" she said.

She yanked Afia from the door, the plastic cage rattling in her arms. Together they slipped on the walkway. Afia fell to her knees. Lissy grabbed the cage and hauled her up. The car was far, far away. They could not run fast enough.

When the blast came, she thought the word: *bomb.* The word seemed to propel her through the air and onto a wet pile of snow by the bushes. Her head slammed hard onto a chunk of ice. When she lifted it, the garage behind them was lit red from the inside. The door lay on the walkway. The cage she'd been holding lay scattered, in shards. She thought she saw a moving slither of white against the wet snow, and then it was gone. Smoke billowed out, a heavy ash.

CHAPTER SIXTEEN

Afia kept moving, moving. You had to keep moving. That was what the survivors had done in the Peshawar bazaar. You stayed and the second blast came, or the snipers. Smoke everywhere; behind her, large things crashed and splintered. Fire, behind the smoke, in the cold air. She kept moving. From the far side of the path came Coach Hayes's weak cry: "Afia!" She crab-walked that way, stumbled over something large—the door, cracked in two—went down on her knees. She reached the car door, the passenger side. Her hand as it pulled the handle was gray with ash. Back out by the street, neighbors' lights were blinking on.

"Miss Hayes," she said when she'd made out the moving form in the snowbank by the hedge. "Coach Hayes, are you injured?" She knelt. Her clothes, she realized, were torn, her scarf gone. "Can you move? Can you speak?"

The coach's face was black with ash, bleeding from the right cheekbone. She waved an arm at Afia. "I can't hear you," she said. She put a hand to her ear and drew it away. No blood there. "I can't hear anything!"

Of course. That happened in the bazaar too, people deaf from the explosion. Strength surged through Afia's limbs. They had to go, now. Shahid had lied. She loved him. She had submitted to him. She wanted to scream not in pain but in grief. If Shahid could harm her, she was lost, lost. And he was a Pashtun, he would not stop. She placed her arms under the coach's shoulders, pulled her up, dragged her to the car, pushed her into the passenger seat, slammed the door.

Move. Fast. Don't stop. Shahid could be coming, Shahid was surely coming, following them from the coach's house, Shahid—oh, Shahid!—would kill them both. *You should scare a little easier*, he'd said. Her brother, her betrayer. The car's motor still purred. Afia had been behind the wheel of a car once before, with Gus, in an empty Smith parking lot. Now she found the *R* on the steering column and pressed the accelerator. The car leaped backward, down the drive, into the street, and hit the curb on the other side before Afia found the brake, thank Allah the brake, and then the *D* and the accelerator again, and they jerked down the street.

Coach Hayes sat crumpled, her hands against her ears as if the sounds were too loud. Trying to control the steering wheel and the accelerator and the brake, the car bucking and heaving from Campus Avenue to Main Street to Pittsfield Road, Afia glanced fretfully to her right. Finally, at the corner of the state highway, Coach Hayes lifted her head. By then the windshield wipers were whipping back and forth: Afia had set them off and didn't know how to stop them. A fire truck passed, its lights cartwheeling. "Can you hear?" Afia asked. "Did you hear the siren?"

"I'm not sure what you said," Coach Hayes answered. "Your voice is a buzz. My ears keep ringing. Afia, a *bomb* went off in that house."

"Yes, I know."

Coach Hayes took her left hand away from where it had been

rubbing her ear and placed it on the steering wheel. "Turn the car around, Afia. We've got to go to the police."

"No." What was she supposed to tell her? *Shahid is killing me. Shahid has to kill me.* Coach Hayes couldn't hear those words. Afia couldn't say them.

"Okay," said the coach. "I'm getting some sound."

Thank Allah. Both of them alive, neither deaf or shattered. Only Gus's house gone, his animals dead, and Shahid—Shahid could be anywhere, he could be behind them, they had to keep moving. Afia pressed the accelerator again and turned onto Route 7.

"The police," Coach Hayes said again, her hand still on the wheel. "The other way, Afia."

Afia shook her head. Keeping her eyes on the dark road, she reached her right hand to the back of the coach's head. A large bump there, and sticky; her hand came away smeared with blood. "You have hematoma," she said. "Maybe concussion. It will heal."

Coach Hayes let go the steering wheel and snatched Afia's wrist. "Stop the goddamn car," she said in a low tone. "Pull off on a side road if you want. This is my car. If someone got the plate, they're going to look for me. Stop the fucking car."

It was too much, too much. Afia's leg started to shake. Ahead, a side road. She turned the wheel and the car skidded to the right. *Brake*, she thought, *brake*, and found it, and with a jolt the car drove into slush and rocked back. She pushed the lever into *P*. Filling her ears was the sound of the heater, the *slup* of the windshield wipers, the soft splat of wet snow falling from branches overhead, and their breaths—the breathing of two women, alive, a soft panting.

Reaching across her, Coach Hayes turned the windshield wipers off, then the headlights. The world went black. Afia gripped the steering wheel tight, to stop her hands from trembling. So. Whatever he had said about a plane ticket, Shahid had lied: He had meant to kill her. To kill her. Her breath sucked in at the thought of it. He would have driven her to get her things at Gus's; would have gunned the car in reverse just as she triggered the bomb. Only because Coach Hayes was driving had he insisted, *you are taking her straight to Northampton*, because he didn't want to kill his coach. He would succeed, eventually, just as the proverb said: *Revenge took a hundred years, because I was impatient.*

But Shahid had once brought her to America, had saved her that way. Maybe he would murder her. But to her last breath she would put herself between him and these *Amreekans* who could never understand.

"There's a ringing in my ears," the coach said, "but it's dying down." She lifted a lever, and the backrest reclined; she leaned her head back. In the darkness, Afia could not tell if her eyes were open or shut. "Try talking," the coach said. "Try telling me what's really going on."

"I'm sorry," Afia said. "Can you hear me?" She felt the coach nod; nothing else moved. "If you are promising, no police," she continued, "you can leave me here. You don't need for to be involved."

"Shahid is my responsibility," Coach Hayes said in a flat voice. "I am involved." She reared up from the reclined seat and reached into the back of the car. She thrust a plastic bottle into Afia's lap. "I'm thirsty," she said.

Her own mouth, Afia realized, tasted of ash. Her throat felt burned. She uncapped the bottle, and for a moment both women drank. The water felt silky.

"And I can't leave you off here," the coach said. "It's the middle of nowhere in February." Her mobile rang with the sound of a black woman singing—shouting—about respect. When she pulled it out and flipped it open, the phone lit her face, gray with ash. She put it to her ear. "Shahid," she said.

Afia gripped her arm. She shook her head, *No, no.*

Coach Hayes pulled away. "We'll need you for the match," she said into the phone. And then, "You're letting me know now. That's the point. Honesty, right?" After another pause, "The question isn't whether you make Wednesday's practice, Shahid. The question is whether you communicate . . . Okay, good . . . One more appointment with Dr. Springer . . . I don't need to know what you talked about. But I wish—" She broke off. Having adjusted to the scant light, Afia could see Coach Hayes's eyes as the coach regarded her. Bright in her ashy face, their expression was confused. "We need to trust each other, Shahid. Loyalty, remember?"

She replaced the phone. In a swift move, she turned off the ignition and pulled out the keys. She popped the seat back up and shifted sideways. "I'm stronger than you," she said calmly to Afia, "so if I want us to go back to Devon and the police, that's where we'll go. If you want something else, you'd better talk to me. Now."

How, Afia wondered, did you begin to fathom this woman? From the start—when Shahid confided in her that not just the coach, but the director of all athletics at Enright, was female—she'd thought Coach Hayes a freak. What sort of woman threw her body around like that? What sort chopped off her hair, shouted at men, let them smell her sweat? Even Coach Hayes's stride, when Afia first saw her on a visit to Enright, looked wrong. The coach moved from the hip and kept her shoulders back, but loosely, not like a warrior. She had a narrow waist, breasts she did nothing to camouflage. She was married, she was a *woman*, not a perverse attempt at a man, yet this life of the body was what she had chosen. Afia had challenged all her teachers in Nasirabad. She had set her sights on being a doctor, no matter how many men teased or harassed her. Ignoring her mother's cautions, she let everyone know she was smarter than her brothers. And still, Coach Hayes made no sense to her. But they were in Coach Hayes's car, and Coach Hayes had just saved her life.

What were the laws in America? They executed people; that much she knew from Khalid. If strangers made trouble, they deported them. And they—not Coach Hayes, maybe, but the police, the judges—hated Muslims. "Someone," she said softly, "is trying to kill me."

"Who? Shahid?"

"No!" she said—too fast, too loud. "Someone else," she added quickly. "My family. I don't know."

"How do you know they weren't after Gus?"

"Maybe they were. It is the same thing."

"Because you're sleeping together."

Afia hid her face. No one else had said those words, not even Gus. And they weren't doing that, not the way Americans meant.

"Afia, don't beat around the bush. A bomb just went off."

"Maybe someone is hurting just Gus. But I do not think." She shut her eyes. *Gus*, she tried to think. Brilliant and gentle and warm Gus, who loved her and would protect her, only now he was in the hospital and somehow she had put him there, and now all his pets were dead and she had killed them.

"Was that an accident Gus had?"

Run from the truth, Afia told herself. *Run*. "Yes," she said. "An accident. He meant for to check those brakes. But he was busy with start of term. He should not have been coming to me," she said. This much was true. "I have been telling him I am engaged, he must stay away. But it was this Valentine's Day custom, he was wanting to bring flowers, chocolates. Chocolates," she repeated, and it sounded like the saddest word in the world.

"I see," said the coach, in a voice that said she was seeing what Afia did not want her to see. "But someone might be wanting to hurt Gus now. And you. And if you just take off—"

"If I am at Gus's garage, they will think it was Shahid who sets a bomb. They will think, he is killing me for honor."

"And if you take off, what will they think? Afia, get your head straight. You had the key to the garage. If you run away, the police will suspect *you*."

That hit her head like a hammer blow. Afia drank more water while she thought it over. The water was icy and sweet. If they suspected her, she could be jailed for a time, maybe even deported. Of course, Gus would try to prove her innocence. And Coach Hayes would march up to the judge and tell him what really happened, how Afia couldn't possibly set a bomb and then walk into it. But still. If she let them catch her on the run; if she confessed. She would turn attention away from Shahid for a few days at least. And in those few days, before they could arrest him, Shahid might leave the country. Because this was not a place where a brother could claim *pashtunwali* as a defense for attempted murder. This was America.

She still felt Shahid's arms against her back, his breath on her shoulder. It was all she needed: to know he loved her. He could not hate her, no matter how *tora* she became, no matter how stained. He was simply obeying Baba. He was doing what brothers must do. Only she could save him from his awful duty.

"I will leave myself here," she said. And with that she opened the car door and stepped out into six inches of frigid slush.

Hours later, Afia sat before a woodstove in a remote cabin, waiting for sleep to give her respite. In Coach Hayes, she thought, she had met her match. The coach had physical strength on her side, Afia strength of will. They shared a deep sense of loyalty, by which Afia would not betray her brother and Coach Hayes would not abandon her. Once Coach Hayes had wrestled her back into the car, they had agreed to one night's truce. Coach Hayes would not report the incident; Afia would not claim to have set the bomb that had almost killed them both. Coach Hayes would find out if Shahid had a solid alibi. Then Afia could come forward with the truth of what had happened at Gus's garage and not fear implicating her brother.

"We can go to Shahid right now," Coach Hayes had said as she maneuvered the car back onto the road. "I just spoke with him. He didn't even know we were going by Gus's place. He thought we were on the road to Northampton."

"Shahid cannot know where I am," Afia had said, her voice firm. She had taken off her shoes and socks; the car's heater blasted at her toes.

"Afia, he'll be concerned. You said he had nothing to do with—with this awful thing."

"Please, Coach Hayes. Just for one night. Do not tell anyone on the team."

"Not even Gus?"

"Gus . . . he will be so sad. His pets."

"Maybe the cats survived. And they were *animals*, Afia. Gus will worry about *you*."

She could only shake her head. Shame was a tide, drowning her.

The coach pressed on. "Why not tell Shahid? You think he might . . . might . . . inform someone else? Someone who is trying to hurt you?"

"I do not know," Afia said, shutting her eyes, "what Shahid will do."

It was the easiest answer, and the truest. After a long pause, Coach Hayes had said, "Okay then. I know where we'll go."

Soon after, Afia had fallen asleep. She had not slept, really, in three nights, not since she'd heard about Gus's accident. Vaguely it occurred to her that Gus might think she, too, had died in the blast. From that thought she drifted into uneasy dreams in which she was dead, only no one seemed to know it. She was tugging at Shahid's sleeve, then Moray's, then Gus's. Baba was in the room, and her uncles, her sisters, all her family. She tried to get them to see how she was dead, her body already rotting. Only one person—Khalid, with his own dead eyes—saw her for the corpse she had become.

She woke with a start. She was in Coach Hayes's car, alone. She sat up. Her hip hurt, and her elbow, where she'd landed hard after fleeing the garage. Outside, the rain had stopped. In front was a convenience shop, lit with cold fluorescence. Swallowing hard—so dead, she had felt, and at the moment she dreamt of Khalid's seeing her, truly dead—she fished her mobile from her pocketbook. Three calls, all from Shahid. Had she slept through the rings, or had they driven through a dead zone? She peered through the window at the two other cars lined up by the shop. Both had New York plates. Then Coach Hayes emerged, a large grocery bag cradled in one arm and her mobile held to her ear with the other. As she opened the driver's door, the interior light came on. The right side of her face was streaked with red, abraded from her fall against the icy snowbank. She handed Afia the grocery bag.

"Just held up here a little," she said into the phone. "Yeah, I think we're making some headway. I'll grab a bite before I drive home. Kiss Chloe. Thanks, sweetheart."

Then she was gone, back to the shop. She returned with two huge plastic jugs of water, which she placed among the athletic gear in the backseat.

"Not a happy dream life you've got there," she said as she slid into the car.

"I'm sorry," Afia said. "Did my phone ring?"

Coach Hayes frowned. She had wiped the black soot from her face. But the abrasion on her cheek was deep and needed cleaning;

the one on the back of her head as well. "Once, maybe twice," she said. "I didn't think you'd want—"

"No. I would not be taking a call. Where are we?"

Coach Hayes started up the car. "Hadley, New York," she said. "I picked up some stuff to eat. I figure you haven't had dinner." She turned onto a country road and put on her high beams. "We've got a camp nearby."

"A camp? For refugees?"

"A weekend house. It's in my husband's family. No one's here in winter. I thought, rather than check in at a motel . . ."

She let the sentence hang. Afia understood: To check in at a motel would be to give a name, a credit card, information that could be traced. The coach was honoring her promise not to let the police know, even by mistake. She was practicing *nanawate*, safe harbor. "Your face is injured," Afia said.

"I picked up some peroxide. We both need disinfecting."

"I'm sorry. You—you should not anything have to do with me."

"I didn't come looking for this. That's for sure." Then, as if realizing she sounded harsh, the coach reached over and squeezed Afia's clammy hand. "Shit happens," she said, the American words of comfort. "We'll figure it out."

Banks of snow rose on either side of the road, but the pavement itself was damp with melt. Holding the groceries, Afia realized she was hungry. She had fetched food from the hospital cafeteria for Gus, but she could not bear to eat more than a few bites herself. He had been so angry, this morning. He never should've trusted his mom's Nissan, he said, she didn't know anything about mechanics, he should've got Charlie at the Gulf station to do a once-over, and now he was out for the season, did Afia get that? And he had all these fucking vet school applications to finish, and you couldn't fall behind in Organic Chem, and what exactly was

Shahid's problem anyway, he sure didn't need his teammate acting like a jealous husband especially when Coach would kiss Shahid's butt, and was Afia sure she wasn't overfeeding the fish? Because if he lost that African cichlid he was going to be majorly pissed. And why was Afia looking at him like that, what the hell was wrong with her? First she broke up with him, now she was back. Why couldn't she look him in the eye?

Because I think my brother tried to kill you, she'd wanted to say, but she'd only sat there, her gaze focused somewhere midway between his chin and the thin hospital blanket. When Gus was dozing, she'd sat by the hospital bed holding his fingers lightly, watching his eyes flutter with dreams.

When Coach Hayes finally bumped onto a short driveway and cut the engine, Afia stepped out into a cold that bit her nostrils. Above, the sky had cleared. For the first time since coming to America, Afia looked up at stars like the stars she used to see on the high plains around Nasirabad—streaming, running together in a thin, cosmic milk.

The coach had left the headlights on. They lit a rambling wooden cabin with a screened porch. Snow rose over the steps. From the back of the car, she pulled out a shovel and proceeded to clear a narrow path, working as fast as a man. "Bring the groceries," she called back to Afia, who quickly obeyed. On the porch, Coach Hayes stomped her feet, protected only by track shoes. She reached up to a beam that supported the porch ceiling. By the side of a door locked with a hasp, she flipped a switch, and yellow light shone over the floorboards, a set of dusty wicker furniture, and a welcome mat that read *Hi. I'm Mat*. "Good thing," Coach Hayes said as she worked a tiny key into the padlock on the door, "the key's still in the same place."

She pushed the door open. Even in the sharp cold, the smell of dead mice overran Afia's senses. Coach Hayes disappeared into the dark space. Afia heard a click, then "Damn" from the coach. A moment later, a floor lamp flickered and came on, its light white and cold compared with the light on the porch. Coach Hayes surveyed the room, then Afia. "Just put those down in there," she said, indicating the groceries.

Afia crossed to a small kitchen in the back, where she heard something scurrying in the cupboards as she set the bag down in the dim light seeping from the main room. Suddenly she wanted to go back—back anywhere, almost, to Northampton or Devon or even Nasirabad, somewhere familiar and clean where she could sort herself out. But that was crazy thinking. She could not go anywhere.

"We'll have to gather wood," the coach called from the main room. She was rooting around somewhere. In another moment a light went on from the lamp that must have burned out its bulb. "I'll get the dead mice. I've got gloves. You can shake out the mattress, check the bathroom. No, skip that. We don't have water."

"No water? But—" Afia stepped to the doorway just as Coach Hayes was heading outside. The coach turned.

"It's not winterized," she said. "You have to drain the place down, or the pipes'll freeze. That's why I brought those jugs. And there's the river, for washing."

Then she was gone. Dazed, Afia looked around the cabin. On the walls were a dozen framed photographs, black-and-whites of an elderly couple and a crowd of children in cotton shirts and plaid shorts; color pictures of the coach and her husband, looking much younger and golden-skinned; other young couples, children, in swimsuits and summer dresses. The main room had a cathedral ceiling with skylights covered in snow; high above the main window hung a crossed pair of wooden racquets. Hesitantly she opened a closet door. Inside stood a broom and dustpan, behind which bed linens were neatly stacked. She pulled out the broom and stepped through another doorway, into a bedroom. There was one bed, double size, on a fine oak frame with a carved headboard. Immediately Afia thought of her bed in Nasirabad. Homesickness washed over her. Baba must have ordered her destroyed, and still she missed him and Moray with an ache deep in her gut. Had Moray wanted her killed, also? What shame she had brought, what disgrace. A family does what it must, and it is the brother who must do it. No *nanawate* for *tora*. Afia was *tor*, she was black, she was rotten.

She swept the floor. Clouds of cold dust billowed before the straw broom. Mouse droppings peppered the kitchen counter. When she pulled the thin mattress from the bed and tried to shake it, she discovered a hole near the bottom, where mice had dug in and stolen stuffing for their nests. Moving quickly as much to keep warm as to get the job done, she continued through the living room and into the sparse kitchen, the pile of refuse before her growing—dead insects and bees, bird feathers, three shriveled mouse carcasses, sawdust that had drifted from the ceiling where insects had bored. She found the kitchen light, an overhead fluorescent that flickered and snapped. A back door was bolted from the inside. She wrenched it open and swept the pile onto the snow-laden stoop. Across a stretch of yard, by the woods, she made out the figure of Coach Hayes, lugging a log carrier. Through the branches of the trees, in the distance, a ribbon of silver: the river. The coach bent to grab a stick of downed wood, then knocked it against a tree trunk to shake off the snow. In the starlight she looked small, too tiny to fight off whatever might come at her in the snow.

By the time Coach Hayes had brought firewood indoors, Afia had dared to open the cupboards. Under the unusable sink she found two live mice, casually nibbling a bar of soap. Immediately she thought of the mouse she'd dropped into Pearl's cage, only yesterday. Pearl, lost now in the snow. The mice scuttled away from the soap. One disappeared behind the cupboard; the other she managed to bludgeon with the broom and sweep into the pan.

"Now let's hope we don't have birds nesting in the stovepipe," the coach said as she crouched before the woodstove jutting out from a stone fireplace.

"There's newspaper," said Afia, practically the only words she had uttered since entering.

"Thank God for that."

As the coach crumpled sheets and shoved them into the stove, Afia noticed the shelves full of board games, books, a box of toys. This was a place for summer vacations, for children to be carefree. "Should I prepare food?" she asked.

Coach Hayes nodded. "Hamburgers was the best I could do at the store. There's propane in the tank, I checked. Should be an iron skillet under the stove. You'll need to light the pilot. You know how?"

Afia nodded. "At home, we have propane." She had been crouching next to the coach, watching her break twigs and tuck them in with the yellowed paper. "Miss Hayes," she began.

"Just call me Coach. Everyone else does."

"Coach, I want to thank you."

Coach shook her head. "I've been telling myself the whole way that I'm crazy. Bringing you here."

"If you understood us—my brother and me—you would not think yourself crazy."

"Well, explain this to me, then." She glanced up, her face pummeled and ashy. "Just this much. You are engaged."

"Yes."

"But not to someone you care about."

"I do not know him, really."

"So this is, what, a forced marriage?"

Afia smiled nervously. "Not forced, no. People here, they use that word, *forced*. It is more an arrangement. A promise the family makes."

"But you have no say in it."

"I do have say. I say yes, or I say no."

"Then why, for all the tea in China," Coach said, lighting the paper, "did you say yes?"

Afia tried explaining about the photograph on the Smith site, about Khalid's showing it to Baba. She imagined, again, her little sisters having stones, or feces, thrown at them as they tried to walk to school. Her mother meeting a sudden silence when she went to the market. "I—I tried," she said. "To do as I must. And then Gus, he is hurt—"

"Right. And now someone's trying to hurt you."

"Shahid says there is another photo. Two more photos."

"Online? But, Afia, if you're still posting—"

"Not me. I think—" Afia caught her breath. She was crouching, watching the match flame lick at the corners of newspaper. She remembered the photo now, the one that had appeared on Taylor's Facebook timeline last week. Some guy from Dartmouth had put it there, Taylor had said. But that couldn't be right. There were a dozen people apple-picking that day, including a couple of Chase's friends. But when Afia was on Gus's shoulders, he'd called to Patty to take a picture, and Patty had grabbed Afia's mobile and snapped it. Afia had never sent the photo anywhere. The only way it could have gotten to Taylor's page was if someone had taken her phone and uploaded the photo before she erased it. That same person had risked even greater shame with a third photo. That same person had armed the device that went off in Gus's garage. Only one person could have done all those things: Shahid. But why?

How could he want so badly to expose her ruin, that he would ruin their whole family? It made no sense.

"Afia?"

"It is . . . it is enemies in Pakistan, I think."

"Which is where Shahid means to send you, tomorrow."

Afia felt herself snagged in her half truths. If she had lost Shahid, she had lost everything. *I am the walking dead*, she wanted to say to Coach Hayes. *Let me go to the police and tell them it was me who lit a fuse at Gus's garage.*

"Okay, then." The wood in the stove had caught fire. Coach closed the door and stood. She was taller than Baba, Afia thought, maybe taller even than Shahid. "Can you make burgers?"

Afia remembered eating with Gus at Local Burger. She'd wolfed the hot sandwich, along with a steaming pile of French fries. Though she had thought she would be sick after, she had kept it all down. But she had never cooked a burger. Now the slimy worms of fat-marbled meat repulsed her. She tried to form them into patties without touching them, using the rusted spoons and spatula she found in a drawer next to the stove. She found matches, got the pilot to sputter to life, and lit two burners. The blue flames, dry and gassy, began to lessen the cold. She found a skillet and swabbed it out with a rag dabbed wet with bottled water, and when it was hot she lifted her ill-formed cakes of meat and dropped them to hiss and spit on the hot iron. She fished heavy stoneware plates from the bottom of the stack in the cupboard, figuring them to be cleaner. In the shopping bag she found a bottle of red wine with a screw top. She filled a tumbler for the coach. Then, pressing her lips together, she filled one for herself.

Her patties fell apart as soon as she tried to nudge them from the skillet. Still, seated at the rickety round table with two lit candle stubs, Coach pronounced them delicious. She also popped open the bag of chips, sour cream and onion, that she'd bought in Hadley. "There's instant coffee for breakfast," Coach said, "and, God help me, Pop-Tarts."

Afia didn't know what a Pop-Tart was, but she nodded. The wine tasted like rotten fruit laced with formaldehyde; she swallowed it and clenched her teeth. Gingerly she ate a chip, the sides of her tongue tasting the artificial flavors. "In living room," she said. "Your husband's family?"

Coach took a bite of her hamburger. "Two sisters. We take turns using the camp. Though no one's been up here recently. They're both married to guys in the city, busy down there."

Afia nodded. "Is the same with us."

"What, your family has a summer place no one uses anymore?"

"No. I mean, when a girl marries. We call it a *gham*. A sorrow," she explained when Coach looked puzzled. "Because your family, they lose you forever. You belong now with your husband. His family."

Coach glanced out at the living room, where the glass frames of the pictures reflected the flames dancing in the woodstove. "I'm from the Midwest," she said. "My mother died when I was twelve."

"Oh. I am sorry."

"Thank you. But I mean I don't have much sense of my own family. And we don't see much of Ethan's. Maybe we should, but it doesn't work out much. Anyway, I don't feel as though I belong to them. I guess Ethan and I just belong to each other."

Coach gave a short laugh, as if she knew how silly and forlorn that sounded. The fire in the woodstove had infused the air with warmth. "We should tend to your wounds," Afia said when they had eaten.

"They're hardly wounds."

"They are very much wounds. Where is brightest light?"

They tried the bathroom, but the bulb had blown out. Bringing a candle, Afia managed to find two wrapped sterile pads and a roll of tape in the medicine chest. She positioned Coach Hayes on the edge of the bed, under the floor lamp. She took what seemed like a clean cloth from the closet, doused it with peroxide, and gently dabbed and stroked the woman's face and the back of her head until the smoke stain and newly formed scabs sloughed off. The head would heal on its own, but the cheek now showed two inches of raw skin that gently oozed blood. Coach Hayes held still, wincing only as the peroxide came near her eye. For all her height and toughness, Afia realized as she set about fitting gauze and tape to the cheek, the coach was a lovely woman, with sculpted cheekbones and the sort of firm, wide jaw Pashtun men admired.

"Tomorrow you should change the dressing," Afia said when she'd finished.

"Thank you."

They stood. "I made up the bed," Afia said, glancing at it. "About other rooms, I don't know—"

"Oh, I'm not staying," said Coach. She looked at herself in the cloudy oval mirror that hung on the wall. "I need to be home with my family. I'll say I dropped you in Northampton. What happened to you after, I have no idea. I can't believe I'll lie to them," she said as she moved out into the sitting room. "I never lie."

"I never have sleep alone, in a house before." Following her, Afia said this almost to herself. She could not bother Coach Hayes further. If Coach was lying, it was Afia's fault. Everything was her fault. But she trembled. She stood in the doorway to the bedroom. "I will not sleep," she said.

Coach turned. The light of the woodstove flickered. "You were alone at Gus's place."

"There were the animals." Saying this, the awfulness of it came thundering through her. Pearl, her body white as an intestine. Voltaire, the iguana, with his throat that fluttered like a leaf in the breeze. Percy, the rat who shared the cage with Voltaire, whom Gus liked to tease her with, by wearing Percy on his head like a beady-eyed cap. And the fish, their radiant colors and translucent bellies, the tiny organs tucked inside, and their eyes round, all-seeing. They were Gus's family, and they were gone, blasted away, like the bodies in the Peshawar bazaar. The morning of one attack, Tayyab had come back early from shopping, his clothes in smoky tatters, his cheeks hollow with fear. *A hand*, he'd said, *there was a hand, and then a head, the head was rolling.*

"Look, I'll call after practice tomorrow," Coach said. "That should give you some time to think over your situation. I doubt there's cell service here, but there's a landline." She nodded toward the wall by the unplugged refrigerator, where an ancient black phone hung with its tangled cord. "The number's unlisted, so no one else will be trying it. You can go to the river for water or melt some snow, to wash your face. Jugs are for drinking. If you pee in the toilet, don't flush it. Don't go far, because I'll be calling you." As she crouched before the woodstove, her voice gentled. "You should plan on speaking to the police tomorrow. They can protect you, Afia."

"But you will not say anything to Shahid. Will you?"

Coach poked the embers and shoved in two more thick, damp branches. "You ever been on a team, Afia?"

"No. But I know there is no *I* in *team*."

"A team"—Coach smiled as she shut the door—"is about honor. Honor as loyalty, as respect, as honesty. I have always respected your brother. I am trying to be loyal to him, honest with him. And you. But you both make it very, very difficult."

"Coach, I—"

"It's all right. I made a choice. But I had to say that. Your people are not the only ones concerned with honor. Now try to sleep. When the fire dies down in the stove, shove some more wood in it."

"Thank you," Afia said.

But Coach had stepped away, was gathering her things, was out the door and starting the car. Afia watched the red taillights disappear down the road. Then she switched off the electric light.

Now she watched flames dance behind the glass door of the woodstove. They were a miniature version, she thought, of the flames that had raged through Gus's house. One set of flames warmed, the other destroyed. Someone would have woken Gus, at the hospital, to tell him of the catastrophe at his garage. He might have rung her. No such call had come, but she was in a dead zone; Coach had said so.

Tomorrow, if she kept her promise to Coach Hayes, she would have to call the police. But call them to say what? That she had not set the bomb, that she had no idea how to make a bomb? That she had run because of fear? Fear of what? The police would guess, soon enough. They would arrest Shahid, who had no idea how to make a bomb either—but this one hadn't worked properly, it had not killed her. They would find evidence and try Shahid, sentence him. They might execute him here, or they might deport him to Pakistan, where Khalid would take him up on his pledge and kill him.

No, she couldn't go to the Devon police. Coach would, eventually, but not until Afia had figured out where to flee, how to disappear. How to find some money, maybe, and cut or dye her hair. Hitchhike onto the highways of America. Send a message to Gus that she would always love him and she was sorry, sorry, so very sorry. And then—she thought as the fire settled and winter's chill retook the room—let Shahid track her down.

CHAPTER SEVENTEEN

Lissy had always been competitive. It was one of the first things Ethan noticed about her, on their third or fourth date after they'd met on the PATH train, he headed to Northern State Prison, she headed to her assistant A.D. job at Rutgers. She had just finished telling him about the injury that had ended her squash career at the Cleveland Classic. She was one competitive lady, Ethan had remarked with a lopsided grin.

Well, she competed, didn't she? To compete without being competitive—that would be like painting without being artistic.

Like talking without speaking, he'd said. Like hearing without listening. And then he'd launched into Simon & Garfunkel. He had a good tenor, even though he was just being silly. She'd thrown a napkin at him.

Still, outside sports, *competitive* was a dirty word. Like *ambitious*. If she'd grown up with a mother, maybe she would have softened her edge, learned to deny herself the thrill of clutching the trophy high over her head. If she had grown up in the world her American players inhabited, full of country clubs and etiquette, maybe she'd have sated her hunger to train harder, practice longer, nail the shots her opponents missed. Maybe, if she'd been introduced early on to pure beauty, or pure affection, she wouldn't have relished the purity of competition—same rules for all, same starting spot, same ineluctable goal—as much as she did. But she had grown up on the scrappy north side of St. Louis, with five brothers and a dad working nights, and one of her last memories of her mother was the glow on her face, her bald head obscured by a blue scarf, as Lissy tore past the hundred-yard finish line ten paces ahead of the closest boy.

Even her choice of sport—squash, claustrophobic and un-American—was etched with ambition. Squash was what they didn't play, on the north side. There were a couple of old courts at the back of the community center and a retired pro who let kids hit for free. But what she wanted was to beat the kids at the private schools, with their clean lines and vaulted ceilings—and when she did, her brothers exploded in whoops and her dad's face came as close to a grin as he could ever manage.

So yes, she told Ethan, she was competitive. Insatiable, rivalrous. She'd come by her ambition honestly, and she wasn't going to be ashamed of it, no matter how crude or unladylike she appeared. But she never cheated, she never lied. And when she came home, she left the competition outside. Those had been her promises.

But now. As she exited the Pike toward Devon she felt the messiness of what she was doing, the impurity of it. The police—she ought to go to the police, tell them where the girl was, help them discover what the hell had happened. Whatever Afia had claimed, Lissy knew what she thought: that Shahid had set a trap for her, had tried to kill her with a bomb at her boyfriend's place. Ethan would think the same. What had he said, about these honor crimes? *It's often the brother doing the meting out.*

But Ethan didn't know everything, and neither did Afia. She, Lissy, knew Shahid inside and out. She had struggled with him through tough matches; she'd watched him find his place on the team and let go, one by one, of his defenses until he became the muscles and sinews of the squad itself. She knew he loved his sister more than life. Honor or no honor, he wouldn't let her come to harm.

So go to the police. If Shahid was innocent, their investigation would pass him by. He'd make his next counseling appointment and then play Harvard. Would beat Harvard, and go on to a brilliant career, coaching or on Wall Street, whatever he chose, the world his oyster.

Except for the girl. Goddammit, the girl. Afia was terrified, and somewhere in her gut Lissy felt certain that her terror would derail Shahid. Would cast suspicion on him, would stir up—what? Trouble, of a kind Lissy sensed faintly but couldn't name. Someone had set that bomb. For now, Gus was in the hospital, safe. Afia was at the camp, also safe. And there were less than five days until the Harvard match that meant everything to her best, her noblest player.

What harm would it do, really, just to wait a little while? To let the girl come to her senses? *All right*, she said to the world as she passed through the sleeping town, *so I want victory. So shoot me.*

At the top of Winter Drive she felt the left side of her cheek tightening and remembered how she looked. Pulling the car over, she flipped up the visor and checked herself out in the mirror—the bandage, the singed hair, the soot. She looked like a blind person's attempt at blackface. She had to clean up and come clean, at least to Ethan.

Oh, baby." He came to sit next to her on the couch when she'd finished describing the explosion. Chloe, thankfully, was asleep. In the kitchen was the Valentine she'd made for Lissy that afternoon. Lissy held a bag of frozen peas to the lump on the back of her head. Ethan pulled her to his shoulder. "You could've been killed."

He smelled wonderfully familiar, the warm musk of his skin. "I'm lucky," Lissy admitted. "Afia cleaned up the one bad spot. I'll have a doozy of a headache in the morning, but—"

"What about Afia? Is she all right? Where is she?"

Lissy lifted her head and adjusted the bag of peas. She hadn't thought what to say. From the beginning, she and Ethan had told each other everything. Old love affairs. Grudges they couldn't let go of. All the stale fantasies that turned them on—she would pretend to be a call girl, he that they were strangers on a cruise. Now she felt honesty slipping away from her, like snow melting off a bank. The camp in Hadley was the best place she could think of, four hours ago, but it wasn't her place. It was Ethan's, and he'd hung on to it over the objections of his sisters, who wanted to sell. It was the place of his happiest memories, he'd told Lissy once, and the place he wanted to pass down to Chloe. Could Lissy inform him that she'd secreted a girl there, a witness to a bombing, a girl who could be at risk from her own brother? He wouldn't share her lurking, inchoate fear. He'd see only her ambition, her determination to push Shahid to a win and get her precious fitness center built.

"And why," Ethan went on while she tried to phrase an answer, "didn't you call the cops?"

Lissy leaned back. She met his worried eyes. "Afia," she said slowly, "seemed more frightened of the police than of the blast. She was talking crazy, Ethan. Like—like someone would be after her, if we went to the police. When I kept on at her about it, she said she'd tell them *she* set a bomb."

"So now she's—"

"Hiding. Somewhere safe. And I don't want to tell you where, honey. Please."

Ethan rose. She heard the clink of ice as he fixed them both a vodka tonic. "Can you tell me," he asked when he came back, "what happened this afternoon?"

"Sure," Lissy said. She described the conversation with Shahid, Afia's willingness to return to Pakistan, her own outrage, Afia asking for Lissy to bring her back to Smith.

"So when you called me to say you were in Northampton," Ethan said—swirling his drink, looking into the fire—"you were lying."

"I'm sorry, honey. I was panicked. I thought somebody could be after her and—"

"You mean you thought Shahid could be after her."

There they were, already, at the place she'd feared. "That doesn't make any sense," she insisted. "Afia agreed to go back to Pakistan. Shahid won."

"Winning's not everything, Liss."

"You know what I mean. He loves her."

Ethan removed his glasses and rubbed the bridge of his nose. "We've got a lot of *ifs* here," he said. "A freak accident—we don't even know it's a crime. Could have been all sorts of stuff stored in that garage. Things combust. What about your player, Gus? His brakes gave out last week, right? Does he have enemies?"

Lissy shook her head, startled. "I don't think so."

"Well, we'll find out quicker," Ethan said, "if you and Afia talk to the police."

"And we will. Let's just give her a couple of days."

Ethan was silent a long time. A log cracked, in the fireplace. He crossed his arms over his chest. Finally he said, very quietly, "You need Shahid. You need him for the Harvard match."

No point in denying it. "I do."

"And you need him not to be facing a bunch of accusations about his sister."

"Ethan, Shahid would not do this. And you know how Muslims get treated, when there's violence. If he and Afia were deported—"

"Tell me where she is, Liss."

The Hadley camp. Why had she been so impulsive? He would never let the girl stay there, if he knew. But just a few days. He didn't have to know, now or ever. Meeting his eyes, she couldn't lie. She could only be stubborn. "Please, Ethan. You've got to trust me on this."

"No, I don't. I've got to be honest with you. And you're making a lousy decision. You're doing it because you care about your player. I know that. And his sister. You care, Liss, but you're wrong. Thank God you didn't come to real harm. But I won't help you if this gets messy. Do not count on me for that."

He unlocked his arms. He put them around her and kissed her ashy hair.

Somehow the next day proceeded. At Enright, Lissy explained her injuries with a story of a fall on the ice in the dark, a crack of her head against stone steps. No one seemed to doubt her, even as the place buzzed with news of the explosion at Gus Schneider's garage. A cat had been rescued; the place was sealed off, police at the scene. At noon, a meeting with university officers about the capital campaign. Don Shears was jolly. Charles Horton, he announced, was coming up from the city for the squash match against Harvard. Depending on the outcome, he would pledge whatever it took to complete a state-of-the art fitness center.

"How much do we figure that would be?" asked Penny DuBois, the faculty dean.

They turned to the comptroller, a spare coffee-skinned guy named Roy Jones. "Counting the initial pledge from Jeff Stubnick and a few other small donations, I'd say it'd take about eight hundred grand to put us over the top," Jones said.

"Pretty nice premium, for a squash match." Don winked at Lissy. "Now, if we could just get Coach Hayes's fund-raising muscle for the new chem labs, we might gain a notch in our academic rankings."

When the meeting broke up, he walked Lissy out. "You got the chops for that Harvard match?" he asked.

"Can't say, Don. Harvard's tough."

"If the injured player—"

"Gus? He plays second string. We'll be fine without him."

Don said, "Poor kid," and Lissy agreed. Turning away, she felt a lump in her throat, as big as the one swelling her cheekbone.

That afternoon, calling the hospital, she learned Gus was discharged. He would know about his garage by now. The other players did. Through the afternoon they streamed into her office—Carlos, Afran, Yanik, Jamil, a few of the girls. Had she heard, they wanted to know. Wasn't it crazy? Carlos had gone by the garage, "And it was a war zone, man, like something on TV." Yanik had talked to Gus, but couldn't get much out of him, the dude was too upset. They had all heard about the rescued cat. Had Coach gotten a call from the police? Because Afran had, also Carlos. They were carpooling down to Gus's mom's place.

No Shahid, Lissy noted. Perhaps he wasn't a good enough liar to come forward. *Not possible*, she fired back at herself. He loved Afia. You couldn't kill what you loved. She didn't give a shit about cultural difference. You couldn't do it and be human.

She was relieved when the phone rang and it was George Bradley from Harvard, calling to talk squash. "I got a tape of your boys against Trinity," he said. "They're eating their Wheaties."

"Working hard," said Lissy. A little pouch of breath that had been trapped in her lungs let go. Coaches, even rival coaches, were the easiest people to talk to.

"Didn't see your main guy. That mean you're cutting us a break?"

"Shahid?" Another pouch of breath caught in a lower lobe, which clamped tight. "He's back now."

"Hope so. I want a good look at him. And I've got a couple of recruits for you. South Africa and Argentina. I'll bring their folders to the match. Consolation prizes."

Lissy hung up. *Hope you've got the chops*, Shears had said, *for that match*. Only with Shahid did Enright have such chops.

Doubts she'd dismissed the night before festered as the day went on. Who was she protecting—Afia, or Shahid? Or herself? The words she used when she lectured her players echoed in her head. *When you're loyal to something that's rotten, it rots your loyalty.* Had Shahid gone rotten? He was her best, her best-loved player. And if she turned Afia over to the police, they would surely finger him. Just a few days, Lissy needed. To know what to do. To beat Harvard in front of Charles Horton. To watch Shahid and understand him, better than she ever had before, so she could bring Afia back to him in safety. A few days, which after all . . . what did they matter? Gus's place was gone, Gus's animals were dead, and no amount of confession would bring them back. And the marriage awaiting Afia in Pakistan—that could wait, too. She reached for her phone and dialed the camp.

Afia's voice was small and tight. "Yes?"

"I'm making sure you're all right."

"I am all right."

"You can't keep staying there. I shouldn't have brought you there."

"I do not think . . . no. I will go from here soon, Coach. But not to the police. How is Gus? You have seen Gus?"

"Not yet. They found his cat."

"Oh, I am so glad. So glad." She was crying. "Facebook and Ebay."

What was the point of telling her: just the one cat? "Afia, I'm going to drive up there tomorrow morning. You need to think seriously. The police will be looking for you. They are your safest alternative. Do you understand me?"

"Yes, Coach."

"I'll be by, I don't know, sometime after nine. We said one day, remember?"

"I know, Coach, but my brother—"

A knock on Lissy's door. "I'll see you tomorrow, Afia."

She checked her watch: 4:25. Practice in five minutes.

"Come in," she called when the knock repeated. She knew from the way the door opened who it would be. She had to lie to him, and this time it wasn't like snow melting but like the twist of a knife. "Shahid," she said—as calmly as she could, but her voice rose like a hiccup on the second syllable—"I thought you'd gone to take your sister to JFK."

"She is not there. She was not in her classes. She does not answer her mobile." He strode into the room, dropped his squash bag, and began pacing, to Lissy's desk and back to the door, to Lissy's desk again. He looked more like the American players, baggy-eyed and unkempt, than like the pro athlete he used to be. He pulled his cell phone from his pocket. His winter jacket hung loose over warm-up pants and squash shoes. "I have this plan," he said. "Anywhere a family member has a phone turned on, yes? I can find her. Only she does not show up, on this plan. She is not anywhere."

"Shahid, settle down." Lissy came out from behind her desk. She stood firm, her arms crossed over her chest. She noted he wasn't asking about the black eye, the bandages. But his overlooking her injuries didn't mean anything—the other guys on the team had probably shared the story of the fall on the ice, and Shahid was distracted. "I don't know your sister that well," she said, watching his pacing slow, like a tired lion, "but she didn't seem eager to give up college and fly back home."

"She's never lied to me. Almost never. Actually, I don't know." He scratched the back of his head. His unwashed hair stuck out. Instinctively Lissy touched the back of her own head, where the lump was slowly shrinking. "But she has to be there. She has to be somewhere. Coach, if I cannot find her, you don't know—" His face twisted as if in grief. If this was acting—if he thought a bomb he had set had killed, or missed killing, his sister—he had a greater talent for acting than for squash. He dropped into a chair and rested his eyes on the heels of his palms. When he looked up, he asked the question Lissy had been dreading. "Did you take her directly to Northampton, yesterday?"

Sharply she recalled Shahid's plea, yesterday, to drive Afia to Northampton himself. Gus's snake; Shahid never saw the cage, couldn't know they were taking it back to the garage. "She wanted to see her professors," she said. "Maybe you need to give her a few more days, Shahid. You can change the ticket. She loves you, she respects you, I didn't get the sense that she would put your family at risk—"

"Damn it, Coach! You don't understand anything!"

Lissy pulled a chair up to face him. Her left side pulled painfully as she sat. She put her hands on Shahid's knees. The right one drummed against the floor. "I understand," she said, "that you are under a lot of pressure. Have you gone for counseling?"

"Once, yes."

"Was that helpful?"

"No. He wants to talk about my sister, about—about—about Gus Schneider, about what's happened to him, I don't know anything about this awful thing with Gus, it's nothing to do with me, only he keeps his hands away from my sister, that's all. Same thing I said to the police."

"The police spoke with you?"

"What do you think? At lunchtime, they find me in the dining hall, they put me to shame in front of everyone. They ask me did I fight with Gus, was Gus dating my sister, where was I yesterday, where is my sister."

"And where," Lissy asked cautiously, "do you think your sister is?"

Dead, he might say. Or *hiding from me*. His brows drew together, hawklike, the way they did on the court. Finally he said, "I am afraid, Coach."

"Of what, Shahid?" *Of yourself?* she wanted to ask. But such questions were Ethan's department. To her, Shahid simply looked the way you look when something out there terrifies you. "Did you give the police," she asked carefully, "all your whereabouts yesterday?"

"Of course I do. Hitting with Afran, then lunch at the dining hall, then the library, and a girl I know saw me. Then your house."

"So you have nothing to fear."

"From the police? No." He shook his head, as if he were talking to a simpleton. "It's for her I'm afraid."

"She's fine, Shahid." Which was, of course, the truth. But she knew he heard empty reassurance. If she could only be sure of him! Could she tell him what she'd told Ethan, everything except Afia's location? She opened her mouth to try.

Then he said, "You talk honor, Coach. But you don't know honor. If I could just—" Plucking one of the hard blue balls from the bin in her office, he squeezed it as if he would crush the pulp out of it. Lissy's impulse shrank, at the fury of his gaze.

"Come on," she said weakly. "Let's work it out at practice."

. . .

By the next day she couldn't stand it. Ethan had avoided all discussion of the bomb. On the surface, nothing had changed. When she told Chloe she'd slipped on the ice, he added for Chloe to be careful about Mommy's boo-boos. Leaving for his office, he'd kissed her on the lips with what seemed like more than the usual warmth. But she sensed him watching her. She felt his disappointment like a bad taste. Canceling her morning appointments, she headed out of town. She had told Afia one day; one day it would be. Shahid had an alibi. Whatever Afia was frightened of could not possibly derail his concentration on the Harvard match. The police would clear them both. He could send her home to Pakistan next week, if he was so determined to send her home.

Then she spotted the blue Hyundai sliding onto the road behind her. *A* blue Hyundai, anyway. No telling if it was the same one she'd seen at the hospital. Its windows were tinted, the sun bouncing off the windshield; she couldn't tell what sort of person was driving. When it followed her off the main road and onto the shortcut around town, her blood froze. Not the driver but the machine itself seemed to follow her. This wasn't any car she knew. Carefully she wound her way south from Devon ten miles to the Mass Pike and headed east instead of west. At the first exit she lined up third at the toll booth. The Hyundai pulled into line behind her. Only when an opening presented itself did she turn the wheel and gun the car over to the next lane. Sailing through with her EZ Pass, she checked the rearview. The Hyundai had lost a spot to a pickup. Off the ramp, Lissy turned left at an amber arrow and wheeled around to reenter the Pike heading west. The blue car, thank God, was nowhere to be seen.

Breathe, she ordered herself. Her hands gripped the steering wheel like a life raft. She had no idea what she was frightened of.

She checked the rearview along the rest of the interstate and after she pulled off, but no blue Hyundai. Few cars generally, though the roads were dry and the sky bright blue.

When she unlocked the hasp at the camp, she found the place cold. "Afia?" she called. No answer came. The back door was shut but unbolted. Panic caught at her breath. Carefully she stepped out the back. From the door of the shed, she saw the girl's eyes peek out, then her body wrapped in her wool coat, an improvised hijab outlining her pale face. "What are you doing out there?" she called.

In her shearling boots Afia stepped gingerly over the snow. "I thought police had come."

Lissy looked her up and down. Afia was shivering. "So you figured you'd escape them? In my shed?"

Afia's arms squeezed against her sides. "There is a closet, in there."

"And you thought I would turn you in. Just like that. Trusting, aren't you?"

"I'm sorry, Coach."

Afia followed her in. Bending to inspect the woodstove, Lissy found the fire died down to embers. "We'll have to clean this out," she said.

"Coach, please. No. I cannot go back."

"Afia, our deal was one night, to get yourself calmed down. You've had two."

"Yes. I know." The girl was hugging herself. Lissy returned to the kitchen, started putting the Pop-Tarts into a grocery bag. "If I could," Afia said from behind her, "if you would be able . . . you have been so kind . . . but I have no one else to ask . . . Gus would do anything, but then he would be of danger again—"

Lissy turned. Afia's blue eyes were twin pools of fear. She placed both her hands on the girl's thin shoulders. "What are you trying to say?"

"I am thinking two hundred dollars would be enough." Afia bit her lip. She looked down at the stove, crackling into life. "I take a bus. Disappear. When they come to ask you, you say you do not know me, you never saw me."

"Two hundred dollars."

"I will repay you. Only if Shahid asks, you do not tell him. And if they come for Shahid, you say he was not at the garage, he could not have done anything."

"I don't have to vouch for Shahid, Afia. He's accounted for his whereabouts. I don't think he's a suspect in whatever happened at Gus's."

"You are sure?"

"It's what he told me. He has an alibi."

Afia chewed her bottom lip. She seemed to be making a calculation. Of how well her brother could lie to the police? Or of how well the police could protect her from whatever else lurked out there? "I cannot go with you, Coach. I am sorry. I am happy for Shahid. Tomorrow, I leave here. By myself. If you cannot loan money—"

"Afia, if you're in the danger you say you are in, leaving here with two hundred bucks won't get you to safety!"

God, the frustration of the girl. Lissy stopped loading the groceries. She'd never seen terror like this before. Would she wrestle Afia to the car? Have her open the door and tumble out on the road? If she reached for her phone and called the police, the girl would bolt; her whole body seemed poised, like a deer's when it senses the rifle. And that blue Hyundai—that hadn't been a coincidence. Someone had tried to track Lissy, someone suspected she would lead them to Afia.

"This is my husband's family home, all right?" she went on. "It's not fair to him. Not fair to me, or to Shahid."

The girl stood mute, stubborn. Her glasses made her eyes look enormous.

"All right." She was pissed at herself, for relenting. But already she was putting the groceries back on the counter. "You can stay another forty-eight hours. That's it. Maybe by then they'll have caught whoever set that bomb. That would make the world look different, wouldn't it?"

Afia fell to her knees, clasped her hands together. "Thank you, Coach."

Lissy checked her watch. "I'll fetch you a few provisions from the local store, then I have to go. So listen up." She took hold of the girl's hands, pulled her up from the floor. She spoke the way she would to a player losing a battle of nerves. "Don't go out except to pee or fetch wood. Use the back door. Bolt it when you're inside. I'll lock the hasp on the front. Tomorrow I'll call the landline. I expect you to pick up. If you have to call me—here's my number—use that line." Tearing off a piece of the grocery bag, she scrawled her cell number. "No other calls except to the Devon police. And I'd appreciate your letting me know if you come to your senses and make that call."

Afia was nodding, her lower lip caught in her teeth. "You are very kind," she said. "I only wonder if . . . if word could get to Gus . . ."

"Oh, no. No no no. I am not contacting anyone until you're ready to make a statement."

"But he will be so worried—"

"He'll have to stay that way."

Impulsively, she drew the young woman's head toward her. She planted a kiss on her forehead, still smelling of ash. She exited from the front, locking the hasp behind her.

CHAPTER EIGHTEEN

There were no body parts, Shahid kept telling himself. Even if Coach—who never lied—had lied about taking Afia to Northampton, and Afia, returning to Gus's garage, had set off that IED, there would have been body parts. He would have heard about it. The police would not have kept asking him where his sister was. So there were no body parts. She wasn't dead. Not necessarily dead. Right? Right?

Not right enough. He called, he texted. He drove to Northampton, collared her roommate. Nothing. *Nothing.* He sat in class, his right knee vibrating like a piston, a hollow core of panic in his chest. Afia hadn't come back to her dorm room Sunday night. Coach had dropped her by the walk and she'd vanished into thin air. Damn it! Only one person in the world wanted to do her harm. He was also the most likely to finish the job on Gus that Shahid had botched. Murderer—Khalid was a murderer. And Shahid had stood next to him on the sidewalk, taken a gun from him, and not shot him where he stood. What a *dawoos*, what an idiot he'd been!

But they had found no body parts, no hands or feet, no spleen, no rolling head. So he had to believe she was alive somewhere, and he could still save her.

Over and over he replayed that half hour at Coach's place. Afia had started out angry, sure. So had he. But when she learned about the third photo, something in her gave way. She had talked to Taylor, she said. She didn't know how the second photo got onto Taylor's page, but Taylor had taken it down. All her friends knew, she said, not to post photos of her, not to tweet about her and Gus, nothing. And now a third photo? The light went out of her eyes. If people were going to ruin her, she said, she was ruined. Then, in English: *Kill me if you must.* At that point Coach had interrupted, while Shahid felt the damning fact of the gun in its white bag back in his room, as if it were rising up, flying to the house on Winter Drive, taking aim at his sister's forehead and firing. No, not that, he'd wanted to yell out, anything but that.

He could have explained the third photo to her. He could have told her Khalid was in the States, here for jihad or honor, it hardly mattered. Khalid had surely taken that third photo from outside Gus's hospital room, while the door stood ajar. If Shahid had warned her, Afia might have been on the alert for Khalid. But he hadn't wanted to frighten her any more. And Khalid had always made Afia nervous, even when he delighted her as a little girl by letting her ride on the back of his motorbike. So Shahid had explained patiently that Afia's *namus* could still be restored, that there would be no more jeers at Sobia and Muska, that Baba's business would be fine, that Moray would forgive her, if only she went back. They could argue all night about whether this love thing was like breathing or like a virus. Nothing they said to each other here would change what was happening in Nasirabad.

Baba, she had said, in Pashto, weeping. *Baba will not forgive me.*

Not so long as you claim this is not your duty, Shahid had told her. *But keep those complaints to yourself and to me. Be meek with Baba. Marry Zardad, and when you have your first child he will love you like always.*

Now she was somewhere out there, and Khalid with all his vengeance in his right hand was out there too, and he was here, a pretend student in a pretend university about to play a pretend squash match, a puppet.

Should he call his father? Should he lie in wait for Khalid, while each day made it more certain that his brother had already cleansed the family honor with Afia's blood? Why had he not asked Khalid for his mobile number? The questions battered him while he stumbled through squash practice, while the police asked him more dumb questions.

The police had been two square-set white men, not in uniform but looking as though they ought to be, who'd collared him as he entered the dining hall. When the taller of the two, McPherson, flashed a badge at him, the first thing he'd thought was, *The car, the brakes, they know about the brakes*. When McPherson explained there had been an explosion, the soft wind outside the dining hall had felt suddenly ice cold, Shahid's arms and legs sticks of ice. "Is she—" he had started. When he couldn't finish, the shorter detective—Barlow—asked where his sister was; they were trying to reach her. "At Smith," he had said, and when they nodded he understood: There hadn't been body parts. Barlow asked if his sister had had a fight with Gus. He called Gus her boyfriend. Had she broken off with Gus over the weekend? Shahid must have looked confused because McPherson asked again. And Shahid saw they were asking not because they were worried but because they were suspicious. Of Afia! He'd strangled a laugh in his throat, a crazy laugh of farce and terror.

And where, McPherson wanted to know, had Shahid spent the day Sunday? "At my coach's house," he'd said—should he mention Afia was there?—"and at the library. I'm behind in a couple of classes. Oh, this girl I know saw me." Valerie, what an ironic joke. There he'd been, trying to block out thoughts of his family and write a paper about China's currency manipulation, and who should saunter into the study area but Valerie. She'd cut her hair and pierced one eyebrow—a little gold ring had glinted there, teasing for a tug. She'd leaned over Shahid's shoulder so he got a look at her cleavage in the V-neck of her cashmere sweater, and he'd smelled the same tempting perfume she'd worn last spring. She'd tried to talk to him like they were old pals. Then she'd made trip after trip through the room, carrying heavy art history books to the color photocopier. Each time he'd looked up, she'd either grinned or winked at him. She'd seen him, all right. She'd made his thing go hard, and he'd pushed his thoughts back to family just to quell it. A disease, Baba had called this love business, and how right he was.

"That'd help," McPherson said. "You got her phone number?"

Before they left, as if it were an afterthought, Barlow turned and asked if he'd quarreled last week with Gus. "Yeah," Shahid had said, not caring anymore what they thought. "He's dating my sister. That's not cool with us."

"Muslims, you mean," Barlow said with a little sneer, and Shahid said no, our family. But it's okay, he insisted, he and Gus were cool; and Barlow wrote that down.

Maybe people disappeared in this country like cats, gone for days then surfacing, their tails twitching in the air. Afia's plump roommate, Patty, wasn't acting worried. Tuesday night she called Shahid, told him to check at the Northampton Price Chopper. "The supermarket?" Shahid had asked, his eyes widening.

"Yeah, it occurred to me. She works there evenings when she doesn't have lab. Bagging, I think."

Bagging! His sister like a sweeper, cleaning up after people, her hands making straight their messes. What else had Afia hidden from him? He burst through the automatic doors and confronted the manager, a spindly man who brought over one of the yellow-haired checkout women. Maybe Afia was with her fella, the woman said pleasantly, poor fella had an accident, did Shahid know? They'd called her cell, the manager said, but she wasn't picking up. He'd give her a couple of days. Her next shift was Wednesday night.

Even Coach didn't seem all that worried about Afia, though she acted suspicious of him. Had he visited Gus? she wanted to know. And was his family really expecting Afia's return? Or had that been planned as a surprise?

By then he was beyond frantic. He moved his second appointment with Dr. Springer up to Wednesday. The therapist knew about Gus's garage; everyone knew. He seemed interested in Afia's disappearing. Wanted to know whether she might have been at the garage. Didn't seem to know his own wife had taken her back to Smith. Speculated on where she might have gone—to a friend's house? A professor's?

"I don't think so, sir. She hasn't gone to her classes, nothing."

"I imagine this is making you pretty jittery."

Just be honest with the guy, Afran had told him, he doesn't bite. "Well, sir, I'm afraid," he said.

"Because the police were questioning you?"

"No, sir. Because my sister could be dead."

Springer frowned. He wrote on the yellow pad. "Did you mention that fear to the police?"

"I talked to campus security, at her school. They said give her a couple of days. But she had a flight to catch!"

"Back to Pakistan, you mean."

"On Monday, yes, and now my father will be calling—"

"But it sounded as though she didn't want to go back. Couldn't she be . . . I don't know . . . hiding from you?"

"No, no. That is not it." Savagely Shahid dug with his pinky at the wax of his right ear. What good would it do, to tell this guy about Khalid? Springer would just send him to the police. If American police started on Khalid's trail—and Shahid didn't even know where that trail started—Khalid would only hasten the business of killing Afia, if he hadn't killed her already. "I don't know how I'm going to play this match," he said, "if I can't get my head straight about her."

Springer told him to call the police if he was really worried about Afia. He gave him a sheet of breathing exercises, ways to get centered. When Afia surfaced, Shahid should talk with her calmly about the best solution. No point forcing her. Of course not, Shahid responded, but Springer's words were so much static to him. He folded the paper and threw it out when he got back to campus for practice.

Hitting the squash ball, he emptied his head. On and on about Gus the other guys went. String of bad luck, Jamil said. Uh-uh, said Chander. Dude is getting targeted. What for? Well, he's Jewish. He keeps weird animals. Who the hell knows?

Shahid just hit the balls.

"You were on fire out there, man," Afran said when they'd showered.

"Yeah, well," said Shahid, his back to his buddy, toweling off. "We got Harvard Friday."

"Seriously. We talked to Coach, you know, we told her to let up on you. I think you'll have it easier now. She doesn't always get what's happening—"

"I don't care about Coach."

"Is it Gus?" Towel cinched around his slender waist, Afran came around to face him. A deep line furrowed his forehead. "I know you guys were wrong-footing each other, but they found his cat, so—"

"I got nothing against Gus. I need to go see him, that's all."

"Then it's your sister. Isn't it? Dude, talk to me."

Shahid's eyes burned. He slumped against his locker. "Everything's wrong," he said. "I should never have brought her here."

"Let's get out of this stinkhole, man. Let's drive around a little."

Sliding into Shahid's Civic, they made their way through town. Most of the story came out. Not draining Gus's brakes, not the sudden appearance of Khalid, but the final decision to send Afia back to Pakistan, to cut short her schooling, and then Afia's vanishing. "You did the right thing," Afran said, nodding. "She'll surface. Later on she'll be grateful to you. You can't blame yourself, dude. Other circumstances, it might have worked. She'd get the degree, go home, tend to women—"

"You don't get it," Shahid said. He stopped the car. They were across from the village green, where middle-aged ladies were taking down the Valentine's Day hearts. "Either someone is trying to hurt her," he said, "or my sister's gone mad."

"Who'd try to hurt her?"

Shahid scanned the green—scanning, he realized, for Khalid. Every thin dark man with a beard looked like Khalid to him, like Khalid had multiplied into a small stealth army. "Maybe there's someone else from my family here. I don't know."

"Or maybe she's just lying low. You don't think she had anything to do with the garage thing? I mean like accidentally."

"I don't think she even knows what happened. She hasn't called anyone."

"How do you know?"

Shahid pulled out his phone and waved it. "I got a family plan," he said. "I can see who she calls. I can track where she is if her phone's on. I never bothered till I found out, you know . . ."

"So where is she?"

Shahid pressed a series of buttons on the phone and showed it to Afran. "Nowhere. The phone's off or dead or she's in a dead zone."

"Do not say *dead*, man. She is not, like, dead." Afran pulled a pack of Twizzlers from his gym bag and handed Shahid one. He chewed thoughtfully on the other, watching the women lit by streetlights, on their ladders, the plastic hearts lifting and spinning in the breeze.

"She is not around." Shahid looked at the Twizzler. He hadn't eaten since breakfast. His mouth felt coated in sawdust. "And I've got these fucking plane tickets. I was supposed to send her home. Two days ago."

"And if you don't, what happens?" Afran ate his Twizzler, chewing thoughtfully. "Let me imagine. Your father is angry with you. Your uncle—what is his name?"

"Omar."

"Uncle Omar withdraws his financial support. You go to financial aid and you explain your position. This is a dramatic tragedy. Americans respond nicely to drama. And they do not want headlines about runaway Muslim squash players. You get my drift?"

"I am really not thinking," Shahid said, his hands on top of the steering wheel and his forehead on the back of his palms, "about how I pay for college, right now."

"Nothing else to think about, man. No one's hurt right now. Well, Gus with his accident, but he'll live. You bought that ticket last week?" Shahid nodded, rubbing his forehead against his hands. "Refundable, then. No harm done. You are not your sister's keeper."

"That's exactly"—Shahid lifted his head, then banged it onto his hands to punctuate each word—"what—I—am."

"Oops, then." Afran pulled out another Twizzler. When Shahid wouldn't take it, he laid it gently on the dash. "That's what you say in this country. Oops."

. . .

Back in his room, Shahid checked the family map again. The bubble popped up on his phone's screen: *Afia is out of range or her phone is off. Please try again later.* Again he texted her; again called and got her voice mail. He stood by the window looking onto the quad. In Nasirabad, it was eight in the morning. Shutting his eyes as he pressed the numbers by heart, he phoned his father.

"I have been so anxious," Baba said when they had made their way past greetings. "Have you bought this ticket, to send her home? I was thinking perhaps she should come into Islamabad. I could drive there, give us the time on the road to talk about what she has done to us, how she can still set things right."

"I—I have bought a ticket, yes, Baba." Did his father know nothing? Or was he pretending, softening Shahid so he would send Afia back to be sacrificed? For Shahid to admit that he had lost track of his sister . . . no. He pressed his forehead against the cold windowpane as he spoke. "But we—we need a few more days."

"She is a clever girl, my son. You need to be strong. This is not her decision."

"I know that, Baba."

"I am a modern man. I listen to my daughter as well as my sons. But she forfeited the right to my listening ear when she forfeited our honor."

"Baba, we still don't know if—"

"No!" his father shouted. "I am tired of discussing this! First I must defend myself—me, the chief of the household!—against a brother-in-law who tells me I fail to do pashtun. Then I have your mother moaning that she will be invited nowhere, she is reduced to ashes. Then my older son telling me I have placed my hopes in the wrong offspring, and what should I have said to him?"

A tear rolled down Shahid's cheek. However short he had fallen of his life's ambitions, never before had he failed to please his father. "What did you say to him?" he asked at last.

"I said," Baba answered, "he had my blessing."

"Blessing?"

Baba sighed. "He has left again. For a longer time, he says. For jihad."

What sort of jihad, Shahid wanted to ask, *is killing your sister?* "But he sent you the third photograph," Shahid said. "I understand, it means a punishment—"

"What third photograph? Your uncle in Peshawar has the Internet. He's said nothing about another photograph."

With the phone to his ear, Shahid opened his laptop. One-handed he typed in his sister's name and clicked *Images*. Photos of Afia brand corn oil popped up; of women named Afia Mazhar and Nura Afia. He checked Facebook pages for Taylor; for Taylor's boyfriend, Chase; for Gus. No photos of Afia, whether kissing Gus in a bed or reaching for apples. "What of Zardad's family?" he managed to ask his father as he tapped keys.

"Inshallah, they still know nothing. No one in town suspects my daughter of anything but ambition. What third photo do you speak of?"

No photos on the Smith College website. On Campusconnect, a pasted version of the image from the old site, Afia with her hand in someone else's, in Gus's. Nothing more. "I—I don't know, Baba. Maybe I am just losing track. She is so sad, to be leaving her studies—"

"She brings it on herself. Get her home soon as you can. Before any third photo, or something worse. I count on you."

As he hung up, Shahid felt his head explode. How blind he had been! He had said it himself to Khalid in Nasirabad: *Shame casts a wide net.* Khalid wasn't about to blast incriminating photos of his sister all over the Internet—he would lose face himself. And at the hospital Afia had said the truth: *There haven't been any other pictures. I'm not stupid.* Afia had not posted the photo he'd seen, briefly—and Baba had seen as well—on Facebook. Khalid had posted it. Khalid had gotten hold of the photo somehow. When? The image had appeared on Taylor's timeline in early January, but it was a photo from fall, an apple orchard. Afia must have had it on her phone, in Nasirabad. You post to a Facebook timeline, there's little chance that the world of Nasirabad will see the photo, but every chance that your siblings in America will, and you can always show it to Baba. You can set things in motion to have your sister's dreams crushed, or even get her killed. You do this not because you want your sister dead. You do not care one way or the other about her; she is nothing. You do it because it will put the brother you hate in a vise. He will bear the brunt of the shame, and if you are very lucky, he will be forced to wield the weapon.

He, Shahid, was the stupid one, the gullible one. His father's business was intact. His little sisters were going to school unmolested. His mother was worried, yes, but she was always worried; no one refused to extend her invitations. Khalid would cause Afia's death not to preserve honor, but to mortify Shahid, setting it up so that Shahid would execute his sister for a crime that no one—save Khalid—had yet condemned. How could he not have seen through this? He clicked on his computer's calendar. Ten days ago, he had spoken with his father, had learned of the photo that Khalid must have posted to Taylor's page. So Khalid could not have arrived in the States earlier than a week ago. Yet there Khalid had been, four days ago, claiming that a photograph that he alone could have taken—after he had tracked down Afia, followed her to the hospital—had already wreaked destruction on all the Satars.

What was that play Afia had helped him with, for his

Shakespeare class, where there hadn't been time for the bad things to have happened? *Othello*, that was it. Iago, the serpent, convincing his master that Desdemona had been unfaithful once, twice, thrice, and only a single afternoon had passed. Khalid was Iago; he, the gullible Othello. "That guy's an idiot," one of the students had said, and they had all laughed, laughed at Othello.

He could kill Khalid with his bare hands. The jealous serpent, the betrayer.

He checked his family map again. Tried Afia's number again. Texted again.

Next morning, his heart like a boulder in his chest, he gathered his books and went to class. Across the quad, he felt eyes following him. But when he turned around, the two cops who'd questioned him were nowhere to be seen. Nothing but bright young students on the thin white carpet of snow, their heads bare to the frigid afternoon sun.

CHAPTER NINETEEN

Thursday night Afia lay awake, conjuring her fate. Enright would play their big game against Harvard Friday afternoon. In another world, she would have persuaded Patty to drive with her to Devon to watch the battle; she would have jumped up and clapped for Shahid at each point, no matter if he won or lost. That world had blown up. The match would happen without her. Maybe without Shahid, if the police had rejected his alibi. If they arrested him, Coach Hayes would step in. To save Shahid, the coach would tell them she was hiding Afia. The police, or the FBI, would soon be driving the winding road up through Hadley. Or no—Shahid would hear of her hiding place, and the moment the police let him go he would take that same road. He could be heading here right now, determined to do his duty to Baba.

Her death was inevitable. No *nanawate* for *tora*. She needed to focus, to prepare herself for it.

In the darkness she lay rigid on her back, expecting the sound of wheels in the icy drive. Footfalls, a knock at the door. But she heard only the owl hoot in the cold trees, the burning wood crack in the stove. The forty-eight hours had come and gone, and Coach Hayes had not fetched her back, had not forced her to make good on her promise to talk to the police. But that was only because of the Harvard match. After the match, Coach Hayes would lose her patience. She would return and bring the police with her. Escaping the bed for a glass of water and to tuck another log into the stove, Afia stared at the wall phone in the kitchen, lit only by moonlight. She knew Gus's number by heart. At the thought of his voice greeting her, the little pet names he used, *M'Afia*, *Afiance*, she felt a burning ache below her ribs. If she couldn't have his touch, she hungered for his voice. But calls from a landline could be traced; she'd seen it, on television. Holding herself back, she listened hard. Only the wind, the owl again, her own staccato breathing.

Shivering, she returned to the bed and huddled, her knees against her chest. Dead, she would be with Allah, she would rest wherever he took her. But where was that, if she was so blackened? She drifted into sleep, startled awake at a dream that vanished, drifted again. As darkness lifted away from the window, she pulled herself from bed and fired up the stove. It was hard to stay focused on death, to prepare yourself for a blow with no set arrival time. By full light, she had warmed her belly with tea, found a pair of clean socks in the bedroom dresser, and laced up the boots Shahid had bought for her. Swathed in all the clothing she had, she unlocked the door and stepped out into pale February light.

Somewhere, in these hills, there had to be a mobile phone signal. The authorities couldn't trace a mobile number—or if they could, it would take them longer. Gus would recognize that she was ringing; he would clutch his phone to his ear, overjoyed that she was alive. He would help her. He would give her the right ideas. In any case, she thought as she crunched clumsily down the road southward, she could not go another day without hearing his voice.

There had been fresh snow most of yesterday, and for at least two miles Afia saw no sign of tire tracks or any human activity—only shuttered country cabins sleeping in the trees. Through the bare trunks, now and then, she glimpsed the silvery snake of the Hudson River, flowing to the sea. She crossed train tracks that ran alongside the road, then crossed back again. At one point thick truck marks emerged from a long driveway that stretched up a steep hill from the road. She checked her phone: no signal. Fifteen minutes later, a truck passed her. The driver, in a checkered cap, waved before spraying a wake of cold white. The day was bright, as it so often was in this country the day after a snowfall, and even in the thin air she began to sweat. She loosened her jacket and wool scarf. A thin white cotton mantle she'd found in a cabin drawer served to cover her hair. She kept checking the phone. No signal at the turn in the road where she saw three deer; no signal where the power lines cut across the road and carved a swath descending the hill into the blue distance; no signal by the ramshackle house with smoke coming from its chimney and a pit bull growling and snapping from a chain on a clothesline.

The sun rose higher. Snow melted and dripped from the conifers. For the first time in her life, no one in her family knew even remotely where she was. Had Zardad's family broken the engagement yet? She remembered the girls in her hall at Smith asking her about arranged marriage, the first semester she'd been there. "Let me get this straight," one of them had said. "You've never kissed a guy, no guy has ever touched you anywhere under your clothes. But the very first night you meet this man someone else picked out for you, you're going to have sex with him."

She had been so flustered. Yes, she had admitted, it was like that, but it wasn't like that. It was two families, joining, it wasn't about what happened that particular night. It was a matter of trust, she'd said, of trusting your parents.

Her parents, who had trusted her. Her eyes burned, thinking of it.

"Just consider this," one of the girls—it might have been Taylor—asked after Afia had done her best to explain how marriage was for Pashtuns. "Consider that there's this guy you really love, and he suggests you try it out."

She had frowned. "Try what out?"

"Marriage. For like a year. Set up housekeeping, live together. See if you're like really compatible. How would that sound, to you?"

Her mouth had gaped, trying to take in what this American girl was proposing. Then she had managed to say, glancing from one pale, eager face to the next, "Not . . . *physically*."

They had laughed. They had all laughed. Now she had some idea what they had been laughing about. And it was something to be ashamed of, something that should make you want to die from shame. But she didn't want to die. She wanted to hear Gus's voice.

She felt a blister growing on her left heel. The houses appeared more often, ranch houses by the road, cars gleaming in the driveways. "You okay, sweetheart?" called one woman shoveling her stoop.

As brightly as she could, Afia called back, "Fine, thanks!"

Finally—after four hours' walking, according to the phone she kept flipping open with her clumsy gloves—she reached the sign for Hadley, and the tiny half pyramid of horizontal lines on the top left of her screen began dancing up and down. Ahead, she saw a sign for the Hadley General Store. Her exhaustion suddenly gone, she trotted along the road and let herself into the shop's warm space. Her eyes, accustomed to the bright sunlight off the snow, blinked in what felt like sudden darkness. In the front, half-bare shelves and a wall of coolers. Toward the back, a counter, a gas fireplace, four little round tables with chairs.

"Sit down, honey," said a thin woman with sandy hair pinned back and a pencil over her ear. "You want coffee?"

"Soup?" Afia tried.

"We got chicken noodle."

"Yes, thank you, please. Chicken noodle."

She slid out a chair and sat. Her toes had gone numb. Her face flushed in the sudden warmth. She was terribly thirsty, and when the thin waitress put a plastic glass of water in front of her she gulped it down.

"Where you from, hon?"

"Just . . . around," she said.

The woman's face roamed over her improvised dupatta, her dark eyebrows. "Didn't see your car pull up."

"I walked."

The woman gave a little bark of a laugh. "Where from? Nobody in this town I don't know."

"I sort of . . . went for a hike," Afia said, trying to Americanize her accent.

"Hmph," the woman said. She retreated behind the counter. Afia noted a phone on the wall. Would she call the police? Afia needed to make her call and get out. She rubbed her hands together, to get the fingers working. There were twenty-one missed calls on her mobile, six from Gus. He'd never rung her mobile before. He knew the number, but she worried Shahid could ask to check her phone. Now it didn't matter. She highlighted the call and pressed the green button. He picked up after two rings. "M'Afia."

She began to cry. "I had to run away," she managed to say. "I'm sorry, I'm so sorry."

"Where *are* you?"

"Somewhere . . . I don't know."

"You all right? I've been nuts, since Sunday night—"

"I am sorry, to be worrying you. Are you out of hospital?"

"Since Monday, for what good that does. I have no home, which you obviously know."

His voice sounded strange—more nasal than usual, as if he were twisting something inside. "I—I do know," Afia said. The waitress brought over the soup and left it on the edge of the table, as if she would rather not come too close. Afia lowered her voice. "I was there, when the bomb went off. It was terrifying. When I think of your pets—"

"What do you mean, you were there? Coach said she took you to Northampton!"

"She—she did. I—I came back. I left my books so I, I borrowed a car. And came back. That's when it happened." Afia's brain felt like the centrifuge they used in bio lab, the words whirring around so fast they lost hold of their meaning.

"And then you just . . . ran off?"

"I sort of, well, I panicked." She should never have phoned, she saw that now. He must suspect her of the worst thing—of setting a bomb at his garage, to explode when he returned there from the hospital. That was what Shahid had done, unless Shahid had meant to bring Afia first to the garage. She would never know which of their deaths, really, her brother had been after. Now Gus's voice sounded full of doubt, and her lying wasn't clearing the doubt away. But she couldn't hang up, not yet. "What of your injuries? You can walk?"

"On crutches, yeah. And they've plastered a brace onto my back. I'm at my mom's place. I should get ninety percent of my mobility back."

"Oh, Gus, I am so glad."

"Where the hell are you, Afia? Why would you *run*?"

"It is complicated. Soon I'm going to be back."

"Well, you'd better. Cops are investigating everything. You're not around, so they're after you. Aren't you hurt?"

"No, no, I'm fine. Some scrapes, yes, but fine. These . . . cops. What do they think happened?"

"They don't know." An edge of irritation in his voice. "That's why it's called an investigation, Afia. You know everyone died but Ebay."

"I did not know. But I thought probably. Yes. I am so, so—"

"And you know what else they're investigating."

That didn't sound like a question, but he paused. Afia lifted a spoonful of soup to her mouth and burned her tongue. "What else?" she said, reaching for the glass of water.

"They're investigating my so-called car accident. They found signs of foul play, Afia."

She didn't like how he kept using her name. It scared her. It reminded her of how her mother had kept using her name, when she first talked about becoming engaged to Zardad. Now Gus was going on about what the police had found. Damage to his brake line; fluid had leaked. They were asking him about enemies he might have, people he might owe money to, crap like that. Trying to tie the two incidents together, the car accident and the explosion. *The brakes*, Afia thought. Twice, Shahid had tried—to kill Gus? To kill her? It hardly mattered. "And all we really know," Gus said, "is that you disappeared. Afia, the fuzz are getting a little curious here."

The nasal edge to his voice hadn't changed. *Fuzz*, what was fuzz? She needed him so badly, and the voice on the other end was listing only her faults. "Gus," she said, tears beginning to drop into the soup, "I love you."

"I love you too, Afiance, but this is not adding up."

"I want to explain everything to you. You can help me so I know what to do."

"What to do was go to the police, Afia. You were at the house when a freaking *bomb* went off, and you didn't go to the police!" His voice was rising, in sound and pitch. "If you have nothing to do with the brakes or that bomb—well shit, Afia, why would you run off? Why don't you come back right now and tell the cops everything?"

Afia tried the soup again. It was warm and salty. She checked the clock on the wall: 1:30 P.M. on a Friday. Normally Gus would be in class. She would just be going to Victorian Lit, where they were finishing *Jane Eyre* with a discussion of Jane's final power over Mr. Rochester. "I do not think," she said softly, "I can ever come back."

"I don't get you, Afia. Two really bad things happen to me, and then you disappear."

"One of those," Afia tried to say, though her voice felt thick, "happened to me. I was almost killed."

"Baby, I know. I know. But we've got to trust each other, okay? You need to tell me where you are."

"I cannot." She needed to get to the bathroom. She needed to vomit. She loved Gus so much that it hurt her inside, because now she could tell he didn't love her any more, he thought she would harm him, he spoke her name now like an accusation. "I have to go," she said. "I'll ring you again soon."

"Afia, fuck! Where are you?"

"I'm so sorry. I—" She wanted to tell him she would make it up to him, would get him back his books, his animals, his happy life. "It isn't you," she said, "they want to hurt. I promise."

"I don't trust you, Afia. This really pisses me off. Afia—"

But she had shut the phone. She was racing toward the back of the shop, to the sign that said *Restrooms*.

CHAPTER TWENTY

If the Enright men's squash team beat Harvard, Shahid would be on his way to a shining future, and Lissy's vision for athletics at Enright would have a clear road before it. If they lost, she had begun to realize, her head could be on the chopping block. Her recruits might finish their four years at Enright, but the athletics department would fall back to where it was when she began, spending precious resources on big-name sports like football without the big players or media-savvy coaches to back them up. But if her kids beat Harvard . . . no, she had to stop going there. Her chest got bunched up; her eyes stung. If they won she would snap her fingers, set everything else to rights. It all began, they'd say years from now, that day they beat Harvard.

Shahid has a big game tomorrow, Afia had said, last time Lissy spoke with her on the phone. *When that is finished, I do something. I make everything all right for Shahid. For Gus, too.*

Lissy had told her not to worry about Gus. Gus had family. She needed to worry about herself, and go to the police. As soon as the Harvard match was finished. Promise?

Promise, Afia had said.

Friday morning, sweating on the stationary bike in the workout room, Lissy ran the afternoon's lineup through her head. Shahid at one, Afran at two, Chander at three. She'd put Yanik at four in spite of his mouth, because he was a fighter and in his last year. Jamil at five, Carlos at six, Johan at seven, Chris at eight. Tom, with a brace on his ankle, in place of Gus at nine. Among the women, Kaitlin was out with mono. She'd put Margot at one, Evie at two, Meaghan at three. . . . When she had run through both teams, she speculated on the Harvard lineups. Amazing how you could set aside what didn't bear thinking about. The blue Hyundai, Gus's dead animals, Afia. Ethan was counting the days, judging her for not going to thc police. Too competitive, too ambitious, pigheaded. The cops themselves had asked her to stop by, answer a few questions.

All of it, she put aside. Only the words remained, looping through her head: *honor crime, honor killing.*

Her players were in their uniforms promptly at 3:45, the Enright blue the color of the sky as the sun dipped. The girls chattered in their excitement; the boys fidgeted. "I am *so* going to lose to that Scottish girl," said Meaghan.

"If she's mine I will punish that bitch," said Margot. "I still remember how she dissed Lydia last year at Nationals. You remember that?"

"They diss everyone," said Afran. "That's their MO."

"Bigots, mon," Jamil chimed in.

Gus hobbled in on crutches, his jersey tight over his back brace, his leg cast extending from foot to midthigh and graffitied in rainbow colors. Men and women rose as one and gave him a standing ovation. He tried to smile. "You guys are the best," he said. Lissy kept half an eye on Shahid, who seemed as glad as the rest but didn't come around to clap Gus on the back. At least, Lissy noticed, he had shaved.

"How you feeling?" she asked Gus, putting her arm around his shoulders while the others started stretching.

"Confused, Coach," he said. His eyes scanned her face. He looked to be the youngest of her players, though he wasn't. It was the freckles and red hair, maybe, or the broad cheeks, the grin without a trace of smirk. He wasn't grinning now. He leaned toward her, spoke softly. "You know who called me just now?"

Lissy frowned. "The police?"

He shook his head. "You can't tell anyone," he said. Lissy nodded. "Afia."

"Really." Lissy held Gus's gaze, her eyes wanting to dart to the nearest exit. She would never be able to bluff her way through this. "Where is she?"

"That's just it. She wouldn't say. Says she went back to my place, after you dropped her in Northampton. That's what triggered the, you know. The bomb. Then she took off. I don't know where. Maybe she's right here in Devon. Just hiding."

Lissy's hand went to her mouth; she spoke through her fingers. "Did you tell the police?"

"Not yet. She seemed so . . . scared." He glanced over at Shahid, doing squats. "Like the thing was meant for her. I really don't want to believe—I mean, the cops already talked to him, right? And he's got a tight alibi. Right?"

"Gus, why would Shahid want to hurt his sister?" She wanted to retract the words as soon as they were out.

Gus shrugged. "He's crazy jealous, Coach. That's all I got. Maybe it's like a Muslim thing. Only I don't think he knows a damn thing about making a bomb."

"Course not." Lissy tried to think. Afia had called Gus. She had to be preparing herself, to set aside her fear and come forward. All to the good. "I don't see where it helps to second-guess the police, Gus. The main thing is, is Afia all right?"

"Yeah. Yeah." With his brows furrowed, Gus looked like a fifteen-year-old puzzling out a knotty problem in calculus. "I think I should talk to him," he said, and started toward Shahid.

Lissy caught his crutch. "Why don't you wait till after the match?"

"I don't see how he can even play, not knowing what's happened to his sister."

"Maybe playing gives him some relief."

"But if he knows she's safe—" he began. He leaned on his crutches. Doubt sliced across his face. "You're right," he said. "I can wait till she calls again."

"Let's talk more," Lissy said, touching his shoulder, "after the match."

He pressed his lips together and tried to smile. "Thanks, Coach."

She took a deep breath: relief, however temporary. Quickly she stepped away from the chattering teams, into the atrium with its picture window onto the quad. She keyed the landline at the cabin into her phone. It rang a dozen times, no answer.

"Coach?" she heard from the hallway.

"Coming," she called back. Returning, she pocketed her phone and clapped her hands. "Ladies and gentlemen," she began. "You look terrific, every one of you. You are ready for this match. You are more than ready. You've been climbing a mountain, and you're on the ridge, you've got the view. So what are we going out there to get?"

"A win!" called Meaghan.

"Wins are nice. They're the peaks, you know, the photo ops. But we are after something bigger. What?"

Chander—the oldest and smallest of the men, a bulldog of an

athlete, hoping for med school—gave the answer. "We are seeking honor."

"Honor, yes," Lissy said. For the first time the word stuck in her throat. "When we are done with the players on Coach Bradley's team, they will hold us in the highest regard. They will set themselves a goal"—she held up one of her hands, flat, palm downward—"to rise to our level." She held out the other hand, a foot higher than the first hand. The fidgeting stopped. She had their attention. "And how do we make that happen?" She rocked the upper hand, keeping it high.

"We play," said Jamil with his broadest Jamaican accent, "our fockin' hearts out."

Afran high-fived him. Lissy dropped her arms. "That's about it," she said. "Keep it clean, ladies and gents. You play for each other. You play for Enright. You play for—for respect."

Then they were jogging out to the courts amid a ripple of applause from the stands.

The men played first. All George Bradley needed to win was his top five. They started with matches six through nine in the lineup. Tom, as Lissy might have predicted, fought valiantly, but he'd come back from his injury too recently and went down in straight games. Johan and Carlos, on the other hand, seemed to thrive on the jeers from the visiting crowd; they nicked and volleyed their way to wins, each in three close games. Chris hung on in the third, trading points to 13 all, then pulled out a pair of boasts that she'd never seen him make in practice, and flung his arms skyward. As the top five starters went on, the match score stood at 3–1 in Enright's favor.

"Your guys came out to play today," Bradley said as he joined her to watch Shahid warm up.

"No different from other days," Lissy said, trying to believe her own words.

Shahid faced off against a short, square Singaporean Chinese whom Bradley had recruited just this year. His warm-up looked relaxed, his legs springy and strong, the ball his genie. Bradley seemed to be watching him as much as his own player. "He looks," he said as the game started in earnest, "as if he plans to slice the flesh from my boy with a neat razor."

"I don't expect your boy will let that happen," Lissy said, though as Shahid captured the first four points in a few strokes, she suspected the Singaporean wouldn't have a lot of choice in the matter.

In the first game, Lissy tried not to hover. The crowd had begun to swell. She stepped into the stands, glad-handing the loyal squash groupies, introducing herself to the sprinkling of parents—the women's parents mostly, who were Americans—who'd driven long distances to watch. At the top of the bleachers she found Ethan, with Chloe in his lap.

"Buenos tardes, Mamí!" Chloe sang out.

Lissy's heart sang, to see her girl here. Every winter was brutal this way, sucking away her time with Chloe. And these weeks—this crazy, dangerous week—had distracted her worse than ever. So, yes, hard for Chloe to come to games and get almost no attention, but Lissy was thrilled to see her. She picked her up and kissed her warm cheek. She thought of the Valentine's card Chloe had made, pinned to the fridge at home: four layers of doilies and precut hearts glued at angles on a sheet of pink construction paper. "You going to cheer on our team?" she asked.

"Go Rockwells!" Chloe shouted.

Lissy chuckled. She set her back down. "You just keep thinking good thoughts, cutie," she said. Quickly she glanced toward the courts. Afran was already behind 2–7; Shahid was holding steady, 6–4. To Ethan she said, "Great of you to come watch."

"I'm as anxious to see this through as you," he said. His smile was strained. He leaned toward her. "Win or lose," he said, "you tell me where that girl is, and we go to the police. Deal?"

"Deal, honey. And thank you." She squeezed his hand, though he didn't respond.

He glanced over her shoulder. "Looks like you've got some VIPs."

Lissy followed Ethan's gaze to the squash center entrance. Sure enough, Don Shears and Charles Horton were shedding their wool coats, glancing around for advantageous seating. "Mommy's got to go," Lissy said. "Keep cheering."

"Yay!" cried Chloe behind her. "Go Rockwells!"

Putting on her most confident face, Lissy approached her boss. "How great of you to come, Don."

"Charles wanted to see what this ragtag group of yours was capable of," Shears said with a meaningful wink.

"This may not be their finest hour." Lissy forced herself to turn to Horton. Under the lights of the gallery his skin looked like soap. His thin lips curled in a predatory smile. "We're up at the moment. But each match goes to the best three of five games. Harvard's ranked second in the nation. We hover between twelfth and fifteenth. Which isn't shabby for a five-year-old program, but—"

"But the hell with school pride," said Horton, his smile fixed on his face, "so long as everyone gets their cardiovascular workout."

Lissy felt stung. She gestured toward the bleachers. "Plenty of school pride here, I think," she said. "And they come for the football games, too."

"Yeah, I know. I know." Horton's gaze was drawn to the first court just as Shahid jumped to smash a volley. A round of clapping from the bleachers. "That's the boy from the dinner, isn't it?"

Lissy nodded. "Shahid Satar," she said. "He's got a shot at winning the individual championships, once the season's done. Nationally, I mean."

He thrust out his lower lip. "Impressive." Then he fixed his cool eyes on her. "I don't like this kind of Europe sport," he said, "and I don't think women should direct athletics or platoons. But you win this thing"—he pointed rapidly to the other courts—"and you've got yourself the fanciest fitness center in the land."

"We'll do our best," Lissy said. She heard the squeak in her voice. "I've got to keep an eye on the courts," she said. "There should be good seats—let me see—" She glanced upward in the gallery. A handful of female players, in their squash clothes, caught her eye and squeezed sideways. When she turned back to Shears and Horton, they were leering like frat boys. "Fourth row center," she offered.

"Suits me," said Horton, pressing Lissy's shoulder as they passed.

At the first break, all of Lissy's starters, except Shahid, were down. Worse, the Harvard supporters had begun their catcalling. Near Jamil they riffed, "He dey Rasta mon, he got joint account in de bank, he bring his spliff dere mon," while Jamil hung his head and sucked on his water. In front of Afran, they minced with towels on their heads. "Call them off, goddammit," Lissy said to Bradley.

"You think they listen to me?" Bradley said. But he hustled the towel-wearers out of the area. Lissy went down the line, encouraging her players. Shahid should keep hammering his big serve. Afran needed to start nicking. Jamil could wear his guy down with lobs. Yanik, who'd lost a first-game squeaker at 14–12, should keep up the straight drives, just tighter and faster. She saw Gus, his casted leg thrust out in front, sitting with Chander, giving him a pep talk. Keep them focused on the game, not on the outcome; that was the mandate. As they went back out, she prowled the aisle in front of the glass cages. Chander and Afran began fighting back, while Shahid took apart his opponent's game with the methodical logic of a surgeon. The razzing from Harvard supporters grew louder. The Enright crowd tried razzing back, but as Yanik flailed and Jamil missed shot after shot, they grew silent and sullen. Like peasants, Lissy thought, at a contest with the lords of the manor. In the middle of the stands, Shears and Horton were engaged in an animated debate, paying no attention to the action on the courts. From the top of the stands, Ethan gave her a thumbs-up. On his left stood a spectator she hadn't seen before, a lithe man in dark fleece and pressed jeans who was cheering for neither Harvard nor Enright. She thought he looked like Shahid, then berated herself for thinking like Horton and the Harvard crowd, as if all dark, brown, lean men were related to each other.

On the courts, something was shifting. Yanik and Jamil lost their second games quickly, but Chander and Afran were trading points with their opponents. Shahid had risen to 10–6 amid squabbles about lets. The Singaporean kid was casting looks out at his supporters, cocking his head toward Shahid as if to say, *Can you believe this raghead?* The match began to tip the other way: 7–10, 8–10, 10–9, 10 all, 11–10. Suddenly Shahid's opponent stretched up for an impossible volley and cracked it across the side and front walls, into the nick, and the second game was over. Playing to best of five, the top five matches now stood at 2–0 Harvard for Yanik and Jamil but one apiece for the other three.

As soon as Shahid was off the court and drinking water, Lissy pulled him aside. They huddled close together on the bench. Shahid was dripping sweat. "Just stay calm," she told him. "Keep steady. You've got him."

"He's calling me names," Shahid said between clenched teeth. "Chinese, you know, they hate us. Singapore Chinese specially. Pakistanis are *dirt* to them."

"We call that bigotry, Shahid. Ignore it."

"I could kill him. Bare-handed. I could—"

"Beat him, Shahid. Just beat him. One point at a time." Lissy sat back. She didn't like the way she was talking. She never told her players to beat anyone. She told them to do their best, to live in the moment, to gain respect. Only the tide *was* turning—she could feel it—and Shahid was at the tip of the wave. She gripped his sweaty shoulder. "Do not retaliate," she said in a low voice. "Just beat him."

When she stood up, she saw Afran exiting his court, beaming. Less than a minute later, Chander came off and high-fived his teammates. Both those matches now stood at 2–1 Enright. Lissy spoke with Afran, then stood back and let the six who had finished move in, joking to ease the tension. The Harvard crowd had quieted. Lissy stepped over to crouch next to Chander. From the corner of her eye she saw Gus hobbling to the other end of the row of glass courts, where Shahid was going back on.

"I think I've got him," Chander said. "He can handle my slice, but when I follow up on that side, he's wrong-footed. I got five points that way."

"Great. But don't count on one shot. Play a series. Use the whole court."

"Where's Shahid at?"

"Way up. Now keep the pressure on."

Shahid was bouncing the ball, preparing to serve, white-hot with anger. Instinctively Lissy glanced toward the bleachers—in previous matches, opposing teams had unfurled banners with slogans like *Smoke the Camels*—but she saw only a tense, buzzing crowd. Horton and Shears were deep in conversation. Ethan, with Chloe in his lap, was still on the top row. The dark stranger stood next to them, holding his chin in his palm. Something hostile in the guy's stance. Who was he? She waved at Chloe and turned back to the court. Shahid was playing a laser-sharp game. He feathered the ball into the corners, attacked from the back wall. His face wore the mask of a vengeful god. And still the score climbed toward Harvard: 3–2, 3–3, 4–3, 4–4, 4–5, 4–6, 4–7.

Behind her, the Enright crowd bloomed into life. "We will, we will ROCKWELL!" the students began chanting as Chander took a quick lead in his fourth game. Afran clawed back from 3–7 to 9–7 in his third. George Bradley was pacing before the courts, stopping to plant his hands on his hips, his face grimly set. The women's squad jumped up and clapped for every point Enright gained.

A strange calm took hold of Lissy. She had felt it before, this slowing of time, this rebalancing of sound. The cheers and jeers of the crowd receded; the footfalls and hot breaths of the players echoed in her ears. She had felt it at the British Open when she reached the round of sixteen. She had known the same feeling just once before as a coach, at Rutgers, when the smallest and bravest of her tennis players fought her way into a third set as the sun slowly sank, and went down in the tiebreaker. The feeling was like a dream of flying, where the destination doesn't matter, only the need to remain aloft. And so she forgot about the fitness center, about the bomb, about Afia. Only these young men mattered—and then Chander won the fourth game, countering Yanik's 1–3 loss and bringing the team score to 4–2, Enright.

Lissy turned to Afran's game. Her breath skipped. The score was 10–7 in favor of Afran. In what seemed like slow motion to Lissy, Afran charged awkwardly across the court in front of his opponent. He tripped, or was tripped, and sailed across the court into the side wall. The crowd groaned. Lissy nodded at the trainer, Sandy, who made his way swiftly through the standing spectators. From the court, Sandy called for a five-minute medical time-out. He brought Afran, limping, off the court, and Lissy shooed the rest of the team away to crouch at his side.

"Is it your ankle?" she asked.

Afran shook his head. As he pulled off his goggles, tears glimmered in his eyes. "Fucker tripped me," he said.

"Call for a stroke. If he tripped you, you can take all the time you need—"

"He'll say I charged him. I know this guy. Anyway, it doesn't matter."

"Why?"

Afran nodded toward his right wrist, which Sandy was examining. As he applied pressure, Afran winced.

"Sprained, I think," Sandy said. "I can tape it, but if there's a fracture—"

"Give me the racquet," Afran said. Lissy handed it to him. He wrapped his fingers around the handle and gripped. Then he let it clatter to the ground.

"If he caused the injury," Lissy said, "it's your match."

"He caused it. But I didn't call it in time."

"You can call it now," Lissy said. She held her breath. Afran's match would make it 5–2 Enright, and a clear win.

"You said we were out for honor, Coach," Afran answered after a pause. "You think waiting five minutes to call dangerous play will gain me any honor?"

Lissy met his eyes. Bursting with sorrow and pride in him, she shook her head. Afran stood. He held his left hand out to his opponent. "Nice match," he said.

Enright was still up, 4–3. She glanced toward Jamil's court. He was in his fourth game, facing match point. "Tough break," Bradley said, coming to stand beside Lissy.

"What do you think happened?"

He glanced sideways at her. "You're going to say my guy tripped yours."

"I'm not saying anything. I'm asking."

"Basil's the sweetest kid on our squad."

"Then I'm sorry they couldn't finish the match."

They looked at one another. There was no going back. Afran might have made the wrong call, but he had done the right thing. "Well, I'm sorry for your guy," Bradley said. "He'll be out a while, I guess."

"Perils of a contact sport," said Lissy wryly.

Then, with her heart shifting in her chest, she looked over to Court One. Shahid had lost the third game; the score stood at 2–1 in favor of his opponent. He was slumped on the bottom bleacher, and Gus sat next to him, the white cast jutting into the lane between bleachers and courts. Gus was leaning close, gesturing with his hands. Slowly Shahid's face widened, eyes and mouth, as if something inside were pressing his bones outward. He turned. He fished in his bag. He bent over, pushing numbers on his cell phone. He stared at it. Then he stood. He began packing his bag.

"Time," Lissy heard Bradley say.

Gus was up, unsteady on his crutches. "Hey, man," he was saying as Lissy pushed through the crowd. "That's supposed to inspire you. You can't *quit*."

Reaching the two players, she leaned close. "What did you tell him?" she hissed at Gus.

"That she's alive, she's okay. He was bummed. He was losing. I thought—"

But Shahid was moving, shaking his head at the guys crowding around him, making his way to the exit. Lissy wove around him and stood at the door, legs apart. She stared him down. "Jamil's losing. That takes us to four all," she said. "It's your match, Shahid."

"Let me go, Coach."

"There's nothing for you to do outside this door. Not right now. Inside, you've got a job."

"I know where she is." His eyes burned at her. His face glowed with sweat. He was going to knock her down.

"No, you don't," she said. Then she saw the cell phone in his hand.

She remembered. *We've got this family map thing.* Afia hadn't called Gus from the cabin. She'd gone somewhere to use her cell, and kept the cell on. "Twenty minutes," she said desperately, "won't make a difference. You owe this to us, Shahid." She nodded at Gus, who had hobbled up next to Shahid. "You owe it," she said in a voice of iron, "to him."

Shahid took a long look at Gus. His eyes traveled from his teammate's pale face to his braced torso and the decorated cast. His hand gripped Gus's shoulder for a moment. "I owe more to her," he said. Then he muscled his way past Lissy, into the hallway and down the metal stairs.

"I'm sorry, Coach," Gus said. "I thought—"

"Don't," she said. She held up a hand. George Bradley was coming her way.

"Looks like your guy's got an emergency," he said.

"Looks like."

"So he's defaulting?"

Lissy fought back tears of panic and frustration. "Looks like," she managed. She turned to the Singaporean, the one who had been calling Shahid names. "Congratulations," she said.

They would lose, now. Team score was tied at 4 all, and Jamil had been down 2–1 in games and 10–6 in the fourth game. Glancing into the stands, she saw Ethan on his feet, his arms raised from the elbow, palms upward, universal for *What the hell?* She shook her head at him. Suddenly Don Shears was at her side. "What in God's name is happening here?"

"I can't explain it, Don. This isn't like Shahid."

"Well, I've got almost a million dollars sitting in the bleachers, says we need a miracle."

Lissy didn't answer. She needed to leave. She needed to try the landline again, or call the Hadley police. Was there a Hadley police? Had Afia even been calling from there, or had she stepped out to the country highway and thumbed a ride into Albany?

"Coach," she heard Chander say. And then Yanik: "Coach, you got to get over here."

Numb, she left Shears to follow her players to the far court, where Jamil sat sucking water from his thermos. Above his court, the game score stood, incomprehensibly, at 2–2. Jamil had won the fourth game 15–13. "It's bash, innit, Coach?" he said, grinning.

"Sure is," said Lissy. She sat next to him. If she had Afia's cell number, she thought, she could reach her, warn her.

"I don't know can I do it or not," Jamil said. "They say Shahid gone and defaulted."

"Don't worry about that, Jamil. What's your strategy?"

"He's a fast little bugger. I wear him down. Way to beat a rabbit is make the rabbit run."

"We're with you, man," Yanik said. "All the way, man."

Jamil went back out. From the way he played the first point—hitting through the ball, pounding the rails, chasing every drop—Lissy knew he would win. It hardly mattered. She seemed to be floating above it all, circling like a hawk over New England, trying to guess where Shahid's red Honda was heading.

"You got one guy on a roll," said Ethan, appearing at her side. He had Chloe in his arms, her jacket over his elbow. "But the other's taken off. What the hell's going on?"

"Do me a favor, honey." Lissy pulled out her phone. "Don't leave yet."

I won't help you, he'd said, *if it gets messy*. But there was no one else to turn to.

"Chloe needs her supper."

"One of the players can take her to the snack shop. Please." She pressed the green button on the phone, and the number at the cabin appeared. "Call," she said, handing it to him. "And keep calling, okay? Every five minutes?"

Ethan stared at the phone. "Lissy, shit," he said. "This is *Hadley*."

"I know." She couldn't meet his eyes. "If she answers—"

"You mean Afia? You took Afia to *Hadley*?"

"Tell her . . . tell her Shahid knows where she is. Tell her he's coming."

"I can't believe you used the camp. My family's camp, Lissy."

"I know. Sweetheart, I know." Quicksand, up to her waist, sucking her down. "And no matter what she says, you should call the police."

"Hadley police? I don't even know if there are—"

"Whoever answers 911."

Ethan set Chloe down. "Are we staying?" Chloe asked.

"For a little bit, honey," Lissy said, trying to keep her voice light. "You can take off your coat. You see Chander, on the first step? Go sit next to him for a second."

Chloe dropped her coat and scampered off. Lissy picked it up. She could see Ethan weaving his way through the spectators, out to the lobby where he could make the call. She started to follow him, but a roar from the crowd drew her back. "Coach, look," Yanik said, grabbing her forearm.

He led her to Jamil's court. Already the score had climbed: 6–3 Jamil, 6–4 Jamil, 7–4 Jamil. A few minutes later, he'd won, 11–6. The team began jumping, pounding each other on the back, pounding Lissy. Chander had Chloe on his shoulders, clapping.

"You pulled it out," said George Bradley, shaking her hand, "with two defaults."

Lissy glanced toward the lobby door. Through the glass she saw Ethan turning in circles, touching the keypad on the phone, putting it to his ear. No answer at the cabin yet. There was time.

There was time. Around her, cheers erupted. She felt like a mole coming into the light, stunned by the reversal of everything she had counted on. Her faith in her squash team, insofar as she had any, had been faith in Shahid Satar. She had urged the others on, listened to their hopes, their fears, their complaints. But she had not believed in them, and she should have. "I'm as surprised as you," she said to Bradley. "Do I still get those recruits?"

He nodded toward her briefcase; two folders peeked from underneath. "And I'm still interested in your boy," he said. "Though he's got some 'splaining to do."

Shears and Horton were making their way down, buttoning their jackets. Quickly she moved in their direction. "Well, Madame Director," said Horton. "You've pulled off a small coup."

"It was a close match," she said. "Our boys are tough."

"Most of them." He looked toward the door. "What happened to that Persian guy?"

"Shahid was . . . he was ill," she said, feeling Shears's gaze. "Fortunately it's a deep team."

"Ought to get even deeper, once they get their fancy-ass machines." He nudged Shears. "Maybe she'll get my son Drew and his buddies on them, who the hell knows?"

"I'm grateful, Mr. Horton. Truly. But if you'll excuse me—"

"Oh, go on, go on. You're a working girl."

Ethan came in from the lobby. "No answer," he said grimly. He handed back the phone. "Now do you want to tell me—"

"I'll explain, I promise. In a sec." Lissy checked her watch. Twenty-five minutes since Shahid had clattered down the stairs. The women's team had massed by the courts. The men were high-fiving, gathering their gear. Chander had Chloe by the snack machine, picking out a treat. Gus, leaning on his crutches by the drinking fountain, was the only idle player. His face was a storm of confusion and anger. She stepped over. "Gus, can you get the girls' team on?"

"What the fuck's up with Shahid?" Gus swallowed. "You think he set that bomb, don't you? You"—he swiped with his sleeve at his nose—"you know where Afia is. You just didn't want Shahid locked up. And there I was practically accusing *her*, on the phone. All because you wanted—"

"Gus, that's not it at all. Look, we'll talk. Really. But can you get the girls on now? Please? Here's the lineup." She handed him the form. He stared at it, wiped his nose again. His eyes were red. He nodded.

Stepping into the lobby, she found Shahid's cell number on her phone and keyed it in. On the second ring, she felt a hand on her shoulder. Ethan. She turned to him. Shahid's number rang again, once more, then cut to voice mail. Shutting her phone, she said in defeat, "I don't know what to do."

Ethan's voice was solid and cold as stone. "You have another match to coach."

"I didn't mean about that."

"You mean about Shahid. About where he's headed."

"Oh, God, Ethan. It's messy." She felt a small hand in hers, Chloe's hand. She gripped it.

"Chloe should get something besides candy bars in her."

"I'm on it."

He crouched. "Take care of Mommy." Standing, he nodded at Lissy's phone. "If you reach the girl," he said, "tell her I'm on my way. If I need to, I'll contact the cops."

Gently he placed his hand on her cheek, thumbed the bruise by her temple. Then he was gone.

CHAPTER TWENTY-ONE

Walking back to the cabin took far longer than walking to Hadley. The road ran uphill, and Afia's blister made her limp. Her throat burned, from vomiting. She had to act, to do something on her own. She knew that now. And she would lose Gus. Maybe she had already lost him. And lost or not, she was sick with love for him. This was what they sang about, in all those Western love songs—the pain, the firing and freezing of the blood, the waiting, the loss. *Better to have loved and lost than never to have loved at all.* She hugged herself as she walked, for the warmth but also the comfort. The sun plummeted behind the pine-thick hills.

She didn't want to prepare for death. She wanted to live. If she could step forward first, if she could lead the police to whatever loose thread would rip apart Shahid's alibi, they would arrest him. Deport him, for having set that bomb. But would they execute him? The Americans, she had read, executed more prisoners than the Chinese.

She opened her phone: no signal. The green numbers read 6:12. She was too far from the village to retrace her steps. If she rang the police, she would have to do it from the cabin, from the landline. And then there would be no saving Shahid.

She tucked the phone into her pocket and stepped up her pace, her blister screaming at her. Once, she had loved her family more than anything. She counted them. Shahid, Sobia, Muska, Moray, Baba, Anâ, her funny uncles and mischievous cousins. Even Khalid. She belonged to them; she was theirs. But that was before the blast, before the lives of Gus and Coach Hayes and all Gus's animals were weighed as nothing against the gold of honor. Now she was pushing down on the other end of the scales. The weight of love for Gus. Love for herself. Selfish love, the heaviest kind.

Stars littered the sky by the time she reached the cabin. Tiny birds flitted among the trees, pecking their last seeds. She let herself in the back door and flicked on the light. Painfully she sat in the kitchen chair and pulled off the boots and socks. On her left heel a clear blister, fragile as an egg sac, had emerged. Shahid had bought these good boots for her, but they weren't meant for so long a trek. Barefoot, she went to stoke the fire. It had died almost to embers. She scraped the ash into the metal bucket, crumpled the last of the newspapers, tucked in the last of the dry kindling, and struck a match. The fire lit noisily, creosote crackling its way up the stovepipe. She freed her hair from the makeshift scarf. From outside came another sound—an owl, a car? She stood up. Was Coach Hayes coming? Had she phoned and found Afia not home? On the other side of the window a black curtain seemed to have fallen; she saw only her reflection. Too easy to imagine danger in the noises of nature. She pushed a log in on top of the kindling. For a long time she crouched, watching the fire dance.

In Nasirabad, she thought, it was first light. Closer to the equator, the days not much different in length summer to winter. Tayyab was stirring already, making tea, preparing his lists for the day, leaning close over the back of an envelope with his weak eyes, scratching his notes in a written Pashto that he'd picked up, the way servants did, from shop signs and advertisements. Outside Charsadda, Lema was stirring next to her husband—what was his name?—and the scar on her face smarted, as it always did when she wasn't too busy to think about it. The baby stirred in Lema's belly and gave her a little ache of hope.

There they all were, dancing in the flames behind the door of the woodstove, where Afia could not reach or touch them. Why had she ever left? To become a doctor. But no doctor could bring back Tayyab's dead daughters. No doctor could heal Lema's face or bring back the mischief that once warmed her smile.

Protecting her blistered feet, Afia tiptoed into the cold kitchen. She stared at the phone, as she had last night, but with emotions whipsawing.

She could wait for Coach Hayes.

No. This wasn't Coach Hayes's problem.

She could send a message, warn Shahid that she would betray him.

Shahid had not warned her. Not of the bomb, not of the brakes on Gus's car.

She had already betrayed Shahid. She had betrayed him when she shamed her family, when she betrayed his trust.

She loved Gus, who had not glossy dark hair but kinky red hair, and no goatee because his beard grew in thin and scraggly, who hit the squash ball with a clumsy swipe, who maybe loved his snakes and fish best but she came in a close second. She loved herself the way you love a dirt floor, because without it you plunge to the earth's bowel. Slowly she lifted the heavy receiver from the phone on the wall. She pressed the numbers Americans pressed when they wanted information, 411. A recorded voice asked for city and state and she whispered, "Devon, Massachusetts." What listing, the voice asked, and she said, "Police." But she must have said it too softly because the recorded voice said to hold for an operator.

From outside, she heard the spin of tires. Headlights scanned the kitchen window. Coach Hayes wouldn't have come back so soon, not after the Harvard match today. Could Gus have found her? Her heart swelled. But she hadn't told him where she was. She hardly knew where she was. An operator came onto the line. "Devon police station," the woman said. "Regular business, or an emergency?"

"I—I don't know," she breathed into the receiver. "Emergency?"

"That would be 911, honey," said the operator. "I'll connect you."

Steps on the back porch. The back door burst open. Framed in its darkness stood not Coach Hayes, not Gus, but Shahid. Her brother, her enemy. A scream died in her throat. She pressed the button down and dropped the receiver. It bounced against the wall, the dial tone a distant drone. She backed away from the wall, away from Shahid, behind the table. Her tongue clamped to the roof of her mouth.

"I knew it," Shahid said in Pashto. Stamping his feet, he stepped into the kitchen. Under the fluorescent light he looked weary and old, like Baba. His hair was disheveled, his face unshaven. Dark circles rimmed his eyes. He was wearing his squash uniform, a jacket loose over the jersey. Clumps of snow followed his footsteps. "I didn't believe it but I knew it. What in the name of Allah did you think you were doing?"

He reached for her. She backed into the sitting room, her injured heels hitting the floor. "I—I was about to ring you," she said. She nodded at the phone.

"But you did ring. You rang from the village. You rang someone else. I saw it on our mobile plan. You didn't know I could do that, did you?"

She shook her head. The cabin felt so warm, unbearably warm.

"I pay extra for the family map, so I can know where you are. So I can protect you, keep you safe. Only I never thought I would have to use it, Afia. And then when I did you weren't anywhere. Till today, and you weren't here, you were down the road, down toward that little town, and I saw you like a little dot, because you were calling someone. You weren't calling me, were you?"

He was on her now. He smelled of dried sweat. He grabbed her above the elbow, where the nerve pinched, and her throat opened and she cried out. "Shahid, stop it! Don't be stupid! Let me go!"

"You were calling *him*. Weren't you?"

She wouldn't answer. Defiantly she met his eyes. "How did you get here?"

"Had to ask, starting at Lake Luzerne. Not many people walk the road around here. After dark especially. I knocked on doors. Said you were mentally ill. One guy said a girl in a scarf headed north. Then another guy'd seen you. And a woman spotted you this morning, going the other way. Last house before the fork, she thought. She'd seen smoke from there."

"What about—about the Harvard match?"

"Forget squash! They are looking for you, back in Devon. Something about a bomb?"

"Bomb?" Afia heard herself laugh, a harsh caw. "You should tell them who set that bomb, Shahid lala. Who wanted to blast me into pieces. But you won't tell them. You're a coward."

"Don't talk that way!" His hand whipped by her face, not quite making the slap. Even so, her cheek stung. But she would not cry in front of him. "You have *no idea*," he said fiercely, shaking her right arm from the wrist, "what danger you are in. Look." With one hand he reached deep into his jacket pocket. He pulled out a small dark object that gradually formed itself into a revolver. Afia's chest went cold. Still holding her, he offered the gun to her on an outstretched palm, as if offering a sweet. "Where do you think this came from?"

With her free hand she snatched the gun from him. She held it behind her back, feeling its weight. She backed away from him into the sitting room, her fettered arm pulling on his hand. She saw his eyes flit to the photos on the wall. "Who is that?" He let go her wrist. She clutched the gun tight behind her back. "Whose place is this?" He flicked on the standing lamp and peered more closely. He looked at Afia, then at the photos again. "Coach Hayes," he said wonderingly. "Coach brought you here."

"I made her, Shahid. It wasn't her fault."

"That cut on her cheek—" He backed away from the picture. "She was with you, wasn't she? When the thing went off?" When Afia didn't answer, he shook his head. "And I thought she never lied."

"Everyone lies, Shahid lala. You lied. You tried to kill Gus."

"I didn't set that bomb."

She managed to meet his gaze. In his bloodshot eyes she saw only grief and torment. This was Shahid, her brother who loved her. He had put up his life to guarantee her honor. He was not reaching for the gun. So he had not come here to hurt her. Something else he wanted. "Who, then?" she ventured.

"I want you back home, Afia. Where you're safe, where they'll forgive you, where everything will be all right."

"And I said I would go, Shahid, and then someone tried to kill me."

"Remember—Afia, remember—you told me that picture of you, in the orchard—"

"Shahid, it was on my mobile. Are you going to admit you uploaded it? I suspected from the start—"

"That someone stole it. Yes, but not me. Think, Afia."

She frowned. She concentrated on the floor, the wide wooden

boards. She pictured herself, back in Nasirabad, fishing for her mobile, finding it in the wrong pocket of her purse, erasing the photo. She had been at the *mehndi*. Plenty of time to take the phone down to Ali Bhai's, to upload the image. She had erased it too late.

"Khalid," she said slowly. She lifted her face, met Shahid's eyes. "But Khalid doesn't know Taylor. He's not even on Facebook."

"He is now. You think Taylor's hard to find, once he's got your phone contacts? It's Facebook, Afia. No one is real, and everyone is everyone's friend. I should've thought it through, once you said you didn't post that damn thing."

Afia's head swirled. "But you said there's another—you said I'm kissing Gus in it—you said our family is dishonored—"

"Our family doesn't know about it. I'm not even sure it exists."

"But you said—"

"There might be another picture, yes." Now Shahid's voice was gentle, the voice he used when they had secrets to share, like the application she made to Smith, like the places Uncle Omar took him to in Peshawar. These were things not for the family to know, just for the two of them, like in meiosis, a dyad. "If there is, Khalid got it, too. But he didn't steal it. He took it."

Khalid. Afia had looked in the fire and seen Tayyab, Lema. She had not seen Khalid. Khalid was in the mountains, planning jihad. Yet some part of her was unsurprised to find Khalid lurking behind these events. "But where did he take—"

"From outside Gus Schneider's hospital room."

"Khalid is in America?" From outside, she heard a new noise. A slow crunch. Quickly she stepped through the kitchen and opened the back door. No moon shone. No car lights. Only the owl, hooting. Sounds of nature. She lifted the heavy, man-made gun and hurled it into the darkness. She heard it land, somewhere near the woodpile, out of reach. Feeling a bit better, she shut the door.

"How can Khalid," she asked—should she believe Shahid? Should she believe anybody?—"be in America?"

"I don't know. It takes months to get a visa. Maybe he's got powerful friends. Maybe they sent him here to wage jihad."

"Or Baba sent him."

"No." Shahid spoke firmly. "No, Afia. Baba wants you home. I told him I was sending you home. Anyway, Baba doesn't have that kind of money or power. Khalid says he has business here."

"Why would he dishonor our family, with such a photo?" She found herself shivering. She crossed her arms over her chest. "Has he gone mad?"

Shahid's chest rose as he took a long breath in, then let it out. He ran a hand through his unruly hair. She knew what he was thinking—*You dishonored us, Afia, you with your lust, you with no morals, no control, you alone, you.* Aloud he said, "He is not mad. He is calculating. To dishonor us would be to dishonor himself."

"Unless I die. Blood cleanses honor, Shahid lala."

"Only if you are sure of shedding it. Look, that photo is not on the Internet. Baba has not seen it. No one in Nasirabad has seen it. Khalid told me about it for one purpose only, and that was to force me against you. And what if I wash away our shame with your blood, but there is no shame to wash? Then I am a bad brother and a bad son. And if I refuse to do it—well, he has the photos. He can kill you himself and show the evidence to Baba, and we are both done for."

"So you—you will not spill my blood?" She backed toward the door.

Slowly, regarding her, he shook his head. "No."

"And Khalid . . . Khalid set that bomb."

"I'd have stopped him if I'd known."

"And now you send me home, and he finds me there. What difference, Shahid lala?"

He approached her, put his hands on her elbows, the thumbs on the inside. They felt hot, his thumbs, as if he ran a fever. "The difference," he said, "is that, inshallah, you will be married to Zardad."

"But I don't love Zardad!" She struggled as he gripped her. "I have to love, Shahid. This is between you and Khalid, this is not—"

"You have to live first!" he said. "We *both* have to live."

"So let me go!"

But he kept hold of her. "Khalid isn't winning this one," he said. "Not on my word of honor to Baba. Now come on. We're leaving."

With one hand Shahid picked up the shearling boots from where they sat dripping on the floor. Holding Afia tight, he moved them both onto the back porch. He propelled her down the steps to the snow. As she stumbled, headlights lit the drive. She threw up an arm, shielding her eyes. Coach Hayes? Had Coach come after Shahid? Had that been the crunch, Coach's car?

Behind the headlights, a door opened and the driver stepped out. Afia screamed. She couldn't see his face, but she knew from the body shape, from the thrust of the long head. Khalid.

"No," she cried. Khalid's arm went up, rested on the top of the door. In his hand a gun. "Khalid lala, no!"

Shahid's hands were around her rib cage. They lifted her, tossed her. Barefoot, into the snow, out of the glare of the lights. She fell on her knees by the woodpile. Twisting her head, she saw Shahid walk slowly toward the car. His hands were up, blocking the glare. "You followed me, didn't you?" he said to Khalid.

"Someone has to keep watch. You don't take care of our father's business, little brother."

"Khalid lala, listen," Afia began. She pushed herself up.

"Quiet, Afia," Shahid hissed. And to Khalid, "You don't want this. Not really."

"Don't I?" Khalid's voice sounded thin. "Baba will be grateful to me."

"No, he won't, Khalid lala," Afia cried. She got to her bare feet in the snow. The cold stung her blister. "Baba wants me home. He'll never forgive you."

"Listen to the whore," Khalid said. "From good parents a black calamity."

"That's a stupid proverb, Khalid," Shahid said. "It's nothing to do with us."

"Her shame," Khalid retorted, "is to do with us." Afia saw Khalid's gun, a tiny black fish, rotate in the dark toward her. "And Baba will know who cleansed it."

"Cleansed it?" Shahid answered. "How about created it, brother? Who sent out that photograph last month, for all to see?"

Afia crouched. She felt in the snow for the gun. So foolish, to fling it! She felt a blow to her hip—Shahid was kicking her. "*Run*," he hissed.

"No!" Her hands scrabbled over the woodpile. She felt more than saw Shahid's form step between her and the headlights.

"The Internet," Khalid was saying, "is out of our control. Step aside, little brother. This is a man's job."

"Afia's mobile wasn't out of your control." Shahid kicked her again. Her hand grasped something cold and hard. The gun. "You stole that photo. You meant for us to think she was ruined."

"I don't turn a blind eye to tora."

"You lied to me about our family. There's no dishonor. You just want her dead and me a murderer."

Afia managed to stand, the gun in her hand. She would pass it to Shahid. She did not want Khalid to die, only to be stopped. Her hand shook like a marionette's. She nudged Shahid's arm with the handle.

He pushed her back behind him. "This is nothing to do with

tora," he went on. "This is your jealousy, Khalid. You cannot stand it that your father loves our moray. That—"

"Stand back, Shahid. Her time has come."

"Who claimed jihad to get to this country? Who sneaked into the hospital—"

"I said stand back."

"And a bomb, Khalid. Good people die, with bombs. You've seen it."

Afia peeked around Shahid's solid form. Khalid had come around, to the side of the headlights. The dark fish in his hands undulated side to side. "I have seen them die like dogs in a ditch," he said, "and with no honor. Move, brother."

If she crawled to him, if she kissed his boots. He would shoot her in the back. She stepped to Shahid's side, in the full light. As she nudged him again with the gun, the dark fish lifted. Shahid swept his left arm wide, shoving her behind him. Something flashed in front of Khalid. A roar. Shahid staggered back, into her.

"Run," he cried. He fell sideways. Afia scrambled away, over the rough gravel, the packed snow. From the dark she looked over her shoulder. Shahid, her brother, her beloved. In the headlights he rose, pushed to his hands and knees, fell back. Blood bloomed in his chest. "Run, Afia!" he cried again, the voice choking now—or maybe it was a voice inside her saying it, *Run*, as Shahid sprawled in the snow. And she did run, but toward him.

The headlights painted his skin white. Blood filled his mouth. His arms twitched, his hands clawed the ground, his knees jerked—and then stopped, like a child arresting a tantrum, the instant she laid her hands on them.

"Don't go," she said. "Shahid, don't go," as if he'd not quite made up his mind. Her hand pressed onto his chest. A faint throb, going, going. Then it was still. His eyes lifted to the black sky.

"Is he—" she heard behind her, and she turned to Khalid taking a step forward. Shadowed though he was, she saw the horror gouging his eyes. His mouth hung slack.

"You've killed him," she said, or thought she said. She couldn't hear her own words. What she heard instead were Shahid's words, again, *Run, Afia*, as he was falling, falling, the bullet in his heart. Gently she passed her bloody hand across Shahid's face, closing his eyelids for him.

For a moment they were there together, Afia and Khalid and Shahid between them. Then Khalid took a step forward. The dark fish rose, and she made herself ready. A whining came into her ears, the sound of death approaching she thought, but then she saw Khalid's eyes widen and remembered. The call she had made, 911. Khalid looked from her to Shahid, lying still on the white snow now, lovely as a sleeping god. Afia pushed back, she stepped out of the light, she saw Khalid's panic. The sirens rose. *Run*, she heard in her head again, and she turned to the dark woods. Her bare feet pushed slowly, then faster. Behind her, one gunshot; another. At the edge of the woods she twisted back, squeezed the trigger of the black thing in her hand, and it jumped high, and she dropped it. Khalid was in the car now. Spinning in the snow, then scraping over the gravel, it roared off, the red eyes at its back receding down the drive. Sirens. *Run.* Shahid lay in darkness. Her feet wheeled beneath her. She stumbled into the trees, her feet numb, branches beneath the snow but she ran, silent now, silent as the birds, only the sound of her breath threatening to betray her.

Book Two

CHAPTER TWENTY-TWO

Khalid sped over the snow, the tires slipping, the car as if it wanted to fly, a flying horse with a will of its own. He couldn't see right. The tears got in his way. A guttural howl came from his throat, like an animal lodged there. Battling the animal, a voice in his head.

This is not the plan. Not the right outcome. Whatever Allah wants of you, it is not this.

What, then? What?

Shahid stepping in front of Afia like that and your finger moving on its own, squeezing the trigger like your heart squeezing? This was a dream of some kind. A dream, yes, you've had those dreams before, those dreams where your finger squeezes, squeezes, and the world flies apart. Those dreams where you are on a flying horse in the snow and it takes leave of the earth. You wake up and you say aloud, "It wasn't real, not real." Say it now. Say it. Wake up, wake up. Wake up.

He passed the police car, its siren rising, blue lights blinking atop like a carnival, but it took no notice of him. He drove across a bridge spanning a wide, half-frozen river, then followed the brightly lit signs to the highway. He was glad for the highway where you couldn't drive accidentally on the left side and find headlights rushing at you, horns blaring. He couldn't bear the noise. He pressed the gas pedal farther, farther, and the car floated down the black lane. Before the headlights, the snow swirled.

He needed to pray. He needed to find that point of light he saw, as if through the place in his forehead that touched the prayer rug, blazing from far off in the darkness. The pure light. All these other lights around him shone dull, yellow, corrupted.

If only Shahid had not stepped forward like that. If only he had let Khalid get off a shot, a clean shot. The bastard, the stupid arrogant bastard. Get in the middle, get yourself killed.

If only Shahid had played his part, the part Khalid had prepared so lovingly for him. So that he, Shahid, would be the one to cleanse their honor. Yes? Giving Shahid the glory, always giving him the glory.

If only! If only his *badal,* his retribution, had been allowed to proceed slowly, as he had meant it to. If only Uncle Omar had not become involved. There was the bastard: Omar. Pushing, always pushing. It was his fault, that bastard Omar's fault.

He floated off the highway. He pulled the car into the parking lot of a Christian church. He needed to get his breathing under control or he would black out. He needed to retrace the map that had brought him to this place, to the cabin he'd just left and his brother's body on the white snow, the red stain blooming behind his head.

It had begun that day he was at Ali Bhai's, deep into the chat room for *pashtunistan*, flipping from the arguments about Imran Khan to some Western media outrage over a girl in the Afghan camps. Same commenters, same pissing matches. One guy wrote that Western universities made sweet Paki girls go stupid and headstrong, and Khalid had clicked on the website for Smith College to see how true that could be. And there she was, his little sister, her hand in that ape's paw.

No. It hadn't begun there, any more than it had begun when he looked into Afia's room and saw the phone on her bed, waiting for him to find the photo of her in an orchard, her legs wrapped horribly around a man's shoulders. It had begun earlier, so much earlier. It had begun—he leaned back in the car and shut his eyes—when he was six years old and his mother, his moray, was dying. How she had loved him! No, she hadn't managed to have more children after him—but he was a boy, after all, and she had cared for him and Baba with all her heart. Then came the thing in her gut, the thing that had kept her from birthing more babies, and it ate away at her from the inside, and she never complained but kept at her duties day and night until she couldn't anymore. Until the day he found her collapsed on the floor by the stove, and Tayyab shouting for the doctor. Yes, that's where it began.

Never forget, she had told him, *you are Pashtun. You are Allah's beloved. You are pure of heart and mind.* So pure, she swore to him, that the mark Allah had bestowed on him, the left foot that turned outward instead of forward and kept him from running as fast as the other boys, was His way of turning Khalid's attention to the poor and the weak, of keeping Khalid from a life of vainglory or foolishness. So pure she had been, herself, that she had welcomed the new wife, Farishta, once her sister-in-law, into the house. Welcomed Farishta's children, Shahid and Afia. Held Khalid's small hand in her large rough one, burning then with fever, and made him promise to look after his new brother and sister, to help Farishta instruct them.

He had tried. By Allah, he had tried. When he saw the eyes his father cast on Farishta, a look he had never seen bestowed on his own mother, he turned away and willed his mind toward higher thoughts. When Farishta's first two pregnancies in Nasirabad ended in miscarriage he cut the skin of his thigh each time he began to gloat, until the cuts were like the hash marks the reapers used to count bales of cotton. When she brought forth two girls in quick succession, he exulted loudly at the births and not at the fact that he remained his father's only true son. He took Shahid under his wing, helping him study and getting him onto the cricket squad.

Only there came what he thinks of now as the terrible Eid, that season in his seventeenth year. First had come Uncle Omar's visit, toward the end of Ramadan, and his singling out Shahid for training in Peshawar. The questions his friends pelted him with—what prizes could Shahid win, would he get to meet the great Jahangir Khan, how rich was this Omar?—were a storm of needles sticking beneath his skin. That he was his father's only son, the one who would inherit the farm, hardly seemed to matter—for what was a farm, when all the glory shone upon this little calf that his father's second wife had brought to Nasirabad?

But worse were the conversations he overheard that same holiday season, after it was decided that Shahid would go to Peshawar. Chatter between Afia, twelve that year, and Tayyab's daughters, as they compared the glass bracelets they had bought with their Eid money. From the day Afia came into his family, a button-eyed toddler, Khalid had warmed to her. She was rival neither to him nor to his dead mother, and he would toss her, laughing, into the air or boost her onto the lowest limb of the mulberry tree. But that Eid, coming back from a holiday cricket match, he heard her on the other side of the courtyard wall, laughing with the servant girls.

"Well, he *couldn't* choose Khalid, could he?" she said. "Khalid walks like a seal! Batting a ball is one thing, but have you seen him run?" There followed a scuffling sound that he imagined was Afia's farcical imitation of the way he ran, with his right leg springing off the foot and his left one dragging. "Oarf! Oarf!" Afia cried, and Tayyab's daughters giggled. His face burning, he had slammed into the *hujra*.

He hadn't wanted to talk to her, hadn't wanted to see her. He was headed into his last year of school then. He'd shown inclinations toward mathematics, toward building things. Baba had urged him to think about engineering. He loved the clean lines of blueprints. They spelled everything his moray had wanted him to become—strong, clean, pure of heart, a man of *ghairat*. He understood why his father had married Farishta. Though he couldn't help resenting his stepmother, it had been the proper match, nothing shameful. But when he shut his eyes at night he pictured the first night of true marriage. His untouched body, and his wife's untouched body—what the Prophet, peace be upon him, had called the twin half of him—coming together in complete union. The wonder of it, like a fire that rises within you both and never destroys you, but only destroys the impurity of your discharge, which transforms into a milky river in which swim your sons and your daughters. By night he fixed his inner eye on the perfection of that act and kept his hands away from his aching, swollen parts. By day he worked to avert his eyes from the village girls.

It was during that same Eid, on the last day of the celebration, that he had left the *hujra* where the men were talking—again!—about Shahid and his athleticism, and how Tofan's brother-in-law would give that boy the chance of a lifetime. He had wandered away, past the mulberry orchard and the first field of cotton, past the willows lining the stream and around the bend toward the deep area they used as a swimming hole. It was late summer then, the heat finally lifting from the earth; and late in the day, too, past the time when the village boys would leap from a tree branch into the deep water. So when he caught a glimpse of a body standing waist-deep in the stream, he took a step back. Then he parted a curtain of willow and looked. Afia stood in a slanting shaft of sunlight, her skin the color of sandalwood, her arms lifted as her hands pushed back her thick hair. She did not see him. The nipples on her wet chest showed only the slightest protrusion, as if they were being tugged out and upward. The rest of her torso looked elongated, no longer a child's simple barrel but beginning to be whittled into a waist, hips. She was humming lightly, one of the songs they had been dancing to at the celebration. Khalid had backed away. His penis had become, suddenly and against his will, a rod of iron. Quickly he turned and ran, toward the house at first and then into a stand of trees. He had crouched and buried his head in his arms. He wanted to cut his sex away with a hatchet; to stab out his eyes. Naked! The Prophet, peace be upon him, had ordered women never to go naked, even with their husbands. How could Afia do such a thing to him, dirty his sight and his mind like that?

There, it had begun. For how could a man live—with such a brother stealing his birthright, with such a sister fouling his eyes? He had said nothing to any of them. But by the next year, to find his way back to purity, he had left home not for the engineering school but for the madrassa. Three years ago he'd gone further, to the high mountains, where men knew there could be no compromise with filth and disorder. Only when a Pakistani army bullet found his shoulder did he come home to heal. He'd passed the time at Ali Bhai's, where he saw that image on the Smith website and began to understand: He could not run away forever. He had to put his family back in order. To put Shahid back in his place, and remove the corruption that had destroyed the pure stepsister he once loved.

He had told Baba of the photo on the Smith website hoping Baba would step in—would lock the girl up and marry her off, put a stop to this creeping rot. *She left Nasirabad to gain knowledge*, he'd argued, *and what does she do but give away her greatest value. And to what? To a Jew!* Yes, he had known it was a Jew, from the very hairs of the hand holding hers. *Willfully*, he had said to Baba, *and without shame, she defiles herself.* But Baba was weak, giving in to Farishta's pleas: There would be an engagement but nothing else, and Afia sent back to the whorehouse she had made for herself.

What does a man do, under such circumstances? He plots. He downloads the website photo. He seizes the photo on Afia's phone, the blurry one in an orchard, her legs wrapped around the Jew's neck. He finds one of Afia's phone contacts, Taylor Saintsbury, on Facebook. He chooses the name Kent Star, *Kent* for Superman's disguise and *Star* the closest he dares come to *Satar*. As Kent Star, he friends Taylor, tags the photo. He returns to the mountains, and waits. The dish of revenge is best served cold.

For Khalid had seen clearly at that point. Only when Afia's shame was cleansed with her blood—he pictured that, he couldn't help himself, blood on her breasts, on her white neck—would they be able to lift their heads as Pashtuns. And Shahid must be made to do the thing. Shahid, too, must be broken, his arrogant hold on their family broken.

Patience had held him steady, through the cold weeks. Only once had he returned to Nasirabad, to show his father the photos, to express his sorrow and press for justice. All in time, it would have happened. But then Omar, who always interfered, had sent a messenger to the camp.

Even as he traveled down the mountain to Peshawar, Khalid had not been naïve. Omar might open his wallet, but he cared nothing for Khalid. Khalid was useful, that was all; his jealousy was useful. And then, as he left Omar's mansion, Khalid saw his true, his final chance: He *could* take care of things. All it took was one more photo, a photo to be shown to no one except Shahid.

What was he hoping for, when he followed Shahid tonight from the squash court to the parking lot and onto the highway? To bear witness, while his coward of a stepbrother finally committed an act for which Baba would never forgive him? To see the blood flow over her white skin? From the number of times Shahid stopped—at a petrol station, a café, a house lit yellow along the road—it was clear he hadn't known quite where he was going. Khalid had had to follow a half kilometer behind and to turn down a different road whenever he saw Shahid's Honda pull over. Just barely had he caught the taillights swerving right, into a long driveway. When the Honda didn't back out, he shut his own lights and rolled, quiet and dark, down the drive. He'd heard the back door open and shut; Afia's voice; the ricochet of a heavy object—the gun, it must have been the gun he'd given Shahid.

What to do, what to do? He'd pulled his own Glock out from under the seat. One action could not be tolerated: for Shahid to take their befouled sister home to be married, as if she had committed no crime greater than the brush of one hand against another. Explicitly, Omar had charged him not to let Shahid abandon his glorious career for such nonsense. No good could come of trying to bleach an indelible stain. Yet there they had come, the open door spilling light onto their faces, Afia barefoot, her features knit tight, and Shahid with his hand on her elbow, guiding her down the steps. They were leaving. He could not let them. Not this time. No. He was a man, a Satar, he would take care of this. And so he had turned the headlights on, raised the Glock.

Allah! How can you account for everything that goes wrong in the world? How could you think a Pashtun brother could lay eyes on such a photo and still send his sister home to be honorably wed? How could you imagine that the recipe for combustion, memorized in the camps above the Khyber Pass, would stutter and delay and fail to kill? How could such a girl disappear, and why would a brother hunt her down for any reason but to seize back his honor? How could a finger on a trigger, once squeezing, fail to stop when a man blocked the target? What, oh what had he been made to do, when all he desired was purity and his rightful place?

He stepped from the car. His left foot throbbed the way it did when his muscles cramped up. The snow had stopped, the sky cleared. Following the constellations, he located the four directions. He knelt, facing east, and in a language that made no sense to him, recited his prayers.

CHAPTER TWENTY-THREE

The place they took Afia wasn't like a prison, not the way she pictured an American prison anyway. She had seen pictures of the cages, the dogs. Her room had a regular door, no bars. Though she was locked in at night, she had a bed and a sink and flush toilet, not a hole in the floor. The place smelled of disinfectant. They allowed her to have books—the jail's small library had even got hold of the textbooks she needed—and she was allotted both paper and pencil, plus two hours a day in the library where there was an Internet connection. No e-mail.

Only one other inmate, a skinny black woman named Thalia who said she was a Muslim, ever spoke to her. Thalia came in two days after Afia, charged with murdering her boyfriend; she'd done two stints behind bars already, she said, and they weren't granting her bail. The other women, a couple dozen at most, avoided Thalia as much as they did Afia. Then there was Officer Jane, the prison librarian, and Sara Desfani, her court-appointed lawyer. Sara—she told Afia to call her Sara—was Muslim, but she wasn't Pashtun or even Pakistani. She tried to get Afia to talk about Baba and

Moray and what they wanted for her, about Shahid and how angry he got when he found out about Gus. Afia didn't see what business Sara had to understand life in Nasirabad. It was all she wanted now. Home. With Moray's cool hands stroking her brow, stroking away the fever that gave her bad dreams in which Shahid was dead and she was locked away forever far from anyone who loved her.

But she wasn't home. She was in the bad dream.

She would not let the name *Khalid* escape her lips. The Americans, if they knew the facts, would want to punish Khalid. But Khalid, for all he'd done to paint the picture of Afia's shame, was not the truly guilty one. She was the guilty one. She was the one who had abandoned her *namus*, who had put Shahid at risk in the first place. *If a tree falls in the woods*, her philosophy teacher had asked, *and no one to hear it, does it make a sound?* If a woman pollutes herself, she could have echoed, and no one to know it, has she brought shame to her family?

The answer, it would seem, was yes.

Shutting her eyes, she saw Shahid's blood on the snow behind the cabin. *Run*, he had cried out, dying. *Run*.

Where should she run now?

From her family, silence. The district attorney, she learned, had spoken to them. All Sara knew was that they had protested Shahid's innocence—he could not have set a bomb, he would not have threatened his sister. They had sent no money for bail. They would not speak with Afia. Sara did not mention Khalid, so Baba must not have mentioned him. Maybe he thought Khalid was still in the mountains; maybe he knew the truth; maybe he had lied to Shahid and sent Khalid to America himself. Afia did not ask.

Alone at night, in her cell, which was never fully dark, always the lights in the hall, she heard her brother's voice, smelled his sweat, rested her closed eyes on the face he always brought home from Peshawar, from the squash tour, from America. His too-wide, silly smile, showing the gums above his teeth. His brown eyes gleaming as she unwrapped her present—a necklace from Dubai, a pair of slippers from America. The tiny mole by his mouth, echoing hers by her eye. *Oh Shahid, Shahid*, she whispered into the silence.

Because of her, Shahid was dead. Shahid had tried to send her home, to save her. But she—she had been in love! With Gus! Even now, in her white room, with her books and her prayer mat—even now with Shahid dead—she felt the secret shame of wanting Gus. He had said all the dear words to her, lying on his bed, their sweat sticking them together. That he loved her. He wanted always to be with her. He would protect her from her family, from her jealous brother. She was the most beautiful girl he had ever seen. He would marry her. How could she ever have thought such foulness sweet, such danger safe?

Gus had not tried to see her, and no wonder. To the police she had claimed she was the one tampering with his brakes, setting a bomb to explode in his home. Why? the police asked. Because, she said, he liked another girl. She was jealous, crazy with jealousy. They claimed she was lying. But could she blame Gus if he believed such a story? A knife pierced her gut every time she thought of him, which was many times every day.

She would never be a doctor now. She would help no one. She had brought death and shame; now she had nothing but death and shame to offer. If they would let her, she thought in the wee hours of the night, under the light they never turned off, she would take poison and be rid of herself.

Once a day they let the women out in the exercise yard. From the back, the building was faced with blond brick; the outside walls were of stone topped by clay tiles. A female guard stood by while Afia walked with Thalia in the cold yard. Thalia talked about revenge. She'd been set up, she said. This guy Hammer had done her boyfriend, all over a bag of coke. When she got out she had a gun stashed away, and she knew how to shoot it and she'd take care of Hammer in a way that she'd never get caught, no ma'am. Thalia talked and Afia tried to listen. Snow banked the gravel path. Toward the center sat a stone fountain that must have been used once as a birdbath, the ice in it slowly melting.

Afia didn't remember much about coming here. That night, at the cabin, she had run until her breath could carry her no farther. There had been stones beneath the stones, sharp twigs, branches that cut her shins and made her fall and rise, fall and rise again. Then she had walked, stumbled, seen the yellow glow of a house lighting its barn. Below her knees, she had felt nothing. She had slipped through the barn door to the familiar odor of animals—a horse, chickens, a pair of goats. In a rough blanket she had rolled herself and spent the night shivering in the stall of the horse, who poked and nuzzled her. In the morning the old man had found her and cried for his wife. By then she was too stiff to move. After rubbing her feet and legs, the wife had swaddled them in a pair of thick wool socks. They had driven her to a hospital. When or how the police came for her, she couldn't remember. When they had pronounced Shahid's name to her, she broke out weeping and would not stop—not in the hospital when they peppered her with questions, not when they pulled her hands behind her back and cuffed her wrists. In the back of the car that brought her to a prison, a different room, she had wept herself to sleep. At some point after that—days, a week, more?—the blisters on her feet proved infected, and they treated her with antibiotics and a stinking plaster. The little toe on her left foot was far gone with frostbite, the doctor reported, and a few days later he gave her an injection to deaden the pain while he cut it off.

She cared about none of it. For a long while, when they came in to ask her questions, she only looked at them and shrugged. Eventually they coaxed words out of her. Eventually she understood: She had to confess that it was she who had killed Shahid, and Shahid who had tried to kill her. That story was the only way to spare her family more grief, just as this was the only place safe from Khalid.

Two weeks had passed; now it was March, the advent of spring. She was watching a red cardinal on the stone fountain when a guard came to lead the women back inside. She had a visitor, the guard said. All the guards, except Officer Jane, were like this one, chunky white women who stood with their arms folded across their chests and barked announcements—LOCKDOWN! LIGHTS OUT! HEAD COUNT!—even when no one stood more than ten feet from them. The cardinal flew off, and she followed the guard to the room with the tables, where other women whispered to their husbands or their lawyers, and more guards stood by the walls. When Coach Hayes came through the armored door, she rose from her folding chair, her knees shaking.

Coach looked like a different woman. Older, paler, her shoulders curled forward as if they bore weight. "Afia," she said when she drew close, and her voice had a rasp in it.

They sat. They were not allowed to touch. All the bad things Afia had done seemed to lie on the table between them. That she had left the cabin. That she had called Gus. That she had failed to lock the back door. But these were not the worst thing. The worst, she had to remind herself, was that she had loosed the bullet to kill Shahid. An easy story to tell—for had she not, in the end, brought death to her brother?—until Coach lifted her pale face and fixed her with those blue eyes. "It's my fault," she said.

Afia's heart squeezed against the wall of her chest. "No," she managed to say.

"Yes. I should have gone to the police. Right away. They would have arrested him. We would have lost the Harvard match." Coach's mouth trembled. She looked down, picked at something on her hand. "And Shahid would be alive."

And I would be dead, Afia thought. But she said only, "You could not know, Coach." And then, because a mountain of lies rose between her and the woman who had tried to rescue her, she said, "How is your family?"

"My family?" Coach snorted. "That was my husband's cabin, where you were hiding. I told him to trust me, that I knew what I was doing."

"He is angry with you."

"You blame him?" She lifted her eyes again. She studied Afia's clothes, the hijab and the black chador. "I never kept anything from Ethan before," she said. Bitterness edged her voice. "It's a . . . a point of honor with us. You people don't have a monopoly on honor."

"I know that, Coach."

"Do you? Then tell me." Coach lifted her forearms to the table, as if she would take Afia's hands. Her tone softened. "What really happened, Afia? Who tried to kill you? How did Shahid die?"

"I—I can't explain." Afia began to weep. Coach Hayes had given her kindness, and she had repaid her with horror and grief. "I never thought to put him in danger."

"But you did. And I did. And he died. Afia, listen to me." Coach Hayes dug in her pocket and pulled out a crumpled tissue, which she passed across the table. "I tried to keep you a secret, and it didn't work out. Now you're keeping a secret. I know you are. My husband tells me I'm imagining things. I go on about a man in a blue car that kept following me, but nobody else saw this man. I'm supposed to believe that Shahid Satar, who I knew like my own son, who I loved—" She broke off. As if a string had been pulled, she sank back in her chair, her large hand over her face. Then she grimaced and sat upright. "I loved him," she repeated, "and I am supposed to believe he was capable of attempted murder. That's what your lawyer wants me to suggest."

"Miss Desfani? She speaks to you?"

"She's preparing a case, Afia. She has to. And the worse Shahid looks, the better the case she wants to build. Well, I'm not buying it, Afia. Not from my husband. Or the police. Or you."

Afia felt as if spiders crawled over her skin. A blue car. Khalid. "Please, Coach," she begged. "No good comes of this. You have your work. You must forget me and—"

Coach's face twisted; a laugh erupted and died. "What work, Afia?"

"The team. The friends of Shahid, they need you—"

"Apparently not that badly. Afia, think about it. I withheld evidence in a criminal investigation. No one thinks I'll go to jail, but it's a scandal. I'm on leave, honey. Administrative leave."

"Leave? That means?"

"Means I don't work, so I won't embarrass the university. Six months from now, we see if this has blown over. Until then . . ." She snorted. She looked away. "I wallow in grief and get eaten up with curiosity. My daughter wets the bed, and my husband . . ." Her voice trailed off.

"I am so sorry, Coach."

"Now do you see? Why it's so important for me to know?"

But Afia felt a wall go up inside her, implacable. She had betrayed everything and everyone else. She would not betray

Baba's only son. "I cannot tell you anything," she said, "that would help."

She felt awful about Coach Hayes. When she saw Sara Desfani, two days later, she asked her not to bother the coach; to make the case without her. "Don't be silly," Sara replied. She had cut and colored her hair since their last meeting. It lifted gently off her forehead and swirled in dark chestnut past her ears. Afia tightened her hijab. "Coach Hayes," Sara went on, "was there when that bomb exploded. Her testimony's essential. She'll come around. Are they giving you time for prayers, here?"

"Yes. But if Coach doesn't want to—"

"Afia, you worry about your own story. Let me worry about the big picture. By the time Ramadan comes—"

"I don't care about Ramadan."

"Neither do I, except to get you out of here by then." Sara glanced at her notes. She tapped a pencil against the side of the table. Her face reminded Afia of Tayyab's wife: full lips and low-slung cheekbones, pouches below the eyes. A stubborn face. No point arguing with her about Coach Hayes. "Your friends at Smith don't consider you especially religious," Sara said.

"I may not have been."

"So it's just since incarceration."

Afia remembered Maryam's wedding. She had spotted her cousin Gulnar wearing full niqab and had wondered how it happened, that those who went away came back more pious. "I cannot explain," she said. "I believe the same as before. But this way"—she demonstrated her clothes, but she meant the Qur'an, the prayer rug, the rituals allotted to her—"I am not so lonely."

"Well, when we go to trial, it would help a lot if you can find your way back to Western clothes. Meanwhile"—Sara opened a folder on the table—"I have some news about your case in Massachusetts."

"Massachusetts," Afia repeated. She had trouble keeping this straight. Shahid had been killed in the state of New York. The explosion at Gus's house and the failure of his brakes had happened in the state of Massachusetts. In Massachusetts no one was charging her with anything, not yet. But the Massachusetts people and the New York ones weren't different tribes, like the Baluchis and the Pashtuns. There was no reason for them to have different laws; they just did.

"No matter what you claim," Sara was going on, "you're off the hook on the brakes. That's good news, sweetheart. Someone from the district attorney's office got hold of a surveillance tape, from the TrueValue just outside Devon."

"I don't want to hear this," Afia said. Like a child, she placed her hands over her ears.

"Honey, he tried to kill you for doing what comes naturally to young people all over the world. And you defended yourself, and now he's dead. You don't have to protect him anymore. He can't hurt you."

Slowly Afia removed her hands. Her eyes widened. Could she mean Khalid, that Khalid was dead? Could the lawyer know about him? She had never mentioned Khalid.

But Sara was lifting another sheet of paper from the folder. "The tape shows your brother Shahid," she said, turning the report in Afia's direction, "buying a wrench, a pair of metal cutters, pliers, a flashlight. Everything you need to drain the brake fluid from a car."

Afia pushed away from the table. She felt blood drain from her face. "You are sure? There was Shahid on a tape? Buying these things?"

"We can't enter this into evidence here. But I've got a buddy over in the Berkshires, he sent me this report. They don't know if your brother was acting alone, but—"

Afia stood up. She walked in a tight circle. She had known, of course; in her heart, she had known. To scare her into acting as she should, Shahid had been ready to take Gus's life. The cruel twist being that she *had* been acting as she should, only when she learned Gus was injured her heart had flown from her chest and gone to him. Shahid had scared her in the wrong direction. "He did," she managed now, emotion strangling her voice, "what he had to."

"What, try to kill your boyfriend? Afia, honey, this sort of code is *primitive*. Believe me. I *know*. Before my family left Iran—"

"I am not from Iran. I am Pashtun." Afia was surprised by the heat in her voice. Spinning around, moving in on Sara with her thick lips and dyed hair, her mud-brown eyes, she could have struck her a blow. She gripped the back of the chair to steady herself. "Gus was *makhtoray*. Our great poet, he says it, the Pashtun man must shoot the seducer of his sister and walk proud to British gallows. Only so do we keep the peace."

"America," Sara said steadily, tightening her red lips, "isn't a British colony. And that is a funny kind of peace."

"My brother loved me."

"All right." Sara nodded, as if Afia had proposed a project. "He loved you. And I'm sure you wish you hadn't had to shoot him."

"I did not—" Afia began. But she saw the trap before she stepped into it. "What is to happen now?"

"With this in hand," Sara said, "I think the rest of the state's case collapses, in Massachusetts. We're left with self-defense. The trial should be scheduled soon."

"And Coach Hayes will testify?"

"I'll subpoena her, if I have to."

"And Gus? Will Gus speak?"

Sara had risen. "I think he has to, honey. Shahid threatened him, and now there's evidence that Shahid meant him harm. His testimony demonstrates your brother's capacity for violence."

"Shahid is not violent!" Afia shouted. From the corner of her eye, she saw a guard, moving toward her. Painfully, she lowered her voice. "He . . . *was* . . . not violent," she managed. "He had to—" She looked away, at the high window, the bright blue of the sky. *Was*, she thought. She felt again how Shahid had pushed her aside, out of harm's way, when the gun flashed. She hadn't had the strength to push back. "He knew," she said as if to herself, "where his duty lay."

CHAPTER TWENTY-FOUR

His sister's trial was like no kind of judgment Khalid had ever witnessed. Here was no *jirga*, no gathering of elders in equal and shared responsibility for the administration of justice. Here, the sides in the dispute—Afia as the wrongdoer and Shahid's supporters as the ones wronged—seemed voiceless in the proceedings. A woman sat high up behind a wooden wall, and the council that would decide the matter—not elders but people of all ages, women alongside men—sat silent and to the side. Those questioning the witnesses had no apparent role in determining the outcome, though they bullied and badgered the people called to the stand as if every word out of a witness's mouth were a snake to be ground beneath the heel.

The issue at hand, he saw immediately, was a foolish misapprehension of Afia for the murderer of Shahid. Somewhere the minions of the devil were laughing. From the bench where he sat, in the rear of the courtroom, Khalid could see the back of Afia's head, covered by a sheer scarf of lavender and blue. Next to her, a stocky Turkish-looking woman in heavy makeup rose to address the woman sitting on high as *Judge*, though she did not perform the role of a judge so much as an administrator, allowing certain procedures and disallowing others. The question at hand, as the stocky woman and her counterpart, a slope-shouldered man with a whine in his voice, made clear, was not who had committed the killing, but why. The stocky woman argued strenuously for self-defense.

Afia could not turn, could not see him seated behind the others in the room, a sparse gathering of the curious and the interested. Even if she could, she might not know him. He had bleached his hair to a cinnamon color and shaved his beard so that his sharp chin felt raw and exposed. Several rows in front of him, he recognized a boy he'd seen with Shahid, the first time he'd spotted his brother on the campus. The rest were strangers. By rights *he* should have been at the front, calling for justice for his dead brother, but no one in this place would understand his claim.

Why Afia was allowing these absurd proceedings to go forward, he thought at first he understood. If she told this assembly what had happened, she would be compelled to confess her own blackness—for it was that blackness that had brought the whole tragedy about. She should be the one dead and under the ground, and she knew it.

The officials at the front had gone through various procedural motions. They had called up two police officers to report on what they had found at the crime scene. They had called up a pinch-faced man who explained what he kept calling "primitive Pathan customs" about family honor and women. When this man had stepped down, the stocky woman stood. "The defense calls Felicity Hayes," she said.

Through the side door came the yellow-haired woman who was Shahid's squash coach. Unbelievable, such a perversion of roles. Shahid had always said *he* when he referred to his coach; Khalid was sure of it. And to think Omar believed his nephew had world-class training! This Felicity Hayes spoke softly but with pride, like a wounded warrior. She had driven Afia to the garage in Devon, she said, and the explosion there had terrified them both. It was impossible that Afia should be involved in such a crime, and yet the thought of the police had panicked her. She had felt sorry for the girl, she said, and so she had given her what she thought was safe harbor.

"Safe from her brother?" the stocky woman asked.

"She wasn't afraid of Shahid."

"You saw them together, that afternoon."

"I did. They'd agreed she would return to Pakistan. She wasn't happy about it. But they loved each other." Felicity Hayes looked around the courtroom, as if beseeching them to confirm this idea. "I can tell you, whatever happened at my husband's cabin, Afia could not have instigated it. She wanted to protect Shahid."

"Because she knew he planted that bomb?"

There was a slight hesitation. "She . . . never said anything like that."

"But you had known him to be violent."

"No," said the coach.

A look of mild disgust crossed the stocky woman's face. Leaning forward, Khalid almost smiled. This lawyer was not getting what she was after. "Tell us about the confrontation you had with Shahid," she said, "the week before."

The coach sat back in her chair. She sighed. She described suspending Shahid from play because he'd missed practices. "He was upset," she said. "He wasn't violent. He went for counseling."

"And three days later," said the stocky woman, "he tried to blow up his sister."

"Objection." The slope-shouldered man had jumped up. "Leading the witness."

"Sustained," said the judge.

The stocky woman sat down a couple of minutes later, and the man rose. As he asked Coach Hayes more questions about Shahid, Khalid's chest and neck began to sweat. They were like snapshots of his brother, her answers to the man's questions. How Shahid had resolved a feud between two other players, his second year at Enright. How he'd brought Afia to America, how he'd bought her the clothes she needed for the cold winters. His hopes for the future, a job at Harvard that would make his father proud. The ghost of Shahid vaulted into the courtroom—his quick grin, the spin of his hips when he feinted with the soccer ball, the light patter of his feet when he used to follow Khalid and the older boys down to the swimming hole. Dead, cold and dead, and buried in this strange land.

Four weeks, now, Khalid had mourned, and prayed, and waited. He had never been so alone. He had told Omar he had comrades in *Amreeka*, and indeed he had found them, a clutch of jihadists masquerading as students, in a dingy flat in South Boston where he had exchanged vague promises of action for a mattress in the corner. But that terrible moment had come when he had to put through a call to Peshawar. Had flames roared over the airwaves and scorched his chest, he could not have felt a hotter wrath than what Omar dealt out. He had been sent to save, and he had killed, he had destroyed everything Omar had built over a decade, he had put out the light of a shining beacon, he had ripped the heart from their family. *Our family*, Omar had said, and by that he meant not Khalid, even though Farishta and her children were meant to belong only to the Satars now—and, were it not for his millions, Omar would have no say in who lived or who died among the

Satars. "It was the girl," Khalid had protested. "It was Afia, she didn't care if he died, she thrust him before her, she knew the gun would go off, she was shameless, it was Afia." But Omar could not, or would not, hear him. Told him only to rot in hell, and then the line went dead.

Now the lawyer was wheedling, pressing the coach. "In your view, then," he was saying, "Shahid Satar would not have attacked his sister. Are you saying you see no reason she would have had to defend herself?"

"In my view," the coach said—again her eyes swept the room, and seemed to stop for a fraction of a second on Khalid—"Afia didn't shoot her brother in self-defense or in murder. I don't think she shot her brother at all. I think something else must be going on."

He needed air. Pushing his way past the others in his row, he slipped from the courtroom. He made his way down the circular staircase, past armed police who looked right through him. Outside, piles of dirt-browned snow lined the sidewalks. Traffic sped by, all automobiles, not a rickshaw or donkey cart in sight. He lit a cigarette—haram, but who was watching?—and inhaled deeply.

He would not rot in hell. He would pick up the shreds of his family's honor and stitch them together with the veins of this blackened sister. Before, yes, his motives had not been entirely pure. Envy had crept in, envy of Shahid, who had been so blindly preferred. Now there was only Afia and the shame she had brought upon them all, Shahid included. Omar had sent no more funds since that telephone call, but Khalid would get by, he would trust in Allah to guide him, his hand would be the hand of righteousness. All he needed was for these people to let Afia go, and he would be waiting for her.

He ground the cigarette under his shoe and returned through the metal detector they had set up in the lobby. Clean-shaven, russet-haired, he was unremarkable to these officers. When he returned to the courtroom, the coach had stepped down. At the tables toward the front of the room, people murmured together. Then the stocky woman straightened. She called a new witness. Gus Schneider.

A side door opened, and a young man entered the room, his torso canted forward, making his way on crutches. For the first time, Khalid's gaze fixed on Afia. Her body strained in the young man's direction, like a plant toward the sun. Yes, this was the one—the one from the hospital, the one whose empty makeshift apartment Khalid had entered by an open window to see the unmade bed, the women's underthings on a chair, the caged creatures staring at him with their glassy eyes while he strung wires around the door frame.

Letting go of one crutch, the young man raised his hand and pledged to tell the truth. His sister's seducer. The Jew. *Gus.*

"Tell us," the stocky woman was saying when he'd made his way clumsily into the witness seat, "about your relationship with Afia Satar."

"She was my girlfriend."

"Meaning you saw a lot of each other?"

Gus's eyes shifted toward Afia, then back. He wore a sport jacket and tie that seemed to squeeze his neck. "She was at Smith. But you know, it was normal. A normal dating relationship."

"And your relationship with Shahid Satar?"

Pressing against the tie, Gus's Adam's apple pulsed. "We were roommates once. We were on the team together. The squash team." Another glance, this time toward the mannish coach in the third row.

"Were you friends?"

"Friends?" Gus's voice slid upward. "Sure. Friends. He was an awesome guy."

"But you fought."

"Once, yeah."

"Over Shahid's sister, Afia." The stocky woman paused a beat, for effect. "The accused," she added.

The boy had begun to sweat. Good. Let him sweat. Let the world begin to see his shame. Khalid made himself breathe. His fingers clutched the front of the wooden seat.

"Yeah," Gus said. "I guess. He didn't like it. You know. The dating. He, uh"—his eyes flicked around the room, trying to follow whatever story he'd been coached to tell—"he could be a pretty scary guy. Jealous, you know."

"So you imagine he could get violent."

"Objection!" This was the slope-shouldered man, jumping up from the table where he sat. "She's asking the witness to speculate."

"I withdraw the question," said the stocky woman. Extraordinary, Khalid thought. That the so-called judge and the council should sit silent while these two hired lawyers spoke in place of the people who were truly involved. Someone should have been demanding atonement from this Gus creature. Not all this thrashing about with words.

Slowly the stocky woman led Gus through the accumulation of lies that would lead his passive audience to think Shahid Satar was a jealous fiend whose intent to harm would be stopped only by a bullet. When she had finished, the slope-shouldered lawyer rose. He had a few questions, he said, and Gus's Adam's apple bobbed again. He should be strangled, Khalid thought. Slowly, with picture wire, until his round eyes bulged in his head and his tongue stuck out like a serpent's.

"About your relationship with the accused, Afia Satar," the lawyer said. "Was it intimate?"

Gus looked confused. His eyes darted to Afia. Khalid's fingers gripped harder. "Could you repeat the question?" Gus asked.

"Was your relationship intimate?" the lawyer said, almost gently. "Was it sexual?"

Shame was a tide, sweeping from Afia back over the courtroom, blanketing Khalid. He barely heard Gus answer, "I don't really want to talk about that."

"So," the slope-shouldered man said, "the answer is yes."

"Objection!" The stocky woman, leaping up next to Afia. "Leading the witness," she said.

"Given what we heard earlier about Pathan customs," said the slope-shouldered man, "the degree of partner intimacy is crucial to the facts in this case."

At last, the judge spoke. Gray-haired and jowly, her elbows in their black sleeves planted wide on the table, she leaned forward. "The court will strike prosecution's inference from the record," she said. "The witness will answer the question."

Gus's cheeks were burning red. "Yes," he said softly. "It was . . . intimate. But not like you're saying. It was—it was normal. That's all."

Normal.

And did the accused, the prosecutor wanted to know, ever complain of her brother's treatment of her? "No, but—" Did she not, in fact, mention that she might prefer her own death to dishonor? "Look, she didn't put it exactly that way. She just said, you know, maybe she'd rather be dead."

Khalid half rose from his seat. *Maybe she'd rather be dead.* At last, they were getting to the heart of the matter. When Gus had stepped down, the court declared a recess. As he followed the rest out of the room, Afia was led away, somewhere else. The Gus guy was not in sight.

He was short on sleep. At the Boston flat he had found nothing useful to do, other than stay up late with the six others crowding the flat, smoking hash and hatching absurd plans for jihad. Now he shut his eyes as he sat on the curved bench rounding the atrium. What did he want, from these curious proceedings? Could they order Afia, as a *jirga* might, to take her own life? He had never heard of such an order in the West. But if they could—or if, as he had heard was possible, they condemned her to execution by the state for the killing of Shahid—would he then be satisfied?

His heart filled with dread. No, he would not. No honor came from such a death, no wiping clean of Afia's shame, no absolution for what she had done, drawing Khalid's fire like that until it hit Shahid. No. He must bring it about himself, this death. And so he must hope for them to let her go, to deliver her up to him.

From a bench outside the courtroom he had been staring at the floor, following the pattern of the tiles, when he felt a body sink next to his and heard a long sigh. He tipped his head sideways. The woman coach, Felicity Hayes. A surge of panic rose within him, but he tamped it down. Up close, with her clean jaw and small mouth, she looked more like a woman, even a beautiful woman. She looked curiously at him. "Long trial, huh?"

He didn't know. What was long, in the West? In the tribal belt, a decision would have been reached in an hour. "Yes," he said.

"Do I know you?"

He widened his eyes. There could be no disguising the accent. "I go to school," he said, "with Shahid."

She frowned. "Enright?" When he nodded her frown went deeper. He thought of the time he had followed her Toyota out of the town to the highway, hoping she would lead him to Afia. "You don't play a sport," she said.

"No, I"—he reached for the easiest lie—"I study engineering."

"But we don't have an engineering school."

"No." He tried to chuckle. It came out as a small yelp. "I am applying elsewhere."

"But you—you were friendly with Shahid. You're Pakistani?"

He straightened up. He needed to get away from this woman. "From Karachi," he said quickly. "I don't know his family. I am only sorry she had killed him. I want justice."

"Well, so do we all, but surely you don't think Afia—"

"Excuse me," he said. He rose and headed for the men's room. She had been with Afia, that night. If the device had gone off properly, she would be dead as well, and her eyes could not bore holes in his back, as they did now while he crossed the atrium, trying to appear—what had this Gus called it?—*normal.*

CHAPTER TWENTY-FIVE

After the verdict, released into the round atrium, Afia looked in vain for Gus. The aunties from the Price Chopper surrounded her, and Sue Glasgow, who had testified as a character witness. And Shahid's friend Afran, his hair cropped close and his eyes full of sadness. A few yards away, gesturing emphatically with her hands, Sara Desfani was giving the news to a reporter. Coach Hayes stood on the other side of the atrium, with a loose-shouldered man Afia recognized from the photos on the wall at that cabin. His cabin, his family's cabin.

"Of course it was self-defense. Poor honey," Esmerelda from the Price Chopper kept saying. "To go through all that and then have them treat you like a criminal. You brave, brave girl."

"Shouldn't never have gone to trial," added Carlotta.

"At least you're out," said Sue Glasgow. And then, after a glance at the security officer who still stood next to Afia, handcuffs dangling from his pocket, "Are you coming back to Smith?"

"I—I don't know."

How had she not thought past this moment? Over and over,

Sara Desfani had told her she would be acquitted, and yet somehow she had held on to the illusion that the court would believe her story, that they would find a way to punish her so Khalid would not have to. She had glimpsed him, leaving the courtroom, his hair hennaed and his face strangely naked. Fear had injected her like a hypodermic. Khalid would bide his time, strike when he chose.

"Course she's going back," Esmerelda said. "Can't stop her, can they?"

"But I have missed classes—"

"You can make those up, I'm sure you can," Professor Glasgow said warmly. "But I don't know if the dorms are open. Spring break, now."

"Spring break," Afia repeated. Of course. Outside the jail, the snow had been steadily melting. On the Smith campus, there would be crocus. She glanced toward the courtroom. It had emptied. The reporter—a bald man with bulging eyes and a recording device in his small hand—had turned from Sara and was approaching Coach Hayes. She looked down the corridor that led to the front of the courtroom. No Gus. She willed her heart to stay afloat.

"You can stay with me," Afran said. He looked older, in street clothes; she had only seen him dressed for squash. "The other guys in my house're in Florida. Plenty of beds."

"You are kind," she said. "But after . . . after what has happened, I don't think—"

"You mean your brother." He waited a beat. "My best friend."

She gaped. She felt the women, clustered around her, begin to close tighter.

"Don't get me wrong. I'm not mad at you," Afran went on—and he didn't sound angry, only nervous, blustering. "But it's messed up, that honor thing. It is totally fucked up. If the dude had just talked to me. . . . Well." He looked around at the other women. "I'm just saying," he finished, meaning there was more to say. "I can be, like, you know. Your other brother. If you need to crash."

"She'll be fine," Carlotta said quickly. "Won't you, honey? You'll be fine."

"Yes," Afia breathed. It dizzied her, being with these people who believed in a lie. She could not go home with Sue Glasgow or the aunties—or, Allah forbid, her brother's friend. "Excuse me," she said.

She made her way past her well-wishers, to the staircase where Coach Hayes's husband stood while his wife gave the reporter tight-lipped responses. "Dr. Hayes," she said.

"It's Springer," he said. "Ethan Springer." He put out his hand, and she let him shake hers. His hand was warm, like his voice. "Glad your ordeal's over," he said. "I am sorry about your brother."

"Thank you." Her throat felt dry. Gus must have gone out a back way, she thought. Avoiding her: what she should have expected. No matter. All she wanted was to go home. Not to a dorm room or the aunties. Home. "I am sorry," she said. "Very sorry. What I do to you."

"Careful, there." Only when his arm went to her elbow did she feel the sinking in her knees. "Let's sit down," he said.

He got her to a bench. He wore thick glasses, like hers, which enlarged his brown eyes, made him look curious or worried, she couldn't tell. Quickly he fetched her water in a paper cone. "Do you want to talk about it?" he asked when she had drunk it dry.

She shook her head. "Only to say, it was not Coach Hayes's fault."

"That's between Lissy and me." After an awkward beat, he added, "I imagine you were panicked."

She nodded, mute. The others drifted over. One by one, they

said good-bye. Carlotta leaned down, pecked Afia on the cheek. Behind her, the reporter was pushing in. Coach's husband stood up and shooed him away. Suddenly the atrium was empty. Even Sara Desfani had disappeared into an office. Only Coach, lingering behind her husband, and the security officer waiting for some sort of formal discharge. With a glance at her, Coach's husband sat back down, next to Afia.

"I understand," he said gently, "you can go back to school."

"It is spring break," she said. She did not say she could no longer imagine Smith, her classes, the labs.

"Is there anywhere you can stay? Where you feel safe?"

She couldn't help it. As she lifted her head, her gaze slid past him, to Coach Hayes. Coach looked better than when she'd come to visit Afia. Her eyes still thirsted for an answer, but she had said her piece at the trial. *I don't think she shot her brother at all.*

Her husband sighed, as if something he'd known all along was coming to light. "I tell you what," he said. "Why don't you come back with us for a few days? Till you get your bearings."

Coach's hand crept onto his shoulder, and he reached back to touch her fingers.

It was strange to leave Glens Falls in a car, to hear the radio; as they pulled away from the courthouse, to pass ordinary people on ordinary sidewalks. As they merged onto the interstate, Afia kept looking into the side mirror, to see if a car might be following them. The light was fading, headlights coming on, and twin beams passed them one after the other. She couldn't keep track. Khalid was out there, she knew, but he would find ways to circle wide of her and pin her down at the moment she failed to look. Best, after all, not to have seen Gus. To see Gus was to put Gus in danger.

As they crossed the Hudson River, the river that had run by the cabin farther north, Coach shifted in her seat and said there was a Muslim cemetery nearby, in the town of Troy. She understood that Shahid had been laid to rest in it. When Afia was ready, she said, they could go there.

Afia strained to look out the window, but night was falling, and all she made out were lights and billboards. "Did you—did you see him?" she asked.

"I did." This was Coach's husband, who had told her to call him Ethan. "I don't think he suffered, Afia. If that's any comfort."

"Comfort," Afia repeated. The word felt alien, like a cloud of gas. "No, I don't think so. But thank you."

It was full dark when they got to the little house by the lake. The last place, Afia thought, where Coach had seen Shahid. Toys and books lay scattered, just as before, over the living room floor. Chloe was asleep, reported the babysitter—a squash player, Afia recognized her. While Ethan drove the girl home, Coach took Afia downstairs, to a sort of TV den on the ground floor, with its own exit toward the lake. There she unfolded a couch, laid out sheets and a blanket. There was only a half bath, Coach said, but she could rustle up a clean toothbrush for Afia, and paste, a set of towels, a nightgown that would be absurdly long but would have to do for now.

"You are very kind," Afia said when Coach returned with these things. She removed her glasses. Fatigue spread across her back, over her shoulders, down her torso to her hips.

"You want something to eat?"

"No, thank you, Coach. I cannot. Your husband . . . he is no more angry?"

"Not with you. And I blame myself more than he ever can. So don't worry about it."

"But I must worry."

"Worry later, then. Get some sleep. Tomorrow we can drive over to Smith, try to fetch your own clothes."

Then Coach did an odd thing. She stepped over to Afia and wrapped her long arms around Afia's back. Pressing Afia to her, she kissed her hair where the scarf had fallen back. "You're safe, now," she said. "That's the main thing."

The nightgown was midnight blue, like water flowing over Afia's body. In the bathroom, she removed the hijab, and her hair caressed her shoulders, her collarbone. The mirror shocked her with her own nakedness, the shadow of breast diving into the silk, the soft delta of skin at her exposed underarm. She lifted the hem to regard her bare feet, the missing toe on the left a nick in the foot's taper, the next toe strangely long and exposed. Sometimes she thought of the vanished toe as the part of her soul that went with Shahid, that would never grow back. Shutting off the light, she brushed her teeth in the dark.

As soon as she had settled in the makeshift bed, sleep pulled her under. But she woke, alert and restless, with the sky paling. She peeked through the Venetian blinds on the outside door. Was Khalid nearby? From the lake came a chorus of spring peepers. The moon rode high, its reflection a shattered plate on the water. For four weeks, she had slept in a locked room and ventured outside only under guard. *Here I am, Khalid*, she thought. Silently, she opened the door and stepped out.

The night air pricked her skin. Against the soles of her feet pressed a wet nubble of grass and weeds, the snow here entirely melted. She scanned all directions—the other houses perched by the shore, their night-lights glinting through the windows; the distant rasp of cars on the state highway; the gray birch branches arching away from the papery white of their trunks. Where ice had vanished from the lake, dwindling stars salted its dark surface. Across the water, movement—her heart listed—but it was only a doe and her fawn, drinking at the edge. From the trees came the lonely hoot of an owl, a flutter of smaller wings. Nothing else stirred. She crouched, hugging her knees around the thin silk. She needed to see, to hear, to taste all this—not for herself, but for Shahid, who never would. Shahid, who with his big strong body would dive into this water, would churn across to the other side and back and emerge, exultant. *Run*, he had ordered her. *Run*. He wanted her to live. But at what price, Shahid lala? What price should be paid, for her little life?

She stretched out on the cold grass. Above, the sky was slate, then taupe. Inside slept a little family—not her family, but a family at least. The doe and fawn a family, the birds quick with their nesting. No one lived long without a family; you were like one of those patients missing kidneys or intestines, you could be kept going with various machines but soon enough you expired. You breathed while you could. You shut your eyes. You felt the world tilt toward the sun.

And then there was Coach's daughter, Chloe, shaking her on the wet grass, shouting, "Mommy! I found her! She's sleeping outside!"

As it turned out, the dorms at Smith were open. Coach brought Afia there the next day. Patty's Hello Kitty clock still rested on the shelf, her iPod in its dock by the leaded windows looking over the walkway where Gus had stood two months ago, begging to be let in. But the room felt achingly lonely. She had heard nothing from Patty or Taylor while in the jail. She imagined their wide eyes, their whispering behind her back: *She, like, shot her own brother. That's wacked, right?* She packed up her books and a few clothes, her Qur'an.

That she would return here after the break, that she would ever be a student again, seemed impossible. What she wanted was to go to the Price Chopper, to see her aunties, even to pick up where she had left off, placing customers' cans and wrapped cold cuts into bags, listening to Carlotta complain of her pothead sons. But she couldn't ask Coach to drive her around all day.

Coach shrugged at this statement. "Why not?" she said. "It's not like I have a job to go to."

"Even now? Now that this trial is finished? Coach, I will go to the boss at Enright, I will explain to him—"

Coach laughed for the first time since that fateful Sunday in February. "Afia, I'll make you a deal," she said. "When you start talking to me about what's still got you so scared, I'll talk to you about my job."

In the driveway by the lake, a blue police car sat waiting. Afia shrank back into her seat. But when Coach Hayes went to talk to the officers who emerged, it seemed they didn't want anything from either of them. The case of the explosion at Gus's garage, one of them explained, was closed. In the back of their car they had the things they had confiscated from Shahid's locker and dorm room—his books, clothes, computer, the sports bag with his wallet in it. The Honda, they said, was still in New York State, but as Shahid's next of kin Afia could reclaim it. They were sorry, they said, for her loss.

At first, Afia recoiled. The officers brought the boxes onto the ground floor of the house and set them in the corner, but she could not touch Shahid's things. It felt like touching the dead. The boxes seemed to whisper to her—of Shahid's life, his little notes and his Facebook page and the assignments still due to his classes, the life he was supposed to be leading.

She opened her own boxes, tried to read *Jane Eyre*, to memorize molecular formulae. She sat on the floor with Chloe and played games. Chloe was like Muska when she was little, bouncy and curious. Did Afia know about Dora? Did she think Purple Monkey was a boy or a girl? Did Afia like purple better, or pink? Could she try Afia's glasses? Why did they make the world look all funny?

Over the next few days she took Chloe to the playground, which was sunny and unseasonably warm. She cooked the family a meal of spicy kebabs and minted raita. She took the bus back to Smith to meet with each of her professors and with the dean, who promised her scholarship would continue through the spring, no matter what her family said or did. She picked up the phone to call Moray in Nasirabad, and put it down; she opened a file on Shahid's laptop to write Moray a letter, and after staring at the blinking cursor, clicked it closed. She was not afraid of what her mother would say, she told Coach. She was afraid of what a phone call, or a letter, would do to her mother. Coach thought she meant grief, hurt feelings. She didn't know what a blackened daughter was, how she could wither whatever part of her family she touched.

Gus called once, twice, three times, and when she would not come to the phone he drove to Coach's house. She sat with him outside, on the deck, a public place where no touching would happen. He still walked with crutches. He had dropped out of school for the spring. Maybe in the fall he'd finish. Vet school the next year, if he was lucky. His eyes flicked over her, then moved to the pattern of wind on the lake, moving cakes of ice around like paper boats. She focused on his sweater, one of those Irish cable knits that she used to see in American movies about blond couples falling in love.

"Without me," she said, "luck will come back to you."

"Is that what you think you brought me, M'Afia? Bad luck?"

"You must not call me that," she said. She kept her voice steady by picturing it as a set of molecules that she had to move carefully in a petri dish, gripping the tweezers hard but never too hard. "I have caused you only pain," she said.

"Hey, you didn't plant a bomb. You didn't mess with my car."

"But you told the police—"

"That it was possible, yeah. But anything's possible, right? You'd run off. The detective said you'd confessed." He leaned across the wrought-iron table on the deck. She could smell his specific odor, the tangy scent that filled her nostrils when they'd lain side by side in his wide bed. "Shahid did the number on my brakes, and I get why. Really. I wasn't paying attention. I put you guys at risk. I messed with your whole family."

She looked at him then. So young, he looked. His face round and full, patchy beard growth around his jawline, freckles framing the short nose.

"My family, you know," he went on, "it's just my mom, plus my dad who's never around. That's it. I used to envy you. All those uncles you had, all those cousins you e-mailed with. And Shahid. I used to imagine being in a little corner of your family. Then I did things—well, the way we do here, you know, guys and girls. Shahid tried to stop me. I didn't listen, so he did what he did. And then Coach . . ." He exhaled a long breath. He looked out over the lake, the sun shooting it with silver between ice cakes. "She never believed in the team," he said. "She believed in Shahid. If she comes back to Enright—"

"Gus, you must blame me. Not her. She wanted all for the best. The team, too."

"Maybe. But I won't play for her anymore. That is, if I can ever play again."

He set his hand flat on the table. She couldn't help herself. She put her own hand over it. Then she lifted it, bent her head toward the fingers, smelled them, touched her lips to his palm.

"Afia, tell me what you're feeling. Can you feel anything for me—"

She set his hand down. Her own went to her ears. Gus looked shocked. She struggled for the words. "Feelings!" she blurted, louder than she'd meant. "Why does everyone ask me about these feelings? To my family I am dead. And Shahid, he is dead, really dead. There is a—a path. That we follow. I am off that path. No way back. Like—like the bird we saw when we were picking apples. The bird that broke its wing. It sits on the ground, and it will die, because it is not flying, and it is supposed to fly. What does it matter, what that bird feels?"

"Afia, you're not going to die."

"Please. Stop talking this way."

"Stop talking about us, you mean."

She looked at his hands, still on the table. She wanted to lift the other hand, to touch her lips to it. She pushed herself up, opened the sliding door to the house, stepped inside. When she turned around, he was gone.

That night, she opened Shahid's computer. She had helped him with his homework enough that she knew the password, *my1Nasir-abad*. There on the desktop were his unfinished papers, his video games, his library of hip-hop and Pashtun songs, the action photos of him leaping for the squash ball, diving to dig it out from the corner. In his goggles he looked like an old-fashioned aviator. That he was cold and dead, under the ground, seemed impossible. A grave in Troy, like the city where Achilles died, also far from home. She should go there, beg his forgiveness. Upstairs, she could hear Coach and Ethan talking softly. Spring break would be over in a few days. They would want her to go back to Smith, to pick up her studies as if the world had not broken into pieces.

She opened Shahid's e-mail. She was spying now, but on what? Could a dead brother have secrets? More than a month ago, he had made a plea to Uncle Omar for funds, that he might go with her as far as Doha. No answer had come. For the first time since her fleeing, she remembered the plan to send her home. "Zardad," she murmured.

Another e-mail, this time to one of his teammates—Carlos, she wasn't sure which one that was. *I can pay u back by graduation man I swear it*, Shahid had written. *Yknow what its like, family emergency.* The response was the record of a funds transfer, two thousand dollars. Then Shahid's note, *Youre the best man, I got yr back anytime*. Then, sure enough, two tickets, bought at the full rate. Her heart swelled and sank. What Baba must have sacrificed, to send Shahid the funds to ship her home! And this boy Carlos, she would owe him now. She opened the file for Shahid's bank account with the same password—silly brother, not bothering to think of a different one—and discovered another five hundred dollars, what was left from the allowance Uncle Omar sent every month. All wasted now, all gone.

Next morning, she told Coach Hayes she was ready to return to Smith. It was a Saturday. Her roommates would be back by now. She could not burden the coach's family any longer.

"You want to go today?" Coach said.

"No!" said Chloe. She grabbed hold of Afia's leg. "I will miss you too much!"

Chloe was a demanding child, Afia thought, crouching down to her. She needed siblings, other small humans with big needs to keep hers in check. "I'll come back and play with you," she promised. "You will teach me Spanish. Sí?"

Coach was meeting the girls' squash team that morning, she

said. It was the only responsibility left to her, at the moment. She wanted to know which starters would be returning in the fall. She'd take Afia to Smith in the afternoon.

When she'd left, Afia went downstairs. She heard Coach's car pull out—then, five minutes later, another car pull in. She glanced out the window of her room but could not see around to the drive. Upstairs, the doorbell sounded, a lackluster buzz. Heavy steps—Ethan's—to the door.

Then his voice. Khalid's. Afia's chest froze. "Hello. Dr. Springer? I am Shahid friend. From Enright University?"

"You're a friend of Shahid's?" Ethan's voice was faint; he was standing at the door, directing his words outside. He was not opening the door to Khalid. "Are you on the team?"

"No, sir, no." Something like a chuckle, from Khalid. "I am not excellent at squash. Not like my unfortunate friend Shahid. No, I am international student. Very close with Shahid."

There was a pause; Ethan said something she couldn't hear. She had backed into a corner, in the shadow by the stairwell.

Then Khalid again. "Yes, very sad. I am close with him. And Afia. He always tell me, 'Take care of Afia.' So now I try. She is here, yes?"

"No," Ethan said. This was louder. "I don't know where she is."

"But I am to take care of her. You take her, yes? From the court."

"How would you know that?"

"Sir, please. I mean no harm. I am friend of Shahid."

Afia felt the sweat running down between her breasts, under her arms, the back of her neck. She couldn't make out what Ethan said next, something about Northampton, that they'd dropped her in Northampton to go back to school.

Then Khalid: "I see, sir. Thank you, sir. Do you mind I get a drink of water?"

Afia held her breath. But only one set of footfalls went to the kitchen and returned to the front door. Then Ethan's voice: "Keep the bottle. Good luck tracking her down."

The door shut with a thunk; she heard the click of the lock. A minute later, the car pulled out and rumbled up the hill. Then, from the top of the stairs, Chloe said, "Daddy? Who was that man?"

"Oh, just a student, honey."

"But Afia's *here*."

"I know, cutie. But she's tired. We don't want to bother her right now. Come help me water the plants."

Afia slipped into her tiny bathroom. She lowered the lid onto the toilet and sat on it, her knees hunched to her chest. She could not go back to the dorm. She would only put Patty and Taylor at risk. Nor could she stay here, to endanger Coach's family. She would have to run, as she had run before, far away, until Khalid found her.

"Shahid," she whispered to herself. "Shahid." As if she could summon his ghost, to tell her what he would have her do. He had wanted her to go home to Nasirabad, to forget her dreams and forget Gus and marry Zardad. Which was, of course, the sensible thing, the only real choice. Zardad. Marriage.

She planted her feet on the cold floor and sat up. *Zardad.* Shahid had assured her, the night he was killed, that no one in Nasirabad knew about that third photo, the one Khalid had taken, the one that showed Gus's face. Maybe, just maybe, there was a chance. If she went back. If she pleaded with Moray. Oh, how she needed her mother, to hold her and scold her, to lash out at her, to beat her if she had to, but to help her in the end, to make her choose the right path. She tiptoed back to her room, around the makeshift bed, to the computer she had repacked and stacked in the corner. Opening Shahid's e-mail again, she clicked on the one-way confirmation for Afia Satar.

Full value of wholly unused ticket, she read, *may be applied toward purchase of a new ticket price at current fare levels upon payment of the cancel fee.*

She went to the airline's site. The difference, with the fee, was just over six hundred dollars. Too much, too much. Wait. The other ticket, Shahid's round trip to Doha. *Charge USD 300.00 for cancel/refund.* More clicks—*Yes* and *Yes* and she entered the information for Shahid's bank account, and the money flowed back, almost three thousand dollars. Her heart pumped so fast that the beats seemed to run together.

Buses left Northampton every day for New York. She had seen the other girls get on them. Today was Saturday. She chose Tuesday. She filled in the numbers, checked the boxes to agree on the rules, the fees. Her fingers had gone cold as porcelain. A half hour later, she brought the computer upstairs. Coach's husband was doing laundry. Chloe was watching cartoons. Safe, safe and happy.

"Excuse me, Ethan?" she said.

"Afia. I thought you'd gone back to bed."

His eyes behind his glasses gave nothing away of the morning's encounter. "I have been working on a project. I wonder, might I use your printer?"

He gestured for her to sit at his desk. His smile was guarded. He was Chloe's baba, Afia thought as he left to pull her away from the TV. Ready to do anything, to protect his child. She printed her new ticket, then went to finish packing.

CHAPTER TWENTY-SIX

As the mulberry trees began to bloom in the spring, Farishta did her best to take up her duties. Six weeks, now, the house had been plunged in grief. The cause was as simple and old as the red dirt of the hills around Nasirabad. A girl had gone rotten, and a boy had lost his golden life. Only these had been her girl, her boy. Birthed between her legs, both of them, from her young first husband, Malook—who had long since faded, in her memory, to a shorter, darker, less even-tempered version of Tofan Satar.

How exultant Malook had been to see his first child, long and honey-colored. Shahid's fat testicles and thumbnail-sized penis had proclaimed success. They had lived in Peshawar, the only couple not part of the sprawling compound in Nasirabad, because Malook was a company major and they had the privilege of military housing. Gray and nondescript, their house had sat in a row of such houses, made safe and therefore privileged by the armed checkpoints at every intersection approaching the neighborhood. Lonely as she was, with Malook gone to the tribal areas three weeks out of every month, the children—Shahid with his restlessness, his thick curling hair; Afia a curious, serious infant—had filled her days. When Malook got leave, they would drive out here, to Nasirabad, where her in-laws would make a fuss over the children. She noticed Tofan especially, even then, the eldest of four boys and a girl, the quietest, with a courtliness that seemed quaint and a laugh that boomed out from the *hujra*. His wife Badrai had been sickly even when Farishta first met her, but solicitous as an older sister. By the time Shahid was big enough to play with their cousins in the courtyard, Badrai's skull beneath her dupatta had gone bald as marble and death was written on her face.

Then the two Punjabis, in uniform, at Farishta's door at dawn one morning in a stinging hot Peshawar summer. An improvised device, in South Waziristan. Five dead, including Malook. Not enough left of his body to bury, though the imam would say the rites and send his soul to paradise. For a time she had moved back home, "home" by then being the fine place her brother Omar had built for their parents and her widowed aunt. What had she felt? A loss, certainly—her husband gone, their life blown away like dust—but she had not known him well. The sweaty couplings in the night; the spurts of anger when she burned the chapatis; the flask of whiskey he kept hidden at the top of the cupboard. At home, she was loved to suffocation, her children whisked from her and taken up by the elders of the household—including Omar, who took a shine to Shahid even then. What a relief it had been, when Badrai, in her illness, managed to travel to Peshawar and extend the offer! To be a second wife. To inherit the husband, the tall, quiet, barrel-chested one with the mustache and the belly laugh. They would be a family again. She and her children would belong to someone.

Gone, now. Like his father, Shahid had given her no body to inter in the plot outside Nasirabad. No one would join her mourning.

The men had said the Janazeh prayer, but she had been shut out from that. Shut out, too, by her mother-in-law and Tofan's sister, Gautana, who knew what evil Farishta had set in motion. Shut out, clearly, by Khalid, who had not responded to the messengers they had sent, had not come down from the mountains. And by Tofan, who grieved his adopted son as if Shahid had sprung from his own loins, but who would not come to Farishta's bed, would not taint his sorrow with hers.

The others had their grief pure; hers was adulterated by failure. For it is from the mother that the daughter learns. When a girl heaps shame on her family, it is her mother who has left the door open, who has allowed shame to enter. Why, oh why, had Afia not simply come home? What sort of madness put a gun in a girl's hands? Better the girl should have loaded her pockets with rocks and waded into the river. Instead her son lay cold in a foreign land. Unless it was a trick, a foul trick. When she dreamed of Shahid he was always alive, lost in a canyon or trapped in a cave, calling ever more faintly, *Moray, Moray.*

Her husband slept in the *hujra*. He asked Tayyab to serve him his meals separately. She heard him, outside in the night, wailing. But he had never struck her, never scolded her. He had put her away, as one puts away a favorite cloth that has become irrevocably stained. Many days she wished he would rage at her, a swifter and surer punishment.

Then, two days ago, she had seen the autorickshaw draw up to the wall, and the girl alight. Tayyab's third daughter, Panra, the brightest of the lot, sent away six years ago to Omar's compound in Peshawar to attend their mother. Tayyab himself, after all, had been a wedding gift from Omar, who by then could not imagine his sister in a household without a cook. A year, now, since Panra's last visit home. Perhaps they had arranged a marriage, though his daughters' marriages thus far had brought Tayyab no good luck.

"Memsahib," Tayyab said the next morning, when she was up early—she rose, now, before dawn each day, unable to bear her own wakefulness—"I have disturbing news."

Tayyab's eyes were failing, milky cataracts inching their way across. Stooped and fussy, he clung to the old ways; you could not lift a tea bag without his coming upon you and shooing you out of the way so he could prepare the whole tray, complete with sweets and napkin. He cared for Farishta and her children with the same intense devotion he gave his own. This time, he drew her back to the courtyard behind the kitchen, even though no one was awake to hear them. He told her that Panra had seen Khalid at Omar's compound, back in the winter. Khalid had not recognized her as she served the tea to him and to Omar. "And so," Tayyab went on, his hands clasped in front of him as if preparing to genuflect, "she heard the sahib say to him, he would fund this trip, he wanted the thing taken care of and his nephew not distracted."

Farishta frowned. Khalid was meant to be in the mountains. Yet in her gut she had known he was not there. Something had been afoot months ago, when Tofan had come to her with a face like a tornado, saying Khalid had found a photo, an objectionable photo. "Take me to your daughter," she said.

Rising from the table in the hut, Panra bowed to her. She was a pockmarked girl with a large nose, but she had always been a hard worker. For her to travel alone from Peshawar to Nasirabad was an act of tremendous daring. She looked exhausted and frightened, like a deer on the chase. "You have come from my brother's home," Farishta said sternly to her.

"Yes, memsahib."

"And you heard him in conversation with my stepson, who was going on a trip."

"Yes, memsahib. To—to *Amreeka*."

Farishta took in a sharp breath. "Tell me exactly what my brother said. Do not be afraid, child. I will not punish you."

The girl raised her eyes. They were large, deep blue, long-lashed, and shot through with red. She licked her lips. "He said," she began, "that a shameless girl was not worth the price."

"What price?"

"The price of a great career, he said. He counted on Khalid sahib to finish the business. When he finished talking, he was very angry. But Khalid sahib was not angry. He ate an orange in the sunlight. Then the driver took him to the airport."

Farishta gave Tayyab two thousand rupees, that the girl might take an autorickshaw back to Peshawar when she was ready, and not be molested. He escorted her back to the house. There, at the threshold, she crumpled. Folded slowly over her knees and ankles. Her arms clasped her shins.

Of course. Of *course*. Her brother Omar—who had no children of his own, who would never have anything other than the dancing boys—treasured Shahid's success above all else. Khalid was not in the mountains, refusing their messengers. Khalid was in *Amreeka*. He had killed her only son, he had killed Shahid. And Afia—who was not so spoiled as to be good as dead, no, but to Omar that didn't matter, she was a nuisance and an impediment—had confessed to the crime herself. She had added Khalid's guilt to her own. What a stupid, brave, loving, ridiculous girl! And yet how could she, Farishta, go on now? To see Omar again, to speak to Omar, was out of the question. She could not tell her husband what she had learned. He would fly into a rage. Would beat Tayyab's daughter, would fire Tayyab. Or if he believed this story, it would circle around, again, to Farishta's own feet. For was not Omar her blood, who had no business interfering in the affairs of the Satars?

She felt Tayyab's hand press lightly on the back of her head. She did not look up. After a moment she heard his feet shuffle away across the courtyard—walking carefully, as he always did now, for fear of tripping on a loose tile.

It was a new grief now. Strange, how a child could be dead differently. What, in the end, is the difference if the end comes through chance or design, by this or that one's hand? But knowing that Khalid had gone across the world to kill her daughter and had ended up, somehow, causing the death of her son was like losing Shahid all over again. She pressed her lips together, she dared not blurt out her new knowledge, but inside a hot wind raged. For Shahid was dead, and this time it all made sense, terrible sense.

Still, she got Sobia and Muska into their uniforms and off to school. She made up the marketing list for Tayyab. She tended to her mother-in-law, who needed her food crushed into a paste and spat half of it out. And then this morning, a bright and breezy Thursday, when the village women went to gather mulberries, she let her daughters pull her along. It had been more than forty days since she had learned of Shahid's death. To continue mourning was shameful, unseemly. She put away her dark clothes and went out.

From the bowed branches of the trees the mulberries hung like fat worms, some purple and others—the sweeter ones—creamy white. In a bright blue shalwar kameez with giant yellow sunflowers printed on the fine cotton, Farishta held the baskets. The others shucked their sandals and climbed the trees. Their men were all in the fields or at the factory; they couldn't see the dupattas slip from their women's heads and shoulders, couldn't hear the jokes they made. Sobia was one of the first to scramble up, her long, narrow feet gripping the trunk as she swung herself onto a branch. Soon a dozen trees sported women like colorful birds, dropping fistfuls of mulberries into Farishta's baskets. When they returned, they would eat the mulberries fresh, bake them into cakes, dry them to put out, months later, in bright woven bowls alongside bowls of pistachios and dates when someone important came to tea.

Muska ran beneath the trees, catching the berries that rained down accidentally as the women shook them loose. She had turned eleven that winter, just old enough to understand what death meant. She didn't ask, as Shahid had asked when his father was killed, when she would see her brother. Many nights she had crawled into Farishta's bed to clutch at her nightgown and sob. At the same time, on days like this one, in the bright morning with dew wet on the long grass, she forgot tragedy and wanted nothing but to stuff her mouth with sweet berries. She didn't know, yet, about Afia, how Afia was as good as dead to them all. She knew only that her sister was still in *Amreeka* and that she was not to pronounce Afia's name in front of her father or uncles. Sobia was more worrisome. She had heard comments from her classmates, Farishta was sure of it, but she would report nothing. She came home, went to her room, did her homework. She was flinty with her younger sister and her grandmother. When Farishta scolded her, she turned her blue eyes on her mother and said, "You wish to instruct me, Moray?" in a tone that could not be punished but left no doubt as to its meaning. Her anguish was buried deep as the emeralds mined in the Kush. Now she took her basket and climbed to the top of the white mulberry tree, where the leaves hid her and only a dangerous sway in the canopy gave her away.

Farishta lifted her eyes. They were below the village, on a slope that led down to the cotton fields. From here you could just make out the road leading down to the highway and the market stalls lining it. At the top of the hill stood a figure in a royal blue burqa. She sighed. So many were covering completely, now. Even the women climbing the trees, when they went to the market, hid their noses and mouths; her sister-in-law Gautana had said the other day that the burqa was the easiest solution, all in one and no worry about slippage. She wondered who the woman was, why she would stand and watch the mulberry picking and not participate. Something familiar in the posture, the set of the swaddled head on the shoulders. Her heart began beating faster, a stone skipping down a hill.

"Muska, my pet. Can you hold my baskets for a few minutes?"

"I'm catching berries!"

"Catch them in a basket. You'll catch more than with your bare hands."

Taking the handle, Muska scarcely glanced at her mother; her eyes were all for the juicy strings tumbling from the trees. Farishta set off across the field, crowded with wildflowers, their stems prickly, the ground beneath mounded and pitted from bicycles taking a shortcut to the river. Ahead lay the warren of houses where the farmworkers lived. Behind their walls of mud and hay sat thatched sheds occupied by goats and cows lazily swatting flies, while grooved canals ran waste from the courtyard latrines down to the fields. Disks of dung, slapped onto the courtyard walls, dried in the sun. She still remembered coming here for the first time, how all the villagers had brought her little gifts, embroidered fans and flour sifters. Shahid had jumped from the rickshaw and run to the stream with the other village boys, as if he had lived here all his short life.

His short, short life.

The woman in the blue burqa stood very still as Farishta approached. In her left hand she carried a small traveling bag. Her shuttlecock mask cast a grid of shadow onto the eyes and nose on the other side. But as she drew close, Farishta had no doubt. Fear and exhilaration grappled in her chest. "Afia," she breathed.

"Moray," came her daughter's voice from within the shroud. "Moray, I've come home."

Farishta's shoulders pulled forward, to wrap her arms around her girl. But anyone could be watching—from the mulberry orchard, from one of the mud houses in the village, from the crowded road below. She kept her arms at her side. From her cheeks she wiped tears of joy. "My sparrow," she said, always her pet name for her oldest daughter, *merghey*, "you've flown such a long way."

"I had to, Moray, you don't know what happened, Shahid and Khalid, they—"

"Ssh. Softly." She patted the air with her hand, tamping it down. "I know."

"So you know it wasn't me. You know—"

"What's done is done." Farishta shook her head. She could not allow this joy to compromise what she knew was right. "You set it in motion, Allah knows."

"I did." Afia took a step forward, Farishta a step back. She could feel the village women's eyes swinging her way from across the field. "That's why I've come, Moray. To set it right. To seek *nanawate*. To do what Shahid wanted me to do—and I was going to, Moray, if he hadn't tried to kill me, I—"

Farishta's blood went suddenly cold. "My son did not try to kill you."

"No, no, Moray, I mean . . ." Afia's voice trailed off. Beneath the burqa she dug into her pants pocket, and Farishta watched her hands behind the shuttlecock mask as she wiped her eyes and blew her nose.

She meant Khalid. But they could not say his name, not like that, not here in Nasirabad. Farishta felt nothing but dismay. "You must be exhausted," she said.

Afia's blue head bobbed. "I haven't slept in three days."

"We must find somewhere for you to stay. While we think what to do."

"I can't—"

"Stay at home? No, my little bird. You would bring shame on us all. I cannot have it."

"But I am trying to do what—what Shahid wanted. He wanted me to come home. To marry Zardad. And I am ready now, Moray. To marry him. To do whatever he orders. I will marry him right away, if you want, and you will never have to lay eyes on me again."

"Afia, Afia." Farishta risked a glance back toward the mulberry orchard. Several women had come down from the trees and stood with their baskets, watching. Sobia and Muska could run up to the road at any moment. She turned and began walking, slowly, down toward the main road, as if she had met this traveler and was helping her on her way. "It is too late for that," she said as Afia followed her. "Zardad's family will have withdrawn the offer. My son"—her voice cracked, she could not speak Shahid's name either—"my son died on account of your sin, and everyone knows it. Inshallah, our family will not lose the respect of the village. There has been no trial here, no proof. But it all depends on your disappearing, Afia. Disappearing from our world. Marriage"—she gave an involuntary, bitter chuckle—"is completely out of the question."

"But, Moray, if I can't come home—" Afia stepped in front of her, then stopped. They were out of sight of the orchard, now. "Where will I go?"

"That is a question only you can answer, my sparrow." Farishta risked a hand reaching out, gripping her daughter's for a moment. "Hide yourself somewhere until the sun is setting," she said. "Then make your way to Tayyab's hut. We can trust him. He knows—he brought me the true story. If I ask, he will shelter you for the night."

"And then?" Afia's voice was weak, pleading.

"I will find what I can to help you on your way. By this time tomorrow, you must be gone from Nasirabad."

That night Farishta lay awake, listening as if something in the darkness would call to her, would ask for her strong hands, her quick tongue to save the thin, sad-looking girl who was all that remained of her first brood. A strange seizure of desire for Tofan crept over her—desire she'd never felt before, when he first took her to his bed and did more slowly and gently what his brother had done with quick dispatch. She hungered for his hands parting her thighs, for his fennel-spiced breath on her neck, for him to fill up the space now left empty inside her. But he slept in the *hujra*. Once, long ago, after Muska was born and the rest of the family was sorrowing over the birth of yet another girl, Tofan had said, "Do you know, my wife, what is the greatest love on earth?"

It had been a riddle, she thought then. The answer could not be the love of Allah, since that was not truly on earth. Nor could it be a woman's love for her man, since such love rubbed elbows with sin and so needed to be kept in check. She had looked into Muska's dark blue eyes and given the obvious answer, though under the disappointing circumstances it seemed weak and insufficient. "A mother's love for her children," she had said.

"You are wrong." He had reached forward a thick index finger, and the baby had latched her little mouth onto it and sucked hard. "A mother loves her children because it is in her nature. She cannot do otherwise. A father loves his sons because they will carry on his family; they will make him proud. But when a father loves a daughter, he loves what will only cost him, and what he is fated to lose. And yet he loves her without condition. That is the greatest love in the world."

Now she lay restless in her anxiety and desire. Tofan had taken both Afia and Shahid as his own children, his own daughter and son. How he would thrill to lay eyes on Afia. But then, loving her, he would have no choice but to lay his hands on her, to wipe away her shame. As dawn crept over the valley, Farishta rose from her lonely bed. Reaching into the bottom of her mending basket, she pulled out the envelope of rupees she kept there, saved from her change at the markets and what the army had paid at her first husband's death. Tucking it inside a finely woven shawl, she slipped across the courtyard. In the covered area outside the stoop, embers still glowed from Tayyab's wife's cooking fire.

CHAPTER TWENTY-SEVEN

Afia woke at first light in Panra's narrow bed. On the floor beside her, Panra slept on a straw mattress. Tayyab had insisted—the young memsahib had had a long journey, she needed her rest, he would not hear of her sleeping on the floor, what would her mother think of him? They had stuffed Afia with chicken and rice and lentils and bread and sent her off when her lids began to droop.

Afia had last been in Tayyab's hut seven years ago. She had gotten her menses and rushed to tell Panra about it. The very next day, her mother had informed her that from then on, as a woman, she was not to play on the dirt floor of the servants' quarters. Panra had understood even before Afia did. They still walked together with Lema to the corner shop for a treat of cherry-red Rooh Afza, but soon after that Panra left school and was sent to work at Uncle Omar's, in Peshawar.

Now Afia rolled over to find Panra with her hands clasped behind her head, staring up at the thatched ceiling. It was their only chance to speak. Nothing of what had happened in America could pass their lips while Tayyab's wife and younger daughters, even his slow-witted son, were gathered close. They had given Afia their condolences for Shahid's death, but as if a disease had carried him off, or a car accident. "Panra," she whispered.

Panra shifted on her pallet. She had a big, plain face, with reddish hair that sprang from her high forehead. She was her parents' eldest daughter now, with the death of her two sisters. Last night, her mother had mentioned a possible husband, a soldier. "But we won't be hasty," Tayyab had said, and Panra had looked relieved.

"Are you all right?" Panra whispered now. "Did you sleep?"

"Like an ox. I'm sure I snored," said Afia, and they giggled. Afia glanced around the still-dark room. Tayyab and his wife slept behind one curtain, their son behind another, and the other girls on cots lining the walls. No one seemed to stir. "Will you go back to Peshawar today?" she asked. "To my uncle's?"

"I don't know. It depends on my father. What about you? If you cannot marry Zardad—"

"I can't give up yet," Afia said. "I thought—maybe, if you go back to my uncle's house—I could go with you. Omar has seen more of the world than my mother has. If he will plead my case—" She stopped. Panra's eyes had gone wide.

"You must not go near him," she said. "He will kill you. If he learned that I brought the truth to your mother, he would kill me."

Slowly, in whispers, Panra told her how Khalid had been sent to America, who had funded him and to what purpose. Afia felt the matchstick house of her future crumble into a brittle pile. "I can go nowhere, then," she said softly.

"Don't say that. You can go to the nuns, in Peshawar. They help women."

The nuns. Afia had seen them, squatting among the polio-stricken at the central market in Peshawar, with their white robes and their earnest faces. "I'll figure something out," she said. "You mustn't get more involved. You've been very brave already, bringing this news to my mother."

"She didn't like hearing it."

"But it answers so much. You do know . . . what happened? Over there?"

Panra picked at the straw sticking out of her mattress. "I can guess."

"Why did you tell my mother? Why take such a risk?"

Even in the dim light, she could see Panra's skin flush pink. She hesitated a long while before speaking. "I—I loved Shahid," she whispered at last. "We all did, but . . . I really loved him. The way they do in movies. You know."

Afia nodded. She did know.

"And I could not live with your mother thinking he would try to hurt you. I had to bring her the truth."

"Ssh," Afia said. Movement, from the other side of the curtain. "We'll talk later," Afia said.

But they never did. As soon as they were up, before Tayyab went to prepare breakfast at the house, Moray knocked softly and slipped inside the hut. Her face was drawn tight, her eyes bleary from lack of sleep. Tayyab's three younger daughters arranged their dupattas and greeted the memsahib. Tayyab's wife went to make tea, but Moray stopped her. Anâ was already awake, she said; she would have to get back quickly. Even yesterday, the village women had questioned her about the stranger she'd spoken with, on the road. Last night she had not been able to concentrate on her duties. Sweeping too vigorously, she had toppled a porcelain vase, one of Badrai's wedding gifts. She could not have suspicion fall on her; if the men of the family knew Afia was in Nasirabad, she could not account for what they might do.

"I didn't mean to bring you trouble, Moray," Afia said. "I only hoped—"

"Hush, child." Her mother had an embroidered shawl draped over her forearm. This she pressed against Afia's chest, bringing Afia's hand up to clutch it there. Afia felt the package, flat and hard, inside.

"Moray, you mustn't," she said. "These are your savings."

"For what else would I save them? Hide them well." As Moray wrapped her arms around her, Afia felt the thickness of the envelope. There had to be fifty thousand rupees inside. "You're so thin," Moray said.

Afia breathed her mother's scent, the tea rinse she used on her hair and the rose oil she liked to dab behind her ears. She felt her mother's plump breasts against the shawl, breasts that had pillowed her head when she'd had a fever or come home distraught from teasing at school. "I don't want to go," she said, her voice muffled by Moray's dupatta.

"There's no choice." Moray pulled away. She lifted Afia's glasses from her face and dabbed Afia's eyes with a corner of her dupatta. Seen without glasses, her familiar face looked blurry, already a face in a dream. "He will not stop," she said. "You know that."

"That's why I came home. If I could only—"

"You have to write down your address for me. So I can send news."

"But I don't know where I'll be, Moray. I don't know where to go."

"Write the university address. Tell them to keep my letters for you. But don't write me back. Do not call. If my words find you, Allah will be sure that I know it."

Leaving her home for the last time, Afia took a bowl of lentils and yogurt from Tayyab and walked slowly down the long hill in the morning light, her burqa enclosing her from the world.

Panra stayed behind. Perhaps she would return tomorrow, to Uncle Omar's compound. Perhaps never. Passing Afia on the road, farmworkers glanced quickly at the screen that hid her face. Then they went on, complaining about the heat and the elections.

"Boy," she said when she reached the main square of the village. A dark, sullen young man lounged against his brightly painted autorickshaw. "How much to Peshawar?"

"Two thousand rupees." He must have thought her burqa looked expensive.

"A thousand."

"Twelve hundred. Get in."

She did as she was told. Strange, how fear seemed to thicken the air. She had traveled alone all the way from Northampton to Nasirabad. Had boarded the shuttle bus, negotiated the swarms of travelers at JFK, bought the burqa at the Qatar airport, made her way past thieves and porters at Peshawar to summon, in her bravest voice, a rickshaw to convey her home. All of it had seized her throat with nervous anticipation. But now that her plan had proved as fragile as a soap bubble, every move felt steep and slow. And to think that Omar, the name that had taken up space in her plans as a refuge, a safe retreat were she not able to marry Zardad—to think that he had been the one hurling death her way in the first place! She felt stupid, like a peasant who cannot read the message on a signboard clear as day.

In Peshawar she paid the rickshaw driver and asked at one street corner and another until she found the house run by the nuns. Even swathed in the blue burqa, she felt exposed, as if the crowds around her could view not just her flesh but her heart, her lungs. *Sisters of Loretto*, the sign outside the house read. But the heavyset nun who answered the door said she was sorry, they had no room for her. They had women there with children, women with burn scars over their bodies, women in danger of being buried alive. They gave her a meal of chickpeas and rice, and sent her on her way. As the afternoon wore on, the air pressed heavier. What if Omar learned why his servant Panra had returned to Nasirabad? What if he discovered Afia in Peshawar? She found the bus station and withdrew two of the bills from her mother's envelope to pay for the coach bus to Islamabad.

Returning to America was not a conscious decision. When she rose the next morning, sleepless but safe in a hotel by the Islamabad airport, it seemed she was already halfway through the only open door. To be in Nasirabad, to be in Peshawar, to be anywhere in Pakistan and yet not be among her family felt like a living death. A woman without a family was nothing. She had no voice, no face.

With Shahid's bank card, she was able to buy a one-way ticket. Less than seventy-two hours after she had landed in Pakistan yearning for home, she was flying away. In the airport she stood in line with the workers headed for the Gulf states to work on oil rigs. Clad in the burqa, she was invisible. They spat on the floor around her; they joked about the *houris* in Qatar. It had been different when she'd flown with Shahid—but Shahid was dead, and she was drifting like pollen back across the oceans. When she'd buckled into her seat on the plane, the tribesman next to her spread himself out, his elbows wide and his bare foot with its dirt-black toenails crossed over his knee. Falling asleep, she heard a loud hissing sound, like someone chasing away chickens. She opened her eyes to the tribesman, eyes wide, hissing and clucking at her.

He needed to use the toilet, but he would not touch her with his hands or speak to her. She was only a body to him, a thing to be gotten out of the way.

In Qatar, she chucked the burqa into a bin. She wrapped her mother's shawl around her shoulders, the money nestled at the bottom of her bag.

Twenty hours later, America—where no one had a family, and no one knew where she was. But as soon as she exited the plane, she began glancing around. She stepped off the bus onto the familiar streets of Northampton. She spent another sleepless night in the Melville Motel. She presented herself to Dean Myers. Not once did she stop sweeping her gaze left and right. She kept whirling about, like a snake catching its own tail, to see what made the odd sound or the threatening silence. Her thinking had gone crooked. She was not herself. Her body was in one piece, but her spirit was like a body after a bombing, scattered and unrecognizable.

In this way, three days passed. "You've got to go to classes, Afia," Patty said. "You'll flunk out if you don't. I'm really sorry about your brother. But you have to get a grip. You want to see a shrink? I know a good one."

"No," Afia said.

Her mobile still worked. They would cut it off eventually, she supposed, unless she used Shahid's computer to pay the bill. But there was no one she wanted to talk to. Thirty missed calls, most of them from Coach Hayes. One from Gus. A handful from Afran, who also left text messages. He'd gotten her number from Coach, he wrote. He was worried because no one had seen her. He had a set of wheels now; he thought he'd come by.

Not possible, she thought. And Afran would give up soon. He didn't need her; no one needed her, not anymore. Not her family, none of whom she'd ever see again, and not the poor women of the tribal areas, for she would never survive long enough to earn her medical degree. Not the other students at Smith. After she'd forced herself to rise from bed and attend a day of classes, Patty and Taylor sat her down and advised her to "lose the hijab." By the weekend Taylor was saying that Afia was creeping her out, and on Tuesday Taylor moved to another suite, leaving Patty and Afia to share a space that felt strangely smaller with just the two of them. That same day, she got a call to meet again with Dean Myers. Dean Myers was a plump woman with a menacing smile and cropped African hair that looked flecked with cotton. Given her situation, Dean Myers said, they had bent all the rules. They had made allowances. Then she had not only disappeared for more than a week, but reappeared insisting that no one but the authorities needed to know of her safe arrival. She was not inspiring trust, Dean Myers said. Was she afraid of something? Dean Myers wanted to help. If Afia would not be forthcoming, she could not help.

She wanted only to focus, Afia said, on her work. So much to make up.

Khalid, she knew, would never give up. He lurked somewhere nearby, his focus unwavering. What was that old story, about Death? How a man journeys far to escape him, only to arrive at the very place where Death patiently waits. Afia had returned to America because Shahid's wishes for her had died with him, because Pakistan would have blotted her out. She had not returned in order to seek out Khalid. But in the end, ten days after she landed, she did exactly that.

CHAPTER TWENTY-EIGHT

The imam at the Al-Hidaya mosque in Albany gave Khalid directions to the grave they had established for Shahid, off a lonely stretch of road outside the city. Only a handful of plots set the field off from the surrounding copse. Shahid's was the newest and simplest, with a verse of the Qur'an and Shahid's name, both in Arabic, on the small stone. With his money dwindling, Khalid took to going there on Fridays. He drove the roads in the rental car he'd never returned, though Uncle Omar had surely canceled the credit card by now. He sat on the stone bench by the side of the graveyard and addressed his brother. Sometimes he waxed angry. What sort of smug bastard was it who thought his selfish successes would rain joy on everyone around him? What had Shahid done with his life? He played a game, that was all, a child's amusement, when everywhere around him were great issues to be addressed. His one job, his one holy responsibility when he came up with the insane notion of bringing their sister to *Amreeka*, was to protect her, and in that he had failed. Now she would die on account of it—and worse, Shahid had caused searing pain to their family, for nothing. Nothing!

Other times, Khalid swept the lingering snow off the bench and sat there, his head hanging heavy from his neck. How had this fate befallen him, that his brother should lie here under the ground while their foul sister was out there unchecked, fornicating with whomever she pleased? What had he done, that he should deserve this fate—to be shaking with cold and hunger in a strange land, his righteous *badal* thwarted, his precious younger brother lost to him, unable to go home? He had tried—oh, he had done everything to achieve the best outcome. Finding the proofs of Afia's shame, planting those proofs carefully so as to properly humble Shahid and wipe away the shame before anyone outside the family heard of it. If only his father could know what Khalid had done, how carefully he had thought it all through, he would want to carry him on men's shoulders through Nasirabad, proclaiming him as a pillar of *pashtunwali*, the son every father dreamed of! But his father could not know because Khalid could not finish the task. And if he failed to track Afia down before his money ran out, he never would. What did Shahid, listening under the ground, think of these events? Was he pleased at Khalid's failure? Why should he so hate Khalid that he would wish such a fate upon him? Did he not remember, or care, about those years Khalid was his big brother, protecting him, teaching him to fly a kite, to properly dribble a football, to behave at school so the teacher would not bring the ruler down on his hands?

Finally, his thoughts would leave Shahid, stubbornly silent in his tiny grave, and roam over Afia. She had disappeared from the coach's house, he was sure of it—he had parked a quarter mile from there after dark and come to look in the windows, and there were only the coach and her husband and child. That husband—he had known, he could tell what Khalid was after. Maybe he had wanted Afia for himself. They were like that, these people, perverse in their desires. Maybe the coach was up to her old tricks, hiding Afia away. He could kidnap the coach's child, force them to reveal the place. No—they'd catch and kill him. Anyway the futility of following both their cars for three days proved that Afia had simply run off, flouting their kindness as she'd flouted her own traditions. Back to the Jew? No, he too seemed alone, moving from his mother's house to the university and back again, and then once or twice with a different girl, big-breasted and fair-skinned. Afia's breasts were not that big, though they must have grown since that time Khalid saw her bathing in the stream. And if she was not with the Jew, who was she with? When he shut his eyes he saw her most vividly, not as she had looked in the courtroom, dressed as demurely as she could in Western clothes, her glasses reflecting the lights; but as she had stood at the cabin in the headlights of the Hyundai, her eyes wide and her hair free, her blouse open at the throat. He had wanted to kill her just like that, just as her high, pleading voice and her half-clothed body called to him. But Shahid, as always, got in his way.

This Friday, as he took to the now-dry bench, he saw that daffodils had emerged from the cemetery's poorly tended grass. Spring. At home, the mulberries would have ripened; the cotton would be thick in the fields. His trail by now had gone cold. Classes had begun again at Smith College, but no Afia in the classrooms where she should have been, and no Afia coming or going from the dorm. At the grocery where she had that filthy job, only older women with brightly dyed hair worked the checkouts. He had asked one of them about Afia Satar, and she had shaken her head sadly. "Don't know where that girl's gone to," she said. "Such a sweet little thing. You aren't a relation, are you?"

No, he had said, only a friend. And he had haunted the Enright campus too, in case one of Shahid's teammates had sheltered her—she would fornicate with one of them in exchange for a safe bed, perhaps, he could envision it but he would not allow himself—but he saw no sign. Strangely, though, in the week since he had given up finding her, he had begun to feel himself followed. A vague unease as he left his motel room. The sound of the door to the men's room at the diner opening and shutting, but when he whipped around from the urinal, no one there. He had left the flat in Boston just as they were drawing up plans to place a bomb at the Homeland Security office there. A few days, he had promised them, then he'd be back to help.

Perhaps they had sent someone after him. Perhaps they thought he was betraying them to the Americans. Perhaps—it occurred to him as a car sloshed down the long dirt drive to the cemetery; he had never seen anyone else at this place—they had tracked him here. A holy place, a place of death. He steeled himself. Standing, he reached for the gun tucked into his waistband. He was a fighter, he tried reminding himself. He had been trained.

The car was a black SUV. It pulled onto a patch of muddy grass, and the imam from the Albany mosque stepped out. He was dressed in black shalwar, with a down vest over his kurta. He was not very old, but overweight, with bags under his eyes; his skin was dark and his nose flattish, African blood. He greeted Khalid with *Asalaam aleikum* and went around to the passenger side. When he had opened the door, Afia stepped down.

Khalid's heart filled his throat. He took a step back. His stepsister was dressed as she had been in the courtroom, but with the scarf wrapped closer so no trace of her thick hair was visible. In muddy boots she stepped gingerly across the terrain. The imam followed. "Asalaam aleikum, Khalid lala," she said. Her voice was breathy.

"What are you doing here?" he said in Pashto, and to the imam in English, "Why you have brought her?"

"Our daughter," the imam said, "is in pain. Your mutual brother"—he gestured toward the cold stone—"is with Allah. But she's asked to be reconciled to you. She is ready to ask forgiveness."

At these words Afia took a step forward. Her glasses were misted over; he couldn't see the expression of her eyes. The flesh of her face looked waxy with fatigue. Slowly she sank to her knees in the mud and bent her head forward to the ground, so all he saw was the silky spread of the dupatta over the back of her shoulders. He could kick at the head right now, kick hard enough to break the neck, and never have to see her face.

"You see," said the imam.

"I do," he managed to say.

"You remember what our Prophet, peace be upon him, said to his enemies at Mecca."

Khalid nodded. His eyes were fixed on the prostrate figure of Afia. What sort of trick was she playing?

"Say it, my son. Repeat what our Prophet said."

"He—he quoted Joseph. He said, 'Let no blame fall upon them.' "

"Exactly. Now, here is your sister. She comes to you of her free will, to seek your forgiveness and love. Up we go." The imam bent with some difficulty and took Afia's upper arm with his thick hand. *Touched* her. A quick flame of rage licked at Khalid's chest, but he tamped it down. This was an imam, *Amreekan* yes, but still a holy man. "You've said," the imam went on, speaking to Afia as she stood, her knees caked in mud, "you want to be left alone with him. Is that still what you want?"

"It is, Imam," she said, her head turned away from Khalid.

The cleric turned to Khalid. "You will keep her safe," he said. "You will do her no harm. She has come to you in peace, brother."

Khalid managed to say he understood, though he couldn't think past the imam's words to anything that made sense. Glancing at Shahid's headstone, the imam expressed condolences for their mutual loss. Then he turned back to Afia. "You sure?" he said.

"I am. Thank you."

The SUV spun its wheels in the mud as it backed out. When it had gone, Khalid took a long time to regard Afia. She stood with her hands folded in front of her. They were chapped, the cuticles bitten raw. He felt the cold butt of the gun against his waist. So much he wanted to know—where had she gone? What had possessed her to return? When had she first committed the sin, and how many times after? But he said only, in Pashto, "How did you find me?"

"I wanted to find where Shahid was buried." Her voice was stronger now. She directed her gaze somewhere to the left of him. "They told me at the police station that the imam would know. He told me you had been coming here on Friday mornings. I waited for Friday, and asked him to bring me. To—to deliver me into your keeping."

"You are a black whore," he said. "You know that."

She nodded. "As you say, Khalid lala. I understand everything now, you see. I understand all that happened, from the start. And I am not running, anymore."

What did she mean, from the start? Did she mean from the call he received from Uncle Omar in the mountains? Or did she mean the moment she first toddled with her mother and brother into the courtyard in Nasirabad and his doom was sealed? "You'll obey me, then," he said.

"I will."

The vision came to him, and he acted on it. "Get in the car," he said.

They drove east and then north, toward the Hudson River. As he navigated the car, quickly checking the map he had been given at the rental place, Afia asked nothing about where he was taking her. She talked, instead, in a stream of soft words, about where she had been and what she had decided, about how much

Shahid and Baba had always loved Khalid, and always, always, of how the blame was hers, not for what she had done but for what she had failed to do, to keep them all first in her heart, to understand what the consequences would be. She spoke almost like one talking in her sleep, the words falling soft and steady as leaves.

He tried to close his ears. He didn't want to hear her voice. At the same time, he couldn't help interrupting: "Nasirabad? You went all the way to Nasirabad? How long were you there?"

"One day only. I saw Moray, and Panra told me about Uncle Omar, how he sent you here and why, it was Shahid's future, I see that now, he had me to fret over and that derailed his future, and I could not go back home. Moray told me this. There is no marriage for me now, no place for me there. So I left—"

"After one day?"

"And a day in Peshawar. I tried to stay with the nuns. But they wouldn't have me, I was not at risk the way their other women were at risk. And then there was nowhere to stay, and I went to Islamabad, and then back to America. And then I knew. I knew you would come back eventually, and you would find me. I would always be looking over my shoulder, all my life, and I couldn't sleep. I couldn't eat. You know the story, Khalid, don't you? Of the man who encounters Death in Damascus, and then he flees overnight to Aleppo?"

Khalid shook his head. He saw the bridge just ahead of them, and a place to pull off. He didn't remember the story. He didn't seem to remember anything. It was all he could do to concentrate on driving, on easing the car off the road, on the next step in the plan that had come to him.

"It's a long, awful journey to Aleppo," Afia went on, still in her dreamy monologue, the words not rushed but not choked back either, floating into the air, "but the man makes it. He's in the market, congratulating himself on having escaped Death. Just then Death comes and taps him on the shoulder, and the man says, 'But you can't be here! I saw you in Damascus yesterday!' And Death says that's why he looked so surprised at their encounter before, because he had an appointment to come for the man the next day, in Aleppo."

Khalid put the car in park. He remembered the old tale now. So she knew what she had come back for. Nothing he could do would surprise her. All her talk amounted to a deathbed confession; she was ready for her fate. "Get out," he said.

There was room for them to walk abreast on the pavement that went by the road and led onto the bridge alongside the traffic. The bridge was painted the color of algae. They were high over an abandoned parking lot, then over bare trees just tipped with green, then over the dark water. This was the wide river he had crossed going to Afia's trial, and returning east, trying to apprehend her. Clouds scudded across the sky. A cold wind had picked up. Afia was still talking. "I want you to know this, Khalid lala," she was saying. "I cannot regret the things I did for their own sake. I am not a believer in that regard. I have studied biology, and we are biological creatures, we feel these desires as other creatures do, and I do not find a place where the Prophet, peace be upon him, ever said we should not feel such things. I read my Qur'an in the prison, Khalid lala. But where Baba is right about love, you know? About love being a disease? It is that when you are in love you forget that what you do in private does not create a world. The world is the world and you are in it. Gus and I, we loved each other like young creatures, but we were in the world. And when I meet Shahid I will tell him I tried. I tried to go home and marry Zardad, and it was too late. And that, you know, was not my doing. So I hope I may hold my head up when I meet him, when I meet Shahid lala."

They were almost at the center of the span, now. On the other side, wire fencing rose higher than a man's head; but on this side there was a chest-high rail, nothing more. Thirty meters below, the cold water flowed southward. Khalid lifted the gun from the waist of his trousers. Holding it close to his body, not to draw attention from a passing car, he gestured with the stock. "Climb," he said.

"Here?" Afia's voice went suddenly small. She backed against the fence. "Here, Khalid lala?" As if all this time she had been spinning a fiction, an idea of what would happen, only here it was and she could not believe it.

"The water," he said. His hand had begun to shake. "The water will wash your sin clean, Afia. Climb."

"Khalid, please." Her eyes behind the glasses were huge, vulnerable. The wind whipped at her hijab. "I haven't finished telling you."

"You've said enough. No point talking. Climb."

"You are sure? Is there no other way—"

Now it was infecting him, this sense that all along he had been inventing what he would do, he had not believed in it. Like the time he had watched a martyr stride into the marketplace and detonate himself, and there were parts of bodies, real bodies, ordinary as meat and it was not an idea any more, it was real as dirt and blood. "No other way," he choked out.

She had a hard time climbing the fence. He wanted to boost her, the way he used to help her climb the mulberry trees when she was little and wanted to grab some of the sweet berries before all the village women harvested them. His hand on her soft bottom, lifting her. But he made himself step back and watch. For a lucky moment, no cars came over the bridge. She got one leg across the rail, then the other. She stood with her hands on the rail, looking into his eyes. She had not met his eyes since she had appeared at the cemetery. He had the sensation of falling, falling from an enormous height. There was only about a foot's breadth between the railing and the drop. Carefully she turned away from him. The water swirled below, ready to suck the body down.

It came in a flash. Not this. Not this. Not the sight of Afia's arm lifting above the waves, then her head, then nothing. Not her lungs straining for air, filling with water. No. He couldn't. He threw an arm over and across her chest. Lifted her up and over the rail. The force of the hoist brought them both down. His shoulder hit one of the girders as they tumbled onto the walkway. The gun clattered to the pavement. Afia crab-walked away. She looked terrified, as she had not looked when she was prepared to jump. To end her life.

"There is another way," Khalid said. Shouted, almost.

"What way?"

"To wash your shame. There is another way." He rose. Energy streamed through his muscles. He could conquer *Amreeka*, he could conquer the world. He reached out a hand. But just as she stretched to take it, he pulled away. Moments before, he had gripped her soft chest, but that was to save her life. Now they must not touch. *He who touches the hand of a woman unlawfully will burn his palms at the Day of Judgment.* He stared at his own hand as, slowly, Afia rose. She came up only to his shoulder.

"Look at me," he said, and her head jerked up. Her breath had the sour tang of fear. "I will marry you," he said.

"What?"

"I will. Marry you. Don't you see? I will do it. I will make it right. You are not my sister, Afia. Not by blood. So you can be my wife. I will make you my wife."

The cars streamed by. What the drivers who bothered to look saw, by the side of the road in the center of the bridge, was a young couple in the midst of a proposal. The young man clenched his hands together and bent one knee slightly, as if in a curtsy or a prayer. They did not see the gun lying on the pavement. They smiled at the prospect of love and returned their eyes to the road.

CHAPTER TWENTY-NINE

Short of stalking her, Lissy didn't know what she could do to get a response from Afia. Though her cell number had her outgoing message, she never picked up or returned calls. Shahid had used that cell plan to track his sister, but clearly she didn't want to be tracked, then or now.

For Lissy, nothing had healed. Night after night she woke from dreams in which she and not the Hadley patrolman had found Shahid's body, had found the receiver dangling from the kitchen wall, had dialed 911, had labored with what she knew of CPR until the medics came and pronounced Shahid dead. She would bend over him in the snow and he would vanish, and there would only be the pink stain, her breath steaming in the air.

Ethan had forgiven her. That was the one miracle. She hadn't understood until he offered Afia a place to stay, after the trial. She had abused his trust, had used the place of his happiest memories, had blundered ahead on her foolish course thinking more about a win over Harvard than about him or Chloe. All these things he had pointed out to her. When he drove her to the trial it had been a gesture, more than she had a right to expect. When he offered Afia safe harbor—then, Lissy knew, he had reached deep and had forgiven her.

And still nothing healed, not really. At Enright, Ernesto Salazar, the football coach, was taking over the athletic directorship until, in Don Shears's words, "things settle down." Ernesto hated the paperwork, he told Lissy over lunch. "The whole business. The stats, the GPAs. The Ask. Get your butt back in the desk as soon as possible, is what I say, and let me back out on the field."

"They'll probably do a search to replace me," Lissy said, "once my contract runs out. There are people on the board—"

"There's Charlie Horton on the board. His kid should've been put on probation three semesters running. I didn't play him before, and I'm not playing him now. What about your guys?"

"You mean the squash team."

"No, I mean your ducklings. Of course the squash team. Men and women both. Your men beat Harvard, for fuck's sake. If I have to be A.D., the least I can demand is that you stay with those squads."

Her squads. Nothing healed, there, though she'd gone to each of them for forgiveness. Chander had been tough. He was graduating and saw his last year as ruined. Jamil was easy, a young man who cried easily and hugged hard. Others, like Yanik, were simply confounded. "What're you asking us to forgive?" he'd said when she met him on campus. "You didn't gun him down."

That was debatable, she thought. Gus Schneider seemed to think she'd killed Shahid as surely as if her finger had been on the trigger. And Afran accused her of bad faith. She'd made him feel, he told Lissy, like they were all members of a family. And okay, Afia was the innocent one, she'd acted in self-defense, whatever. But she hadn't been part of the family, and Shahid had. How could Coach choose her over Shahid?

She didn't, she told him, think she was choosing.

"Oh, dude, Coach, one of them was going to die." Afran shook his head. "You get to that point, someone dies."

Margot, from the girls' squash team, sent Lissy a poem by Theodore Roethke, about a student who had fallen from a horse. Roethke mourned the girl's death but claimed he had "no rights in the matter, neither father nor lover."

"Shahid, Shahid," Lissy whispered aloud on the cold deck under the brooding spring sky, the lake patterned with melting ice cakes. "What did I want for you? The world, the universe. What did you want, Shahid? What did you want? What did I take from you?"

Shutting her eyes, she saw the sweat in the hollow of his collarbone, the span of his shoulders, his small ears that always needed cleaning. She was no poet. She had no words that added up to Shahid alive, that could put their arms around the whole of him and name the canyon of loss. She fell into it and tried to claw her way out, and fell again, and there seemed no bottom to it.

Then the stranger showed up at their door, looking for Afia, and suddenly grief gave way to a renewed suspicion. He'd thought she was being paranoid, Ethan said. But looking into the guy's wolfish eyes, he recognized the man who'd sat next to him on the bleachers, at the Harvard match. "Something about him," he said when Lissy returned from taking Afia to Smith. "Both times I laid eyes on him. Made my blood run cold. I don't know if he killed Shahid, but he was definitely after that girl."

Now Afia didn't return calls, and she seemed to have disappeared from Smith. Lissy's mood began to swing, from panic that whoever was after Afia had found her, to relief that this time, Ethan shared her suspicions; to panic that she ought to be doing something, anything, to derail some ghost train of disaster. When the panic seized at her throat, she changed to shorts and went up into the empty squash center, where she banged balls against the cool surfaces of the court. Even now she preferred the hard, fast ball of her childhood, pitching back at her furiously, to the softer ones the pros all played with these days. She came home sweaty and spent. At night she lay on her back next to Ethan, neither of them sleeping.

"We should try the police again," she said after a fortnight.

"With what?" Ethan's voice, in the night, was heavy with patience. "A blue Hyundai, no plate numbers? A guy who says he's majoring in engineering and you've got no engineering school? Not exactly a criminal case, Liss."

"You think his hair was dyed."

"Definitely. And still, something . . . He was South Asian, but more than that. Some kind of family resemblance to Shahid. Tall, angular, you know, and then maybe the shape of the jaw. Not like a brother, but a sort of family resemblance."

He reached out and pushed at the mobile hanging over their bed. Chloe had made it, in preschool, during the awful month between the murder and the trial. Chloe knew that one of Mommy's players had died and Mommy was sad. She started acting out, crying furiously at small boo-boos, wetting her bed. At school, they were making "hearts and flowers," dropping tiny plastic beads onto a pegboard with preset designs, which the teachers ironed until the beads fused together into a shape the children could bring home. Chloe had brought home a great stack, and one noontime Lissy had woken—she lay in bed later and later during those weeks, grief pressing her into a limbo between sleep and waking—to find the hearts and flowers dangling above her head from a set of wire hangers that Ethan must have strung up. *Now you will feel better,* Chloe had said that day, climbing onto the bed to blow at the mobile. *When you wake up, you can see flowers and hearts, and you won't be so sad.*

"You know how Afia printed something, on your computer?" Lissy said now, while the plastic shapes spun. "I bet it was a boarding pass. Her roommate at Smith said she saw her for ten minutes. Afia told her she was going on a trip. She packed a small suitcase, like for a weekend."

"Well, we can't file a missing person report," Ethan said. "Not with testimony like that. Not when we don't have a claim on her."

"She's got to be somewhere."

"Somewhere alive? Or somewhere dead?"

Lissy shuddered. "Can you kill someone in Massachusetts and dump her body? And have no one ever know?"

"Happens all the time. Those guys I used to work with, at the prison? Someone cared about the women they went after. Barring that . . ."

"But someone cares about Afia. I mean, we do. Other people, too. She's got a family."

"That," Ethan said, "could be the main problem here."

When Lissy went to the Devon Price Chopper the next week, she wasn't looking for Afia, but for decent lettuce. As she held the two wilted, stringy heads of green and red leaf, she debated driving to Guido's Market in Pittsfield; considered that she didn't have a paycheck to splurge on organic produce flown up from Mexico; pondered the differences among Price Choppers; and remembered. The Price Chopper ladies, the ones who'd sat in the courtroom.

She put the lettuce back and left her grocery cart empty. The roads were clear, the snow visible only in shady patches under the green-tipped trees. In Northampton, the Price Chopper was bigger and shinier than Devon's. Lissy scanned the checkout lanes. At the third one over, an older woman with severely dyed black hair moved items across her scanner while she gossiped with the bagger, an obese black kid with a complicated haircut. *Carlotta*, her name tag read. Lissy loitered until the customer had paid and the lane was empty. Before she could speak, the woman's face brightened.

"I know you!" she said. "You're the one testified for Afia! Professor, right?"

"No, I'm . . ." Lissy paused. "I was her brother's coach."

"Well, you have my condolences." Carlotta leaned close. Cupping a leathery hand dramatically by her mouth, she whispered, "Though he must've been a piece of work. That poor girl."

"Have you seen anything of her? Since the verdict?"

"Funny you should ask. 'Scuse me a moment."

A customer loaded a large cart's worth of groceries onto the belt. While Carlotta was scanning them, another checkout worker closed her station and stepped over. Her name tag read *Esmerelda*. "I'm going on break," she said in a gravelly voice. She looked at Lissy. "Land sakes," she said.

"Tell her," Carlotta said as she turned a package of frozen chicken nuggets around, trying to get the machine to read its code, "about our girl."

Esmerelda's hair was dyed the color of cornsilk and piled onto her head. "What a puzzle that girl is," she said.

"You've seen her?" Lissy said.

Esmerelda motioned Lissy to step outside with her. There, she lit a Newport and inhaled gratefully. "She come in yesterday," she said, crossing her free arm across her torso and balancing the other elbow on her wrist. She took another drag, squinting against the smoke. "She's back in school, that's the good news. Got a lot of catching up to do, but that is one smart girl. She could make it if she wanted."

Lissy's heart lifted. "She's living in the dorms?"

"And going to her classes." Esmerelda stared at the cigarette's filter as if she'd like to break it off.

"What's the bad news then?"

"Shouldn't be bad news. She's engaged."

Lissy felt her head jerk up, as if yanked by a string. "You mean, like, to be—"

"Married, yeah."

Shahid in her house, she remembered. Begging his sister, finally ordering her—to go back home, to be married to some man she'd never met. Afia with her head bent, acquiescing. Never, back then, would Lissy have seen this as a good outcome. But now. She did have a family, after all. "So she'll be returning to Pakistan?"

"She says she's marrying some cousin. Guess they do that, those people. But I tell you, Professor, she don't look like a happy bride. She was my daughter, I'd take her to get her head examined." Esmerelda took a last drag and ground the Newport under her sneaker. "Must be losing her brother made her so crazy. But I tell you. She looks like the firing squad's coming at dawn."

Good news, Lissy kept saying to Ethan that evening. Good news that Afia was safe, was at school, was going to classes. Good, even, that she was engaged. It meant her family was speaking to her again, welcoming her back into the fold. "But you know, I went by her dorm after, and I left an urgent message for her to call me. She has no reason not to. I mean, we did nothing except to help the girl, right? You offered her a place to stay—"

"Maybe she's not comfortable with you, Liss. You were horrified the first time, remember? About the engagement?"

"That's not it. That's not it. I'm sure that's not it." Lissy was pacing the living room. Downstairs, in the room where Afia had slept,

Chloe was watching a Dora cartoon. Her giggles floated up the stairwell. "Someone's threatening her. That guy at the door, most likely. And last time she leaned on me for protection, it didn't work out so well, you know, her brother ended up dead. So now she's keeping her head down, but it doesn't mean she's safe, it means—"

"Lissy. Liss." Ethan had been washing dishes. He dried his hands and stepped into the sitting room. Blocking her path, he took her by the elbows. His glasses were steamed from the hot water of the sink. His hands were warm. The pressure of his thumbs on her inner elbows halted her monologue, stripped away her agitation. "I understand," he said with a wobble in his voice, "that you came to care about this girl. You think she's in danger, and you want to help. You're a good person. You're a coach. You're a natural-born rescuer. But it's not the danger to this girl that's got you so worked up. You know better than to tie yourself in knots helping someone who doesn't want it. When other kids don't return your phone calls, you call them rude and let it go. So what's this really about?"

She felt her jaw clench. Grief crystallized to a point. "Afia did not kill Shahid," she said.

"Yeah, I got that. I'm on your page about that."

"So someone else did. Right? That guy who talked to me at the trial. Who came to the door. He's a murderer, and he's out there. And Shahid is dead. And I loved him, Ethan. Not just as a player. But as a boy. As a man. Not like a lover but—but like something. And I want—"

A wave of frustration shook her body. She butted her head into Ethan's chest. As he reached up to stroke her hair, the truth pushed its way out.

"Justice, dammit," she said. "I want blood."

CHAPTER THIRTY

The sun rose. The hours crawled by. The sun set. The only advantage, as far as Afia could see, of attending classes was that being at Smith gave her a place to sleep away from Khalid.

Poised over the river, she had been ready for death. A moment in the cold water, a brief struggle. But he had plucked her away—her brother, her killer, her brother's killer, and now . . . her husband? That was death, truly. To marry Khalid. To marry your murderer. If the man who ran from Damascus to Aleppo had been a woman, would this have been waiting for her? Death, transformed into a bridegroom?

But oh, how it fit with tradition. If she told Patty the circumstances of her engagement, Patty would be horrified. Marry your first cousin? Marry your brother's murderer? And yet how many thousands of marriages had been contracted out of just those relations? Marrying such a man as Khalid was a time-honored solution. It kept the *khel* together. It prevented *badal* and further bloodshed. It produced children who would bind the old wounds.

But how could she. How could she. *Oh, Shahid lala*, she whispered to herself in the shortening nights, but she had run out of things to say to her brother's ghost.

Her only hope lay in the dilemma of money. Khalid wanted—he had told her this over a cheap dinner at a restaurant that billed itself as Indian but was run by a family from Karachi—to bring them both home to Nasirabad in time for Eid, at the end of Ramadan, in June. There, he would ask Baba formally for her hand. It was not proper for Afia to marry for a year after her brother's death, but as an engaged woman she could be welcomed back into the family. Khalid would leave the training camp, finish his degree. Eventually he would take over the farm, while Afia remained safely in purdah.

But Baba did not and must not know that Khalid was in the United States. And Khalid knew better than to leave Afia alone here. She was weak; she had demonstrated that; she would only bring further shame on their heads, and he would have to end her life. Khalid was thinking aloud as he said these things. His fingers had drummed noisily on the Formica tabletop. He needed money, he said, and he needed to get it here, where he could keep an eye on her. He wanted to know her class schedule; the names of her friends; the code for her dorm building. When Afia, knowing the answer, asked what financial resources he'd found to bring him to the United States in the first place, he told her not to be wondering. That funding option, he said, was closed now. And Afia, being the foolish woman she was, had wasted the money Shahid had left them.

The money Shahid left us. She shuddered later, remembering those words. As if Shahid were not her one full, beloved brother and Khalid's bloody victim, but a rich elder who had endowed them with a way back home. She should have been relieved, she supposed, to learn that Uncle Omar wasn't firing advice, or funds, from across the globe. Relieved that Khalid was scheming ways to get money and not ways to kill her. But rather than death, she faced this limbo: the days, the nights, the classes where she failed to concentrate. She faced the meals Khalid insisted on, twice a week, where he stared at her the way she had seen Gus's lizard stare at a cricket before darting out its tongue to snap the insect into its mouth. Oh, where could she go, where? Not to Coach Hayes, whose life she had already almost destroyed. Not to Gus, who no longer loved her. Except for the dinners with Khalid, she had left campus only once, with Patty, to buy tampons at the Price Chopper, where she got to see her aunties. But as soon as she had told them of her engagement, they had gotten so happy and excited, she couldn't bear to explain the stranglehold she felt herself in.

At least, with Khalid, she would be able to go home. So she told herself, over and over. Home to Moray and Baba, to Sobia and Muska, to Lema . . . if she were allowed to see Lema, which she never would be.

Then Khalid would drive her back to the campus in the rental car that he seemed to be sleeping in—it reeked of body odor and stale food—and watch as she reentered her dorm. He kept his gun tucked into his pants at all times. Once, as he went inside a gas station to pay for his gas, she opened the glove box to see the rental agreement, in case he would be arrested for stealing the car. And there, in the shallow pocket, lay another gun. A small black one, like a toy. She lifted it out; it lay heavy in her palm. Then, as she saw him walking back, she slipped it into her pocketbook and shut the glove box. Now, at least, she had a way to end her own life quickly, if she could only summon the courage.

Afia, stay a minute," Sue Glasgow said this afternoon as they all rose from their desks in Organic Chemistry. It had been more than two weeks since the awful moment on the bridge.

Classes were starting to wrap up. Afia had shifted to the back of the room, where she hoped she would not be called on. Now she gathered her library textbooks and made her way to the front.

"I have failed the exam," she said as Sue Glasgow lifted a sheet from the pile on her desk. She had been allowed to take the mid-term late, but the questions had swum in her vision. *Suppose you allowed cyclohexene to react with* Br_2 *in water. What would you expect?* You would expect nothing, because you would be in purdah, pregnant with your enemy's child. "I am sorry."

"I'm not worried about the exam, Afia. I'm worried about you. You had a terrible winter. Terrible. And now you look ill. Should you be in school right now?"

"Professor Glasgow." Afia tugged at her hijab. She felt warm on her neck. "I have nowhere else to go."

"Well, there's the hospital."

A little snort escaped her. "They have no medicine for me, Professor."

"Talk to me about it. Afia, please. I know you're estranged from your family, but—"

"It is private, Professor. I cannot."

"I thought we were friends."

Afia managed to lift her eyes. Friends? Here stood this well-meaning, brilliant teacher, ignorant as a rock. "Perhaps I should not come to class—"

"That's absurd." Sue Glasgow waved the sheet, filled with red *X*'s, then slid it across the desk at Afia. "I'm going to speak with Dean Myers," she said.

Afia nodded. She took the exam, its F circled at the top. She stepped out into the cool sunshine. How startling it had been, more than a year ago when she first came here, to see bright blue sky and yet walk out into frigid air. Now she was used to it. She pulled her wool cardigan close. Three months ago, she would have felt devastated to hear Sue Glasgow speak to her that way. Now it felt like her missing toe, an absence of what should have been pain.

Her eyes were on the walkway when she heard a familiar voice. "I thought you agreed I could be, like, your brother."

She looked up. "Afran!"

He held out a cardboard cup. "Tea?"

She surveyed the area before accepting it. Khalid had not admitted watching her movements on campus, but neither had he told her what he did all day, except to say he was getting the money. She imagined he was dealing drugs, up at the state university where there were plenty of buyers. Looking nervously around, all she saw were American girls chattering as they hustled between classes. "What—what brings you here?" she asked.

But his eyes had followed hers, flicking left and right. "Let's step into another building," he said.

"Afran, I cannot invite you—"

"Not your dorm. Here." He gestured with his head at the library. "They let you bring tea partway inside. I checked."

The feeling as she followed him up the steps to the library was so alien that she had trouble naming it. Happiness. She was happy to see him. Happy as she would not have been to see Coach Hayes, or even Gus, the thought of whom made her gut constrict in shame and confusion. Afran found a bench in a corner outside the main desk and motioned her to sit. She uncapped the tea and sipped. It was hot, sweet, spiced. They called this *chai* in America, not knowing that all tea, in Pakistan, was chai. It tasted delicious, and she said so.

Afran nodded. He'd reverted to his squash clothes, the blue warm-up jacket and loose pants. The uniform Shahid had died in. He looked older than she remembered him. Quieter, somehow.

"Coach might lose her job," he said, as if this were an answer to a comment about tea.

"She did not think she would."

"That's because she's being nice to you." He drank the tea the way men did from a teacup in Nasirabad, lifting the rim with thumb and fingers and sucking out the liquid. "You going to call her?"

Afia felt her neck grow hot. Of the unanswered calls on her mobile, at least half were from Coach Hayes. Before, she had been the one to prod the coach into taking her to a place of safety. This time, she feared, the opposite would be true. And yet of all the people Afia knew in America, Coach Hayes was the one she wanted most to talk to. Like her, Coach had loved Shahid first and foremost. If anyone could see a way to honor Shahid now, it would be Coach. "I will try," she said lamely. "I have been so busy."

"Busy? Like, with school?"

"School, yes." She stared into the dark tea, the silhouette of her face reflected on its surface.

"No more . . . legal stuff."

"No."

"You're missing Shahid, aren't you?"

"Every day." For a moment, the image of Shahid flung backward onto the snow floated into her mind. They came, these awful apparitions, and she squeezed her eyes shut and tried to make them go away.

"Coach doesn't think you killed him."

"Coach does not know everything."

"Maybe because you don't tell her." Afran set his cup down. He turned to her. "You still engaged?"

"I . . ." Her hand holding the tea shook; she steadied it with the other hand. Then she remembered: Zardad. "Yes," she said, her voice tight. "Still engaged."

"To some guy in Pakistan, Gus said."

She hesitated. But they would be in Pakistan, when it really happened. "Yes."

"And what about your brother? Your other one, I mean."

"I don't understand you, Afran."

"I think you do." He reached across the bench. He touched her fingers. Even as a charge of fear went through her, she didn't draw them away. "You're hiding something, Afia. Shahid was hiding things, too. Not your brother—he told me you guys had a brother. But he hid other stuff. And it didn't work out very well."

She couldn't lie to him. Any moment now, he would say again, *your other brother*, and her flinch would give her away. "This is to do with me only," she said. "And it is for the best, Afran. No one else is at risk—"

"You think not?" He withdrew his fingers. He was shaking his head quickly, as if to rid himself of confusion. "Then why is Gus getting this creepy feeling?"

"What creepy feeling?"

"Like he's being followed everywhere. Like this car that ran a red light in Pittsfield, right where he was crossing the street from his doctor's office, wasn't just some crazy dude. Another guy yanked him back or he'd've been dead. I mean, if anyone's got a right to paranoia, it's our boy Gus. On the other hand"—he tipped his head and smirked—"I know the rule."

She couldn't help herself. Her heart burned. "What kind of car?"

"Ah. So that matters."

She pressed her lips together. She needed to think.

"The rule," Afran went on, "is you don't just punish the girl. Not if you want a clean slate. The guy has to go, too. Even if they're not . . . you know. The fact is it happened. To make it unhappen, you've got to go after everyone."

She struggled to stick to a lie that kept everyone safe. A story where there was no Khalid, no murder of Shahid, no engagement to Khalid. Any other story put Afran, too, in danger. She looked at him. He had offered to be her brother. He did not look afraid. But he was not her brother, and this *badal* was not his. "Tell Gus," she said, "I will phone him."

"That'd be a start."

Afia reached out and took Afran's hand. She squeezed it too hard, and for a very long time.

She needed a plan. It would be weeks before Khalid earned—or begged, or stole—enough to fly them both to Nasirabad. Weeks of Khalid's regarding her like brother and sister, like warden and captive, before he could marry her and possess her body. During those weeks, it was unlikely she could meet Gus for tea, go with Taylor to watch him play squash, even walk down the sidewalk by his side without Khalid being driven to murderous rage. No, worse. The longer Khalid needed to guard her, here, the more his *badal* would turn toward Gus, the man who had seduced her and paid no price beyond a broken leg and a lost home. And Ramadan would only stiffen his resolve.

Once—in what felt like another life—she had explained to Sara Desfani that by her people's law Gus was *makhtoray*, that Shahid had had the right to kill him. But Shahid was gone, and Gus was not subject to this law. She was ready to sacrifice herself to Khalid. She wasn't ready to sacrifice Gus to Khalid's honor.

Like he's being followed everywhere. In hundreds of places Gus could be alone, unprotected. How could she stop Khalid from killing him, if that was Khalid's intent? *Think*, she told herself as she lay awake at night, her books untouched. *Think*.

Khalid would not walk proud to the gallows, as in that old saying. He wanted to live; to bring Afia home with him. He would wait his chance to kill Gus in a place where he wouldn't be caught; or he would kidnap Gus, drive him into the mountains, destroy him there and bury the body. Alone in the dorm room that Thursday night, Afia pulled out the gun she'd taken from Khalid's glove compartment. She checked the chamber and found it loaded. Holding the handle out from her chest with both hands, the way Thalia had shown her in prison, she tried to sight down the barrel, to imagine her stepbrother in the crosshairs. Then she remembered how the other gun had gone off, at the edge of the wintry woods, how it had kicked hotly back at her and she had dropped it. She would be useless, trying to fend off Khalid. Nor could she predict when he might move against Gus, or where.

The next morning, trembling, she found the last missed call from Gus on her mobile and pressed the green button.

"Afia," came his familiar voice, smooth and boyish. "I've been worried about you."

"I need to see you."

She heard him sigh. "Look, Afia," he said—not *M'Afia*, no more nicknames, sweet words—"Afran told me. You're going back to Pakistan. This whole thing . . . well, it's awful. I'm going to blame myself the rest of my life."

"It's not for that I call, Gus—"

"So I don't think I should see you, Afia. Not that I don't love you. I really do. But it's not going to work if—"

"I have something to give you, Gus. We must meet somewhere . . . somewhere safe." She waited through a long silence. "Gus?"

"I don't like," he said, "where this is going."

"Not I neither. Tell me a safe place."

"On one condition. When we meet you'll tell me"—she caught the hard edge of his voice, same as when she'd rung him up from the store in Hadley—"what the hell is going on."

They agreed on the squash center, where he'd started trying to hit the ball again. It was off season, no one else would be there. She would text him about the time; she had to beg Esmerelda for a ride. She checked her watch. She had Sue Glasgow's final biology class this morning. No matter. She would fail the class, anyway. Wrapping the gun in a scarf, she thrust it deep into her backpack and set off across campus, to the road that led out of Northampton Center to the Price Chopper.

The day was warm, true spring at last. Tulips clustered in front of the businesses on State Street. Clouds scudded across the sky, and she felt almost cheered, walking her old route to work. At the Price Chopper, Esmerelda fretted about stretching her break too far. Was it important? she wanted to know, and Afia said yes, very important, and Esmerelda's dimples showed as she asked if this was about Afia's fella. And Afia reminded her that she was engaged, but Esmerelda laughed and said she'd give that four Pinocchios, and if Afia could wait in the sun for an hour, she'd scoot her over to Devon, only she'd have to get a lift back or take the bus through Springfield.

Afia sat weary but with a bubble of hope in her chest. Maybe there was no danger. But at least she would be giving Gus two weapons—the gun, and the truth. Part of the truth, at least. As much as he needed to know. After that, Allah would have to protect him. Flipping open her mobile, she sent the text. *Squash centre 2:00.* A breeze blew across her face. When the door opened from the Price Chopper, the sweet smell of their bakery drifted out.

Car doors slammed every few minutes, in the parking lot.

Why she bolted awake when Khalid's slammed, she didn't know. But she was upright as he came at her, his face unshaven and his eyes like nail heads.

"Khalid lala!" she said. She moved away from her backpack. "Why are you here?"

"You think I don't watch your classes?" He took hold of her arm at the elbow. "You go to classes so that I know you are safe! Are you playing truant, now? Must I fetch you back each time you wander away?"

"Khalid lala, please." She made her voice soft, tried to press the panic out of it. "You don't care about my education. Why does it matter—"

"I am not such a fool. You have no strength. This place has corrupted you through and through. In class, in your room, you stay safe. You stay mindful. But this place!" He flung an arm out at the Price Chopper. "I knew when I saw those women, they were dangerous for you. Now get in the car. We'll go back to your school. You wander off again, I can't answer for what I'll do."

"Do you mean"—she edged back toward the backpack now, ready to obey him—"you've been checking on my class attendance? But Khalid lala, you need to earn money, you said so."

"And how can I," he said, pulling her toward the blue car, "when you have no self-control?"

"I am sorry. So sorry. I didn't think. I wanted only to see my aunties here—"

"You'll see them when I say you can see them."

"Of course. You're right. Now let me just—"

"I'll get it." He pushed her into the car and went for the backpack, still on the bench. *No*, she thought. *Please, no.* But as soon as he lifted the handle, he seemed to know. He loosened the cord at the top. He pulled out the scarf. His face, as he flung the empty bag into the car, was a raging storm. In the driver's seat, he removed the gun from its wrapping and tucked it into his waistband. For a full minute he sat staring straight ahead. Afia heard his breath going in and out of his nostrils. She heard her own breath, the battering of her heart. "Give me your mobile," he said at last.

"Khalid lala, I don't think I have it with me, I—"

He twisted in the seat and wrenched the backpack up from the floor behind him. Rifling through its outer pockets, he found the little flip phone. Afia looked out the window. She willed Esmerelda to come out. She would run to Esmerelda. Khalid wouldn't dare fire on an innocent woman in a crowded parking lot. But shoppers went in and out of the automatic doors, and no Esmerelda.

Khalid scrolled through the phone's numbers; through the messages. When he turned to Afia his voice was calm and flat, like a computer voice. "Where is he."

"Who?"

He held the phone up. Though she couldn't make out the number on the screen, she knew it was Gus's. "Tell me or you die."

"I die, then." She said the words easily. A decision she should have made weeks ago. She met his eyes without flinching.

He put the car in gear. "I will find him first," he said, "and then we will talk about living or dying."

The car spun around and down the aisle of the lot; a women with a baby perched on a shopping cart yanked the cart back in alarm. "Where are we going?" Afia asked when she had her breath.

"Somewhere," Khalid said in that same flat voice, "from which you cannot wander off."

CHAPTER THIRTY-ONE

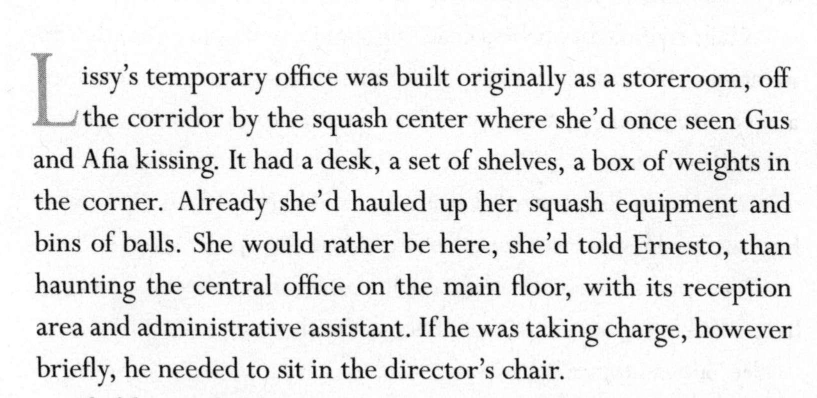

Lissy's temporary office was built originally as a storeroom, off the corridor by the squash center where she'd once seen Gus and Afia kissing. It had a desk, a set of shelves, a box of weights in the corner. Already she'd hauled up her squash equipment and bins of balls. She would rather be here, she'd told Ernesto, than haunting the central office on the main floor, with its reception area and administrative assistant. If he was taking charge, however briefly, he needed to sit in the director's chair.

She'd attended her last meeting about the capital campaign, along with Ernesto, who kept squinting at the rows of figures; he was too vain for reading glasses. Charlie Horton, Don Shears had reported, was making good on his pledge. They would break ground on the fitness center in the fall. "Congratulations," she'd said to Shears as she made her swift exit.

He'd caught her arm. "You might call Horton," he said. "Thank him. Say good things about football."

"Don, when I got here—"

"Just call him, okay?" He'd placed his hand, a little too heavily, on her shoulder. "Keep the lines open."

She turned this advice over in her head as she began unpacking boxes. It felt good to pack, to unpack, to arrange. Grief was like any season, forced eventually to give way. The terrible choices she had made in February, and their terrible consequences, felt like a great glob of cold earth that she had swallowed and planted inside her, to grow however it must.

She pulled her clock out of the first box and set it. One fifty-five. In a couple of hours she'd fetch Chloe. Ethan had expanded his practice in the past month, saying little about it, but Lissy knew he was preparing in case they were reduced to one income. And what if she had to go on the market, apply for a coaching spot in Nebraska or South Carolina? No, she couldn't. Ethan loved their house even more than she did. Loved getting down to professional meetings in New York, loved seeing his sisters there. He'd talked—angrily—about selling the family camp in Hadley, now that death had spoiled the place. But Chloe was getting bigger. He'd want to take her fishing on the Hudson.

Three taps, at her door. She looked up at the grinning, freckled face of Gus Schneider. "Look, Mom," he said, spreading his arms wide. "No crutches."

"Good job." She smiled at him. "I thought you dropped out of school."

"Just for spring. I'll be back in the fall. Thought I could practice with the team, you know, till I graduate in December." He picked up a plaque from an open box, an award she'd gotten for assistant coaching, her last year at Indiana. "If you're coaching, I mean."

She snorted lightly. "I thought you considered me unqualified. After what happened."

"Hey, Coach, cut me a little slack, okay? This was the winter from hell for me. I wanted to blame someone."

"And did you?"

"Yeah. Finally. Myself." He put the plaque back. In his right hand he held a squash racquet. He picked one of the hard balls out of her yellow basket and bounced it on the strings. "If I'd talked to Shahid in the first place, none of this shit would've gone down."

"Only if you'd stayed away from Afia. And you loved her."

His eyes followed the blue ball, up, up, up. "I did, yeah. Maybe I still do a little, but . . . I don't know." He caught the ball. "I think I'm ready to move on. She called me this morning."

"Really." She stuck the plaque in a drawer of the gray metal desk. Below it lay a pile of faded photos—her with the Rutgers team, her at eighteen with her hair in a dirty-blond ponytail, her dad at the one national tournament he attended. "She say anything about how she's . . . adjusting?"

"She's engaged again."

"How do you feel about that?"

"I don't know." He began tossing the ball up with his free hand. "There's something else going on," he said. "My mom says it's my imagination. She wants me to see, you know, like your husband."

"You've been pretty traumatized."

"It's not that." He dropped the ball back into the bin. "Look, she's coming up here," he said. Now his eyes lit up, a vestige of the old Gus, the puppy in love.

"Afia? You mean like to the squash center?"

"She wanted somewhere private. You going to be around awhile?"

"An hour or so."

"Maybe we can hit. You know, after I talk to her."

"I'd like that." Her lips curled. "I've been smacking the ball myself, a little. It's a great tension reliever."

"I could use that." He started out of the door, then turned

back. "If things get weird, you know, between us? Me and Afia? Maybe we could stick our heads in here. Talk to you."

"Sure," Lissy said. Though as Gus went out, she considered what a lousy advisor she'd be—for a pair of star-crossed lovers, for a young man frightened of shadows, for a girl relieved to have the choice of a fixed marriage.

She'd have been happy to see Afia—to scold her, she supposed, for ingratitude, and to make one last vain attempt to learn the truth. But she shut her door to give them privacy. Reaching into the box, she pulled out another photo, framed: Shahid, three years ago. He'd just placed third in the nationwide individuals, and he showed his white teeth in a wide grin. Standing next to him, Lissy herself looked like the proverbial canary-fed cat, ready to burst.

You looked so fierce, Ethan said once, when she asked him why he'd first started talking to her on that train. *And you looked so alone. It was a challenge.*

Why had she cared so hugely, too hugely, about Shahid? Why was it her task to harbor Afia, or to save her now? Was it about honor? Or winning? Or pasting together a family? She ran her thumb over the glass protecting Shahid's face. More than anything else, his family had been Afia.

She checked the clock. Two twenty. She realized she'd been hearing Gus, out in the squash center, hitting balls while he waited for Afia. But the slap of ball on wood had stopped some minutes ago. Afia was late. Now came the hum of the elevator rising from the lobby. Steps through the atrium. She cracked her door, listened for Afia's voice. But what came was a man's voice, harsh and accented.

"Your name," the man said, "is Gus Schneider?"

"Yeah, man," Gus said, sounding very young. "Who're you?"

"I am Khalid. Brother to Afia. You destroy our family."

"Now wait a second, dude. I don't even know your family, and Afia and I—"

"Shut up."

"Whoa. Dude. Put those away, okay? I never touched her. Honest. This is all a mistake, this—"

Lissy shut off her light. Gingerly she stepped into the dark hallway. Directly in front of her, next to the bleachers, stood the tall man who had been in the top bleacher at the Harvard game. His long face the face at the wheel of the blue Hyundai. In both his hands, centered in front of his chest, a black handgun. From where she stood, she couldn't see Gus, but the light was shining from the third court. Her hand went to the cell phone in her pocket. But there was no time to call for help.

"You must know why you die. You must know"—the tall man's hands shook just a little, holding the gun—"what filth you do to her."

Khalid, she thought. On the top bleacher; driving the blue Hyundai. Ethan had encountered him at their front door. His name was Khalid.

"Don't shoot me, man. Please. This is like a misunderstanding. I'm my mom's only kid. Please."

"Get your knees on."

She needed a weapon, any weapon. Silently she stepped back into her office. In the blue glow of the computer she spotted her squash racquet, and the yellow bin of hard balls. She'd almost thrown them away when she packed her office. Now she reached and plucked three from the pile. Two she slipped into her pocket. The third she kept in her left hand. Silently she stepped back into the dark hallway. Gus was facing her, but she hoped he couldn't make her out, or at least that a flicker of his eyes would not give her away.

"Her I forgive," Khalid was saying. "Her I marry."

"You? You're the guy she's marrying? Not the guy in—"

"Shut up."

"I mean, congratulations, man. I have all respect for you. Honest."

"Shut up."

The light silhouetted his back. He stood maybe thirty feet away, the length of a squash court. She had one chance. Overhead serve, the high-risk serve. She lowered her left arm, lifted the blue ball. It rose, going dark and then invisible, into the high space, as her knees bent. Her right arm arced back, looking for power. Muscle memory, the blindfold over the eyes. She sprang. At the *pock* of the strings, Khalid started to turn, but too late. Ninety miles an hour. The hard ball hit between his shoulder blades.

"*Ungh*," he breathed. His back arched. The hand with the gun flung upward. A shot exploded into the glass wall of the squash court. Gus began to rise from his knees—too slowly, his leg still weak. Lissy dropped the racquet. Her legs churned. Khalid was recovering; he still had the gun, he was wheeling around. She hurtled forward. Her head connected with his torso, her arms on his hips. He was taller than she was, but not strong like Shahid. She felt the breath push out of him as he staggered, and they both went down. Over her head, the world exploded. Her head whipped back, struck the carpet. Above her she saw Khalid regain his feet. His shoulder blazed red. He was waving his weapon, firing. Lissy sliced out with her right leg, catching him at the ankle, and then he was down, and she pulled up from the floor, her head clanging, and with a great lurch she landed on top of him, her arms pinning his arms, the rich soup of blood filling her shirt, the stench of it, and Khalid's choked breath at her mouth, and she was grunting and sobbing at once until she heard Gus say, "Okay, Coach. It's okay. I got the gun."

CHAPTER THIRTY-TWO

In the years to come, Afia would lose count of the times she woke from a dream with the horrible knowledge that she had killed her brother, that he was gone forever, that no power on earth or in heaven would bring him back. She would lie in the dark and breathe rapidly, then more slowly. At last, in the ordinary silence, she would realize it had been only a dream and that Khalid was still alive, though not likely ever to walk the earth as a free man.

Or sometimes she would have the same dream and wake to realize, yet again, that it was a dream only in its details—details where she wielded a knife or cut a rope, or watched her brother drown—and that he was indeed snuffed out, his life no more than the shape of a cloud that dissipates with the next gust of wind. *Shahid*, she would whisper, *Shahid*, as if he could answer her and forgive her. But again there was only the most dull and ordinary silence in the gray light before dawn.

Sometimes it would breed in her a white fury that Khalid should still stand and walk, even in a cell, while Shahid lay still forever. The brother who had opened his heart lay cold in his grave; the brother obsessed with jealousy and revenge dined every night on his success. If she had pulled the gun from her backpack and aimed it, instead of handing it meekly over, Khalid, too, would be under the ground. And then she would rise shakily from her bed and fetch a glass of cold water. In the bathroom she would remember Baba, who would never again speak to her, and be glad that at least he had a son living, that he could look out at the moon and imagine Khalid looking at that same moon in the mirror image of his day.

Through the mornings after these restless nights she would stumble with dry, itching eyes and a strain at the hinge of her jaw. If she had more than two or three bad nights in a row she would pop a blue pill and drift to the bottom of an ocean, pressed down by the weight of sleep, rising only when her alarm chimed and she was late to work.

Work was Malloy's diner, on the edge of downtown Northampton, a place where early-morning truckers and late-night students crossed paths in the summer dawn. She had told Coach Hayes she would stay on at Smith. She had petitioned for asylum. The cascade of events had cost her her scholarship, but Dean Myers said they would work with her. They didn't hang their people out to dry, the dean had said. Afia didn't know this expression, but she pictured herself, thin and hollow and hanging on a clothesline, the breeze trying to blow her off and only the clothespins at her shoulders keeping her in place. Many days, that was how she felt.

Some of the truckers tried to flirt with her, when she had an early shift. But she kept her head down, and they ended up saying things about Indian girls, how uptight they were. She didn't tell them she was not Indian.

"I think it will take me too long to finish the degree," she said to Coach Hayes when the coach came to see her in August. She had withdrawn from the spring semester, but now she was getting ready to register for fall classes. She was living in a furnished room, a block from campus. She would take only Immunology and Advanced Calculus, which was all the new scholarship money would cover. "And when it's all done, I won't be able to go back. To Pakistan, I mean."

"No need to rush," Coach said. "And why would you want to go back?"

It's my home, Afia thought of saying. And now that she could never return, she missed the house in Nasirabad with an ache so painful she had to bite her fist, sometimes, to silence a wail of longing. She missed the garlic and cumin of her mother's cooking, the chatter of Sobia and Muska, even the clack of Anâ's knitting needles and the quiet sobs of Tayyab when he thought no one could hear him. She missed the damp-wool odor of her bedroom rug during monsoon. She missed her carved bed, the particular squeak of the springs on the side toward the wall. She missed the way the sun glanced off the walls of their compound. The sweet lament of the muezzin she missed, every night as the sun set. The wildly painted rickshaws, the call of the sugarcane juice wallah, the night watchman's whistle, the odor of petrol and sugar and dust in the air. The ripe purple strings of the mulberries, the flat disks of drying dung on the village walls, the shouts of the lucky boys who were allowed to jump into the stream, its water milky with limestone runoff. Lema. Her uncles with their cruel giggles and their warm, rough hands.

But Nasirabad, she knew, was not her home any longer. Her mother had turned her away after she'd made the exhausting journey back, ready to marry Zardad, ready to do whatever was needed to make the past recede and the future begin. She had not even been allowed to set foot inside her home. Only the back of Tayyab's hut, on the pallet next to Panra, and that for one night only. "I wanted," she told Coach, "to help the women in the villages. They cannot see male doctors, and there are not enough females. People die because of this."

"They die in a lot of places, all around the world," Coach said. "You're going to make a big contribution, Afia."

"I don't know," Afia said. She lingered with Coach, in a booth at the back of the diner. Coach had given her a framed photo of herself and Shahid, from the first year he'd come to America. She'd insisted Afia should have it. And so Shahid's nineteen-year-old self smiled up from the table, holding a shiny trophy. Afia couldn't look at it, but neither would she turn the photo over and bury Shahid's face.

It was the end of her shift; she still wore the apron the diner gave her, and the little name tag above her left breast. She covered her head, but with a bandanna, like the other waitresses; the Arab thing, the owner had said, made customers nervous. She made better money than in the Price Chopper. Some days the aunties stopped in after their shift, to drink Cokes and eat French fries. Other days, Afran stopped and had hot tea at the counter. "I might not be able to complete the degree. Without . . ."

"Without Shahid," Coach finished for her.

"I betrayed him," Afia said, her voice going flat the way it always did when guilt pressed its hot weight upon her. "And for what? A boy who told me I was pretty."

"You know what we call your relationship with Gus?" Coach asked. Afia shook her head. "Puppy love," Coach said. "Here we consider it a kind of practice."

"Practice for what?"

"For love. The real thing. We think it's good to have a sort of warm-up game, before you choose a life partner. Shahid had some puppy love too, you know."

Afia tipped her head, frowned. "I did not know."

"Sure. With a girl, Valerie, I think, and they broke up. I don't think he was betraying you."

"It is different for a man. Even here, it is different. This is a shame I will never wipe clean, Coach. Do not try with me."

Coach moved the saltshaker around the table. "Would you really have married him?"

"Khalid?" Afia nodded. At Coach's shocked look, she said, "It is like a mathematical equation, no? I am shame. Khalid kills Shahid. To . . . to nullify?" Coach nodded. "To nullify the badal, the revenge, you know, someone must seek revenge for him killing my brother. To nullify the revenge he can marry me, erase the shame. Khalid is my brother step—"

"Stepbrother," Coach interrupted.

"Stepbrother, but also we are cousins. This is good, in my culture, to marry one cousin. To keep family together. Now my father can give forgiveness to Khalid, and my mother has no more shame. It is small, this—what do you call it?—sacrifice."

Her eyes slid over to the photo of Shahid. What *would* he have wanted? For a day and a night she'd cried for help from the closet Khalid had locked her into, at the Pioneer Motel outside Northampton where he'd been staying. Only when the cleaning woman, ignoring the *Do Not Disturb* sign in the morning, had turned the latch did Afia burst out and beg the manager to call the police in Devon.

By then it was all over. No more did she need to imagine Gus lying in a pool of blood. Never again would her body shrink in on itself as she pictured Khalid pounding babies into her, back in

Nasirabad, while her mind tunneled underground. Coach Hayes had saved her, a second time.

In the diner, Coach was stirring her coffee. She was still talking about love. "Romance," she was saying, "may not be the best foundation for marriage. But people fall in love everywhere, Afia. Here and in Pakistan, and now and since forever. Sometimes it's great and sometimes it hurts like hell. But it's the opposite of a betrayal. It's a kind of . . . of keeping faith. With the heart."

Afia's own heart took a small skip. At least twice a week, now, Afran drove out from his summer job in Boston. They went for walks along the old logging roads west of town. He did not touch her. But he no longer offered to behave toward her like a brother. He told her about his home in Turkey, the olive groves and the mountains rising up from the Black Sea. He would go back, he said, but to Istanbul, where there was money to be made.

"Afia," Coach said, "you're smiling."

"I am thinking," Afia said, blushing, "that Shahid had this romance."

"So what about you?"

"Me?"

"You've got your life ahead of you, don't you? You going to spend it beating yourself up?"

Afia looked around the coffee shop. Her life. Would it be here, in this place smelling of pork fat and coffee beans? Even when she had lain in Gus's arms, she had never imagined the rest of her life without her parents, her uncles and aunts, her brothers. Now she had only the molded tables with their shiny surfaces, and a glimmer of salvaged light in the courses at Smith. And, she thought with a tiny sliver of hope, Afran. Maybe this, after all, was what Shahid would have wanted . . . but then Shahid had never wanted, like her, to be dead. "Maybe," she said.

"So you'd rather have stayed home in Pakistan, let your parents arrange a marriage, give up your dreams of being a doctor."

Afia looked at her in gentle surprise. "And have Shahid alive?" Her eyes went to the photo, to her young, exultant brother. "Oh yes, Coach. Forever, yes."

Lissy left the diner and drove back along sun-dappled roads to Devon. Had she kept her nose out of Shahid Satar's affairs, she thought, Afia would be dead and Shahid alive. End of story. No, not the end. Gus dead, too. Khalid at large, and the feud between brothers set to end the way it ended for the Greeks in their tragedies.

What if, what if. An hour northward, Khalid Satar was pacing his cell at the maximum-security unit in Shirley. The D.A. at the trial, Mike Kelley, had told Lissy the feds might render the guy to the Pakistanis, who were not likely to treat him as well as the State of Massachusetts. But what if Tofan Satar had influence, over there, and managed eventually to free his son? Had Khalid's thirst been satisfied? Or would he again try to wipe out the stain that was Afia, to erase the sacrifice of Shahid? Even now, it took only the name in her head, *Shahid*, to knot her heart.

As, clearly, it knotted Afia's. The girl's healing was still pasted together, still fragile. The bones of her face stood out more than before, and the eyes behind the glasses shone less brilliantly. Hesitance and a weary cynicism had replaced the stubbornness and gumption she'd had that distant night, when they'd driven to Lissy's cabin. Then, of course, Afia had believed herself a loved woman. From now on she might prove a hard woman to love.

Lissy swung into the parking lot by Chloe's day care. For a moment, while the big beech tree shading the playground hid her car, she watched her daughter. Chloe was gripping the monkey bars, swinging her legs, getting her momentum up to grapple her way across. She let go with her left hand, gripped the next bar, swung her right hand ahead, lost her grip, and dropped to the sand. "You okay, honey?" called one of the teachers—Kaitlin, from the Enright squash team. "Fine," Chloe called back. She stood up, dusted off the sand, climbed back up the ladder, reached again, clambered across two rungs, fell. Behind her, a chunky girl in a yellow dress followed and tried to swing from the bars; falling right away, the girl burst into tears. Chloe crouched by her, patted her back. Pulling her up, she led the girl over to the sand table. She was shooting a longing glance back toward the monkey bars when she spotted Lissy. "Mommy!" she cried.

"Hey, cutie."

"You're *early*."

"Is that okay?" Lissy unlatched the playground gate and stepped in. "Today's a big day."

"I know," Chloe said matter-of-factly. She took Lissy's hand; hers was grainy with sand. "We sang to me," she said, "at lunch."

"Did your friends like Daddy's cupcakes?"

Chloe nodded. "Specially the sprinkles."

"I saw you on those monkey bars. You're really getting it."

Chloe pulled her down. She whispered, "But we can't do it now, Mommy. Megan'll follow me and fall, and when she cries I cry."

Kaitlin brought out the clean cupcake pan. She was a midsized, muscular girl with curly brown hair flecked gold by the sun and skin that had tanned nut-brown. "Hey, Coach. Looking forward to training in a few weeks."

"You know I can't coach the team till November."

"And by then you'll be back in the A.D.'s office. You'll barely have time for us."

Lissy's heart hurt, when her players talked this way. They saw only a division between innocent and guilty, victim and victimizer. They loved her. They would do their utmost for her. Last week, construction had begun on the fitness center. With Shahid exonerated, Lissy's series of missteps last winter presented itself to the world as gutsy instinct. Already Ernesto had promised he wouldn't arm-wrestle her. "I like my boys," he'd said, "but I can't deal with these suits." And Jeff Stubnick was threatening to withdraw his pledge if Coach Hayes was not reinstated. In her heart, she felt the pull toward her vocation. The joy of the kids—okay, they weren't kids, but once a day or twice a week they got to play as if they were. And she was good at managing the department, massaging the other coaches' egos, subduing resentments, stoking hopes. She was even good, apparently, at the Ask.

But she didn't know, yet, if she trusted herself to keep her priorities straight.

"You might go out for soccer in the fall," she said to Kaitlin. "It would help your footwork."

"Naw, Gus has got me playing tennis," Kaitlin said. "We want to set up a club league. Mixed doubles."

"Not a bad idea. How is Gus?"

They'd been dating, she knew, since midsummer. She wondered if Afia knew. It had to seem strange to her, the joining and unjoining of young Americans, meeting and parting as casually as bees and flowers.

"He's great. He aced the bio GRE. Oh, and he's been coaching Tom. Tom's dying to be a starter this year."

"He keeps working, he'll have a shot. You?"

"I'm your girl. And we want the honor speech. You know, the one you always give."

Lissy grinned, to hide the dagger of dread that drove home that word. "I'll tell you this," she said. "You and the rest. It's going to be my honor to work with you."

"Bye, Kaitlin!" Chloe singsonged.

"Happy birthday, Monkey," Kaitlin said. She leaned down to kiss Chloe's head.

They called her Monkey, Chloe reported as they drove home, not because of Purple Monkey—whom she still held tight, ragged though he was getting—but because of the bars. And she wanted squash lessons. Didn't Mommy start playing squash when she turned four?

"Tennis at first, and I was five. And I didn't take lessons."

"Why not?"

Because, Lissy thought, there was no money. And no thought of tall, willful little girls being athletes. "Sometimes," she said, "it's fun to just play."

"Kaitlin says you like to win."

Lissy chuckled. "She should talk."

Chloe had stopped wetting the bed. Today she was turning four, another petal unfolded from the swirled knot. They would all grow bigger soon enough, or older, ready for the perils of being fully open. Meanwhile Shahid was still dead, would always be dead, that bloom cut off in its first flowering.

She turned into the driveway. Balloons hung from the porch, a *Happy Birthday* banner from the lintel. Chloe clapped her hands. "Do you think there's cake?" she said. "Can we eat it outside?"

From trimming the hedges, Ethan straightened. He wore a faded Obama T-shirt and a pair of cutoffs. His legs, burnished with a summer tan, were ropy and taut. His neck glowed with sweat. He pulled off his glasses and wiped his face with a handkerchief from his back pocket. While Chloe banged into the house, he would pull Lissy to him and kiss her, his mouth smelling of beer and sweat, his shirt dampening hers. He knew, now, that she could lie to him. He knew and he loved her regardless. "We can eat wherever you like," Lissy said to her daughter, and gratitude lifted her from the car, onto the green lawn.

In Nasirabad, Farishta put the finishing touches on her letter. She had written it on paper she'd found on her husband's desk and tucked it into an envelope from his drawer, adding two extra stamps from the roll in his basket of paper clips and tape. It didn't say much, only news of the farm, the girls' work in school, how Anâ was slowly failing. But Afia would know, at least, that someone still thought of her from home. Painstakingly she copied the English address from the slip of paper Afia had given her: *Afia Satar, Smith College, Northampton, Massachusetts, USA*. She tucked it behind the stacks of spices she kept on the far side of the counter. Tayyab might see it, but he wouldn't disturb the paper without asking her.

Then she set to arranging her receiving room. With Ramadan over, her visitors would revel in the pleasure of cakes and tea in midafternoon. Sobia was too young for a commitment to marry. Everyone knew that. Her monthly cycle had started less than a year ago; she had just fasted through her first Ramadan. The visiting family—the Munawars, her husband's cousins through his grandfather, on his mother's side—was setting out more to prove to the community that Satar's second daughter was marriageable than to make an offer. Young Tahir Munawar was at the university in Peshawar, studying to be an engineer. His mother and aunties had plenty of time for teas, for the light conversations that led to negotiations. But it was generous of them to come first to Farishta. It reestablished her.

And in light of the request to come to tea, her husband had forgiven her. Forgiven her failure to bring up a virtuous daughter, her setting in motion the cascade of kismet that had left him without sons. More than any restored honor in the eyes of the community, his forgiveness gave her back her strength. He had been a good husband. Not as successful in business as her brother, but a landowner with a *khel* that went back many centuries on this land, and the quiet dignity that came with such history. He had not once held the specter of Badrai over her, but had treated her as his life partner from the day of their marriage.

Looking back, she saw she had begun to lose his respect when she failed with Khalid—failed to take the earnest, watchful, motherless boy and find a way to make him love her. It was easy to say it was Khalid who had brought on the tragedy in America. But the fact remained that Farishta had failed with him, and failed with her own child too, when Afia forgot everything she had been so carefully taught.

How hard it had been to turn her away! Afia had dared what Farishta could never have dreamed: to make the journey across oceans and continents, through a day and a night, unprotected, among men of no scruples and no honor. And not only that, but to walk alone into the most dangerous place on earth for a blackened woman, her family home. But to embrace her would have been to condemn her—and not only that, to put Sobia and Muska, and Tofan's livelihood, under threat. Foolish, foolish girl, that she thought her mother could do otherwise than to send her off with a warning. Some mothers—she thought of her sister-in-law Gautana—might have put an end to the girl themselves.

For weeks after, she had wondered. Was her girl on the streets of Peshawar, barefoot like the Gypsies, her thin hands held out for rupees? Had the money Farishta gave her helped her to safety? Or had she been beaten and robbed, like too many girls in the cities? Had she given up on everything and found her way to Karachi, where she could sell her body to the Iranians who brought their goods into port? Where could a girl go, without family?

Back to *Amreeka*, of course. Farishta should have known. But in all her prayers, all her appeals for a vision, a dream at least, where she could glimpse Afia and know what had become of her, she had never thought her daughter could find the strength to retrace her journey to the jaws of the beast who would devour her. Nor would she have known without the news that came, five weeks after Farishta watched Afia leave the courtyard forever, of Khalid's arrest.

Strange, so strange. The moment Tofan got the shocking news, he forgave Farishta. At first she had been puzzled to the point of alarm. Then the story filtered down, by way of Roshan to his son Azlan and then to Tayyab and back to Farishta: Khalid had been engaged in jihad, planning a great action against the military who rained drones down upon innocent families in the mountains. He might be tortured, he might be detained for life in *Amreeka*, but he was a hero. Everyone in Nasirabad sang his praises and gave credit to his family. Their reputation was restored.

Nothing in this fantastic story had mentioned Afia. But Farishta knew from her husband's grave, unspoken relief that the arrest of Khalid meant the end of retribution. It meant that Afia—though dead to them, as dead as Shahid in his cold grave half a world away—would live. *The greatest love is a father's love for his daughter.* And there were still the two girls at home to bring them hope. A month ago, Tofan had come back to Farishta's bed just as the sunset gave them permission, and he had tasted of her before he tasted of either food or water.

She went in to Tayyab. "The English cakes look very sweet," she said.

The old man nodded and made a little bow. "Yes, memsahib, but we have the salty biscuits as well, and little pots of kheer."

"Now, I don't want you carrying the tray. That's Sobia's job."

"Yes, memsahib."

Sobia was in her room, trying on one shalwar kameez after another. It was all still pretend, to the girl. For some time she had longed for her big sister and would retreat, weeping, to her new room when she was scolded for mentioning Afia's name. But now she was enjoying the role of the big sister, the first who would be married—not now, of course, too soon, but whenever her mother decreed it was time. She would go, then Muska would go, and then it would be only Farishta and her husband unless Khalid was released and made his triumphant return.

That last thought sent a shudder through Farishta's body. Strange, how Shahid had been a hero to lead an American squash team and be on his way to a Harvard degree; and now Khalid was a hero for supposedly performing jihad in America, where Omar's money had sent him. When Farishta thought of the Eid celebration that had ended Ramadan, she felt ill. It was the one time each year that Omar and her mother came to Nasirabad, for the great feast. Tofan had never liked his brother-in-law. He would have been relieved to skip the invitation, the lavish meal, Omar's flaunting of his cosmopolitan wealth. But if he ever came to understand why Farishta would not, could not, break bread again with her only brother, he would set out to kill Omar, and no power in the world would hold him back. So she had treaded softly; she had forced her bile down; remembering the children she had left, she had allowed her brother to cross her threshold without harm.

The sitting room was perfect. Sobia, in a cherry-red shalwar kameez with embroidery of gold and royal blue, was in the kitchen practicing tea service with Tayyab. Farishta stepped onto the veranda that looked over the valley and the mulberry trees, stripped now of their fruit. Sometimes, when she squinted, she could see Shahid and Afia climbing the trees barefoot with their baskets, gobbling as many berries as they gathered. Now, along the dirt road that ran by the orchard, she spied a village boy on a bicycle, sheaves of sugarcane strapped to the back fender. He was going into town, to supply the sugarcane wallah. "Boy!" she cried out. "Boy, come here!"

While the boy pushed his bicycle up the long slope, Farishta retreated to the kitchen. "What do you think, Moray?" Sobia said, turning in her outfit.

"Pretty," Farishta said. "But let's curl a couple of locks"—licking a finger, she drew her daughter's bangs out from her dupatta and wrapped them into spirals—"to decorate your forehead. I'll be right back," she said.

She pulled the stamped envelope out from behind the spices. If Tayyab saw her, he gave no sign. He was, he could always claim later, half blind. From the drawer she pulled out a ten-rupee coin. Then she strode quickly back to the veranda. The boy had leaned his bike against a tree and made the rest of his way up on foot. "Yes, memsahib?" he said eagerly. For the Satars were still, or again, known as a big family, and if the mistress of the family wanted you, it must be for a lucrative errand.

"Tuck this envelope in your kameez," she told the boy. "But do not get your sweat on it. When you pass the post box by the sugarcane wallah, you take this out and pass it through the slot. If anyone asks you, you say you have written away to a contest. You understand?"

The boy nodded. She slipped the envelope under his shirt, by his thin chest—thin as Shahid's, at that age—and offered the coin. His eyes danced. "Allah's blessings on you, memsahib," he said.

"Allah hafez," Farishta said. And she watched him spin away down the road, carrying her words across the world to her child.

READERS GUIDE

A SISTER TO HONOR

by Lucy Ferriss

DISCUSSION QUESTIONS

1. The book opens with the Pashtun proverb "Woman is the lamp of the family." What do you think this means? Do you agree with the sentiment expressed?

2. Were you familiar with traditional Pakistani culture before reading *A Sister to Honor*? Did any aspects of it surprise you?

3. Throughout the book, Afia's family seems conflicted about the Westernization of their children. On the one hand, they take pride when their children succeed in America; on the other, they hold disdain for the host country. What are some examples of this paradox? Do you sympathize with this contradiction, or are you frustrated by it?

4. In Chapter Thirteen, Shahid claims Afia commits a "lie of omission" by not telling him about her relationship with Gus. Do you believe that omitting information is the same as telling a lie? Are there certain circumstances where it's understandable to withhold information?

5. Pakistani women are expected to maintain a strict modesty, especially when compared to the behavior of the American girls in this novel. How are American girls, such as Afia's roommates,

Patty and Taylor, characterized? Do you think this is an accurate depiction?

6. Discuss how the concept of honor plays a role in the novel. What authorities define honor? Which characters do you think were honorable—or, to the contrary, dishonorable?

7. In Chapter Sixteen, Coach Hayes states, "Your people are not the only ones concerned with honor." While cultural dissimilarities prevail more often than not in *A Sister to Honor*, there are similarities to be found between characters and cultures. What are some other instances of this? Why do you think the author included these comparisons rather than solely focusing on clashes between cultures?

8. Throughout the novel, Shahid and Afia compare their life in America to what they've seen in American movies. Based on your experiences, do you think mainstream movies are an accurate representation of American society, or is the portrait misleading? Do American films romanticize love and sex?

9. The American judicial system and *pashtunwali*, the code of the Pashtuns, have very different ideas about who has the right to judge an action and punish a crime. Compare these two systems. What are the flaws and benefits of each?

10. The phrase "You're in America now" is used several times to counter Shahid and Afia's defense of their Pashtun customs. Do you think they should have sacrificed their traditions and adapted? To what extent?

11. Despite the heavy focus on honor, it is love that seems to drive some of the riskiest actions and largest sacrifices in this book. Can you think of any examples of this?

12. The Pakistani women in *A Sister to Honor* are expected to have an arranged marriage. What do you think of this custom? Would you marry for anything other than love?

13. Who has power in *A Sister to Honor*, and why—is it money, gender, or position? How do characters use their power, and what limits or weakens them? Are there characters who are completely powerless?

notes